The Tale of Beowulf

FLAME TREE PUBLISHING

LANGFEÐGATAL **LANGEBEK, 1, 3**	**FLATEYARBÓK** **CHRISTIANIA, 1860, 1, 27**
Voden þan kollvm ver Oden	Voden, *er ver kollum* Odinn
Frealaf	Frilafr, *e.v.k.* Bors
Finn	Burri, *e.v.k.* Finn
Godvlfi	Godolfr
Eat	
Beaf	Beaf, *e.v.k.* Biar
Scealdna	Skialldin, *e.v.k.* Skiolld
Heremotr	Heremoth, *e.v.k* Hermod
Itermann	Trinaan
Athra	Atra
Bedvig	Beduigg
Seskef vel Sescef	Seseph

The Tale of Beowulf

of

Edited & Introduced by Dr. Victoria Symons

General Editor: Jake Jackson

FLAME TREE PUBLISHING

This is a FLAME TREE Book

FLAME TREE PUBLISHING
6 Melbray Mews
Fulham, London SW6 3NS
United Kingdom
www.flametreepublishing.com

First published 2022

ISBN: 978-1-83964-992-9

The text in this book is based on the following sources:
*The Story of Beowulf: Translated from Anglo-Saxon into Modern
English Prose* by Ernest J.B. Kirtlan (Thomas Y. Cromwell
Company Publishers and Hazell, Watson and Viney LD, 1914)

*Beowulf: An Introduction to the Study of the Poem with a Discussion of the
Stories of Offa and Finn* by R.W. Chambers (Cambridge University Press, 1921)

The Finnsburh Fragment, 'Deor' and 'Widsith'
translated by Dr. Victoria Symons.

A copy of the CIP data for this book is available from the British Library.

Printed and bound in the UK by Clays Ltd, Elcograf S.p.A

Contents

Series Foreword

STRETCHING BACK to the oral traditions of thousands of years ago, tales of heroes and disaster, creation and conquest have been told by many different civilizations in many different ways. Their impact sits deep within our culture even though the detail in the tales themselves are a loose mix of historical record, transformed narrative and the distortions of hundreds of storytellers.

Today the language of mythology lives with us: our mood is jovial, our countenance is saturnine, we are narcissistic and our modern life is hermetically sealed from others. The nuances of myths and legends form part of our daily routines and help us navigate the world around us, with its half truths and biased reported facts.

The nature of a myth is that its story is already known by most of those who hear it, or read it. Every generation brings a new emphasis, but the fundamentals remain the same: a desire to understand and describe the events and relationships of the world. Many of the great stories are archetypes that help us find our own place, equipping us with tools for self-understanding, both individually and as part of a broader culture.

For Western societies it is Greek mythology that speaks to us most clearly. It greatly influenced the mythological heritage of the ancient Roman civilization and is the lens through which we still see the Celts, the Norse and many of the other great peoples and religions. The Greeks themselves learned much from their neighbours, the Egyptians, an older culture that became weak with age and incestuous leadership.

It is important to understand that what we perceive now as mythology had its own origins in perceptions of the divine and the rituals of the sacred. The earliest civilizations, in the crucible of the Middle East, in the Sumer of the third millennium BC, are the source to which many of the mythic archetypes can be traced. As humankind collected together in cities for the first time, developed writing and industrial scale agriculture, started to irrigate the rivers and attempted to control rather than be at the mercy of its environment, humanity began to write down its tentative explanations of natural events, of floods and plagues, of disease.

Early stories tell of Gods (or god-like animals in the case of tribal societies such as African, Native American or Aboriginal cultures) who are crafty and use their wits to survive, and it is reasonable to suggest that these were the first rulers of the gathering peoples of the earth, later elevated to god-like status with the distance of time. Such tales became more political as cities vied with each other for supremacy, creating new Gods, new hierarchies for their pantheons. The older Gods took on primordial roles and became the preserve of creation and destruction, leaving the new gods to deal with more current, everyday affairs. Empires rose and fell, with Babylon assuming the mantle from Sumeria in the 1800s BC, then in turn to be swept away by the Assyrians of the 1200s BC; then the Assyrians and the Egyptians were subjugated by the Greeks, the Greeks by the Romans and so on, leading to the spread and assimilation of common themes, ideas and stories throughout the world.

The survival of history is dependent on the telling of good tales, but each one must have the 'feeling' of truth, otherwise it will be ignored. Around the firesides, or embedded in a book or a computer, the myths and legends of the past are still the living materials of retold myth, not restricted to an exploration of origins. Now we have devices and global communications that give us unparalleled access to a diversity of traditions. We can find out about Indigenous American, Indian, Chinese and tribal African mythology in a way that was denied to our ancestors, we can find connections, match the archaeology, religion and the mythologies of the world to build a comprehensive image of the human adventure.

The great leaders of history and heroes of literature have also adopted the mantle of mythic experience, because the stories of historical figures – Cyrus the Great, Alexander, Genghis Khan – and mytho-poetic warriors such as Beowulf achieve a cultural significance that transcends their moment in the chronicles of humankind. Myth, history and literature have become powerful, intwined instruments of perception, with echoes of reported fact and symbolic truths that convey the sweep of human experience. In this series of books we are glad to share with you the wonderful traditions of the past.

Jake Jackson
General Editor

Introduction

The Manuscript

ON THE EVENING of 23 October 1731, a fire broke out in the library of Ashburnham House, in Westminster. A house fire is never good news, but this one was particularly disastrous. Ashburnham House was at the time a temporary storage facility for an extensive and priceless collection of manuscripts amassed a century earlier by Sir Robert Cotton, including some of the most significant survivals of ancient and medieval Europe. Desperate attempts were made to salvage as much of the collection as possible. Priceless manuscripts were flung by the handful from open windows; bookshelves were lifted wholesale and carried from the building. By morning, approximately one third of the collection had been reduced to ashes.

Amongst the survivors of the blaze was a somewhat innocuous manuscript from around the turn of the eleventh century, charred along the edges where its shelf had already started to smoulder. This manuscript has little to immediately tempt a casual reader. There are some illustrations but no great decorative flourishes as we see in more celebrated manuscripts like The Lindisfarne Gospels, no works by Bede or any other famous literary figures of the early medieval period. It was not targeted for rescue from the fire, but rather swept up in the general evacuation. Nevertheless, buried in its singed pages was one of the greatest survivals of the medieval period: the poem *Beowulf*.

That manuscript, known as the Nowell Codex, is today amongst the most celebrated treasures of the British Library. It contains the only copy of Beowulf, now considered a cornerstone of English literature. Once upon a time, not all that long ago, leafing through the pages of the Nowell Codex would have been its own sort of heroic quest. You would need to arrange a trip to London; clutching a letter of recommendation and a well-rehearsed reason. Once admitted – if you got that far – you'd also need steady nerves under the gaze of a watchful senior librarian. Nowadays, however, the entire manuscript is digitized and freely available online. It can be viewed anywhere, any time, at the click of a mouse.

If you were to open the manuscript – either digitally or in person – this is what you would find. Like all books from the period, it is written on parchment made from animal skin, and it is written by hand. The whole manuscript is the work of two scribes, switching partway through *Beowulf* at line 1,939 (folio 94a). We can tell from these scribes' handwriting styles that they were working at either the close of the tenth century or the start of the eleventh, although Beowulf itself is almost certainly older. In addition to *Beowulf*, the Nowell Codex also contains works of Old English prose: St Christopher, The Marvels of the East (which includes some fantastic illustrations of said marvels) and The Letter of Alexander to Aristotle. Next comes *Beowulf,* followed by another Old English poem called *Judith*. It has been argued – and is perhaps significant – that these texts all make reference to monsters, monstrous humans or fantastic beings.

Today, each page of the Nowell Codex is mounted in a paper frame, intended to protect the fire-damaged extremities from crumbling further. Some text has been lost at the edge of each page, and there is a great deal of scholarly debate about what some of those words may originally have been. Although it is poetry, *Beowulf* is written in unbroken lines that look like prose. It has no title, no ascribed author, little punctuation and no line numbers. This is all usual for poetry of the period. All Old English poems, including those discussed in this introduction, are referred to today by titles given them by modern editors.

While the poem lacks a title, the first scribe has left us a hint as to what contemporary readers may once have called it. On line 53, Scyld's son Beow is briefly mentioned. However, if you were to open the manuscript to f. 133r, and look to the middle of the first line of the second text block, you would see that the scribe has written not the name 'Beow' but 'Beowulf'. The actual Beowulf, the hero of the poem, is not introduced for several further generations, and his name is withheld until line 343 (you can see it on f. 139v, towards the end of the fourth line: *Beowulf is min nama*, 'Beowulf is my name'). This scribal slip is often silently corrected in modern translations (in the translation below, Beow is called 'The Danish Beowulf'), but it's worth noting. Coming upon a character whose name resembled that of the anticipated hero, our scribe corrected what looked like an error. Beowulf is a modern title, but this poem was clearly considered to have been a tale 'of Beowulf'.

Old English Poetry

When we talk about Old English poetry, we mean poems composed in the vernacular language of early medieval England between approximately the seventh and eleventh centuries. The extant canon comprises about 30,000 poetic lines, the majority of which are contained within just four manuscripts: the Exeter Book, the Vercelli Book, the Nowell Codex, which we have discussed above, and the Junius Manuscript. This is not all that much to represent four centuries of literary tastes and styles. A scattering of poems comes to us from other sources, written into the margins of manuscripts, carved on to monuments, or preserved in the body of prose works. Whatever their origins, almost all Old English poems survive today in single copies. This is the case for *Beowulf*. For comparison, no fewer than 55 manuscripts from the later medieval period contain complete or near-complete copies of Geoffrey Chaucer's *The Canterbury Tales*. A great deal has been lost.

Amongst what remains, *Beowulf* looms large. It is by far the longest work in the corpus. At 3,120 lines, it accounts for a little over a tenth of all poetry surviving from the period. Andreas, which tells the story of St Andrew the Apostle, is barely half as long at 1,722 lines. But it's not just in its length that *Beowulf* stands out. Where other extended Old English poems tell the tales of saints or holy figures, as with *Judith* from the same manuscript, *Beowulf* alone gives us the life and deeds of a secular – or non-religious – hero. We do know that other poems like *Beowulf* once existed. In 797, Alcuin wrote a scathing letter to the Bishop of Lindisfarne. With the famous question 'Quid enim Hinieldus cum Christo?' – 'What has Ingeld to do with Christ?' – he admonished the monks at Lindisfarne for preferring poems of secular heroes over religious instruction. We will have to imagine the stories of Ingeld that so entranced the Lindisfarne monks, for only passing references to the hero survive. He is mentioned briefly in *Beowulf*, as Hrothgar's foe, and also in the much shorter poem *Widsith*. Today, our best sources for the legend of Ingeld come from Old Norse literature.

In spite of the slenderness of the canon, what does survive is rich and incredibly varied. We have a number of longer religious poems, including lives of both biblical and English saints. 'Genesis' and 'Exodus', as their titles suggest, are adaptations of biblical narratives. The Exeter Book manuscript boasts a collection of nearly 100 Old English riddles, with solutions as divergent as storms and ploughs, swans and swords, not to mention a handful of heavily euphemistic domestic objects. A group of poems known today as the 'Old English elegies' also come from the Exeter Book. Their modern titles – 'The Wanderer', 'The Seafarer', 'The Wife's Lament' – hint at the predicaments of their speakers. Narrated in the first person, these elegies tell individual tales of suffering, shot through with universal emotions of isolation, loneliness, impotence and grief. A number of Old English poems are military in nature, celebrating victories or decrying defeats. Some are charms.

Of these chance survivors, three merit particular mention in the context of *Beowulf*. All three of these poems can be found in translation in the appendix at the end of this volume. The first is The Finnsburh Fragment. As its name suggests, this is a fragment of what was once a longer poem. Its survival is as remarkable as that of the *Beowulf* manuscript, though somewhat less dramatic. George Hickes, an early scholar of Old English, is said to have copied the poem from a loose leaf found in the archives of Lambeth

Palace Library. Having copied the text, he dutifully slotted the leaf between the pages of another manuscript... and it has never been seen again. What remains of the poem narrates a battle between Danes and Frisians at a place called Finnsburh. What is remarkable is that a version of this narrative is also given in *Beowulf*. The exact relationship between the two poems is hotly debated; the main points are teased out by R.W. Chambers in the second part of this volume (where he refers to it by its as the Finnsburg Fragment).

We also have two shorter poems, 'Deor' and 'Widsith'. These are both catalogue poems, which seems to have been a popular style in the early medieval period but is not so favoured by readers today. A catalogue poem is really a collage, a gathering of sayings, maxims, stories or wisdom, presented in such a way as to demonstrate the wit and learning of the poet, and test that of the audience. 'Widsith' is a catalogue of kings, nations and heroes drawn from classical and Germanic legend. It assumes a great deal of knowledge from its audience – knowledge that in many cases we struggle to supply today – and gives us a tantalizing glimpse into just how many heroic narratives must once have been in circulation. It does not mention *Beowulf*, although some of the poem's secondary characters are included. 'Deor', meanwhile, gives slightly fuller treatment to a much smaller selection of heroic tales. Once again, *Beowulf* does not make an appearance.

These three poems give us some sense of the kinds of longer, secular poems that must have been in circulation at the same time as Beowulf. For more analogues, we must look further afield. Many of the scenes and characters in *Beowulf* are echoed in surviving Old Norse literature. These analogues are explained in detail, and translated at length, in chapters by R.W. Chambers below.

Language and Style

Old English poetry had a distinct structure that sets it firmly apart from its later medieval or early modern counterparts. The opening lines of *Beowulf* in the original language look like this:

> *Hwæt! We Gardena in geardagum,*
> *þeodcyninga, þrym gefrunon,*
> *hu ða æþelingas ellen fremedon.*

At first glance, this poetry can seem quite forbidding, and not just because of the obscurity of the language. The poetic form itself is quite different from what we are used to thinking of as 'poetry' today. The Old English poetic line is divided into two halves, separated in the middle by a gap (the 'caesura'). Each half-line contains two stressed syllables and a varying number of unstressed syllables. At least one stressed syllable in the first-half line will alliterate with the first stressed syllable in the second. This is what we call 'metrical alliteration', and it is what renders the line poetic. From these blocks of half-lines, cemented together through alliteration, are built the entire edifice of the Old English poetic corpus. It is a very constrained, somewhat stylized literary form, and early medieval poets seem to have delighted in the challenges it presented.

Metrical alliteration would eventually be replaced by end-rhyme in the poetry of the later medieval period. So, Chaucer favours rhyme rather than metrical alliteration in his poetry (the Parson in *The Canterbury Tales* refers sneeringly to alliterative verse as 'rom, ram, ruf'). However, we still find metrical alliteration used to great effect in some later works. For example, the anonymous poet who composed four long poems in the late fourteenth century, including *Sir Gawain and the Green Knight* and *Pearl*, wrote using both rhyme and metrical alliteration.

The Origins of Beowulf

We have seen that the sole surviving copy of *Beowulf* was written down sometime around the beginning of the eleventh century, dateable by the styles of handwriting employed by its two scribes. We can be a lot less certain of when *Beowulf* was first composed. This is largely due to the nature of manuscript culture. The society of early medieval England was what we call 'proto-literate', meaning that much of its literature would initially have been composed orally, and passed on by word of mouth, for several decades or even centuries before it was written into manuscripts. In turn, those written works would themselves have been copied into new manuscripts by successive generations of scribes. It is very likely that a history of this sort lies between the first iteration of *Beowulf* and the version we find in the Nowell Codex. Scholars have made very detailed arguments, based on everything from staining on the manuscript's pages to the scribes' use of vowels, in an attempt to pinpoint the time and place of the poem's composition. The most widely accepted view is that *Beowulf* is probably a poem of the eighth century. Such a dating means that as many as three hundred years may separate this 'original' *Beowulf* from the writing of the Nowell Codex.

What is more, the poem itself is set earlier still. Beowulf is not a historic figure, but some of the poem's secondary characters are. They lived in sixth-century Scandinavia, and it is here – both in time and place – that *Beowulf* is set. It was once argued that the Old English poem may even be a direct translation of a Scandinavian original. This is unlikely. However, it is important to note that the story and setting of *Beowulf* were already old when the poem itself was composed, and much older still when it was written into the Nowell Codex. There is enough of a remove for the poem to celebrate the trappings of heroic culture whilst critiquing its many shortcomings. *Beowulf* is a poem with nostalgia built in, but nostalgia tempered by the reality that heroic actions have human costs.

For the same reason that it is difficult to date the poem, it is also very difficult to talk about the 'Beowulf poet'. Each performance, and each scribal production, would certainly involve changes to the poem. When scholars and critics today refer to the poet of *Beowulf*, they are often referring to the poem's narrative voice and the worldview it embodies. The first-person narrator pauses often to pass comment on the poem's events, actions and characters. A recurring phrase is *þat was god cyning* – 'that was a good king'. Elsewhere, the narrator comments approvingly on the wealth of

Scyld's funeral ship, and confidently tells us the moment Grendel's fate has changed, though even the monster himself is not yet aware. The narrator is not the poet, of course, but these scattered asides and first-person interjections breathe a bit of life into the anonymity that otherwise shrouds the poem's origins.

One of the most notable moments of narrative commentary comes towards the start of the poem, when the Danes find themselves seriously outmatched by Grendel and resort to making sacrifices. This, we are told, was their custom, 'the hope of the heathen', in the translation below (Section II), because 'the Creator they knew not'. Though the characters of *Beowulf* are pagan, its setting, narrator and intended audience are all explicitly Christian. Grendel himself is descended from the biblical Cain, and God's workings, though hidden from the pagan characters, are repeatedly made clear to the audience. It has been suggested that this mismatch between the poem's Christian narrator and its pagan heroes must mean that the Christian elements are a late addition, awkwardly bolted on to a pre-Christian poem already in circulation. However, the balancing of Christian and pagan perspectives is more closely woven into the fabric of the poem than this explanation allows. *Beowulf* is an eleventh-century copy of a possibly eighth-century composition, telling the story of sixth-century characters. Its layering of perspectives and values, religion and worldviews is a literary rendering of the poem's own layered history.

The Story of Beowulf

The story that Beowulf tells is this: The Danish people, having suffered many years without the protection of a king, one day find an infant washed up on their shore. They make him their leader. Scyld, as he is called, grows up to be everything a king should be: fearsome to foreigners, generous to his own people, and the father of a son. That son, Beow, does as his father did, and so this Danish dynasty is founded. All goes well for a few generations, until Hrothgar – Scyld's great-grandson – takes it upon himself to build the mightiest hall known to man. This, it seems, is a step too far. The monster Grendel bursts on to the scene in a cannibalistic fury, snatching up armfuls of Danes to devour back in his underwater lair, rendering this dazzling building useless.

Meanwhile, across the sea in Geatland, a young prince hears of the Danes' troubles. He packs up with his band of loyal retainers and goes to test his strength against the monster. After a good bit of boasting and verbal sparring, Beowulf's offer is accepted. That night he meets Grendel in hand-to-hand combat. Beowulf literally disarms him, tearing the monster's limb off at the shoulder. Grendel limps back to his lair to die, and the Danes are jubilant. Their celebrations are short-lived, however, for the very next night Grendel's mother comes to avenge her son. Her violence is more restrained, but more pointed. Instead of wholesale slaughter, she scoops up a single Dane – Hrothgar's most trusted *eaxl-gestealla*, 'shoulder companion' – along with her son's actual arm, and drags them both away. Once again, Beowulf steps up. He meets Grendel's mother in her own home, ultimately overpowering her in a fight that is markedly more evenly matched than the previous struggle with Grendel.

Beowulf's second victory is met with rather less celebration than his first. Gazing at the weapons Beowulf has retrieved from the lair of Grendel and his mother, Hrothgar delivers a speech bordering on a sermon, decrying greed and the corruption of power. Beowulf is sent on his way, with treasure and thanks and a firm farewell.

Back in Geatland, Beowulf recounts his adventures to his uncle, the Geatish king Hygelac. Then, in the span of a single half-line, fifty years go by. Beowulf is now himself an old king. This time, it's his own kingdom at peril, harassed by a fire-breathing dragon, and once more Beowulf takes it upon himself to face the monster. As the poem's narrative fractures into increasingly lengthy digressions, we learn about Beowulf's path to kingship, the deaths of first his uncle and then his nephew, his own feud with the Swedes. But it is the dragon fight that ends the poem. Whether Beowulf's insistence on meeting the dragon alone is the noble sacrifice of a selfless king or one last stab at glory by a hero past his prime is left unstated. Either way, it is an error. The dragon outmatches Beowulf, and it is a younger warrior called Wiglaf who eventually dispatches it. Beowulf himself is mortally wounded in the encounter. He leaves his people with the dragon's treasure, but no actual heir. At the end of the poem the Geats find themselves where the Danes began: leaderless and vulnerable.

Feuding Families

We saw above that the poem's layering of perspectives allows it to strike a balance between the contradictory theologies of its pagan heroes and Christian audience. There are many other examples of this sort of layering, and the complexity they bring to the text. For example, the appearance of Grendel's mother follows immediately on from two scenes of human women. In the first, Hrothgar's court poet recounts the tale of Hildeburh, a Danish princess married to the Frisian king Finn (Sections XVI–XVII in the translation below). One winter, her brother and his retinue come to stay and old animosities boil over. By the time spring arrives, Hildeburh has lost her son, her Danish brother, and her Frisian husband. She herself is carted back to Denmark along with the rest of the 'ornaments and jewels' looted from Finn's home. As Hildeburh's story comes to an end, Hrothgar's queen Wealtheow enters the hall (Sections XVII–XVIII). She praises Beowulf, but urges her husband to entrust his wealth and kingdom to their nephew Hrothulf. In doing so, she attempts to secure the future of her own young sons. We know from Old Norse analogues that she has chosen poorly; after Hrothgar's death, Hrothulf makes a grab for power and both boys are killed. Finally, as Wealtheow retires to bed, Grendel's mother bursts into the hall (Section XIX). These three scenes form a triptych of maternal impotence; each of the three women, human or monster, failing to save their sons from the violence of a feuding society. But it is left to the audience to decide what conclusions should be drawn from these parallels. The poet presents them without comment.

These familial feuds lie at the beating heart of *Beowulf*. Most notably, Grendel's descent and the root of his monstrosity are traced back to Cain, whose biblical fratricide leads to exile from both God and human society. But it is not just the poem's monsters that are touched by domestic strife. Hygelac becomes king only after the accidental killing of his eldest brother by his youngest. Beowulf tosses accusations of fratricide at Unferth, and Hrothulf – as we have seen above – is quick to shed his cousins' blood. Beowulf's father was a troublemaker; the hero's voyage to Denmark seems to be partly an attempt to find a father figure in Hrothgar. Grendel himself has no father. Hrothgar worries, later in life, that his brother was the 'better man'. These neglected sons are given their counterpoint towards the end of the poem, when Beowulf imagines a father's anguish at the death of his only child. As much as it is about monsters, *Beowulf* is also about families. It is about absent fathers and sons desperate to prove themselves, about greed and loyalty, parental grief, sibling rivalry and violence handed from one generation to the next. These themes are writ large in the poem's three monsters, but they colour almost every action of its human characters and the world they inhabit too. It is in this interplay of humans and monsters, family and foe, hero and villain, that the poem speaks most forcefully to us today.

The Present Volume

It is an irony that *Beowulf* is certainly more widely circulated today than ever before in its history. There are a wealth of translations, in prose and verse, into both modern English and a great many other languages. It has been adapted to film, television, stage, video games and even opera. It hardly needs saying that the modern fantasy genre, both on the screen and the page, is heavily indebted to *Beowulf*. The poem's influence on J.R.R. Tolkien's *The Lord of the Rings* trilogy, in particular, has ensured the former's lasting legacy. The version of *Beowulf* presented in this volume is a prose translation by Ernest

J.B. Kirtlan. In addition, this volume also contains extracts from R.W. Chambers' influential study *Beowulf: An Introduction to the Study of the Poem.* The extracts chosen for this volume demonstrate Chambers' extensive knowledge of the poem's history and analogues. You will find translations of a number of Old Norse texts that tell comparable tales of monsters, dragon fights and wandering heroes, as well as a wealth of folktales, genealogies, histories and archaeological parallels.

Dr. Victoria Symons

Victoria Symons is a medievalist specializing in the language, literature and manuscripts of early medieval England. She is the author of *Runes and Roman Letters in Anglo-Saxon Manuscripts*, co-editor of 'The Riddle Ages' blog, and has written articles for both academic and general readership on Old and Middle English riddles, charms and poetry.

Beowulf

The Story of Beowulf

IT IS OFTEN a surprise to new readers that *Beowulf* starts not in Geatland with the poem's hero, but several generations earlier in Denmark. This prelude nevertheless introduces many of the poem's most central themes: wealth, power, treasure, and the nature of a 'good' king. The story proper picks up in the next section, several generations later but still in Denmark, when the Danish king Hrothgar commissions a magnificent hall, Heorot. It is this hall that soon attracts Grendel's wrath, and the monster bursts on to the stage in Section II. Beowulf himself arrives some years later, and the poem's central story of three monster slayings takes shape from there. The Danish coastguard who challenges Beowulf's arrival in Section IV draws a distinction between "words and works", but the poem *Beowulf* is driven by both.

Alongside the hero's superhuman fights, many of the poem's most striking passages are speeches. Hrothgar's description of the Grendels' murky lair (Section XX), is one such example. Later, Beowulf gives his own moving account of his ascent to the Geatish throne (Sections XXXIV–XXXV). One of the most famous speeches is the so-called 'Lay of the Last Survivor' (Section XXXII), a meditation on the transitory nature of life and wealth that casts an elegiac shadow over all of the glory and great deeds of the poem.

The Prelude

NOW WE have heard, by inquiry, of the glory of the kings of the people, they of the Spear-Danes, how the Athelings were doing deeds of courage. Full often Scyld, the son of Scef, with troops of warriors, withheld the drinking-stools from many a tribe. This earl caused terror when at first he was found in a miserable case. Afterwards he gave help when he grew up under the welkin, and worshipfully he flourished until all his neighbours over the sea gave him obedience, and yielded him tribute. He was a good king. In after-time there was born to him a son in the Court, whom God sent thither as a saviour of the people. He saw the dire distress that they formerly suffered when for a long while they were without a prince. Then it was that the Lord of Life, the Wielder of glory, gave to him glory. Famous was Beowulf. Far and wide spread his fame. Heir was he of Scyld in the land of the Danes. Thus should a young man be doing good deeds, with rich gifts to the friends of his father, so that in later days, when war shall come upon them, boon companions may stand at his side, helping their liege lord. For in all nations, by praiseworthy deeds, shall a man be thriving.

At the fated hour Scyld passed away, very vigorous in spirit, to the keeping of his Lord. Then his pleasant companions carried him down to the ocean flood, as he himself had bidden them, whilst the friend of the Scyldings was wielding words, he who as the dear Lord of the Land had ruled it a long time. And there, in the haven, stood the ship, with rings at the prow, icy, and eager for the journey, the ferry of the Atheling.

Then they laid down their dear Lord the giver of rings, the famous man, on the bosom of the ship, close to the mast, where were heaps of treasures, armour trappings that had been brought from far ways. Never heard I of a comelier ship, decked out with battle-weapons and weeds of war, with swords and byrnies. In his bosom they laid many a treasure when he was going on a far journey, into the power of the sea. Nor did they provide for him less of booty and of national treasures than they had done, who at the first had sent him forth, all alone o'er the waves, when he was but a child. Then moreover they set a golden standard high o'er his head, and let the sea take him, and gave all to the man of the sea. Full sad were their minds, and all sorrowing were they. No man can say soothly, no, not any hall-ruler, nor hero under heaven, who took in that lading.

The Tale

I

MOREOVER THE Danish Beowulf, the dear King of his people, was a long time renowned amongst the folk in the cities (his father, the Prince, had gone a-faring elsewhere from this world). Then was there born to him a son, the high Healfdene; and while he lived he was ruling the happy Danish people, and war-fierce and ancient was he. Four children were born to him: Heorogar the leader of troops, and Hrothgar, and Halga the good. And I heard say that Queen Elan (wife of Ongentheow) was his daughter, and she became the beloved comrade of the Swede. Then to Hrothgar was granted good speed in warfare and honour in fighting, so that his loyal subjects eagerly obeyed him, until the youths grew doughty, a very great band of warriors. Then it burned in his mind that he would bid men be building a palace, a greater mead-hall than the children of men ever had heard of, and that he would therein distribute to young and to old, as God gave him power, all the wealth that he had save the share of the folk and the lives of men.

Then I heard far and wide how he gave commandment to many a people throughout all the world, this work to be doing, and to deck out the folkstead. In due time it happened that soon among men, this greatest of halls was now all ready. And Hart he called it, whose word had great wielding. He broke not his promise, but gave to them rings and treasures at the banquet. The hall towered on high, and the gables were wide between the horns, and awaited the surging of the loathsome flames. Not long time should pass ere hatred was awakened after the battle-slaughter, twixt father-in-law and son-in-law.

Then it was that the powerful sprite who abode in darkness, scarce could brook for a while that daily he heard loud joy in the hall. There was sound of harping, and the clear song of the bard.

He who knew it was telling of the beginning of mankind, and he said that the Almighty created the world, and the bright fields surrounded by water. And, exulting, He set the sun and the moon as lamps to shine upon the earth-dwellers, and adorned the world with branches and leaves. And life He was giving to every kind of living creature. So noble men lived in joy, and were all blessed till one began to do evil, a devil from hell; and this grim spirit was called Grendel. And he was a march-stepper, who ruled on the moorlands, the fens, and the stronghold. For a while he kept guard, this unhappy creature, over the land of the race of monsters, since the Creator had proscribed him. On the race of Cain the Eternal Lord brought death as vengeance, when he slew Abel. Nor did he find joy in the feud, but God for the crime drove him far thence. Thus it was that evil things came to their birth, giants and elves and monsters of the deep, likewise those giants who for a long while were striving with God Himself. And well He requited them.

II

Then he went visiting the high house after nightfall, to see how the Ring-Danes were holding it. And he found there a band of Athelings asleep after feasting. And they knew not sorrow or the misery of men. The grim and greedy wight of destruction, all fierce and furious, was soon ready for his task, and laid hold of thirty thanes, all as they lay sleeping. And away he wended, faring homeward and exulting in the booty, to revisit his dwellings filled full of slaughter. At the dawn of day the war-craft of Grendel was seen by men. Then after his feeding they set up a weeping, great noise in the morning.

The glorious Lord, the very good Atheling, sat all unblithely, and suffered great pain, and endured sorrow for his thanes, when they saw the track of the loathly one, the cursed sprite. That struggle was too strong, loathsome and long. And after but one night (no longer time was it) he did them more murder-bale, and recked not a whit the feud and the crime. Too quick was he therein. Then he who had sought elsewhere more at large a resting-place, a bed after bower, was easily found when he was shown and told most truly, by the token so clear, the hate of the hell-thane. He went away farther and faster, he who would escape the fiend. So he ruled and strove against right, he alone against all of them, until the best of houses stood quite idle. And a great while it was – the friend of the Danes suffered distress and sorrows that were great the time of twelve winters.

Then was it made known to the children of men by a sorrowful singing that Grendel was striving this while against Hrothgar, and waged hateful enmity of crime and feud for many a year with lasting strife, and would hold no truce against any man of the main host of Danes, nor put away the life-bale, or settle feud with a fee, nor did any man need to hope for brighter bettering at the hand of the banesman. The terrible monster, a dark death-shadow, was pursuing the youth and the warriors, and he fettered and ensnared them, and ever was holding night after night the misty moorlands. And, men know not ever whither workers of hell-runes wander to and fro. Thus the foe of mankind, the terrible and lonesome traveller, often he did them even greater despite. And he took up his dwelling in the treasure-decked Hall of Hart in the dark night, nor could he come near the throne the treasure of God, nor did he know His love. And great was the evil to the friend of the Danes, and breakings of heart. Many a strong one sat in council, and much they discussed what was best for stout-hearted men to do against the fearful terror. And sometimes they went vowing at their heathen shrines and offered sacrifices, and with many words pleaded that the devil himself would give them his help against this menace to the nation. For such was their custom, the hope of the heathen. And ever of Hell they thought in their hearts; the Creator they knew not, the Judge of all deeds, nor knew they the Lord God, nor could they worship the Protector of the heavens, the Wielder of glory. Woe be to that man who shall shove down a soul through hurtful malice into the bosom of the fire, and who hopes for no help nor for any change – well shall it be with that one who after his death day shall seek the Lord and desire protection in the embrace of the Father.

III

So Beowulf, son of Healfdene, ever was brooding over this time-care, nor could the brave hero avert woe. That conflict was too strong, loathsome and long, that terrible and dire distress, the greatest of night-bales which came to the people.

Then the thane of Hygelac, the good man of the Geats, heard from home of the deeds of Grendel. And on the day of this life he was the strongest of main of all men in the world; noble was he and powerful. He bade a fair ship be made, and said that he would be seeking the War-King, the famous prince, over the swan path, and that he needed men. And the proud churls little blamed him for that journey, though dear he was to them. They urged on the valiant man and marked the omen. The good man of the Geats had chosen champions of those who were keenest, and sought out the ship. And one, a sea-crafty man, pointed to the land-marks. Time passed by; the ship was on the waves, the boat under the cliff, and the warriors all readily went up to the stern. And the currents were swirling, with sea and sand. And men were carrying on to the naked deck bright ornaments and splendid war-armour. Then they shove forth the ship that was well bound together; and it set forth over the waves, driven by the wind, this foamy-necked ship, likest to a bird; until about the same time on the next day, the ship with its twisted stern had gone so far that the sailing men could see the land, the shining sea-cliffs, the steep mountains, and the wide sea-nesses. Then they crossed the remaining portion of the sea. The Geats went up quickly on to the shore, and anchored the ship. War-shirts and war-weeds were rattling. And they gave God thanks for their easy crossing of the waves. Then the ward of the Swedes, who kept guard over the sea-cliffs, saw them carry down the gangways the bright shields and armour, all ready. And full curious thought tortured him as to who these men were. He, the thane of Hrothgar, rode down to the beach on his charger, and powerfully brandished the spear in his hand and took counsel with them.

'Who are ye armour-bearers, protected by byrnies, who come here thus bringing the high vessel over the sea, and the ringed ship over the ocean? I am he that sits at the end of the land and keep sea-guard, so that no one more loathsome may scathe with ship-army the land of the Danes. Never have shield-bearers begun to come here more openly, yet ye seem not to know the password of warriors, the compact of kinsmen. Nor ever have I seen a greater earl upon earth, than one of your band, a warrior in armour. And except his face belie him, he that is thus weapon-bedecked is no hall-man; but a peerless one to see. Now must I know your lineage before you go farther with your false spies in the land of the Danes. Now O ye far-dwellers and sea-farers, hear my onefold thought – haste is best in making known whence ye are come.'

IV

Then the eldest gave answer, and unlocked his treasure of words, the wise one of the troop: 'We are of the race of the Geats and hearth-comrades of Hygelac. My father was well known to the folk, a noble prince was he called Ecgtheow. And he bided many winters, ere as an old man he set out on his journeys away from the dwelling places. And wellnigh every councillor throughout all the world remembered him well. We through bold thinking have come to seek thy lord, the son of

Healfdene, the protector of the people. Vouchsafe to us good guidance. We have a great business with the lord of the Danes, who is far famed. Nor of this shall aught be secret as I am hoping. Well thou knowest if 'tis true as we heard say, that among the Danes some secret evil-doer, I know not what scather, by terror doth work unheard-of hostility, humiliation, and death. I may give counsel through greatness of mind to Hrothgar as to how he, the wise and good, may overcome the fiend, if ever should cease for him the baleful business and bettering come after and his troubles wax cooler, or for ever he shall suffer time of stress and miserable throes, while the best of all houses shall remain on the high stead.'

Then the watchman, the fearless warrior, as he sat on his horse, quickly made answer: 'The shield-warrior who is wide awake, shall know how to tell the difference between words and works, if he well bethink him. I can see that this band of warriors will be very welcome to the Lord of the Danes. Go ye forth, therefore, bear weapons and armour, as I will direct you. And I will command my thanes to hold against every foe, your ship in honour, new tarred as it is, and dry on the sands, until it shall carry the dearly loved man, that ship with the twisted prow, to the land of the Geats. To each of the well-doers shall it be given to escape scot-free out of the battle rush.' Then they went forth carrying their weapons. And there the ship rested, fastened by a rope, the wide-bosomed vessel secured by its anchor. The Boar held life ward, bright and battle-hard and adorned with gold, over the neck-guard of the handsome Beowulf. There was snorting of the war-like-minded, whilst men were hastening, as they marched on together till they caught sight of the splendid place decked out in gold. And it was the most famous of palaces, under the heavens, of the earth-dwellers, where the ruler was biding. Its glory shone over many lands. Then the dear one in battle showed them the bright house where were the brave ones, that they might straightway make their way towards it. Then one of the warriors turned his horse round, and spake this word: 'Time it is for me to go. May the Almighty Father hold you in favour, and keep you in safety in all your journeyings. I will go to the sea-coast to keep my watch against the fierce troops.'

V

The way was paved with many coloured stones, and by it they knew the path they should take. The coat of mail shone brightly, which was firmly hand-locked. The bright iron ring sang in the armour as they came on their way in their warlike trappings at the first to the great hall. Then the sea-weary men set down their broad shields, their shields that were wondrous hard 'gainst the wall of the great house, and bowed towards the bench. And byrnies were rattling, the war-weapons of men. And the spears were standing in a row together, the weapons of the sea-men and the spear grey above. And the troop of armed men was made glorious with weapons. Then the proud chieftain asked the warriors of their kindred: 'From whence are ye bringing such gold-plated shields, grey sarks and helmets with visors, and such a heap of spears? I am the servant and messenger of Hrothgar. Never saw I so many men prouder. I trow it was for pride and not at all for banishment, but for greatness of mind that Hrothgar ye are seeking.'

Then answered the brave man, the chief of the Geats, and spake these words, hard under helmet: 'We are the comrades at table of Hygelac. Beowulf is my name. I will say fully this my errand to the son of Healfdene the famous chieftain, unto thy lord and master, if he will grant us that we may salute him who is so good.'

Then spake Wulfgar (he was Prince of the Wendels). His courage was known to all, his valour and wisdom. 'I will make known to the Prince of the Danes, the Lord of the Scyldings the giver of rings the famous chieftain as thou art pleading, about thy journey, and will make known to thee quickly the answer which he the good man thinks fit to give me.' Quickly he turned then to where Hrothgar was sitting, old and very grey with his troop of earls. The brave man then went and stood before the shoulders of the Lord of the Danes. Well he knew the custom of the doughty ones. Wulfgar then spoke to his lord and friend: 'Here are come faring from a far country over the wide sea, a people of the Geats, and the eldest the warriors call Beowulf. And they are asking that they may exchange words with thee, my lord. O gladman Hrothgar, do not refuse to be talking with them. For worthy they seem all in their war-weeds, in the judgement of earls. At least he is a daring Prince who hither hath led this band of warriors.'

VI

Then spake Hrothgar the protector of the Danes: 'Well I knew him when he was a child, and his old father was called Ecgtheow. And to him did Hrethel of the Geats give his only daughter, and his son is bravely come here and hath sought out a gracious friend.' Then said the sea-farers who had brought the goodly gifts of the Geats there for thanks, that he the battle-brave had in his hand-grip the main craft of thirty men. 'And the holy God hath sent him for favour to us West Danes, and of this I have hope, 'gainst the terror of Grendel. I shall offer the goodman gifts for his daring. Now make thou haste and command the band of warrior kinsmen into the presence. Bid them welcome to the people of the Danes.' Then went Wulfgar even to the hall-door, and spake these words: 'My liege lord, the Prince of the East Danes, commands me to say that he knows your lineage. And ye who are bold of purpose are welcome hither over the sea-waves. Now may ye go in your war-weeds, under your visored helmets to see Hrothgar. Let your swords stay behind here, the wood and the slaughter-shafts and the issue of words.' Then the Prince rose up, and about him was many a warrior, a glorious band of thanes. And some bided there and held the battle-garments as the brave man commanded. And they hastened together under the roof of Hrothgar as the man directed them. The stout-hearted man went forward, hard under helmet till he stood by the dais.

Then Beowulf spake (and the byrny shone on him, the coat of mail, sewn by the cunning of the smith): 'O Hrothgar, all hail! I am the kinsman and comrade of Hygelac. Many marvels I have set on foot in the days of my youth. The affair of Grendel was made known to me in my native land. Sea-farers told how this best of all palaces stood idle and useless to warriors, after evening light came down under the brightness of heaven. Then my people persuaded me, the best and the proudest of all my earls, O my lord Hrothgar, that I should seek thee, for they well knew my main strength. For they themselves saw how I came forth bloodstained from the power of the fiend, when I bound the five, and destroyed the giant's kin, and slew 'mongst the waves, sea-monsters by night, and suffered such dire distress, and wreaked vengeance for the strife of the Geats (for woe they were suffering), and I destroyed the fierce one. And now all alone I shall settle the affair of Grendel the deadly monster, the cruel giant. And one boon will I be asking, O Prince of the Bright Danes, thou lord of the Scyldings, Protector of warriors and friend of the folk, that thou wilt not refuse, since so far I am come, that I and my troop of earls, this crowd of brave men, may alone cleanse out Hart. I have heard say also that the monster because of his rashness recks not of weapons. And, if Hygelac the blithe-minded will be my liege lord, I will forgo to carry to the battle a sword, or broad shield all yellow; but I will engage by my hand-grip with the enemy, and strive for life, foe with foe. And he whom Death taketh shall believe in the doom of the Lord. And I doubt not he will fearlessly consume the people of the Geats, if he may prevail in the war-hall as he has often done with the strong men of the Danes. And thou shalt not need to hide my head if Death take me, for he will seize me all bloodstained, and will bury the slaughter all bloody, and will think to taste and devour me alone and without any sorrow, and will stain the glens in the moorland. And thou needest not to sorrow longer over the food of my body. And if battle take me, send to Hygelac this best of coats of mail, the noblest of garments. It is the heirloom of Hrethel the work of Weland; and let Weird go as it will.'

VII

Hrothgar gave answer, the protector of the Danes: 'O my friend Beowulf, now thou hast sought us, for defence and for favour. Thy father fought in the greatest of feuds. He was banesman to Heatholaf amongst the Wylfings, when for battle-terror the King of the Geats could not hold him. Thence he sought the folk of the South Danes over the welter of waves. Then first was I ruling the Danish folk, and in my youthful days possessed the costly jewels, the treasure city of heroes. Then Heregar was dead, my elder brother not living was he, the child of Healfdene. He was a better man than I was. Then a payment of money settled the matter. I sent to the Wylfings ancient presents over the sea-ridges. And he swore to me oaths. And it is to me great sorrow in my heart to tell any man what Grendel hath done in Hart through his malice, of humiliation and sudden horror. My hall-troop has grown less, the crowd of my thanes; Weird has swept them towards the terror of Grendel. But easily may the good God restrain the deeds of the foolish scather. And drunken with beer the warriors full often boasted o'er the ale-cup that they would bide in the beer-hall the battle of Grendel with the terror of swords. Then was the mead-hall all bloodstained in the morning when dawn came shining, and all the benches were wet with gore, the hall with sword-blood. And so much the less did I rule o'er dear doughty ones whom death had taken. Now sit down to the banquet and unbind thy thoughts, thy hopes to the thanes, as thy mind inspires thee.' Then was there room made in the beer-hall for the Geats all together. And there they went and sat down, the strong-hearted men, proud of their strength. And a thane waited on them, who bore in his hands the ale-cup bedecked, and he poured out the sparkling mead, while the clear-voiced bard kept singing in Hart. There was joy to the heroes, and a very great gathering of Danes and of Geats.

VIII

Spake then Unferth, the son of Eglaf, who sat at the feet of the Lord of the Danes and opened a quarrel. (For the journey of Beowulf, of the brave sea-farer, was vexation to him, for he could not brook that ever any other man than he himself should obtain greater fame in all the earth.)

'What!' said he, 'art thou that Beowulf who didst contend with Breca, and strovest for the mastery in swimming o'er wide seas, when ye two for pride were searching the waves and for foolish boasting risked your lives in the deep waters? No man could dissuade you from that sorrowful journey, neither friend nor foe, when ye two swam in the sea, when ye two enfolded the waves with your arms and measured the sea-ways and brandished your arms as you glided o'er the ocean. The sea boiled with waves the wintry whelming. And for seven nights long ye were toiling in the stress of seas. But he o'erpowered thee in swimming, for greater strength had he. Then at the morning tide the sea bore him up to the land of the Heathoremes. Thence he was seeking the friend of his people his own dear country, the land of the Brondings, the fair city of refuge, where he had his own folk, and a city and rings. The son of Beanstan soothly fulfilled his boasting against thee. So do I deem it a worse matter, though thou art everywhere doughty in the rush of battle and grim warfare, if thou shalt be daring to bide near Grendel a night-long space.'

Then Beowulf spake, the son of Ecgtheow: 'What! my friend Unferth, drunken with beer, many things thou art saying about that Breca and talkest of his journey. But soothly I tell thee that I had the greater strength in that swimming, and endurance in the waves. We two agreed when we were youngsters, and boasted (for we were both still in the days of our youth) that we in the ocean would be risking our lives. And so in deed we did. We had a naked sword hard in our hands when we were swimming. We two were thinking to guard us 'gainst whale fishes. Nor over the sea-waves might he be floating a whit far from me, more quickly on the waters. Then we together were in the sea for the space of five nights until the flood, the boiling waters drove us asunder. And the coldest of weather, and the darkening night, and a wind from the north battle-grim turned against us, and rough were the waves. And the mind of the mere-fishes was stirred when my shirt of mail that was hand-locked gave to me help against the foe. The decorated battle-robe lay on my breast all adorned with gold, and the doomèd and dire foe drew to the bottom, and fast he had me grim in his grip. Still to me was granted that I reached to the monster with the point of my sword. And the mighty sea-deer carried off the battle-rush through my hand.'

IX

'So then evil-doers did often oppress me. And I served them with my dear sword as was most fitting. Not at all of the feasting had they any joy. Evil destroyers sat round the banquet at the bottom of the sea, that they might seize me. But in the morning, wounded by my sword, they lay up on the foreshore, put to sleep by my weapon so that they hindered no more the faring of the sea-goers. Light came from the eastward, the bright beacon of God. The waves grew less that I could catch sight of the sea-nesses, the windy walls. Weird often saveth the earl that is undoomed when his courage is doughty. Nevertheless it happened that I slew with my sword nine of the sea-monsters. Nor have I heard under vault of heaven of a harder night-struggle, nor of a more wretched man on the sea-streams. Still I escaped from the grasp of the foes, with my life, and weary of the journey. When the sea bore me up, on the flood tide, on the welling of waves, to the land of the Finns. Nor have I heard concerning thee of any such striving or terror of swords. Breca never yet, nor either of you two, did such a deed with shining sword in any battle-gaming (not that I will boast of this too much), yet wast thou the slayer of thy brother, thy chief kinsman. And for this in hell shalt thou suffer a curse, though thy wit be doughty. And soothly I tell thee, O son of Eglaf, that Grendel that hateful monster never had done such terrors to thy life and humiliation in Hart if thy mind and thy soul were as battle-fierce as thou thyself dost say. But he has found that he needed not to fear the feud the terrible sword-thrust of your people the Danes. He taketh forced toll, and spareth none of the Danish people, but joyfully wageth war, putteth them to sleep and feedeth on them, and expecteth no fight from the Danes. But I shall ere long offer him in war the strength and the courage of the Geats. Let him go who can to the mead all proudly when morning light shall shine from the south, another day over the children of men.'

Then in the hall the giver of rings was grey-haired and battle-brave. The Prince of the Danes was hopeful of help. The guardian of the folk fixed on Beowulf his firm-purposed thought. There was laughter 'mong heroes, din resounded, and words were winsome. Wealtheow went forth, the Queen of Hrothgar, mindful of kinship and decked out in gold, she greeted Beowulf in the hall. And then the lovely wife first proffered the goblet to the Lord of the East Danes, and bade him be blithe at the beer-drinking, he who was dear to all his people. And gladly he took the banquet and hall-cup, he the victorious King. The lady of the Helmings went round about every one of the youthful warriors, and proffered the costly cup, until the time came that the ring-adorned Queen, most excellent in spirit, bore the mead-cup then to Beowulf. She, the wise in words, greeted the Geats and gave thanks to God that she had her desire that she might trust in any earl for help against such crimes. He gladly received it, he the battle-fierce warrior, from the hand of Wealtheow, and then began singing, inspired by a warlike spirit.

Beowulf spake, the son of Ecgtheow: 'I had intended at once to work out the will of this your people when I set forth over the sea and sat in my sea-boat with the troop of my people, or that I would fall in the slaughter fast in the fiend's grip. I shall yet acquit myself as befitteth an earl, or in the mead-hall await my last day.' And well the lady liked the words, the boasting of the Geat. And that lovely queen went all decked out in gold to sit by her lord. Then mighty words were spoken in the hall as before, by the people in joyance and the noise of the victors, until the son of Healfdene straightway would be seeking his evening rest. And he knew that a battle was doomed in the high hall to the monster when no longer they could see the light of the sun, or darkening night came stalking over all the shapes of shadows. The troop of warriors rose up, the Lord greeted the other, Hrothgar greeted Beowulf, and wished him good health and the warding of that wine-hall, and he spake the word: 'Since the time that I could lift my hand or my shield, never have I given the mighty hall of the Danes into the care of any, except now to thee. Have now and hold thou this best of houses, be thou mindful of honour, and show thyself courageous, and wakeful 'gainst foes. Nor shalt thou lack joy if thou escapest from that brave work with life.'

X

Then Hrothgar departed with his troop of heroes, he the Prince of the Scyldings; out of Hall went he, for the battle-chieftain would be seeking out Wealtheow his Queen, that they might go to rest. The glory of kings had appointed a hall-ward, as men say, against Grendel. A thane was in waiting on the Prince of the Danes, and his watch was keeping against the giant. The Lord of the Geats readily trusted the proud strength, the favour of God. Then doffed he the iron coat of mail and his helmet from his head, and gave his sword bedecked, the choicest of weapons, to a thane that was serving, and bade him to hold ready his armour. Then the good man spoke some words of boasting: 'I reck not myself meaner in war-powers and works of battle than Grendel doth himself. For I will not with sword put him to sleep and be taking his life away, though well I might do it. He knows not of good things, that he may strike me, or hew my shield, though brave he may be in hostile working – but we two by right will forbear the sword if he dare be seeking warfare without weapon, and then God all-knowing, the holy Lord, shall adjudge the glory on whichever side He may think meet.' Then the bold in fight got him to rest, and the pillow received the head of the earl, and many a keen sea-warrior lay down on his bed in the hall about him. None of them thought that he thence would ever seek another dear home, folk or free city where he was a child; for they had heard that fell death had taken, ere this too many, in that wine-hall, of the people of the Danes. But the Lord gave weavings of war-speed to the people of the Geats, both comfort and help. So that they all overcame their enemies through the craft of one man and by his might only. And truly it is said that God Almighty doth wield for ever the race of men. Then came in the wan night the shadow-goer gliding. Warriors were sleeping when they should have been keeping guard over that palace; all save one only. It was well known to men that their constant foe could not draw them into shadowy places when the Creator was unwilling. But he, ever wakeful, in angry mood, and fiercely indignant against the foe, was waiting the issue.

XI

Then came Grendel, stalking from the moors among the misty hill-slopes, and he bore God's anger. And the wicked scather of human kind fully intended to ensnare a certain one in the high hall. So he wended his way under the welkin to where he knew that the best of wine-halls, the gold-hall of man, was adorned with gold plating. Nor was that the first time that he sought out the home of Hrothgar. Nor ever in former or later days did he find a harder welcome from hall-thanes. Then the creature bereft of all joy came to the great hall, and the door, strongly bound with fire-bands, soon sprang open at his touch. And the evil-minded one in his fury burst open the door of the palace. And soon after this the enemy, angry in mind, was treading o'er the doomèd floor. And a fearsome light streamed forth from his eyes likest to a flame. And he could see many a warrior in that palace, a troop of peace-lovers asleep together, a company of kinsmen, and he laughed aloud. Then the terrible monster fully intended to cut off from life every one of them there, when he was expecting abundance of meat. But that fate was not yet, that he should lay hold of any more of human kind after that night.

Then did Beowulf, kinsman of Hygelac, see the dire distress, how the wicked scather would fare with sudden grip. Nor did the monster think to delay, but at the first he quickly laid hold of a sleeping warrior, and tore him to pieces all unawares, and bit at the flesh and drank the streaming blood, and devoured huge pieces of flesh. And soon he had eaten up both feet and hands of the man he had killed. Then he stepped up to the great-hearted warrior where he lay on the bed, and took him in his hands. He reached out his hand against the enemy, and quickly received him with hostile intent, and sat upon his arm. The Keeper of crimes soon was finding that he never had met in all the quarters of the earth amongst other men a greater hand-grip. And in mind and heart he was fearful, and eager to be gone and to flee away into darkness to seek the troop of devils. But that was not his fate, as it had been in days of yore. Then the good kinsman of Hygelac remembered the evening talk, and stood upright and laid hold upon him. His fingers burst. The giant was going forth, but the earl stepped after. The famous one intended to escape more widely, howsoever he might, and to flee on his way thence to the sloping hollows of the fens. That journey was sorrowful, which the harmful scather took to Hart. The lordly hall resounded. And great terror there was to all the Danes, the castle-dwellers, to each of the brave. And both the mighty guardians were fiercely angry. The hall resounded. Then was it great wonder that the wine-hall withstood the bold fighters, and that it fell not to the earth, that fair earth-dwelling. But very firm it was standing, cunningly shaped by craft of the smith, within and without. Then on the floor was many a mead-bench, as I have heard tell, decked out with gold, where the fierce ones were striving. Nor did the wise Danes formerly suppose that any man could break down a hall so noble and decorated with antlers, or cunningly destroy it, unless the bosom of flame swallowed it up in smoke. The roaring went up now enough. And an awful terror came to the North Danes, to each one of those who heard weeping from the ramparts, the enemy of God singing a fierce song, a song that was empty of victory, and the captive of hell lamenting his sorrow. For he that was strongest of men in strength held him fast on the day of his life.

XII

The Prince of earls would not at all let go alive the murderous comer, nor did he count his life as of use to any of the peoples. And many an earl of Beowulf's brandished the old heirloom, and were wishful to defend the life of their far-famed liege-lord, if they might do so. And they knew not, when they entered the battle, they the hard-thinking ones, the battle-men, and they thought to hew on all sides seeking out his spirit, that not any choice iron over the earth nor any battle weapon could be greeting the foe, but that he had forsworn all victorious weapons and swords. And miserable should be his passing on the day of this life, and the hostile sprite should journey far into the power of devils. Then he found out that, he who did crimes long before this with mirthful mind to human kind, he who was a foe to God, that his body would not last out; but the proud kinsman of Hygelac had him in his hands. And each was loathsome to the other while he lived. The terrible monster, sore with wounds was waiting. The gaping wound was seen on his shoulder. His sinews sprang open; and the bone-lockers burst. And great victory was given to Beowulf. Thence would Grendel, mortally wounded, flee under the fen-slopes to seek out a joyless dwelling. The more surely he knew he had reached the end of his life, the number of his days. Joy befell all the Danes after the slaughter-rush. So he had cleansed the hall of Hrothgar – he who had come from far, the proud and stout-hearted one, and saved them from strife. He rejoiced in the night-work and in the glorious deeds. His boast he had fulfilled, this leader of the Geats, which he made to the East Danes, and likewise made good all the distresses and the sorrows which they suffered of yore from the foe, and which through dire need they had to endure, of distresses not a few. And when the battle-brave man laid down the hand, the arm and shoulder under the wide roof, that was the manifest token.

XIII

Then in the morning, as I have heard say, was many a battle-warrior round about the gift-hall. Came the folk-leaders from far and from near along the wide ways to look at the marvel. Nor did his passing seem a thing to grieve over to any of the warriors of those who were scanning the track of the glory-less wight, how weary in mind he had dragged along his life-steps, on the way thence doomed and put to flight, and overcome in the fight at the lake of the sea-monsters. There was the sea boiling with blood, the awful surge of waves all mingled with hot gore. The death-doomèd one dyed the lake when void of joys he laid down his life in the fen for refuge. And hell received him. Thence after departed the old companions, likewise many a young one from the joyous journeys, proud from the lake to ride on mares, the youths on their horses. And there was the glory of Beowulf proclaimed. And many a one was saying that no man was a better man, no, none in the whole wide world under arch of the sky, of all the shield-bearers, neither south nor north, by the two seas. Nor a whit did they blame in the least their friend and lord, the glad Hrothgar; for he was a good king.

Meanwhile the famed in battle let the fallow mares leap and go faring forth to the contest, wherever the earth-ways seemed fair unto them and well known for their choiceness: and the thane of the king, he who was laden with many a vaunt, and was mindful of songs, and remembered a host of very many old sagas, he found other words, but bound by the truth. And a man began wisely to sing the journey of Beowulf, and to tell skilful tales with speeding that was good, and to interchange words. He told all that ever he had heard concerning Sigmund, with his deeds of courage, and much that is unknown, the strife of Waelsing; and the wide journeys which the children of men knew not at all, the feud and the crimes, when Fitela was not with him, when he would be saying any of such things, the uncle to the nephew, for always they were comrades in need at all the strivings. They had laid low very many of the giant's race by means of the sword. And after his death-day a no little fame sprang up for Sigmund when he, the hard in battle, killed the worm, the guardian of the hoard. He alone the child of the Atheling, hazarded a fearful deed, under the grey stone. Nor was Fitela with him. Still it happened to him that his sword pierced through the wondrous worm, and it stood in the wall, that doughty iron, and the dragon was dead. And so this monster had gained strength in that going so that he might enjoy the hoard of rings by his own doom. He loaded the sea-boat and bore the bright treasures on to the ship's bosom, he the son of Waels. The worm melted hot. He was of wanderers the most widely famous in deeds of courage, amongst men, the protector of warriors. He formerly throve thus.

Then the warfare of Heremod was waning, his strength and his courage, and he was betrayed among the giants into the hands of the foes, and sent quickly away. And too long did whelming sorrow vex his soul. He was a source of care to his people, to all the nobles, and many a proud churl often was lamenting in former times the way of life of the stout-hearted, they who trusted him for the bettering of bales, that the child of their lord should always be prospering, and succeed to his father's kingdom, and hold the folk, the hoard and city of refuge, the kingdom of heroes, the country of the Danes. But Beowulf Hygelac's kinsman was fairer to all men; but crime assailed Heremod.

Sometimes they passed along the fallow streets contending on mares. Then came the light of morning and hastened forth. And many a stiff-minded messenger went to the high hall to see the rare wonder. Likewise the King himself, the ward of the hoard of rings, came treading all glorious and with a great suite, forth from the bridal bower, and choice was his bearing, and his Queen with him passed along the way to the Mead-hall with a troop of maidens.

XIV

Hrothgar spake. He went to the hall and stood on the threshold and saw the steep roof all decked out with gold and the hand of Grendel. 'Let thanks be given quickly to God for this sight,' said he. 'Often I waited for the loathsome one, for the snares of Grendel. May God always work wonder after wonder, He the Guardian of glory. It was not long ago that I expected not a bettering of any woes for ever, when, doomed to blood, this best of all houses stood all stained with gore. Now has this Hero done a deed, through the power of the Lord, which none of us formerly could ever perform with all our wisdom. Lo! any woman who gave birth to such a son among human kind, may say, if she yet live, that the Creator was gracious unto her in bearing of children. Now, O Beowulf, I will love thee in heart as my son. Hold well to this new peace. Nor shall there be any lack of joys to thee in the world, over which I have power. Full oft I for less have meted out rewards and worshipful gifts to a meaner warrior, one weaker in strife. Thou hast framed for thyself mighty deeds, so that thy doom liveth always and for ever. May the All-wielder ever yield thee good as He now doth.'

Beowulf spake, the son of Ecgtheow: 'We framed to fight that brave work with much favour, and hazarded a deed of daring and the might of the unknown. I quickly gave you to see the monster himself the enemy in his fretted armour ready to fall. I thought to twist him quickly with hard grip on a bed of slaughter so that he should lie in the throes of death, because of my hand-grip, unless he should escape with his body. But I could not cut off his going when the Creator willed it not. I cleft him not readily, that deadly fiend. He was too strong on his feet. Nevertheless he left behind his hand as a life protection to show the track, his arm and his shoulders. But not by any means thus did that wretched creature get any help, nor by that did the evil-doer, brought low by sin, live any longer. But sorrow hath him in its fatal grip closely encompassed with baleful bands. There shall a man covered with sins be biding a mickle doom as the shining Creator will prescribe.'

Then was the man silent, the son of Ecglaf, in his boasting speech about deeds of battle, when the Athelings looked at the hand high up on the roof, by the craft of the earl, and the fingers of the foe, there before each one. And each of the places of the nails was likest to steel, the claw of the heathen, the uncanny claw of the battle warrior. Every one was saying that no very good iron, of any of the brave ones, would touch him at all, that would bear away thence the bloody battle-hand of the monster.

XV

Then was it bidden that Hart should be decked by their hands on the inside. And many there were of the men and wives who adorned that wine-hall the guest-chamber. And the tapestries shone along the walls brocaded with gold; many a wonderful sight for every man who stareth upon them. And that bright dwelling was greatly marred, though within it was fast bound with iron yet the door-hinges had sprung apart. The roof alone escaped all safe and sound when the monster turned to flight despairing of life and doomed for his crimes. Nor will it be easy to escape from that fate, whosoever may try to, but he shall get by strife the ready place of the children of men of the soul-bearers, who dwell upon earth, by a fate that cannot be escaped where his body shall sleep after the banquet fast in the tomb.

Then was the time for Healfdene's son to go into the hall, when the King himself would partake of the banquet. Nor have I ever heard tell that any people in greater numbers bore themselves better about their treasure-giver. And the wealthy ones sat down on the bench and rejoiced in their feeding. And full courteously their kinsmen took many a mead-cup, they the stout-hearted Hrothgar and Hrothulf in the high hall. And within was Hart filled with friends. And by no means were the Danes the while framing treacheries. Then the son of Healfdene gave to Beowulf the golden banner, the decorated staff banner as a reward for his conquest, and the helm and the byrny. And many a one saw the youth bear in front the bejewelled sword. Beowulf took the cup in the hall. Nor did he need to be ashamed of the fee-gift in the presence of warriors. Nor have I heard tell of many men giving to others on any ale-bench, four gifts gold-decked, in friendlier fashion. The outside rim wound with wires gave protection to the head on the outer side around the crown of the helmet. So that many an heirloom could not hurt fiercely the helmet that was hardened by being plunged in cold water when the shield-warrior should attack the angry one. The Protector of earls commanded eight horses to be brought in under the barriers, with bridles gold plated. And a varicoloured saddle was fixed upon one of them, decked out with treasures, and this was the battle-seat of the high King when the son of Healfdene would be doing the sword-play. Never in the van did it fail the warrior so widely kenned when the helmets were falling. Then the Prince of the Danes gave to Beowulf the wielding of them both, of horses and weapons; and bade him well enjoy them. And thus in manly fashion the famous chieftain, the treasure-guardian of heroes, rewarded the battle onslaught with horses and treasures so as no man can blame them, whoever will be saying rightly the truth.

XVI

Then the Lord of earls as he sat on the mead-bench gave glorious gifts to each one of those who had fared with Beowulf over the ocean-ways, and heirlooms they were; and he bade them atone for that one with gold whom formerly Grendel had wickedly killed as he would have done more of them unless Almighty God and the spirit of Beowulf had withstood Weird. The Creator ruleth all of human kind, as still He is doing. And good understanding is always the best thing, and forethought of mind. And he who long enjoys here the world in these strife-days, shall be biding both pleasant and loathsome fate. Then was there clamour and singing together in the presence of the battle-prince of Healfdene, and the harp was sounded and a song often sung, when Hrothgar's scop would tell forth the hall-mirth as he sat on the mead-bench.

'When Fear was befalling the heirs of Finn, the hero of the Half-Danes, and Hnaef of the Danes must fall in the slaughter of the Frisian People. Not in the least did Hildeburh need to be praising the troth of the Jutes. For sinlessly was she deprived of her dear ones in the play of swords of children and brothers. By fate they fell, wounded by arrows. And she was a sad woman. Nor without reason did the daughter of Hoc mourn their doom. When morning light came, and she could see under the sky the murder of her kinsmen where she before in the world had the greatest of joy. For warfare took away all the thanes of Finn except a mere remnant, so that he could not in the place where they met fight any warfare at all with Hengest, nor seize from the Prince's thane the woful leavings by fighting. But they offered him terms, so that they all made other room for them on the floor, and gave them halls and a high seat that they might have half the power with the children of the Jutes; and the son of Folcwalda honoured the Danes every day with fee-givings, and bestowed rings on the troop of Hengest, yea, even great treasures plated with gold, so that he would be making the kin of the Frisians bold in the beer-hall. Then they swore on both sides a treaty of peace. Finn swore with Hengest and all without strife that he held in honour the woful remnant by the doom of the wise men, and that no man there by word or work should break the treaty, or ever annul it through treacherous cunning, though they followed the slayers of their Ring-giver, all bereft of their lord as was needful for them. But if any one of the Frisians by daring speech should bring to mind the murderous hate between them, then should the edge of the sword avenge it. Then sworn was that oath, and massive gold was lifted up from the hoard. Then was Hnaef, the best of the warriors, of the bold Danes, ready on the funeral pyre. And the blood-stained shirt of mail was easily seen, the golden boar, in the midst of the flame, the iron-hard boar, and many an Atheling destroyed by wounds. Some fell on the field of death. Then Hildeburh commanded her very own son to be thrust in the flames of the pyre of Hnaef, his body to be burned and be put in the fire. And great was the moaning of the mother for her son, and dirge-like lamenting as the warrior ascended. And the greatest of slaughter-fires wound its way upwards towards the welkin and roared before the cavern. Heads were melting, wounds burst asunder. Then blood sprang forth from the wounds of the body. Flame swallowed all, that most cruel of ghosts, of both of those folk whom battle destroyed. Their life was shaken out.

XVII

'Then the warriors went forth to visit the dwellings which were bereft of friends, and to look upon the land of the Frisians, the homesteads and the high town. And Hengest was still dwelling with Finn, that slaughter-stained winter, all bravely without strife. And he thought on the homeland, though he could not be sailing his ringed ship over the waters. The sea boiled with storm and waged war with the wind. And winter locked up the ice-bound waves till yet another year came in the court, as still it doth, which ever guards the seasons, and the glory-bright weather. Then winter was scattered, and fair was the bosom of the earth. And the wanderer strove to go, the guest from the court. And much more he thought of vengeance for the feud than of the sea-voyage, as to how he could bring about an angry encounter, for he bore in mind the children of the Jutes. And so he escaped not the lot of mortals when Hunlafing did on his arm the best of swords, the flashing light of the battle, whose edge was well known to the Jutes. And dire sword-bale after befel the fierce-minded Finn, even in his very own home, when Guthlaf and Oslaf lamented the grim grip of war and the sorrow after sea-journeys, and were charging him with his share in the woes. Nor could he hold back in his own breast his fluttering soul. Then again was the hall adorned with the bodies of foemen, and Finn was also slain, the King with his troop, and the Queen was taken. And the warriors of the Danes carried to the ships all the belongings of the earth-king, such as they could find in the homestead of Finn, of ornaments and jewels. They bore away also the noble wife Hildeburh down to the sea away to the Danes, and led her to her people.'

So a song was sung, a lay of the gleemen, and much mirth there was and great noise from the benches. And cup-bearers offered wine from wondrous vessels. Then came forth Queen Wealtheow in her golden circlet, where the two good men were sitting, the uncle and his nephew. And still were they in peace together, and each true to the other. Likewise Unferth the Spokesman sat there at the foot of the Lord of the Danes. And each of them trusted Unferth's good heart and that he had a great soul, though he was not loyal to his kinsmen at the sword-play.

Then spake the Queen of the Danes: 'Take this cup, O my liege lord, thou giver of rings. Be thou right joyful, thou gold-friend to men; do thou speak mild words to the Geats, as a man should be doing. Be glad of thy Geats and mindful of gifts. Now thou hast peace both near and far. There is one who told me that thou wouldst have the battle-hero for thy son. Now Hart is all cleansed, the bright hall of rings. Enjoy whilst thou mayest many rewards, and leave to thy kinsmen both folk and a kingdom when thou shalt go forth to look on eternity. I know my glad Hrothulf will hold in honour this youth if thou, O Hrothgar the friend of the Danes, dost leave the world earlier than he. I ween that he will yield good to our children if he remembers all that has passed – how we two worshipfully showed kindness to him in former days when he was but a child.' Then she turned to the bench where were her sons Hrothric and Hrothmund and the children of heroes, the youths all together. There sat the good man Beowulf of the Geats, by the two brothers.

XVIII

And the cup was borne to them, and a friendly invitation given to them in words, and twisted gold was graciously proffered him, two arm-ornaments, armour and rings, and the greatest of neck-rings of which I heard tell anywhere on earth. Ne'er heard I of better hoard jewels of heroes under the sky, since Hama carried away the Brosinga-men to the bright city, ornaments and treasure vessel. It was he who fled from the cunning plots of Eormanric and chose eternal gain. Hygelac of the Geats next had the ring, he who was the grandson of Swerting, when under the standard he protected the treasure and defended the plunder. And Weird carried him off when he, because of pride suffered woes, the feud with the Frisians. Then carried he the jewels, the precious stones over the sea, he who was the ruling prince, and he fell under shield; and the life of the king and the coat of mail and ring together came into possession of the Franks. And worse warriors plundered the slaughter after the war. And the corpses of the Geats held the field of death. The hall resounded with noise when Wealtheow spake these words in the midst of the court:

'Enjoy this ring, dearest Beowulf, and use this coat of mail, these national treasures, and good luck befall thee! Declare thyself a good craftsman, and be to these boys gentle in teaching, and I will be mindful of thy guerdon for that thou hast so acted that men will esteem thee far and near for ever and ever, even as widely as the sea doth encompass the windy earth-walls. Be a noble Atheling as long as thou livest. I give thee many treasures. Be thou kindly in deed to my sons, joyful as thou art. For here is each earl true to his fellow, and mild of mood, and faithful to his liege-lord. Thanes are gentle, the people all ready. O ye warriors who have drunk deep, do as I tell you.' She went to the seat where was a choice banquet, and the men drank wine. They knew not Weird, the Fate that was grim, as it had befallen many an earl.

Then evening came on, and Hrothgar betook him to his own quarters, the Prince to his resting-place, and a great number of earls kept guard o'er the palace as often they had done in former days. They laid bare the bench-board and spread it over with beds and bolsters. And one of the beer-servants eager and fated went to his bed on the floor. And they set at his head war-shields, that were bright. And over the Atheling, there on the bench was easily seen the towering helmet and the ringed byrny, the glorious spear. It was their wont to be ready for war both at home and in battle, at whatever time their lord had need of them. The season was propitious.

XIX

Then they sank down to sleep. And sorely some of them paid for their evening repose, as full often it had happened to them since Grendel came to the gold-hall and did evil, until an end was made of him, death after sins. It was easily seen and widely known to men that an avenger survived the loathsome one, for a long time after the war-sorrow. A woman, the mother of Grendel, a terrible wife, bore in mind her woes. She who was fated to dwell in the awful lake in the cold streams since Cain became a sword-slayer to his only brother, his father's son. He then went forth marked for the murder, and fled from human joys and dwelt in the waste. And thence he awoke many a fatal demon. And Grendel was one of them, the hateful fierce wolf, who found the man wide awake awaiting the battle. And there was the monster at grips with him, yet he remembered the main strength the wide and ample gift which God gave to him, and trusted in the favour of the Almighty for himself, for comfort and help by which he vanquished the enemy and overcame the hell-sprite. Then he departed abject, bereft of joy, to visit the death-place, he the enemy of mankind.

But his mother, greedy and sad in mind would be making a sorrowful journey that she might avenge the death of her son. She came then to Hart, where the Ring-Danes were asleep in that great hall. Then soon there came misfortune to the earls when the mother of Grendel entered the chamber. Yet less was the terror, even by so much as the craft of maidens, the war-terror of a wife, is less than that of men beweaponed – when the sword hard bound and forged by the hammer, and stained with blood, cuts the boar on the helmet of the foe with its edge. Then in the hall, the hard edge was drawn, the sword over the seats, and many a broad shield, heaved up fast by the hand. And no one heeded the helmet nor the broad shield when terror seized upon them. She was in great haste, she would go thence her life to be saving when she was discovered. Quickly she had seized one of the Athelings fast in her grip when forth she was fleeing away to the fen-land. He was to Hrothgar the dearest of heroes, in the number of his comrades by the two seas, a powerful shield-warrior, whom she killed as he slumbered, a youth of renown. Beowulf was not there. To another the place was assigned after the treasure-gift had been bestowed on the famous Geat. Then a great tumult was made in Hart, and with bloodshed she had seized the well-known hand of Grendel her son. And care was renewed in all the dwellings. Nor was that a good exchange that they on both sides should be buying with the lives of their friends.

Then was the wise King, the hoar battle-warrior, rough in his mood when he came to know that the dearest of his chief thanes was dead and bereft of life. And Beowulf quickly was fetched into the bower, he, the man all victorious. And at the dawning went one of the earls, a noble champion, he and his comrades, where the proud man was waiting, to see whether the All-wielder will ever be causing a change after woe-spells. And the battle-worthy man went along the floor with his band of followers (the hall wood was resounding) so that he greeted the wise man with words, the Lord of the Danes, and asked him if he had had a quiet night in spite of the pressing call.

XX

Hrothgar spake, he the Lord of the Danes: 'Ask not after our luck, for sorrow is renewed to the folk of the Danes. Aeschere is dead, the elder brother of Yrmenlaf; he was my councillor and my rune-teller, my shoulder-companion when we in the battle protected our heads; when troops were clashing and helmets were crashing. He was what an earl ought to be, a very good Atheling. Such a man was Aeschere. And a wandering slaughter-guest was his hand-slayer, in Hart. I know not whither that dire woman exulting in carrion, and by her feeding made famous, went on her journeys. She was wreaking vengeance for the feud of thy making when thou killedst Grendel but yesternight, in a violent way, with hard grips, because all too long he was lessening and destroying my people. He fell in the struggle, gave his life as a forfeit; and now comes another, a mighty man-scather, to avenge her son, and the feud hath renewed as may seem a heavy heart-woe to many a thane who weeps in his mind over the treasure-giver. Now lieth low the hand which availed you well, for every kind of pleasure. I heard land-dwellers, and hall-counsellors, and my people, say that they saw two such monstrous March-steppers, alien-sprites, holding the moorland. And one of them was in the likeness of a woman as far as they could tell; the other, shapen wretchedly, trod the path of exiles in the form of a man, except that he was greater than any other man, he whom in former days the earth-dwellers called by name Grendel. They knew not his father, whether any secret sprite was formerly born of him. They kept guard over the hidden land, and the wolf-slopes, the windy nesses, the terrible fen-path where the mountain streams rush down under mists of the nesses, the floods under the earth. And it is not farther hence than the space of a mile where standeth the lake, over which are hanging the frosted trees, their wood fast by the roots, and shadowing the water. And there every night one may see dread wonders, fire on the flood. And there liveth not a wise man of the children of men who knoweth well the ground. Nevertheless the heath-stepper, the strong-horned hart, when pressed by the hounds seeketh that woodland, when put to flight from afar, ere on the hillside, hiding his head he gives up his life.

'Nor is that a canny place. For thence the surge of waters riseth up wan to the welkin when stirred by the winds, the loathsome weather, until the heaven darkens and skies weep. Now is good counsel depending on thee alone. Thou knowest not the land, the terrible places where thou couldest find the sinful man; seek it if thou darest. I will reward thee for the feud with old world treasures so I did before, with twisted gold, if thou comest thence, on thy way.'

XXI

Beowulf spake, the son of Ecgtheow: 'Sorrow not, O wise man. It is better for each one to avenge his friend, when he is much mourning. Each one of us must wait for the end of his world-life. Let him work who may, ere the doom of death come; that is afterwards best for the noble dead. Arise, O ward of the kingdom. Let us go forth quickly to trace out the going of Grendel's kinswoman. I bid thee do it. For neither in the bosom of the earth, nor in forests of the mountains, nor by the [ways of the sea, go where she will, shall she escape into safety. Do thou this day be patient in every kind of trouble as I also hope to be.' The old man leapt up and gave thanks to God, the mighty Lord, for the words of Beowulf.

Then was bridled a horse for Hrothgar, a steed with twisted hair, and as a wise prince he went forth in splendid array. The troop of shield-warriors marched along. And the traces were widely seen in the forest-ways, the goings of Grendel's mother over the ground. Forwards she had gone over the mirky moorlands, and had borne in her grasp, bereft of his soul, the best of the thanes who were wont to keep watch over Hrothgar's homestead. Then Beowulf, the Atheling's child, stepped o'er the steep and stony slopes and the narrow pathways, and the straitened single tracks, an unknown way, by the steep nesses, and by many a sea-monster's cavern. And one of the wise men went on before to seek out the path, until all at once he found some mountain trees, overhanging the grey stones, a forest all joyless. And underneath was a water all bloodstained and troubled. And a grievous thing it was for all the Danes to endure, for the friends of the Scyldings, and for many a thane, and distressful to all the earls, when they came upon the head of Aeschere on the cliffs above the sea. The flood boiled with blood and with hot gore (the folk looked upon it). And at times the horn sounded a battle-song ready prepared.

All the troop sat down. And many kinds of serpents they saw in the water, and wonderful dragons searching the sea, and on the cliff-slopes, monsters of the ocean were lying at full length, who at the morning tide often make a woful journey on the sail-path; and snakes and wild beasts they could see also. And these living things fell down on the path all bitter and angry when they perceived the noise, and the blast of the war-horn. And the Prince of the Geats killed one of them with his bow and arrows and ended his wave-strife, and he was in the sea, slower at swimming as death swept him away. And on the waves by fierce battle hard pressed, and with boar-spears savagely barbed, the wondrous sea-monster was assailed in the struggle and drawn up on the headland. And men were looking at the awful stranger. And Beowulf put on him his armour, that was fitting for an earl, and by no means did he lament over his life, for the hand-woven coat of mail, which was ample and of many colours, was destined to explore the deeps, and knew well how to defend his body, so that neither battle-grip nor the hostile grasp of the treacherous one might scathe breast or life; and the white helmet thereof warded his head, that which was destined to search out the bottom of the sea and the welter of waters, and which was adorned with treasures and encircled with noble chains, wondrously decked and set round with boar-images, as in days of yore a weapon-smith had made it for him, so that no brand nor battle-sword could bite him. And by no means was that the least of aids in battle that the Spokesman of Hrothgar lent him at need, even the hilted sword which was called Hrunting. And it was one of the ancient treasures. Its edge was of iron, and poison-tipped, and hardened in battle-sweat. And never did it fail in the fight any man who brandished it in his hands, or who dared to go on fearful journeys, to the field of battle. And that was not the first time that it was to do deeds of courage. And Unferth did not think, he the kinsman of Ecglaf, crafty of strength, of what he formerly had said when drunken with wine, he had lent that weapon to a braver sword-warrior. He himself durst not risk his life in the stress of the waters and do a glorious deed. And thereby he lost his doom of famous deeds. But thus was it not with that other, for he had got himself ready for the battle.

XXII

Beowulf spake, the son of Ecgtheow: 'O kinsman of Healfdene, thou far-famed and proud prince, thou gold-friend of men, now that eager I am for this forth-faring, bethink thee now of what we two were speaking together, that if I should lose my life through helping thee in thy need, thou wouldst be always to me in the place of a father after my death. Be thou a guardian to my kinsmen, my thanes, and my hand comrades, if battle should take me. And dear Hrothgar, send thou the gifts, which thou didst give me, to Hygelac. And the Lord of the Geats, the son of Hrethel, when he looks on the treasure and perceives the gold, will see that I found a giver of rings, one good and open-handed, and that while I could, I enjoyed the treasures. And do thou let Unferth, the man who is far-famed, have the old heirloom, the curiously wrought sword with its wave-like device, with its hard edge. I work out my fate with Hrunting, or death shall seize me.'

After these words the Lord of the Weder-Geats courageously hastened, and by no means would he wait for an answer. The whelming sea received the battle-hero. And it was a day's while before he could see the bottom of the sea. And very soon the fierce and eager one who had ruled the expanse of the floods for a hundred years, she, the grim and greedy, saw that a man was searching out from above the dwelling of strange monsters. Then she made a grab at him, and closed on the warrior with dire embrace. But not at first did she scathe his body, safe and sound. The ring surrounded it on the outside, so that she could not pierce the coat of mail or the interlaced war-shirt with loathsome finger. Then the sea-wolf, when she came to the bottom of the sea, bore the Ring-Prince towards her house so that he might not, though he was so strong in soul, wield any weapon; and many a wonder oppressed him in the depths, many a sea-beast broke his war-shirt with his battle-tusks, and monsters pursued him.

Then the earl saw that he was in he knew not what hall of strife, where no water scathed him a whit, nor could the sudden grip of the flood touch him because of the roof-hall. He saw, too, a firelight, a bright pale flame shining. Then the good man caught sight of the she-wolf, that monstrous wife, down in the depths of the sea. And he made a mighty rush with his sword. Nor did his hand fail to swing it so that the ringed mail on her head sang a greedy death-song. Then Beowulf the stranger discovered that the battle-blade would not bite or scathe her life, but the edge failed the lord in his need. It had suffered many hand-blows, and the helmet, the battle-dress of the doomed one, it had often cut in two. That was the first time that his dear sword-treasure failed him. Then he became resolute, and not by any means did he fail in courage, that kinsman of Hygelac, mindful of glory. And this angry warrior threw away the stout sword, bound round with jewels with its wavy decorations, and with its edge of steel, so that it lay prone on the ground; and henceforth he trusted in his strength and the hand-grasp of might. So should a man be doing when he thinketh to be gaining long-lasting praise in fighting, and careth not for his life. Then the Lord of the Geats seized by the shoulder the mother of Grendel (nor at all did he mourn over that feud), and he, the hard in battle, threw down his deadly foe, when he was angry, so that she lay prone on the floor. But she very quickly, with grimmest of grips, requited him a hand-reward, and made a clutch at him. And the weary in soul, that strongest of fighters, he the foot-warrior stumbled and fell. Then she sat on that hall-guest, and drew forth her axe, broad and brown-edged, and would fain be avenging the death of her child, of her only son. But on his shoulder was the coat of mail all woven, which saved his life and prevented the entrance of the point and the edge of the sword. And the son of Ecgtheow, the Prince of Geats, would have surely gone a journey under the wide earth unless that warlike coat of mail had given him help, that hard war-net, and unless the Holy God He the cunning Lord, and the Ruler in the heavens, had wielded the victory, and easily decided the issue aright; then he straightway stood up.

XXIII

Then among the weapons he caught sight of a sword, rich in victories, an old weapon of the giants, and doughty of edge, the glory of warriors. It was the choicest of weapons, and it was greater than any other man could carry to the battle-playing, and all glorious and good, a work of the giants. And he seized it by the belted hilt, he the warrior of the Danes, rough and battle-grim, and he brandished the ring-sword; and despairing of life, he angrily struck so that hardly he grasped at her neck and broke the bone-rings. And the point pierced through the doomed flesh-covering. And she fell on the floor. The sword was all bloody, and the man rejoiced in his work. Shone forth the bright flame and a light stood within, even as shineth the candle from the bright heavens. And then he looked on the hall, and turned to the wall. And the thane of Hygelac, angry and resolute, heaved hard the weapon, taking it by the hilt. And the edge was not worthless to the battle-warrior, for he would be quickly requiting Grendel many a war-rush which he had done upon the West Danes, many times oftener than once when in sleeping he smote the hearth-comrade of Hrothgar, and fed on them sleeping, of the Danish folk, some fifteen men, and bore forth yet another one, that loathly prey. And well he requited him, this furious champion, when he saw the war-weary Grendel lying in death, all void of his life as formerly in Hart the battle had scathed him. His body sprang apart when after his death he suffered a stroke, a hard battle-swing; and then he struck off his head.

Right soon the proud warriors, they who with Hrothgar, looked forth on the sea, could easily see, that the surging water was all stained with blood and the grey-haired ancients spoke together about the good man, that they deemed not the Atheling would ever again come seeking the famous Prince Hrothgar glorying in victory, for it seemed unto many that the sea-wolf had destroyed him.

Then came noonday. The valiant Danes left the headland, and the gold-friend of men went homeward thence. And the strangers of the Geats, sick in mind, sat and stared at the water. They knew and expected not that they would see again their liege-lord himself. Then the sword began to grow less, after the battle-sweat, into icicles of steel. And a wonder it was that it all began to melt likest to ice, when Our Father doth loosen the band of frost and unwinds the icicles, He who hath power over the seasons, He is the true God. Nor in these dwellings did the Lord of the Geats take any other treasure, though much he saw there, except the head and the hilt, decked out with jewels. The sword had melted, and the decorated weapon was burnt up. The blood was too hot, and so poisonous the alien sprite who died in that conflict. Soon Beowulf was swimming, he who formerly awaited the onset of the hostile ones in the striving, and he dived upwards through the water. And the weltering surge and the spacious lands were all cleansed when the alien sprite gave up his life and this fleeting existence.

He the stout-hearted came swimming to shore, he the Prince of the sea-men enjoying the sea-spoils, the great burden of that which he had with him. They advanced towards him and gave thanks to God, that glorious crowd of thanes, and rejoiced in their lord that they could see him once more. Then was loosed quickly from that valiant man both helmet and shield. The sea became turbid, the water under welkin, all stained with blood. And rejoicing in spirit the brave men went forth with foot-tracks and passed over the earth, the well-known pathways. And a hard task it was for each one of those proud men to bear that head away from the sea-cliff. Four of them with difficulty on a pole were bearing the head of Grendel to the gold-hall, until suddenly, valiant and battle-brave, they came to the palace, fourteen of the Geats marching along with their liege-lord who trod the field where the mead-hall stood. Then this Prince of the thanes, this man so bold of deed and honoured by Fate, this battle-dear warrior went into the hall to greet King Hrothgar. Then over the floor where warriors were drinking they bore Grendel's head, a terror to the earls and also to the Queen. And men were looking at the splendid sight of the treasures.

XXIV

Beowulf spake, the son of Ecgtheow: 'Lo, son of Healfdene, lord of the Danes, we have brought thee this booty of the sea all joyfully, this which thou seest as a token of glory. And I hardly escaped with my life, and hazarded an arduous task of war under water. And nearly was the battle ended for me, but that God shielded me. Nor could I in that conflict do aught with Hrunting, though the weapon was doughty. But the Ruler of men granted me to see hanging on the wall a beauteous sword mighty and ancient (often He guides those who are bereft of their comrades), and I drew the weapon. And I struck in that striving the guardian of the house when I saw my chance. Then that battle-sword that was all decked out, burned up so that blood gushed forth, the hottest of battle-sweat. But I bore off that hilt thence from the enemy, and wrought vengeance for the crimes, the deaths of the Danes, as it was fitting. And here I bid thee to take thy rest all sorrowless in Hart, with the troop of thy men and each of the thanes of thy people, the youth and the doughty ones. O Lord of the Danes, no longer need'st thou fear for them, because of earls' life-bale as before thou didst.' Then was the golden hilt, the work of the giants, given into the hand of the old warrior, the hoary battle-chief. This work of the wonder-smiths went into the possession of the Lord of the Danes after the destruction of devils; and when the man of the fierce heart, the adversary of God guilty of murder, forsook this world, it passed to the best of world-kings by the two seas, of these who in Sceden Isle dealt out treasures. Hrothgar spake and looked upon the hilt, the old heirloom on which was written the beginning of the ancient feud since the flood, the all-embracing ocean slew the giant race, when they bore themselves presumptuously. They were a folk strangers to the eternal God, to whom the ruler gave their deserts through whelming of waters. Thus was there truly marked on the sword guards of shining gold, by means of rune-staves, set down and stated by whom that sword was wrought at the first, that choicest of weapons, with its twisted hilt, adorned with a dragon. Then spake the wise man the son of Healfdene, and all kept silence: 'He who doeth truth and right among the folk, and he who can recall the far-off days, he the old protector of his country may say that this earl was well born. Thy fair fame is spread throughout the wide ways, among all peoples, O my friend Beowulf. Thou dost hold all with patience, and might, with the proud of mind. I will perform the compact as we two agreed. Thou shalt be a lasting aid to thy people, a help to the heroes. Not so was Heremod to the sons of Egwela, the honour-full Danish folk. For he did not become a joy to them, but slaughter and death to the Danish people. But in a fury he killed the table-companions his boon comrades; until he alone, the famous chieftain, turned away from human joys. And though the mighty God greatly exalted him by the joys of strength over all people and rendered him help, yet a fierce hoard of hate grew up in his soul; no rings did he give to the Danes, as the custom was; and joyless he waited, so that he suffered troublesome striving and to his people a long time was baleful. Do thou be learning by that example and seek out manly virtues. I who am old in winters sing thee this song. And a wonder is it to say how the mighty God giveth wisdom to mankind through wideness of mind, lands, and earlship. He hath power over all. Sometimes he letteth the thought of man of famous kith and kin be turning to love, and giveth him earth-joys in his own country, so that he holdeth the city of refuge among men, and giveth him to rule over parts of the world, and very wide kingdoms, so that he himself foolishly never thinketh of his end. He dwelleth in weal; and neither disease nor old age doth deceive him a whit, nor doth hostile sorrow darken his mind, nor anywhere do strife or sword-hate show themselves; but all the world doth go as he willeth.

XXV

'He knoweth no evil until his share of pride wasteth and groweth, while sleepeth the guardian, the ward of his soul. And the sleep is too deep, bound up in afflictions, and the banesman draweth near who shooteth cruelly his arrows from the bow. Then in his soul under helmet is he stricken with bitter shaft. Nor can he save himself from the crooked behests of the cursed ghost. And little doth he think of that which long he hath ruled. And the enemy doth covet, nor at all doth he give in boast the plated rings, and he then forgetteth and despiseth his fate his share of honour which God before gave him, He the Wielder of wonder. And in the end it doth happen that the body sinks fleeting and doomed to death falleth. And another succeeds thereto who joyfully distributeth gifts, the old treasure of the earl, and careth not for terrors. Guard thee against malicious hate, O my dear Beowulf, thou noblest of men, and choose for thyself that better part, eternal wisdom. Have no care for pride, O glorious champion. Now is the fame of thy strength proclaimed for a while. Soon will it be that disease or sword-edge or grasp of fire or whelming of floods or grip of sword or flight of arrow or dire old age will sever thee from strength, or the lustre of thine eyes will fail or grow dim. Then forthwith will happen that death will o'erpower thee, O thou noble man. Thus have I for fifty years held sway over the Ring-Danes under the welkin and made safe by war many a tribe throughout the world with spears and swords, so that I recked not any man my foeman under the sweep of heaven. Lo! then there came to me change in my homeland, sorrow after gaming, when Grendel, that ancient foe became my invader. And ever I bore much sorrow of mind through that feud. And may God be thanked, the eternal lord, that I lingered in life, till I looked with mine eyes on that head stained with sword-blood after the old strife. Go now to thy seat and enjoy the feasting, thou who art glorious in war. And when morning cometh there shall be a host of treasures in common between us.'

And the Geat was glad of mind, and soon he went up to the high seat as the proud chief had bidden him. Then renewed was fair chanting as before 'mongst these brave ones who sat on the floor. And the helmet of night grew dark over men. And the noble warriors arose. The venerable king wished to go to his bed, the old prince of the Danes. And the Geat, the shield-warrior, desired greatly to go to his rest. And straightway a hall-thane guided the far-comer, weary of his journey, he who so carefully attended to all his needs such as that day the ocean-goers would fain be having. And the great-hearted one rested himself. The House towered on high that was spacious and gold-decked. The guest slept within until the black raven heralded the joy of heaven.

Then came the sun, hastening and shining over the earth. Warriors were hurrying and Athelings were eager to go to their people. The bold-hearted comer would visit the ship far away. He the hardy one bade the son of Ecglaf carry forth Hrunting, and commanded him to take his sword, that lovely piece of steel. And he gave thanks for the lending, and said he reckoned him a good war-comrade and crafty in fighting. Not at all did he blame the edge of the sword. He was a proud man. When ready for the journey were all the warriors, then Beowulf the Atheling, of good worth to the Danes, went up to the dais where was Hrothgar the faithful and bold, and greeted him there.

XXVI

Beowulf spake, the son of Ecgtheow: 'Now we the sea-farers, that have come from afar, desire to say that we are hastening back to Hygelac. And here have we been nobly waited on, and well thou hast treated us. And if I then on earth can gain a whit further greater heart-love from thee, O Lord of men, than I have gained already, in doing war-deeds, thereto I'm right ready. And if I shall hear o'er the sheet of waters that terrors are oppressing those who sit round thee, as erewhile thine enemies were doing upon thee, I will bring here a thousand thanes, heroes to help thee. And I know that Hygelac, the Lord of the Geats, the guardian of my folk, though young in years, will help me by word and works to bring to thee honour and bear spear to thine aid, the help of strength, if thou hast need of men. And if Hrethric the Prince's child should ever take service in the court of the Geat, he may find there many a friend. It is better for him who is doughty himself to be seeking far countries.'

Hrothgar spake and gave him answer: 'The all-knowing Lord doth send thee words into thy mind. Never heard I a man speak more wisely, so young in years, thou art strong of main and proud of soul, and of words a wise sayer. I reckon that if it cometh to pass that an arrow or fierce battle should take away the children of Hrethel or disease or sword destroy thy sovereign, the protector of the folk, and thou art still living, that the Sea-Geats will not have to choose any better king, if thou wilt hold the kingdom of the kinsmen. Thou hast brought about peace to the folk of the Geats and the Spear-Danes, and a ceasing of the strife and of the enmity which formerly they suffered. And whilst I am ruling the wide kingdom, treasures shall be in common between us. And many a man shall greet another with gifts over the sea. And the ring-necked ship shall bear over the ocean both offerings and love-tokens. I know the two peoples to be steadfast towards friend and foe, and blameless in all things in the old wise.'

Then in that hall the prince of the earls, the son of Healfdene, gave him twelve treasures, and bade him be seeking his own people in safety and with the offerings, and quickly to come back again. Then the King, the Prince of the Danes, he of good lineage, kissed the best of thanes, and embraced his neck. And tears were falling down the face of the old man. And the old and wise man had hope of both things, but most of all of the other that they might see each the other, those thoughtful men in council.

For Beowulf was so dear to him that he could not restrain the whelming in his bosom, but a secret longing fast in the bonds of his soul was burning in his breast against his blood. So Beowulf the warrior, proud of his golden gifts, went forth o'er the grassy plain rejoicing in treasure. And the sea-goer was awaiting her lord where she lay at anchor. And as he was going he often thought on the gift of Hrothgar. He was a king, blameless in every way, until old age, that scather of many, bereft him of the joys of strength.

XXVII

So many a proud young warrior came to the seaside. And they were carrying the ring-net, the interlaced coats of mail. And the ward of the shore noticed the going of the earls, as he did their coming. Nor with evil intent did he hail the guests from the edge of the cliff, but rode up to them, and said that welcome and bright-coated warriors went to the ship to the people of the Geats. Then on the sand was the spacious craft laden with battle-weeds, the ringed prow with horses and treasures, and the mast towered high over Hrothgar's gifts. And he gave to the captain a sword bound with gold, so that by the mead-bench he was by that the worthier because of the treasure and the heirloom. Then he went on board, the deep water to be troubling, and finally left the land of the Danes. And by the mast was one of the ocean-garments, a sail fast by a rope. The sea-wood thundered. Nor did the wind hinder the journey of that ship. The ocean-goer bounded forth, the foamy-necked one, over the waves, the bound prow over the ocean streams, till they could see the cliffs of the Geats' land, the well-known headlands.

Then the keel thronged up the shore, driven by the wind, and stood fast in the sand. And the harbour-master was soon on the seashore, who of yore eagerly had seen from afar the going forth of the dear men. And he made fast the wide-bosomed ship, by the anchor chains, so that the less the force of the waves could tear away that winsome ship. He commanded the treasure of the nobles to be borne up the beach, the fretted armour and the plated gold. And not far thence it was for them to be seeking the giver of treasure, Hygelac, Hrethel's son, for at home he dwelleth, he and his companions near to the sea-wall. And splendid was that building, and the Prince was a bold King, and the halls were high, and Hygd his wife was very young and wise and mature in her figure, though the daughter of Hæreth had bided in that city but a very few years. But she was not mean nor niggardly of gifts and of treasures to the people of the Geats.

But Thrytho was fierce, for she had committed a terrible crime, that bold Queen of the folk. There was none that durst risk that dire thing of the dear companions, save only her lord, that he should stare on her with his eyes by day; but if he did he might expect that death-bands were destined for himself, for after the hand-grip a weapon was quickly prepared, that the sword that was curiously inlaid should bring to light and make known the death-bale. Nor is it a queenly custom for a woman to perform, though she might be peerless, that she should assail the life of a peace-wearer, of her dear lord, after a pretended insult. At least King Offa, the kinsman of Hemming, checked her in that. But otherwise said the ale-drinkers, namely that she did less of bale to her people and of hostile acts, since the time when she was first given all decked with gold to the young champion, to her dear lord, since she sought the Hall of Offa over the fallow flood by the guidance of her father, where on the throne whilst she lived she well did enjoy her fate, that woman famous for good works. And she kept great love for the prince of heroes, and of all mankind he was, as I have learned by asking, the greatest by two seas. For Offa was a spear-keen man in gifts and in warfare, and widely was he honoured. And he ruled his people wisely. And to him and Thrytho Eomær was born to the help of heroes, he the kinsman of Hemming, the nephew of Garmund, was crafty in battle.

XXVIII

Then the hardy one himself, with his troop set forth to tread the seashore, going along the sands, the wide sea-beaches. The candle of the world shone, the sun that was shining from the South. And joyfully they journeyed, and with courage they marched along, to where they heard by inquiring, that the good Prince of earls, the banesman of

Ongentheow the young war-king, was giving out rings within the city. And quickly was made known to Hygelac the coming of Beowulf, that he the Prince of warriors, the comrade in arms, was returning alive and hale from the battle-play, was coming to the palace. And straightway was there room made for the foot-guests on the floor of the hall by command of the King. And he that had escaped scot-free from the contest sat with the King, kinsman with kinsman, and the lord with courteous speech saluted the brave man with high-swelling words. And the daughter of Hæreth poured forth from the mead-cups throughout that great hall, for she loved well the people, and carried round the drinking-stoups to each of the warriors. And Hygelac began to question his comrade as curiosity prompted him as to the journey of the Sea-Geats. 'How went it with thee, dear Beowulf, in thy faring, when thou didst bethink thee suddenly to be seeking a contest o'er the salt waters, in battle at Hart? And thou didst requite the widely known woe which Hrothgar was suffering, that famous lord. And I brooded o'er that mind-care with sorrow-whelmings, for I trusted not in the journey of the dear man. And for a long time I bade thee not a whit to be greeting the murderous stranger, but to let the South Danes themselves wage war against Grendel. And I now give God thanks that I see thee safe and sound.'

Beowulf answered, the son of Ecgtheow: 'O Lord Hygelac, it is well known to many a man, our famous meeting, and the battle we fought, Grendel and I, on the wide plain, when he was working great sorrow to the Danes and misery for ever. All that I avenged, so that no kinsman of Grendel anywhere on earth needed to boast of that uproar by twilight, no not he of that kindred who liveth the longest, encircled by the fen. And first, to greet Hrothgar, I went to the Ring-hall. And straightway the famous kinsman of Healfdene, when he knew my intention, gave me a place with his own son; and the troop was all joyful. Nor ever have I seen greater joy amongst any hall-dwellers under the arch of heaven. Sometimes the famous Queen, the peace-bringer of the folk, walked over the whole floor and encouraged the young sons. And often she gave to the man a twisted ring ere she went to the high seat. And sometimes for the noble band the daughter of Hrothgar carried the ale-cups to the earls at the end of the high table. And I heard those who sat in that hall calling her Freawaru as she gave the studded treasure to the heroes. And she, young and gold-decked, is betrothed to the glad son of Froda. The friend of the Danes and the guardian of the kingdom has brought this to pass, and taken that counsel, so as to set at rest by that betrothal many a slaughter-feud and ancient strife. And often it happens that a little while after the fall of a people, the deadly spear seldom lieth at rest though the bride be doughty. And this may displease the lord of the Heathobards and all of his thanes of the people, when he with his bride walketh over the floor, that his doughty warriors should attend on a noble scion of the Danes, and the heirloom of the ancients should glisten on him, all hard, and the ring-sword, the treasure of the Heathobards, whilst they might be wielding weapons.

XXIX

'Till the day on which they risked their own and their comrades' lives in the battle. Then said an old spear-warrior who remembered all that had happened, the death of men by spears (his mind was grim), and he began with sorrowful mind to seek out the thought of the young champion by broodings of the heart, and to awaken the war-bales, and this is what he said: "Canst thou recognize, my friend, the dire sword which thy father carried to the battle, under the visored helm, on that last journey, when the Danes slew him and had the battle-field in their power, when Withergyld lay dead after the fall of the heroes? Now here the son of I know not which of the slayers, all boasting of treasures, goeth into the hall and boasteth of murder and carrieth the gift which thou shouldst rightly possess." Then he exhorteth and bringeth to mind each of the occasions with sorrowful words, until the time cometh that the thane of the bride dieth all stained with blood for the deeds of his father by the piercing of the sword, having forfeited his life. But the other thence escapeth alive, for he knows the land well. Then the oath-swearing of earls is broken on both sides when deadly enmities surge up against Ingeld, and his love for his wife grows cooler after whelming care. And for this reason I reckon not sincere the friendliness of the Heathobards towards the Danes or the troop-peace between them, the plighted troth.

'Now I speak out again about Grendel, for that thou knowest full well, O giver of treasure, how went that hand-to-hand fight of the heroes. When the jewel of heaven glided over the world, then the angry sprite, the terrible and evening-fierce foe, came to visit us where we were dwelling in the hall all safe and sound. There was battle impending to Hondscio, the life-bale to the doomed one. And he first fell, the champion begirt. For Grendel was to the famous thane a banesman by biting, and devoured whole the dear man. Nor would he, the bloody-toothed slayer, mindful of bales, go out empty-handed any sooner again, forth from the gold-hall; but he proved my strength of main, and ready-handed he grasped at me. An ample and wondrous glove hung fast by cunning bands. And it was cunningly fashioned by the craft of devils, and with skins of the dragon. And the fierce doer of deeds was wishful to put me therein, one among many. But he could not do so, for I angrily stood upright. And too long would it be to tell how I requited all evil to that scather of the people, where I, O my liege-lord, honoured thy people by means of good deeds. He escaped on the way, and for a little while he enjoyed life-pleasures. But his right hand showed his tracks in Hart, and he sank to the bottom of the sea, all abject and sad of heart. And the lord of the Danes rewarded me for that battle-rush with many a piece of plated gold, and with ample treasure, when morning came and we had set ourselves down to the feasting. And there was singing and rejoicing. And the wise man of the Danes, who had learned many things, told us of olden days. And the bold in battle sometimes touched the harp-strings, the wood that was full of music, and sometimes he gave forth a song that was true and sad – and sometimes, large-hearted, the King related a wondrous spell well and truly. And sometimes the old man encumbered by years, some ancient warrior, lamented his lost youth and strength in battle. His heart was tumultuous when he, of many winters, recalled all the number of them. So we rejoiced the livelong day until another night came down upon men. Then was the mother of Grendel quickly ready for vengeance, and came on a woful journey, for Death had carried off her son, that war-hate of the Geats. And the uncanny wife avenged her child. And Aeschere, that wise and ancient councillor, departed this life. Nor when morning came might the Danish people burn him with brand, that death-weary man, nor lay the beloved man on the funeral pyre. For she bore away the body in her fiendish grip under the mountain-streams. And that was to Hrothgar the bitterest of griefs which for long had befallen the Prince of the people. Then the Prince, sad in mood, by thy life entreated me that I should do a deed, worthy of an earl, midst welter of waters, and risk my life and achieve glory. And he promised me rewards. I then discovered the grim and terrible guardian of the whelming waters, at the sea's bottom, so widely talked of. There was a hand-to-hand engagement between us for a while, and the sea boiled with gore; I cut off the head of Grendel's mother in the hall at the bottom of the sea, with powerful sword. And I scarce saved my life in that conflict. But not yet was my doomsday. And afterwards the Prince of earls gave me many gifts, he the son of Healfdene.

XXXI

'So in good customs lived the King of the people. Nor had I lost the rewards, the meed of strength, for the son of Healfdene bestowed upon me treasures according to my choice, which I will bring to thee, O my warrior-King, and graciously will I proffer them. Again all favour depends on thee, for few chief kinsmen have I save thee, O Hygelac.' He commanded them to bring in the boar, the head-sign, the battle-steep helmet, the hoary byrny, the splendid war-sword, and then he chanted this song: 'It was Hrothgar, that proud prince, who bestowed upon me all this battle-gear. And a certain word he uttered to me, that I should first give thee his kindly greeting. He said that Hrothgar the King of the Danes possessed it a long while. Nor formerly would he be giving the breast-weeds to his son the brave Heoroward, though dear he was to him. Do thou enjoy all well.'

Then I heard that four horses, of reddish yellow hue, followed the armour. And thus he did him honour with horses and gifts. So should a kinsman do. By no means should they weave cunning nets for each other, or with secret craft devise death to a comrade. His nephew was very gracious to Hygelac, the brave in strife, and each was striving to bestow favours on the other. And I heard that he gave to Hygd the neck-ring so curiously and wondrously wrought, which Wealtheow a daughter of royal birth had given him, and three horses also slender and saddle-bright. And her breast was adorned with the ring she had received.

And Beowulf, son of Ecgtheow, so famous in warfare and in good deeds, bore himself boldly and fulfilled his fate, nor did he slay the drunken hearth-comrades. He was not sad-minded, but he, the battle-dear one, by the greatest of craft known to man held fast the lasting and generous gift which God gave him. For long had he been despised, so that the warriors of the Geats looked not upon him as a good man, nor did the lord of troops esteem him as of much worth on the mead-bench. Besides, they thought him slack and by no means a warlike Atheling. Then came a change from all his distresses to this glorious man. Then the Prince of Earls, the battle-brave King, commanded that the heirloom of Hrethel all decked out in gold should be brought in. For of swords there was no more glorious treasure among the Geats. And he laid it on the bosom of Beowulf, and gave him seven thousand men and a building and a throne. And both of them held the land, the earth, the rights in the land as an hereditary possession; but the other who was the better man had more especially a wide kingdom.

And in after-days it happened that there were battle-crashings, and Hygelac lay dead, and swords under shields became a death-bane to Heardred, when the brave battle-wolves, the Swedes, sought him out among the victorious ones and assailed with strife the nephew of Hereric, and it was then that the broad kingdom came into the possession of Beowulf. And he held sway therein fifty winters (and a wise King was he, that old guardian of his country) until on dark nights a dragon began to make raids, he that watched over the hoard in the lofty cavern, the steep rocky cave. And the path thereto lay under the cliffs unknown to men. And what man it was who went therein I know not, but he took from the heathen hoard a hall-bowl decked with treasure. Nor did he give it back again, though he had beguiled the guardian of the hoard when he was sleeping, by the craft of a thief. And Beowulf found out that the dragon was angry.

XXXII

And it was by no means of his own accord or self-will that he sought out the craft of the hoard of the dragon who inflicted such evil upon himself, but rather because being compelled by miseries, the slave fled the hateful blows of heroes, he that was shelterless and the man troubled by guilt penetrated therein. And soon it came to pass that an awful terror arose upon the guest... And in the earth-house were all kinds of ancient treasures, such as I know not what man of great thoughts had hidden there in days of old, the immense heirlooms of some noble race, costly treasures. And in former times death had taken them all away, and he alone of the warriors of the people who longest lingered there, full lonely and sad for loss of friends was he, and he hoped for a tarrying, that he but for a little while might enjoy the ancient treasures. And this hill was quite near to the ocean-waves, and to the sea-nesses, and no one could come near thereto.

And he the guardian of rings carried inside the cave the heavy treasures of plated gold, and uttered some few words: 'Do thou, O earth, hold fast the treasures of earls which heroes may not hold. What! From thee in days of yore good men obtained it. Deadly warfare and terrible life-bale carried away all the men of my people of those who gave up life. They had seen hall-joy. And they saw the joys of heaven. I have not any one who can carry a sword or polish the gold-plated cup, the dear drinking-flagon. The doughty ones have hastened elsewhere. The hard helmet dight with gold shall be deprived of gold plate. The polishers sleep the sleep of death who should make ready the battle grim, likewise the coat of mail which endured in the battle was shattered over shields by the bite of the iron spears and perishes after the death of the warrior. Nor can the ringed byrny go far and wide on behalf of heroes, after the passing of the war-chief.

'No joy of harping is there, nor mirth of stringed instruments, nor does the goodly hawk swing through the hall, nor doth the swift horse paw in the courtyard. And death-bale hath sent away many generations of men.' Thus then, sad at heart he lamented his sorrowful plight, one for many, and unblithely he wept both day and night until the whelming waters of death touched his heart. And the ancient twilight scather found the joyous treasure standing open and unprotected, he it was who flaming seeks the cliff-sides, he, the naked and hateful dragon who flieth by night wrapt about with fire. And the dwellers upon earth greatly fear him. And he should be seeking the hoard upon earth where old in winters he guardeth the heathen gold. Nor aught is he the better thereby.

And thus the scather of the people, the mighty monster, had in his power the hall of the hoard three hundred years upon the earth until a man in anger kindled his fury. For he carried off to his liege-lord the plated drinking-flagon and offered his master a treaty of peace. Thus was the hoard discovered, the hoard of rings plundered. And a boon was granted to the miserable man. And the Lord saw for the first time this ancient work of men. Then awoke the dragon, and the strife was renewed. He sniffed at the stone, and the stout-hearted saw the foot-mark of his foe. He had stepped too far forth with cunning craft near the head of the dragon. So may any one who is undoomed easily escape woes and exile who rejoices in the favour of the Wielder of the world. The guardian of the hoard, along the ground, was eagerly seeking, and the man would be finding who had deprived him of his treasure while he was sleeping. Hotly and fiercely he went around all on the outside of the barrow – but no man was there in the waste. Still he gloried in the strife and the battle working. Sometimes he returned to the cavern and sought the treasure vessels. And soon he found that one of the men had searched out the gold, the high heap of treasures. The guardian of the hoard was sorrowfully waiting until evening should come. And very furious was the keeper of that barrow, and the loathsome one would fain be requiting the robbery of that dear drinking-stoup with fire and flame. Then, as the dragon wished, day was departing. Not any longer would he wait within walls, but went forth girt with baleful fire. And terrible was this beginning to the people in that country, and sorrowful would be the ending to their Lord, the giver of treasure.

XXXIII

Then the Fiend began to belch forth fire, and to burn up the glorious palace. And the flames thereof were a horror to men. Nor would the loathly air-flier leave aught living thereabouts. And this warfare of the dragon was seen far and wide by men, this striving of the foe who caused dire distress, and how the war-scather hated and harmed the people of the Geats. And he hurried back to his hoard and the dark cave-hall of which he was lord, ere it was day-dawn. He had encircled the dwellers in that land with fire and brand. He trusted in his cavern, and in battle and his cliff-wall. But his hope deceived him. Then was the terror made known to Beowulf, quickly and soothly, namely that his very homestead, that best of houses, that throne of the Geats, was dissolving in the whelming fire. And full rueful was it to the good man, and the very greatest of sorrows.

And the wise man was thinking that he had bitterly angered the Wielder of all things, the eternal God, in the matter of some ancient customs. And within his breast gloomy brooding was welling, as was by no means his wont. The fiery dragon had destroyed by flame the stronghold of the people, both the sea-board and neighbouring land. And therefore the King of the Weder-Geats devised revenge upon him.

Now Beowulf the Prince of earls and protector of warriors commanded them to fashion him a glorious war-shield all made of iron. For he well knew that a wooden shield would be unavailing against flames. For he, the age-long noble Atheling, must await the end of days that were fleeting of this world-life, he and the dragon together, though long he had held sway over the hoard of treasure. And the Prince of rings scorned to employ a troop against the wide-flying monster in the great warfare. Nor did he dread the striving, nor did he think much of this battle with the dragon, of his might and courage, for that formerly in close conflict had he escaped many a time from the crashings of battle since he, the victorious sword-man, cleansed the great hall in Hart, of Hrothgar his kinsman, and had grappled in the contest with the mother of Grendel, of the loathly kin.

Nor was that the least hand-to-hand fight, when Hygelac was slain there in the Frisian land when the King of the Geats, the friendly lord of the folk, the son of Hrethel, died in the battle-rush beaten down by the sword, drunk with blood-drinking. Then fled Beowulf by his very own craft and swam through the seas. And he had on his arm alone thirty battle-trappings when he went down to the sea. Nor did the Hetware need to be boasting, of that battle on foot, they who bore their linden shields against him. And few of them ever reached their homes safe from that wolf of the battle.

But Beowulf, son of Ecgtheow, swam o'er the expanse of waters, miserable and solitary, back to his people, where Hygd proffered him treasures and a kingdom, rings and dominion. She did not think that her son Heardred would know how to hold their native seats against strangers, now that Hygelac was dead. Nor could the wretched people prevail upon the Atheling (Beowulf) in any wise to show himself lord of Heardred or to be choosing the kingship. Nevertheless he gave friendly counsel to the folk with grace and honour until that he (Heardred) was older and held sway over the Weder-Geats.

Then those exiles the sons of Ohthere sought him over the seas; they had rebelled against the Lord of the Swedes, the best of the sea-kings, that famous chieftain of those who bestowed rings in Sweden. And that was life's limit to him. For the son of Hygelac, famishing there, was allotted a deadly wound by the swing of a sword. And the son of Ongentheow went away thence to visit his homestead when Heardred lay dead, and left Beowulf to sit on the throne and to rule the Goths. And he was a good King.

XXXIV

He was minded in after-days to be requiting the fall of the prince. He was a friend to the wretched Eadgils, and helped Eadgils the son of Ohthere with an army with warriors and with weapons, over the wide seas. And then he wrought vengeance with cold and painful journeyings and deprived the king (Onela) of life. Thus the son of Ecgtheow had escaped all the malice and the hurtful contests and the courageous encounters, until the day on which he was to wage war with the dragon. And so it came to pass that the Lord of the Geats went forth with twelve others and inflamed with fury, to spy out the dragon. For he had heard tell of the malice and hatred he had shown to men, whence arose that feud.

And by the hand of the informer, famous treasure came into their possession; he was the thirteenth man in the troop who set on foot the beginning of the conflict. And the sorrowful captive must show the way thither. He against his will went to the earth-hall, for he alone knew the barrow under the ground near to the sea-surge, where it was seething, the cavern that was full of ornaments and filagree. And the uncanny guardian thereof, the panting war-wolf, held possession of the treasures, and an ancient was he under the earth. And it was no easy bargain to be gaining for any living man.

So the battle-hardened King sat down on the cliff, and took leave of his hearth-comrades, he the gold-friend of the Geats. And his heart was sad, wavering, and ready for death, and Weird came very near to him who would be greeting the venerable warrior and be seeking his soul-treasure, to divide asunder his life from his body. And not long after that was the soul of the Atheling imprisoned in the flesh. Beowulf spake, the son of Ecgtheow: 'Many a war-rush I escaped from in my youth, in times of conflict. And well I call it all to mind. I was seven years old when the Lord of Treasures, the friendly lord of the folk, took me away from my father – and King Hrethel had me in thrall, and gave me treasure and feasted me and kept the peace. Nor was I a whit less dear a child to him than any of his own kin, Herebald and Hæthcyn or my own dear

Hygelac. And for the eldest was a murder-bed most unhappily made up by the deeds of a kinsman, when Hæthcyn his lordly friend brought him low with an arrow from out of his horn-bow, and missing the mark he shot through his brother with a bloody javelin. And that was a fight not to be atoned for by gifts of money; and a crime it was, and wearying to the soul in his breast. Nevertheless the Atheling must unavenged be losing his life. For so is it a sorrowful thing for a venerable man to see his son riding the gallows-tree when he singeth a dirge a sorrowful song, as his son hangeth, a joy to the ravens. And he, very old, may not give him any help. And every morning at the feasting he is reminded of his son's journey else-whither. And he careth not to await another heir within the cities, when he alone through the fatality of death hath found out the deeds.

'Heartbroken he looks on the bower of his son, on the wasted wine-hall, become the hiding-place for the winds and bereft of the revels. The riders are sleeping, the heroes in the tomb. Nor is any sound of harping, or games in the courts as erewhile there were.

XXXV

'Then he goeth to the sleeping-place and chanteth a sorrow-song, the one for the other. And all too spacious seemed to him the fields and the dwelling-house. So the Prince of the Geats bore welling heart-sorrow after Herebald's death, nor a whit could he requite the feud on the murderer, nor visit his hate on that warrior with loathly deeds, though by no means was he dear to him. He then forsook the joys of life because of that sorrow-wound which befell him, and chose the light of God, and left to his sons land and towns when he departed this life as a rich man doth. Then was there strife and struggle between the Swedes and the Geats, and over the wide seas there was warfare between them, a hardy battle-striving when Hrethel met with his death. And the children of Ongentheow were brave and battle-fierce, and would not keep the peace on the high seas, but round about Hreosnaborg they often worked terrible and dire distress. And my kinsmen wrought vengeance for that feud and crime as all men know, though the other bought his life with a hard bargain. And war was threatening Hæthcyn the lord of the Geats. Then I heard tell that on the morrow one brother the other avenged on the slayer with the edge of the sword, whereas Ongentheow seeketh out Eofor. The war-helmet was shattered, and the Ancient of the Swedes fell prone, all sword-pale. And well enough the hand kept in mind the feud and withheld not the deadly blow. And I yielded him back in the warfare the treasures he gave me with the flashing sword, as was granted to me. And he gave me land and a dwelling and a pleasant country. And he had no need to seek among the Gifthas or the Spear-Danes or in Sweden a worse war-wolf, or to buy one that was worthy.

'And I would always be before him in the troop, alone in the front of the battle, and so for ever will I be striving, whilst this sword endureth, that earlier and later has often stood me in good stead, since the days when for doughtiness I was a hand-slayer to Day Raven the champion of the Hugs. Nor was he fated to bring ornaments or breast-trappings to the Frisian King, but he the guardian of the standard, he the Atheling, fell on the battle-field, all too quickly. Nor was the sword-edge his bane, but the battle-grip broke the whelmings of his heart and the bones of his body. Now shall my sword-edge, my hand and hard weapon, be fighting for the hoard.'

Beowulf moreover now for the last time spake these boastful words: 'In many a war I risked my life in the days of my youth, yet still will I seek a feud, I the old guardian of the people will work a glorious deed if the wicked scather cometh out from his earth-palace to seek me.'

Then he saluted for the last time each of the warriors, the brave wearers of helmets, the dear companions. 'I would not carry a sword or weapon against the dragon if I knew how else I might maintain my boast against the monster, as I formerly did against Grendel. But in this conflict I expect the hot battle-fire, both breath and poison. Therefore I have both shield and byrny. I will not flee from the warder of the barrow a foot's-space, but it shall be with me at the wall of the barrow as Weird shall direct, who created all men. I am strong in soul so that I will refrain from boasting against the war-flier. Await ye on the barrow guarded by byrnies, O ye warriors in armour, and see which of us two will better survive his wounds after

the battle-rush. This is no journey for you nor fitting for any man
save only for me, that he should share a conflict with the monster
and do deeds worthy of an earl. I will gain possession of the gold by
my courage, or battle and deadly evil shall take away your lord.'

Then the strong warrior, hard under helm, arose beside his shield
and carried his shirt of mail under the rocky cliffs and trusted in the
strength of himself alone. Nor was that a coward's journey. Then Beowulf,
possessed of manly virtues, who had escaped in many a conflict and
crashing of battle when men encountered on foot, saw standing by the
wall of the barrow an arch of rock, and a stream broke out thence from
the barrow, and the whelming of that river was hot with battle-fires.
Nor could he survive any while near to the hoard unburnt because of
the flame of the dragon. Then in a fury the Prince of the Weder-Geats
let a torrent of words escape from his breast and the stout-hearted one
stormed. And his war-clear voice resounded under the hoar cliffs. And
hatred was stirred, for the guardian of the hoard recognized well the
voice of Beowulf. And that was no time to be seeking friendship. And
the breath of the monster, the hot battle-sweat, came forth from the
rock at the first and the earth resounded. The warrior, the Lord of the
Geats, raised his shield under the barrow against the terrible sprite. Now
the heart of the dragon was stirred up to seek the conflict. The good
war-king had formerly drawn his sword, the ancient heirloom, not slow
of edge. And each of them who intended evil was a terror the one to the
other. And the stern-minded one, he the Prince of friendly rulers, stood
by his steep shield, and he and the dragon fell quickly together. Beowulf
waited warily all in his war-gear. Then the flaming monster bent as he
charged, hastening to his doom. The shield well protected life and body
of the famous warrior for a lesser while than he had willed it if he was to
be wielding victory in that contest on the first day; but Weird had not so
fated it. And the Lord of the Geats uplifted his hand, and struck at the
horribly bright one heavy with heirlooms, so that the edge stained with
blood gave way on the bone and bit in less strongly than its master had
need of when pressed by the business. Then after the battle-swing the
guardian of the barrow was rough-minded and cast forth slaughter-fire.
Battle-flames flashed far and wide. And the son of the Geats could not

boast of victory in the conflict. The sword had failed him, naked in the battle, as was unfitting for so well tempered a steel. And it was not easy for the famous son of Ecgtheow to give up possession of the bottom of the sea, and that he should against his will dwell in some place far otherwhere, as must each man let go these fleeting days sooner or later. And not long after this Beowulf and the monster met together again. The guardian of the hoard took good heart, and smoke was fuming in his breast. And fierce were his sufferings as the flames embraced him, he who before had ruled over the folk. Nor at all in a troop did his hand-comrades stand round him, that warrior of Athelings, showing courage in the battle, but they fled into a wood their lives to be saving. And the mind of one of them was surging with sorrows, for to him whose thoughts are pure, friendship cannot ever change.

XXXVI

Wiglaf was he called, he who was the son of Weohstan, the beloved shield-warrior, the Prince of the Danes and the kinsman of Aelfhere. He saw his lord suffering burning pain under his visor. Then he called to mind the favour that he (Beowulf) had bestowed upon him in days of yore, the costly dwelling of the Waegmundings and all the folk-rights which his father had possessed. Then he could not restrain himself, but gripped the shield with his hand, the yellow wood, and drew forth the old sword which was known among men as the heirloom of Eanmund, the son of Ohthere, and in the striving Weohstan was banesman by the edge of the sword to that friendless exile and bore away to his kinsman the brown-hued helmet, the ringed byrny, and the old giant's sword that Onela had given him, the war-weeds of his comrade, and the well-wrought armour for fighting. Nor did he speak of the feud, though he slew his brother's son. And he held possession of the treasures many years, both the sword and the byrny, until such time as his son should hold the earlship as his father had done. And he gave to the Geats a countless number of each kind of war-weeds, when he in old age passed away from this life, on the outward journey. That was the first time for the young champion that he went into the war-rush with his noble lord.

Nor did his mind melt within him, nor did the heirloom of his kinsman at the war-tide. And the dragon discovered it when they two came together.

Wiglaf spake many fitting words, and said to his comrades (for his mind was sad within him): 'I remember the time when we partook of the mead, and promised our liege-lord in the beer-hall, he who gave to us rings, that we would yield to him war-trappings both helmets and a hand-sword, if such need befell him. And he chose us for this warfare, and for this journey, of his own free will, and reminded us of glory; and to me he gave these gifts when he counted us good spear-warriors and brave helmet-bearers, although our lord, this guardian of the people had it in his mind all alone to do this brave work for us, for he most of all men could do glorious things and desperate deeds of war. And now is the day come that our lord hath need of our prowess and of goodly warriors. Let us then go to the help of our battle-lord while it lasts, the grim terror of fire. God knows well of me that I would much rather that the flame should embrace my body together with that of my lord the giver of gold. Nor does it seem to me to be fitting that we should carry shields back to the homestead except we have first laid low the foe and protected the life of the Prince of the Weders. And well I know that his old deserts were not that he alone of the youth of the Geats should suffer grief and sink in the fighting. So both sword and helmet, byrny and shield shall be common to both of us together.'

Then he waded through the slaughter-reek, and bore the war-helmet to the help of his lord, and uttered a few words: 'Beloved Beowulf, do thou be doing all things, as thou of yore in the days of thy youth wast saying that thou wouldst not allow thy glory to be dimmed whilst thou wast living. Now shalt thou, the brave in deeds and the resolute noble, save thy life with all thy might. I am come to help thee.' After these words came the angry dragon, the terrible and hostile sprite yet once again, and decked in his various hues of whelmings of fire, against his enemies, the men that he hated. And the wood of the shield was burnt up with the waves of flame, and his byrny could not help the young spear-warrior; yet did the youth bravely advance under the shield of his kinsman when his own had been destroyed by the flames. Then again the war-king bethought him of glory, and struck a mighty blow with his battle-sword so that it fixed itself in his head, forced in by violence. And Naegling, Beowulf's sword old and grey, broke in pieces, and failed in the contest. It was not given to him that sharp edges of swords should help him in battle. His hand was too strong, so that it overtaxed every sword, as I have been told, by the force of its swing, whenever he carried into battle a wondrous hand-weapon. And he was nowise the better for a sword. Then for the third time, the scather of the people, the terrible Fire-dragon, was mindful of feuds, and he rushed on the brave man when he saw that he had room, all hot and battle-grim, and surrounded his neck with bitter bones. And he was all be-bloodied over with life-blood, and the sweat welled up in waves.

XXXVII

Then I heard tell that the Earl of the King of the People showed in his time of need unfailing courage in helping him with craft and keenness, as was fitting for him to do. He paid no heed to the head of the dragon (but the brave man's hand was being burnt when he helped his kinsman), but that warrior in arms struck at the hostile sprite somewhat lower in his body so that his shining and gold-plated sword sank into his body, and the fire proceeding therefrom began to abate. Then the good King Beowulf got possession of his wits again, and drew his bitter and battle-sharp short sword that he bore on his shield. And the King of the Geats cut asunder the dragon in the midst of his body. And the fiend fell prone; courage had driven out his life, and they two together had killed him, noble comrades in arms. And thus should a man who is a thane always be helping his lord at his need. And that was the very last victory achieved by that Prince during his life-work.

Then the wound which the Earth-dragon had formerly dealt him began to burn and to swell. And he soon discovered that the baleful venom was seething in his breast, the internal poison. Then the young noble looked on the giant's work as he sat on a seat musing by the cliff wall, how arches of rock, firmly on columns held the eternal earth-house within. Then the most noble thane refreshed his blood-stained and famous Lord, his dear and friendly Prince with water, with his own hands, and loosened the helmet for the battle-sated warrior. And Beowulf spake, over his deathly pitiful wound, for well he knew that he had enjoyed the day's while of his earthly joy: and the number of his days was all departed and death was coming very near.

'Now,' said Beowulf, 'I would have given battle-weeds to my son if any heir had been given to me of my body. I held sway over these peoples fifty years. And there was no folk-king of those who sat round about who dared to greet me with swords, or oppress with terror. At home have I bided my appointed time, and well I held my own, nor did I seek out cunning feuds, nor did I swear many unrighteous oaths. And I, sick of my life-wounds, can have joy of all this. For the Wielder of men cannot reproach me with murder of kinsmen when my life shall pass forth from my body. Now do thou, beloved Wiglaf, go quickly and look on the hoard under the hoar stone, now that the dragon lieth prone and asleep sorely wounded and bereft of his treasure. And do thou make good speed that I may look upon the ancient gold treasures and yarely be feasting mine eyes upon the bright and cunning jewels, so that thereby after gazing on that wealth of treasure I may the more easily give up my life and my lordship over the people, whom I have ruled so long.'

XXXVIII

Then straightway I heard tell how the son of Weohstan, after these words had been spoken, obeyed the behest of his lord, who was sick of his wounds, and carried the ring-net and the coat of mail adorned, under the roof of the barrow. And as Wiglaf, exulting in victory, came by the seat, he saw many gems shining and shaped like the sun and gleaming gold all lying on the ground, and wondrous decorations on the wall, and he saw too the den of the dragon, the ancient twilight-flier, and flagons standing there and vessels of men of days long gone by, no longer polished but shorn of adornment. And there also was many a helmet, ancient and rusty, and many arm-rings cunningly twisted.

The possession of treasure and of gold on the earth may easily make proud all of mankind, let him hide it who will. Likewise he saw the all-gilded banner lying high over the hoard, that greatest of wondrous handiwork and all woven by the skill of human hands. And therefrom went forth a ray of light, so that he could see the floor of the cave, and look carefully at the jewels. And there was no sign of the dragon, for the sword-edge had carried him off.

Then I heard tell how in that barrow one at his own doom plundered the hoard, that old work of giants, and bore away on his arms both cups and dishes. And the banner also he took, that brightest of beacons. Beowulf's sword, with its iron edge, had formerly injured him who had been the protector of these treasures for a long time, and had waged fierce flame-terror, because of the hoard fiercely welling in the midnight hour until he was killed.

The messenger was in haste, and eager for the return journey, and laden with jewels, and curiosity tormented him as to whether he would find the bold-minded Prince of the Geats alive on the battle-field, and bereft of strength where before he had left him. Then he with the treasures found the glorious lord, his own dear master, at the last gasp, and all stained with blood. And he began to throw water upon him, until the power of speech brake through his mind, and Beowulf spake, and with sorrow he looked upon the hoard.

'I would utter words of thanks to the Lord and wondrous King, to the eternal God, for the treasures which now I am looking upon that I have managed to obtain them for my dear people before my death-day. Now that I have in exchange for this hoard of treasure sold my life in my old age, and laid it down, do thou still be helping the people in their need, for I may no longer be lingering here. Do thou bid the famous warriors erect a burial-mound, after the burning of the funeral pyre, at the edge of the sea, which shall tower aloft on Whale's Ness, as a memorial for my people, and so the sea-farers shall call it the Hill of Beowulf, even those who drive the high ships from afar through the mists of the flood.'

Then he the bold Prince doffed from his neck the golden ring. And he gave it to his thane, to the young spear-warrior, the gold-adorned helmet, the ring, and the byrny, and bade him enjoy it well. 'Thou, O Wiglaf,' he said, 'art the last heir of our race, of that of the Waegmundings. Weird has swept away all my kinsmen to their fated doom, all the earls in their strength, and I shall follow after them.'

Now that was the very last word of the old warrior's breast thoughts, ere he chose the funeral pyre the hot wave-whelmings. And his soul went forth from his breast to be seeking the doom of the truth-fast ones.

XXXIX

Then had it sorrowfully come to pass for the young warrior that he saw his most beloved in a miserable plight on the earth at his life's end. Likewise the terrible dragon, his slayer, lay there bereft of life and pressed sore by ruin. And the coiled dragon could no longer wield the hoard of rings, but the iron edges of the sword, well tempered and battle-gashed; the hammer's leavings, had carried him off, so that the wide-flier, stilled because of his wounds, fell to the earth near to the hoard-hall. And no more in playful wise at the midnight hour, did he drift through the air; this dragon, proud in his gainings of treasure, showed not his face, but was fallen to the earth because of the handiwork of the battle-warrior.

And as I have heard, it would have profited but few of the mighty men, even though they were doughty in deeds of all kinds, though they should rush forth against the flaming breath of the poisonous scather, even to the very disturbing of the Ring-Hall with their hands, if they should have found the guardian thereof awake, and dwelling in the cliff-cave. Then Beowulf's share of lordly treasure was paid for by his death. And both he and the dragon had come to an end of their fleeting days.

And not long after that, the laggards in battle, those cowardly treaty-breakers, ten of them together, came back from the woodlands, they who erewhile had dreaded the play of javelins when their lord had sore need of their help. But they were filled with shame, and carried their shields, and battle-weeds, to where the old prince was lying. And they looked on Wiglaf; he the foot-warrior sat aweary near to the shoulders of his lord, and sought to rouse him by sprinkling water upon him, but he succeeded not at all. Nor could he, though he wished it ever so much, keep life in the chieftain or avert a whit the will of the Wielder of all things. Every man's fate was decided by the act of God, as is still the case. Then was a grim answer easily given by the young man to these who erewhile had lost their courage.

Wiglaf spake, he the son of Weohstan, the sad-hearted. 'He who will speak truth may say that the lord and master who gave you gifts, and warlike trappings, in which ye are now standing, when he very often gave on the ale-bench to them who sat in the hall, both helmet and byrny, the Prince to his thanes, as he could find any of you most noble far or near, that he wholly wrongly bestowed upon you war-trappings when war befell him. The King of the folk needed not indeed to boast of his army comrades, yet God, the Wielder of Victory, granted to him that alone he avenged himself with the edge of the sword when he had need of strength. And but a little life-protection could I give him in the battle, yet I sought to help him beyond my strength. The dragon was by so much the weaker when I struck with my sword that deadly foe. And less fiercely the fire surged forth from his head. Too few were the defenders thronged around their lord when his fated hour came. And now shall the receiving of treasure, and the gift of swords, and all joy of home and hope cease for ever to men of your kin. And every man of you of the tribe must wander empty of land-rights, since noble men will learn far and wide of your flight and inglorious deed. Death would be better for earls than a life of reproach.'

XL

Then he bade them announce that battle-work at the entrenchment up over the sea-cliff where that troop of earls sat sorrowful in soul through the morning-long day, holding their shields and in expectation of the end of the day and the return of the dear man. And he who rode to and fro o'er the headland was little sparing of fresh tidings, but said to all who were sitting there, 'Now is the joy-giver of the people of the Geats fast on his death-bed, and by the deed of the dragon he inhabits the place of rest gained by a violent death. And by his side lieth the enemy of his life, sick of his dagger-wounds. Nor could he inflict with the sword any wound on that monster. Wiglaf sits over Beowulf, he the son of Weohstan, the earl over the other one who is dead, and reverently keeps ward over the loathèd and the belovèd. But there is an expectation of a time of war to the people, since to Franks and Frisians the fall of the King has become widely known. The hard strife was shapen against the Hugs, when Hygelac came with a fleet into the Frisian lands where the Hetware overcame him in battle, and by their great strength and courage brought it to pass that the shield-warrior should stoop. He fell in the troop. Nor did the Prince give jewelled armour to the doughty ones. The mercy of the Merewing was not always shown to us. Nor do I expect aught of peace or good faith from the Swedish People. But it was well known that Ongentheow bereft Hæthcyn the son of Hrethel of life over against Ravenswood, when because of pride the warlike Swedes first sought out the people of the Geats. Soon Ongentheow the wise father of Ohthere, the ancient and terrible, gave him (Hæthcyn) a return blow, destroyed the sea-kings, and rescued his bride (Queen Elan) he the old man rescued his wife bereft of gold, the mother of Onela and of Ohthere, and then followed up the deadly foe until with difficulty they retreated all lord-less to Ravenswood. And he attacked the remnant with a great army, weary though he was with his wounds. And the live-long night he vowed woe upon the wretched troop, and said that on the morrow he would by the edge of the sword slay some and hang them up on the gallows-tree for a sport of the birds. But help came to the sorrowful in soul at the dawn of day, when they heard the horn of Hygelac and the blast of his trumpet when the good man came on the track faring with the doughty warriors of the people.

XLI

'And the blood-track of both Swedes and Geats, the slaughter-rush of warriors, was widely seen how the folk stirred up the feud amongst them. The good man, wise and very sad, went away with his comrades to seek out a stronghold. Earl Ongentheow turned away to higher ground, for he the war-crafty one had heard of the prowess of Hygelac the proud. He had no trust in his power to resist, or that he would be able to refuse the demands of the seamen, the ocean-farers, or defend the treasure he had taken, the children and the bride. Thence afterwards, being old, he sought refuge under the earth-wall. Then was chase given to the people of the Swedes and the banner of Hygelac borne aloft; and they swept o'er the field of peace when the sons of Hrethel thronged to the entrenchment. And there too, was Ongentheow, he the grey-haired King of the People driven to bay at the edge of the sword, and forced to submit to the sole doom of Eofor. And angrily did Wulf, son of Wanred, smite him with weapon, so that from that swinging blow blood-sweat gushed forth in streams under the hair of his head. Yet the old Swede was not terrified thereby, but quickly gave back a terrible blow by a worse exchange when the King of the people turned thither. Nor could Wulf the bold son of Wanred give back a blow to the old churl, for Ongentheow had formerly cut his helmet in two, so that he, stained with blood, fell prone perforce to the ground. But not yet was he doomed, but he raised himself up, though the wound touched him close. And the hardy thane of Hygelac (Eofor) when his brother lay prostrate, caused the broad sword, the old giant's sword, to crash through the wall of shields upon the gigantic helmet. Then stooped the King, the shepherd of the people, mortally wounded. And there were many who bound up his kinsman and quickly upraised him when room had been made so that they might possess the battle-field, while one warrior was plundering another. One took the iron shield of Ongentheow, and his hard-hilted sword, and his helmet, and carried the trappings of the old man to Hygelac. And he received the treasures, and fairly he promised reward for the people, and he did as he promised. The lord of the Geats (Hygelac) son of Hrethel, rewarded with very costly gifts the battle onset of Eofor and Wulf when he got back to his palace, and bestowed upon each of them a hundred thousand, of land and locked rings. Nor could any man in the world reproach him for that reward, since they had gained glory by fighting; and he gave to Eofor his only daughter, she who graced his homestead, to wed as a favour. And this is the feud and the enmity and hostile strife of men, which I expect the Swedish people will seek to awaken against us when they shall hear we have lost our Prince, he who in days of yore held treasure and kingdom against our foes after the fall of heroes, and held in check the fierce Swede, and did what was good for the people and deeds worthy of an earl. Now is it best for us to hasten to look upon our King and bring him who gave to us rings to the funeral pyre. Nor shall a part only of the treasure be melted with the proud man, but there is a hoard of wealth, an immense mass of gold, bought at a grim cost, for now at the very end of his life he bought for us rings. And the brands shall devour all the treasures and the flames of the funeral fire, they shall enfold them, nor shall an earl carry away any treasure as a memorial, nor shall any maid all beauteous wear on her neck ring adornments, but shall go sad of soul and bereft of gold, and often not once only tread an alien land now that the battle-wise man (Beowulf) has laid aside laughter, the games and the joys of song. And many a morning cold shall the spear in the hand-grip be heaved up on high, nor shall there be the sound of harping to awaken the warriors, but the war-raven, eager over the doomed ones, shall say many things to the eagle how it fared with him in eating the carrion while he, with the wolf, plundered the slaughtered.'

Thus then was the brave warrior reciting loathly spells. And he lied not at all in weird or word. Then the troop rose up together, and all unblithely went under Eagles' Ness, to look on the wonder, and tears were welling. Then they found him on the sand in his last resting-place, and bereft of soul, who had given them rings in days gone by, and then had the last day drawn to its close, for the good man Beowulf, the warrior King, the Lord of the Weder-Goths, had died a wondrous death.

But before this they had seen a more marvellous sight, the dragon on the sea-plain, the loathsome one lying right opposite. And there was the fire-dragon grimly terrible, and scorched with fire. And he was fifty feet in length as he lay there stretched out. He had had joy in the air awhile by night, but afterwards he went down to visit his den. But now he was the prisoner of death, and had enjoyed his last of earth-cares. And by him stood drinking-cups and flagons, and dishes were lying there and a costly sword, all rusty and eaten through as though they had rested a thousand winters in the bosom of the earth. And those heirlooms were fashioned so strongly, the gold of former races of men, and all wound round with spells, so that no man could come near that Ring-hall, unless God only, Himself the true King of victories, gave power to open up the hoard to whom He would (for He is the Protector of men) even to that man as it seemed good to Him.

XLII

Then was it quite clear to them that the affair had not prospered with the monster, who had hidden ornaments within the cave under the cliff. The guardian thereof had slain some few in former days. Then had the feud been wrathfully avenged. And it is a mystery anywhere when a valiant earl reaches the end of his destiny, when a man may no longer with his kinsman dwell in the mead-hall. And thus was it with Beowulf when he sought out the guardian of the cavern and his cunning crafts. And he himself knew not how his departure from this world would come about. And thus famous chieftains uttered deep curses until the day of doom, because they had allowed it to come to pass that the monster should be guilty of such crimes, and, accursed and fast with hell-bands, as he was, and tormented with plagues that he should plunder the plain. He (Beowulf) was not greedy of gold, and had more readily in former days seen the favour of God.

Wiglaf spake, the son of Weohstan: 'Often shall many an earl of his own only will suffer misery, as is our fate. Nor could we teach the dear lord and shepherd of the kingdom any wisdom so that he would fail to be meeting the keeper of the gold treasures (the dragon) or to let him stay where he had been long time dwelling in his cavern until the world's end. But he held to his high destiny. Now the hoard is seen by us, grimly got hold of, and at too great a cost was it yielded to the King of the people whom he enticed to that conflict. I was within the cavern, and looked upon all the hoard, the decoration of the palace, when by no means pleasantly, room was made for me, and a faring was granted to me in under the sea-cliff. And in much haste I took a very great burden of hoard-treasures in my hand, and bore it forth hither to my King. He was still alive, wise and witting well. And he the ancient uttered many words in sadness, and bade me greet you, and commanded that ye should build after death of your friend a high grave-mound in the place of the funeral pyre, a great and famous monument, for he himself was the most worshipful of men throughout the earth, while he was enjoying the wealth of his city. Let us now go and see and seek yet once again the heap of treasures, the wonder under the cliff. I will direct you, so that ye may look at close quarters upon the rings and the wealth of gold. Let the bier be quickly made ready when we come forth again, and then let us carry the dear man our lord when he shall enjoy the protection of the Ruler of all things.'

Then the son of Weohstan, the battle-dear warrior, ordered that commandment should be given to many a hero and householder that they should bring the wood for the funeral pyre from far, they the folk-leaders, to where the good man lay dead.

'Now the war-flame shall wax and the fire shall eat up the strong chief among warriors, him who often endured the iron shower, when the storm of arrows, strongly impelled, shot over the shield-wall, and the shaft did good service, and all eager with its feather, fear followed and aided the barb.' Then the proud son of Weohstan summoned from the troop the thanes of the King, seven of them together, and the very best of them, and he the eighth went under the hostile roof. And one of the warriors carried in his hand a torch which went on in front.

And no wise was it allotted who should plunder that hoard, since they saw some part unguarded remaining in the Hall, and lying there fleeting.

And little did any man mourn when full heartily they carried forth the costly treasures. Then they shoved the dragon the worm over the cliff-wall, and let the wave take him and the flood embrace that guardian of the treasures. Then the twisted golden ornaments were loaded on a wagon, an immense number of them. And the noble Atheling, the hoar battle-warrior, was carried to Whales' Ness.

XLIII

Then the People of the Geats got ready the mighty funeral pyre, and hung it round with helmets and battle-shields, and bright byrnies as he had asked. And in the midst they lay the famous Prince, and they lamented the Hero, their dear lord. Then the warriors began to stir up the greatest of bale-fires on the cliff-side. And the reek of the wood-smoke went up swart, over the flame, which was resounding, and its roar mingled with weeping (and the tumult of winds was still), until it had broken the body, all hot into the heart. And unhappy in their thinkings, and with minds full of care, they proclaim the death of their lord, likewise a sorrowful song the Bride…

And heaven swallowed up the smoke. Then on the cliff-slopes the people of the Geats erected a mound, very high and very broad, that it might be beholden from afar by the wave-farers; and they set up the beacon of the mighty in battle in ten days. And the leavings of the funeral fire they surrounded with a wall, so that very proud men might find it to be most worthy of reverence.

And they did on the barrow rings and necklaces, and all such adornments as formerly warlike men had taken of the hoard. And they allowed the earth to hold the treasure of earls, the gold on the ground, where it still is to be found as useless to men as it always was. Then the battle-dear men rode round about the mound, the children of the Athelings, twelve of them there were in all, and would be uttering their sorrows and lamenting their King, and reciting a dirge, and speaking of their champion. And they talked of his earlship and of his brave works, and deemed them doughty, as is fitting that a man should praise his lord in words and cherish him in his heart when he shall have gone forth from the fleeting body. So the People of the Geats lamented over the fall of their lord, his hearth-companions, and said that he was a world-king, and the mildest, the gentlest of men, and most tender to his people, and most eager for their praise.

Further Notes on Beowulf

Part I

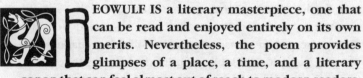

BEOWULF IS a literary masterpiece, one that can be read and enjoyed entirely on its own merits. Nevertheless, the poem provides glimpses of a place, a time, and a literary canon that can feel almost out of reach to modern readers. The following excerpts from R.W. Chambers' landmark study, *Beowulf: An Introduction to the Study of the Poem* (1921), are a solid starting point for anyone looking to venture a little further into the world of the poem.

The study of *Beowulf* is its own tale to tell. The poem was originally read primarily as historical material. Passing references to individual kings, heroes, places and battles were painstakingly matched with Latin chronicles. Descriptions of weapons and armour, ships and buildings were compared to archaeological finds, and linguists used the poem as evidence for the development of Old English and other early Germanic languages. That all changed in 1936, when a lecture by J.R.R. Tolkien deftly shifted the focus of the field. In arguing, eloquently and persuasively, for *Beowulf*'s value as 'a work of art' as much as a historical document, Tolkien paved the way for the modern study of the poem, and of Old English literature more generally.

Chambers' work somewhat straddles these differing approaches to *Beowulf* scholarship. He identifies in the poem two strands which he feels are never quite reconciled. The first is the historical or pseudo-historical elements: the Danish and Geatish royal families, their feuds and courts. This leans towards the older school of Beowulf studies. The second, which is the focus of the excerpts presented here, is what Chambers calls the 'old wives' fables of struggles with ogres and dragons'. Fables though they may be, it is in his minute tracing of the parallels between various literary and folkloric sources that Chambers' work on *Beowulf* truly shines. The excerpts in this first chapter trace those parallels in detail, starting with *Grettis saga*, then *Hrólfs saga kraka*, and further literary analogues, followed by the specific characters Scyld and Beow. The texts discussed here are then presented in translation in the following chapter. The opening genealogical table is an invaluable reference point, giving the names and relationships of all the main characters of *Beowulf*, the royal houses to which they belong, and the names of corresponding characters from Scandinavian literature.

Naturally, Chambers is a scholar of his time. Not included amongst the following excerpts are the many pages of Latin sources that he presents entirely untranslated, confident that his readers would be as familiar with that ancient language as with modern English. His focus on the minutiae of the poem's details, and in particular his efforts to completely reconcile the poem's narrative with historical events, is also of its time. A study of *Beowulf* today is as likely to consider its literary themes, or its narrative craftsmanship, and we are more comfortable allowing for ambiguities or contradictions in the text. Nevertheless, for anyone hoping to see the world of *Beowulf* a little more fully, there is no better place to start than the wealth of stories, fables, histories and archaeology presented below.

Genealogical Tables

T HE NAMES OF the corresponding characters in Scandinavian legend are added in italics; first the Icelandic forms, then the Latinized names as recorded by Saxo Grammaticus.

The Danish Royal Family

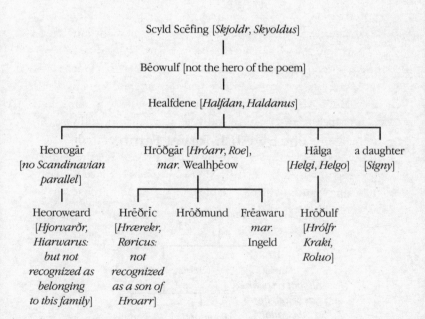

Scyld Scēfing [*Skjoldr, Skyoldus*]

Bēowulf [not the hero of the poem]

Healfdene [*Halfdan, Haldanus*]

Heorogār
[*no Scandinavian parallel*]

Hrōðgār [*Hróarr, Roe*], *mar.* Wealhþēow

Hālga [*Helgi, Helgo*]

a daughter [*Signy*]

Heoroweard
[*Hjorvarðr, Hiarwarus: but not recognized as belonging to this family*]

Hrēðrīc
[*Hrærekr, Røricus: not recognized as a son of Hroarr*]

Hrōðmund

Frēawaru *mar.* Ingeld

Hrōðulf
[*Hrólfr Kraki, Roluo*]

The Geat Royal Family

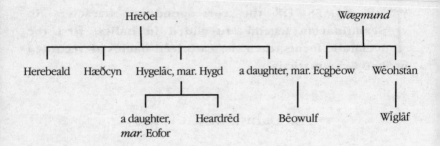

Hrēðel — Herebeald, Hæðcyn, Hygelāc (mar. Hygd), a daughter (mar. Ecgþēow)

Wægmund — a daughter (mar. Ecgþēow), Wēohstān

Hygelāc, mar. Hygd — a daughter, *mar.* Eofor, Heardrēd

Ecgþēow — Bēowulf

Wēohstān — Wīglāf

The Swedish Royal Family

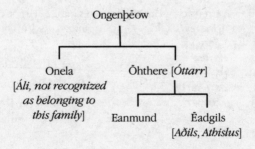

Ongenþēow — Onela [*Áli, not recognized as belonging to this family*], Ōhthere [*Óttarr*]

Ōhthere — Eanmund, Ēadgils [*Aðils, Athislus*]

The Scandinavian Parallels –
Grettir and Orm

T HE *GRETTIS SAGA* tells the adventures of the most
famous of all Icelandic outlaws, Grettir the strong. As
to the historic existence of Grettir there is no doubt:
we can even date the main events of his life, in spite of
chronological inconsistencies, with some precision. But
between the year 1031, when he was killed, and the latter
half of the thirteenth century, when his saga took form,
many fictitious episodes, derived from folk-lore, had woven
themselves around his name. Of these, one bears a great,
if possibly accidental, likeness to the Grendel story: the
second is emphatically and unmistakably the same story as
that of Grendel and his mother. In the first, Grettir stops at a
farm house which is haunted by Glam, a ghost of monstrous
stature. Grettir awaits his attack alone, but, like Beowulf,
lying down.

Glam's entry and onset resemble those of Grendel: when Grettir closes
with him he tries to get out. They wrestle the length of the hall, and
break all before them. Grettir supports himself against anything that
will give him foothold, but for all his efforts he is dragged as far as
the door. There he suddenly changes his tactics, and throws his whole
weight upon his adversary. The monster falls, undermost, so that Grettir
is able to draw, and strike off his head; though not till Glam has laid
upon Grettir a curse which drags him to his doom.

The second story – the adventure of Grettir at Sandhaugar
(Sandheaps) – begins in much the same way as that of Grettir and
Glam. Grettir is staying in a haunted farm, from which first the farmer
himself and then a house-carl have, on two successive Yuletides,
been spirited away. As before, a light burns in the room all night,

and Grettir awaits the attack alone, lying down, without having put off his clothes. As before, Grettir and his assailant wrestle down the room, breaking all in their way. But this time Grettir is pulled put of the hall, and dragged to the brink of the neighbouring gorge. Here, by a final effort, he wrenches a hand free, draws, and hews off the arm of the ogress, who falls into the torrent below.

Grettir conjectures that the two missing men must have been pulled by the ogress into the gulf. This, after his experience, is surely a reasonable inference: but Stein, the priest, is unconvinced. So they go together to the river, and find the side of the ravine a sheer precipice: it is ten fathom down to the water below the fall. Grettir lets down a rope: the priest is to watch it. Then Grettir dives in: "the priest saw the soles of his feet, and then knew no more what had become of him." Grettir swims under the fall and gets into the cave, where he sees a giant sitting by a fire: the giant aims a blow at him with a weapon with a wooden handle ("such a weapon men then called a *hefti-sax*"). Grettir hews it asunder. The giant then grasps at another sword hanging on the wall of the cave, but before he can use it Grettir wounds him. Stein, the priest, seeing the water stained with blood from this wound, concludes that Grettir is dead, and departs home, lamenting the loss of such a man. "But Grettir let little space come between his blows till the giant lay dead." Grettir finds the bones of the two dead men in the cave, and bears them away with him to convince the priest: but when he reaches the rope and shakes it, there is no reply, and he has to climb up, unaided. He leaves the bones in the church porch, for the confusion of the priest, who has to admit that he has failed to do his part faithfully.

Now if we compare this with *Beowulf*, we see that in the Icelandic story much is different: for example, in the *Grettis saga* it is the female monster who raids the habitation of men, the male who stays at home in his den. In this the *Grettis saga* probably represents a corrupt tradition: for, that the female should remain at home whilst the male searches for his prey, is a rule which holds good for devils as well as for men. The change was presumably made in order to avoid the difficulty – which the *Beowulf* poet seems also to have realized – that after the male has been slain, the rout of the female is felt to be a deed of less note – something of an anti-climax.

The sword on the wall, also, which in the *Beowulf*-story is used by the hero, is, in the *Grettir*-story, used by the giant in his attack on the hero.

But that the two stories are somehow connected cannot be disputed. Apart from the general likeness, we have details such as the escape of the monster after the loss of an arm, the fire burning in the cave, the *hefti-sax*, a word which, like its old English equivalent (*hæft-mēce*, *Beowulf*, 1457), is found in this story only, and the strange reasoning of the watchers that the blood-stained water must necessarily be due to the hero's death.

Now obviously such a series of resemblances cannot be the result of an accident. Either the *Grettir*-story is derived directly or indirectly from the *Beowulf* epic, more or less as we have it, or both stories are derived from one common earlier source. The scholars who first discovered the resemblance believed that both stories were independently derived from one original. This view has generally been endorsed by later investigators, but not universally. And this is one of the questions which the student cannot leave open, because our view of the origin of the *Grendel*-story will have to depend largely upon the view we take as to its connection with the episode in the *Grettis saga*.

If this episode be derived from *Beowulf*, then we have an interesting literary curiosity, but nothing further. But if it is independently derived from a common source, then the episode in the *saga*, although so much later, may nevertheless contain features which have been obliterated or confused or forgotten in the *Beowulf* version. In that case the story, as given in the *Grettis saga*, would be of great weight in any attempt to reconstruct the presumed original form of the *Grendel*-story.

The evidence seems to me to support strongly the view of the majority of scholars – that the *Grettir*-episode is not derived from *Beowulf* in the form in which that poem has come down to us, but that both come from one common source.

It is certain that the story of the monster invading a dwelling of men and rendering it uninhabitable, till the adventurous deliverer arrives, did not originate with Hrothgar and Heorot. It is an ancient and widespread type of story, of which one version is localized at the Danish court. When therefore we find it existing, independently of its Danish setting, the presumption is in favour of this being a survival of the old independent story. Of course it is *conceivable* that the Hrothgar-Heorot setting might have been first added, and subsequently stripped off again so clean that no trace of it remains. But it seems going out of our way to assume this, unless we are forced to do so.

Again, it is certain that these stories – like all the subject matter of the Old English epic – did not originate in England, but were brought across the North Sea from the old home. And that old home was in the closest connection, so far as the passage to and fro of story went, with Scandinavian lands. Nothing could be intrinsically more probable than that a story, current in ancient Angel and carried thence to England, should also have been current in Scandinavia, and thence have been carried to Iceland.

Other stories which were current in England in the eighth century were also current in Scandinavia in the thirteenth. Yet this does not mean that the tales of Hroar and Rolf, or of Athils and Ali, were borrowed from English epic accounts of Hrothgar and Hrothulf, or Eadgils and Onela. They were part of the common inheritance – as much so as the strong verbs {52}or the alliterative line. Why then, contrary to all analogy, should we assume a literary borrowing in the case of the *Beowulf-Grettir*-story? The compiler of the *Grettis saga* could not possibly have drawn his material from a MS of *Beowulf*: he could not have made sense of a single passage. He conceivably *might* have drawn from traditions *derived* from the Old English epic. But it is difficult to see how. Long before his time these traditions had for the most part been forgotten in England itself. One of the longest lived of all, that of Offa, is heard of for the last time in England at the beginning of the thirteenth century. That a Scandinavian sagaman at the end of the century could have been in touch, in any way, with Anglo-Saxon epic tradition seems on the whole unlikely. The Scandinavian tradition of Offa, scholars are now agreed, was not borrowed from England, and there is no reason why we should assume such borrowing in the case of Grettir.

The probability is, then, considerable, that the *Beowulf*-story and the *Grettir*-story are independently derived from one common original.

And this probability would be confirmed to a certainty if we should find that features which have been confused and half obliterated in the O.E. story become clear when we turn to the Icelandic. This argument has lately been brought forward by Dr Lawrence in his essay on "The Haunted Mere in *Beowulf*." Impressive as the account of this mere is, it does not convey any very clear picture. Grendel's home seems sometimes to be in the sea: and again it seems to be amid marshes, moors and fens, and again it is "where the mountain torrent goes down under the darkness of the cliffs – the water below the ground (i.e. beneath overhanging rocks)."

This last account agrees admirably with the landscape depicted in the *Grettis saga*, and the gorge many fathoms deep through which the stream rushes, after it has fallen over the precipice; not so the other accounts. These descriptions are best harmonized if we imagine an original version in which the monsters live, as in the *Grettis saga*, in a hole under the waterfall. This story, natural enough in a Scandinavian country, would be less intelligible as it travelled South. The Angles and Saxons, both in their old home on the Continent and their new one in England, were accustomed to a somewhat flat country, and would be more inclined to place the dwelling of outcast spirits in moor and fen than under waterfalls, of which they probably had only an elementary conception. "The giant must dwell in the fen, alone in the land."

Now it is in the highest degree improbable that, after the landscape had been blurred as it is in *Beowulf*, it could have been brought out again with the distinctness it has in the *Grettis saga*. To preserve the features so clearly the *Grettir*-story can hardly be derived from *Beowulf*: it must have come down independently.

But if so, it becomes at once of prime importance. For by a comparison of *Beowulf* and *Grettir* we must form an idea of what the original story was, from which both were derived.

Another parallel, though a less striking one, has been found in the story of Orm Storolfsson, which is extant in a short saga about contemporary with that of Grettir, *Ormsþáttr Stórólfssonar*, in two ballads from the Faroe Islands and two from Sweden.

It is generally asserted that the *Orm*-story affords a close parallel to the episodes of Grendel and his mother. I cannot find close resemblance, and I strongly suspect that the repetition of the assertion is due to the fact that the *Orm*-story has not been very easily accessible, and has often been taken as read by the critics.

But, in any case, it has been proved that the *Orm*-tale borrows largely from other sagas, and notably from the *Grettis saga* itself. Before arguing, therefore, from any parallel, it must first be shown that the feature in which Orm resembles Beowulf is not derived at second hand from the *Grettis saga*. One such feature there is, namely Orm's piety, which he certainly does not derive from Grettir. In this he with equal certainty resembles Beowulf. According to modern ideas, indeed, there is more of the Christian hero in Beowulf than in Orm.

Now Orm owes his victory to the fact, among other things, that, at the critical moment, he vows to God and the holy apostle St Peter to make a pilgrimage to Rome should he be successful. In this a parallel is seen to the fact that Beowulf is saved, not only by his coat of mail, but also by the divine interposition. But is this really a parallel? Beowulf is too much of a sportsman to buy victory by making a vow when in a tight place. *Gǽð ā wyrd swā hīo scel* is the exact antithesis of Orm's pledge.

However, I have given in the Second Part the text of the *Orm*-episode, so that readers may judge for themselves the closeness or remoteness of the parallel.

Bothvar Bjarki

WE HAVE SEEN that there are in *Beowulf* two distinct elements, which never seem quite harmonized: firstly the historic background of the Danish and Geatic

courts, with their chieftains, Hrothgar and Hrothulf, or Hrethel and Hygelac: and secondly the old wives' fables of struggles with ogres and dragons. In the story of Grettir, the ogre fable appears – unmistakably connected with the similar story as given in *Beowulf*, but with no faintest trace of having ever possessed any Danish heroic setting.

Turning back to the *Saga of Rolf Kraki*, we *do* find against that Danish setting a figure, that of the hero Bothvar Bjarki, bearing a very remarkable resemblance to Beowulf.

Bjarki, bent on adventure, leaves the land of the Gautar (Götar), where his brother is king, and reaches Leire, where Rolf, the king of the Danes, holds his court; [just as Beowulf, bent on adventure, leaves the land of the Geatas (Götar) where his uncle is king, and reaches Heorot, where Hrothgar and Hrothulf (Rolf) hold court].

Arrived at Leire, Bjarki takes under his protection the despised coward Hott, whom Rolf's retainers have been wont to bully. The champions at the Danish court [in *Beowulf* one of them only – Unferth] prove quarrelsome, and they assail the hero during the feast, in the *Saga* by throwing bones at him, in *Beowulf* only by bitter words. The hero in each case replies, in kind, with such effect that the enemy is silenced.

But despite the fame and splendour of the Danish court, it has long been subject to the attacks of a strange monster – a winged beast whom no iron will bite [just as Grendel is immune from swords]. Bjarki [like Beowulf] is scornful at the inability of the Danes to defend their own home: "if one beast can lay waste the kingdom and the cattle of the king." He goes out to fight with the monster *by night*, accompanied only by Hott. He tries to draw his sword, but the sword is fast in its sheath: he tugs, the sword comes out, and he slays the beast with it. This seems a most pointless incident: taken in connection with the supposed invulnerability of the foe, it looks like the survival of some episode in which the hero was unwilling [as in Beowulf's fight with Grendel] or unable [as in Beowulf's fight with Grendel's mother] to slay the foe with his sword. Bjarki then compels the terrified coward Hott to drink the monster's blood. Hott forthwith becomes a valiant champion, second only to Bjarki himself. The beast is then propped up as if still alive: when it is seen next morning the king calls upon his retainers to play the man, and Bjarki tells Hott that now is the time to clear his reputation. Hott demands first the sword, Gullinhjalti, from Rolf, and with this he slays the dead beast a second time. King Rolf is not deceived by this trick; yet he rejoices that Bjarki has not only himself slain the monster, but changed the cowardly Hott into a champion; he commands that Hott shall be called Hjalti, after the sword which has been given him. We are hardly justified in demanding logic in a wild tale like this, or one might ask how Rolf was convinced of Hott's valour by what he knew to be a piece of stage management on the part of Bjarki. But, however that may be, it is remarkable that in *Beowulf* also the monster Grendel, though proof against all ordinary weapons, is smitten *when dead* by a magic sword of which the *golden hilt* is specially mentioned.

In addition to the undeniable similarity of the stories of these heroes, a certain similarity of name has been claimed. That *Bjarki* is not etymologically connected with *Bēowulf* or *Bēow* is clear: but if we are to accept the identification of Beowulf and Beow, remembering that the Scandinavian equivalent of the latter is said to be *Bjár*, the resemblance to *Bjarki* is obvious. Similarity of sound might have caused one name to be substituted for another. This argument obviously depends upon the identification *Bēow = Bjár*, which is extremely doubtful: it will be argued below that it is more likely that *Bēow = Byggvir*.

But force remains in the argument that the name Bjarki (little bear) is very appropriate to a hero like the Beowulf of our epic, who crushes or hugs his foe to death instead of using his sword; even if we do not accept explanations which would interpret the name "Beowulf" itself as a synonym for "Bear."

It is scarcely to be wondered at, then, that most critics have seen in Bjarki a Scandinavian parallel to Beowulf. But serious difficulties remain. There is in the Scandinavian story a mass of detail quite unparalleled in *Beowulf*, which overshadows the resemblances. Bjarki's friendship, for example, with the coward Hott or Hjalti has no counterpart in *Beowulf*. And Bjarki becomes a retainer of King Rolf and dies in his service, whilst Beowulf never comes into direct contact with Hrothulf at all; the poet seems to avoid naming them together. Still, it is quite intelligible that the story should have developed on different lines in Scandinavia from those which it followed in England, till the new growths overshadowed the original resemblance, without obliterating it. After nearly a thousand years of independent development discrepancies must be expected. It would not be a reasonable objection to the identity of *Gullinhjalti* with *Gyldenhilt*, that the word *hilt* had grown to have a rather different meaning in Norse and in English; subsequent developments do not invalidate an original resemblance if the points of contact are really there.

But, allowing for this independent growth in Scandinavia, we should naturally expect that the further back we traced the story the greater the resemblance would become.

This brings us to the second, serious difficulty: that, when we turn from the *Saga of Rolf Kraki* – belonging in its present form perhaps to the early fifteenth century – to the pages of Saxo Grammaticus, who tells the same tale more than two centuries earlier, the resemblance, instead of becoming stronger, almost vanishes. Nothing is said of Bjarki coming from Gautland, or indeed of his being a stranger at the Danish court: nothing is said of the monster having paid previous visits, visits repeated till king Rolf, like Hrothgar, has to give up all attempt at resistance, and submit to its depredations. The monster, instead of being a troll, like Grendel, becomes a commonplace bear. All Saxo tells us is that "He [Biarco, i.e. Bjarki] met a great bear in a thicket and slew it with a spear, and bade his comrade Ialto [i.e. Hjalti] place his lips to the beast and drink its blood as it flowed, that he might become stronger."

Hence the Danish scholar, Axel Olrik, in the best and most elaborate discussion of Bjarki and all about him, has roundly denied any connection between his hero and Beowulf. He is astonished at the slenderness of the evidence upon which previous students have argued for relationship. "Neither Beowulf's wrestling match in the hall, nor in the fen, nor his struggle with the firedrake has any real identity, but when we take a little of them all we can get a kind of similarity with the latest and worst form of the Bjarki saga." The development of Saxo's bear into a winged monster, "the worst of trolls," Olrik regards as simply in accordance with the usual heightening, in later Icelandic, of these early stories of struggles with beasts, and of this he gives a parallel instance.

Some Icelandic ballads on Bjarki (the *Bjarka rímur*), which were first printed in 1904, were claimed by Olrik as supporting his contention. These ballads belong to about the year 1400. Yet, though they are thus in date and dialect closely allied to the *Saga of Rolf Kraki* and remote from Saxo Grammaticus, they are so far from supporting the tradition of the *Saga* with regard to the monster slain, that they represent the foe first as a man-eating she-wolf, which is slain by Bjarki, then as a grey bear [as in Saxo], which is slain by Hjalti after he has been compelled to drink the blood of the she-wolf. We must therefore give up the winged beast as mere later elaboration; for if the Bjarki ballads in a point like this support Saxo, as against the *Saga* which is so closely connected with them by its date and Icelandic tongue, we must admit Saxo's version here to represent, beyond dispute, the genuine tradition.

Accordingly the attempt which has been made to connect Bjarki's winged monster with Beowulf's winged dragon goes overboard at once. But such an attempt ought never to have been made at all. The parallel is between Bjarki and the Beowulf-Grendel episode, not between Bjarki and the Beowulf-dragon episode, which ought to be left out of consideration. And the monstrous bear and the wolf of the *Rímur* are not so dissimilar from Grendel, with his bear-like hug, and Grendel's mother, the 'sea-wolf.'

The likeness between Beowulf and Bjarki lies, not in the wingedness or otherwise of the monsters they overthrow, but in the similarity of the position – in the situation which places the most famous court of the North, and its illustrious king, at the mercy of a ravaging foe, till a chance stranger from Gautland brings deliverance. And here the *Rímur* support, not Saxo, but the *Saga*, though in an outworn and faded way. In the *Rímur* Bjarki is a stranger come from abroad: the bear has made previous attacks upon the king's folds.

Thus, whilst we grant the wings of the beast to be a later elaboration, it does not in the least follow that other features in which the *Saga* differs from Saxo – the advent of Bjarki from Gautland, for instance – are also later elaboration.

And we must be careful not to attach too much weight to the account of Saxo merely because it is earlier in date than that of the *Saga*. The presumption is, of course, that the earlier form will be the more original: but just as a late manuscript will often preserve, amidst its corruptions, features which are lost in much earlier manuscripts, so will a tradition. Saxo's accounts are often imperfect. And in this particular instance, there is a want of coherency and intelligibility in Saxo's account, which in itself affords a strong presumption that it *is* imperfect.

What Saxo tells us is this:

At which banquet, when the champions were rioting with every kind of wantonness, and flinging knuckle-bones at a certain Ialto [Hjalti] from all sides, it happened that his messmate Biarco [Bjarki] through the bad aim of the thrower received a severe blow on the head. But Biarco, equally annoyed by the injury and the insult, sent the bone back to the thrower, so that he twisted the front of his head to the back and the back to the front, punishing the cross-grain of the man's temper by turning his face round about.

But who were this "certain Hjalti" and Bjarki? There seems to be something missing in the story. The explanation [which Saxo does not give us, but the *Saga* does] that Bjarki has come from afar and taken the despised Hott-Hjalti under his protection, seems to be necessary. Why was Hjalti chosen as the victim, at whom missiles were to be discharged? Obviously [though Saxo does not tell us so], because he was the butt of the mess. And if Bjarki had been one of the mess for many hours, his messmates would have known him too well to throw knuckle-bones either at him or his friend. This is largely a matter of personal feeling, but Saxo's account seems to me pointless, till it is supplemented from the *Saga*.

And there is one further piece of evidence which seems to clinch the whole matter finally, though its importance has been curiously overlooked, by Panzer and Lawrence in their arguments for the identification, and by Olrik in his arguments to the contrary.

We have seen above how Beowulf "became a friend" to Eadgils, helping him in his expedition against King Onela of Sweden, and avenging, in "chill raids fraught with woe," *cealdum cearsīðum*, the wrongs which Onela had inflicted upon the Geatas. We saw, too, that this expedition was remembered in Scandinavian tradition. "They had a battle on the ice of Lake Wener; there King Ali fell, and Athils had the victory. Concerning this battle there is much said in the *Skjoldunga saga*." The *Skjoldunga saga* is lost, but the Latin extracts from it give some information about this battle. Further, an account of it *is* preserved in the *Bjarka rímur*, probably derived from the lost *Skjoldunga saga*. And the *Bjarka rímur* expressly mention Bjarki as helping Athils in this battle against Ali on the ice of Lake Wener.

Olrik does not seem to allow for this at all, though of course aware of it. The other parallels between Bjarki and Beowulf he believes to be mere coincidence. But is this likely?

To recapitulate: In old English tradition a hero comes from the land of the Geatas to the royal court of Denmark, where Hrothgar and Hrothulf hold sway. This hero is received in none too friendly wise by one of the retainers, but puts his foe to shame, is warmly welcomed by the king, and slays by night a monster which has been attacking the Danish capital and against which the warriors of that court have been helpless. The monster is proof against all swords, yet its dead body is mutilated by a sword with a golden hilt. Subsequently this same hero helps King Eadgils of Sweden to overthrow Onela.

We find precisely the same situation in Icelandic tradition some seven centuries later, except that not Hrothgar and Hrothulf, but Hrothulf (Rolf) alone is represented as ruling the Danes, and the sword with the golden hilt has become a sword named "Golden-hilt." It is *conceivable* for a situation to have been reconstructed in this way by mere accident, just as it is conceivable that one player may have the eight or nine best trumps dealt him. But it does not seem advisable to base one's calculations, as Olrik does, upon such an accident happening.

Parallels from Folklore

HITHERTO we have been dealing with parallels to the Grendel story in written literature: but a further series of parallels, although much more remote, is to be found in that vast store of old wives' tales which no one till the nineteenth century took the trouble to write down systematically, but which certainly go back to a very ancient period. One particular tale, that of the Bear's Son (extant in many forms), has been instanced as showing a resemblance to the *Beowulf*-story. In this tale the hero, a young man of extraordinary strength, (1) sets out on his adventures, associating with himself various companions; (2) makes resistance in a house against a supernatural being, which his fellows have in vain striven to withstand, and succeeds in mishandling or mutilating him. (3) By the blood-stained track of this creature, or guided by him in some other manner, the hero finds his way to a spring, or hole in the earth, (4) is lowered down by a cord and (5) overcomes in the underworld different supernatural foes, amongst whom is often included his former foe, or very rarely the mother of that foe: victory can often only be gained by the use of a magic sword which the hero finds below. (6) The hero is left treacherously in the lurch by his companions, whose duty it was to have drawn him up...

Now it may be objected, with truth, that this is not like the *Beowulf*-story, or even particularly like the *Grettir*-story. But the question is not merely whether it resembles these stories as we possess them, but whether it resembles the story which must have been the common origin of both. And we have only to try to reconstruct from *Beowulf* and from the *Grettis saga* a tale which can have been the common original of both, to see that it must be something extraordinarily like the folk-tale outlined above.

For example, it is true that the departure of the Danes homeward because they believe that Beowulf has met his death in the water below, bears only the remotest resemblance to the deliberate treachery which the companions in the folk-tale mete out to the hero. But when we compare the *Grettir*-story, we see there that a real breach of trust is involved, for there the priest Stein leaves the hero in the lurch, and abandons the rope by which he should have drawn Grettir up. This can hardly be an innovation on the part of the composer of the *Grettis saga*, for he is quite well disposed towards Stein, and has no motive for wantonly attributing treachery to him. The innovation presumably lies in the *Beowulf*-story, where Hrothgar and his court are depicted in such a friendly spirit that no disreputable act can be attributed to them, and consequently Hrothgar's departure home must not be allowed in any way to imperil or inconvenience the hero. A comparison of the *Beowulf*-story with the *Grettir*-story leads then to the conclusion that in the oldest version those who remained above when the hero plunged below *were* guilty of some measure of disloyalty in ceasing to watch for him. In other words we see that the further we track the *Beowulf*-story back, the more it comes to resemble the folk-tale.

And our belief that there is some connection between the folk-tale and the original of *Beowulf* must be strengthened when we find that, by a comparison of the folk-tale, we are able to explain features in *Beowulf* which strike us as difficult and even absurd: precisely as when we turn to a study of Shakespeare's sources we often find the explanation of things that puzzle us: we see that the poet is dealing with an unmanageable source, which he cannot make quite plausible. For instance: when Grendel enters Heorot he kills and eats the first of Beowulf's retinue whom he finds: no one tries to prevent him.

The only explanation which the poet has to offer is that the retinue are all asleep – strange somnolence on the part of men who are awaiting a hostile attack, which they expect will be fatal to them all. And Beowulf at any rate is not asleep. Yet he calmly watches whilst his henchman is both killed and eaten: and apparently, but for the accident that the monster next tackles Beowulf himself, he would have allowed his whole bodyguard to be devoured one after another.

But if we suppose the story to be derived from the folk-tale, we have an explanation. For in the folk-tale, the companions and the hero await the foe singly, in succession: the turn of the hero comes last, after all his companions have been put to shame. But Beowulf, who is represented as having specially voyaged to Heorot in order to purge it, cannot leave the defence of the hall for the first night to one of his comrades. Hence the discomfiture of the comrade and the single-handed success of the hero have to be represented as simultaneous. The result is incongruous: Beowulf *has* to look on whilst his comrade is killed.

Again, both Beowulf and Grettir plunge in the water with a sword, and with the deliberate object of shedding the monster's blood. Why then should the watchers on the cliff above assume that the blood-stained water must necessarily signify the *hero's* death, and depart home? Why did it never occur to them that this deluge of blood might much more suitably proceed from the monster?

But we can understand this unreason if we suppose that the story-teller had to start from the deliberate and treacherous departure of the companions, whilst at the same time it was not to his purpose to represent the companions as treacherous. In that case some excuse *must* be found for them: and the blood-stained water was the nearest at hand.

Again, quite independently of the folk-tale, many *Beowulf* scholars have come to the conclusion that in the original version of the story the hero did not wait for a second attack from the mother of the monster he had slain, but rather, from a natural and laudable desire to complete his task, followed the monster's tracks to the mere, and finished him and his mother below. Many traits have survived which may conceivably point to an original version of the story in which Beowulf (or the figure corresponding to him) at once plunged down in order to combat the foe corresponding to Grendel. There are unsatisfactory features in the story as it stands. For why, it might be urged, should the wrenching off of an arm have been fatal to so tough a monster? And why, it has often been asked, is the adversary under the water sometimes male, sometimes female? And why is it apparently the blood of Grendel, not of his mother, which discolours the water and burns up the sword, and the head of Grendel, not of his mother, which is brought home in triumph? These arguments may not carry much weight, but at any rate when we turn to the folk-tale we find that the adventure beneath the earth *is* the natural following up of the adventure in the house, not the result of any renewed attack.

In addition, there are many striking coincidences between individual versions or groups of the folk-tale on the one hand and the *Beowulf-Grettir* story on the other: yet it is very difficult to know what value should be attached to these parallels, since there are many features of popular story which float around and attach themselves to this or that tale without any original connection, so that it is easy for the same trait to recur in *Beowulf* and in a group of folk-tales, without this proving that the stories as a whole are connected.

The hero of the Bear's son folk-tale is often in his youth unmanageable or lazy. This is also emphasized in the stories both of Grettir and of Orm: and though such a feature was uncongenial to the courtly tone of *Beowulf*, which sought to depict the hero as a model prince, yet it *is* there, even though only alluded to incidentally, and elsewhere ignored or even denied.

Again, the hero of the folk-tale is very frequently (but not necessarily) either descended from a bear, nourished by a bear, or has some ursine characteristic. We see this recurring in certain traits of Beowulf such as his bear-like method of hugging his adversary to death. Here again the courtly poet has not emphasized his hero's wildness.

Again, there are some extraordinary coincidences in names, between the *Beowulf-Grettir* story and the folk-tale. These are not found in *Beowulf* itself, but only in the stories of Grettir and Orm. Yet, as the *Grettir*-episode is presumably derived from the same original as the *Beowulf*-episode, any *original* connection between it and the folk-tale involves such connection for *Beowulf* also. We have seen that in *Grettis saga* the priest Stein, as the unfaithful guardian of the rope which is to draw up the hero, seems to represent the faithless companions of the folktale. There is really no other way of accounting for him, for except on this supposition he is quite otiose and unnecessary to the *Grettir*-story: the saga-man has no use for him. And his name confirms this explanation, for in the folk-tale one of the three faithless companions of the hero is called the Stone-cleaver, *Steinhauer*, *Stenkløver*, or even, in one Scandinavian version, simply *Stein*.

Again, the struggle in the *Grettis saga* is localized at Sandhaugar in Barthardal in Northern Iceland. Yet it is difficult to say why the saga-teller located the story there. The scenery, with the neighbouring river and mighty waterfall, is fully described: but students of Icelandic topography assert that the neighbourhood does *not* at all lend itself to this description. When we turn to the story of Orm we find it localized on the island Sandey. We are forced to the conclusion that the name belongs to the story, and that in some early version this was localized at a place called Sandhaug, perhaps at one of the numerous places in Norway of that name. Now turning to one of the Scandinavian versions of the folk-tale, we find that the descent into the earth and the consequent struggle is localized in *en stor sandhaug*.

On the other hand, it must be remembered that if a collection is made of some two hundred folk-tales, it is bound to contain, in addition to the essential kernel of common tradition, a vast amount of that floating material which tends to associate itself with this or that hero of story. Individual versions or groups of versions of the tale may contain features which occur also in the *Grendel*-story, without that being any evidence for primitive connection. Thus we are told how Grendel forces open the door of Heorot. In a Sicilian version of the folk-tale the doors spring open of themselves as the foe appears. This has been claimed as a parallel. But, as a sceptic has observed, the extraordinary thing is that of so slight a similarity (if it is entitled to be called a similarity) we should find only one example out of two hundred, and have to go to Sicily for that.

Yet there are other features in the folk-tale which are entirely unrepresented in the *Beowulf-Grettir* story. The hero of the folk-tale rescues captive princesses in the underworld (it is because they wish to rob him of this prize that his companions leave him below); he is saved by some miraculous helper, and finally, after adopting a disguise, puts his treacherous comrades to shame and weds the youngest princess. None of these elements are to be found in the stories of Beowulf, Grettir, Orm or Bjarki, yet they are essential to the fairy tale.

So that to speak of *Beowulf* as a version of the fairy tale is undoubtedly going too far. All we can say is that some early story-teller took, from folk-tale, those elements which suited his purpose, and that a tale, containing many leading features found in the "Bear's son" story, but omitting many of the leading motives of that story, came to be told of Beowulf and of Grettir.

Scef and Scyld

OUR POEM begins with an account of the might, and of the funeral, of Scyld Scefing, the ancestor of that Danish royal house which is to play so large a part in the story. After Scyld's death his retainers, following the command he had given them, placed their beloved prince in the bosom of a ship, surrounded by many treasures brought from distant lands, by weapons of battle and weeds of war, swords and byrnies. Also they placed a golden banner high over his head, and let the sea bear him away, with soul sorrowful

and downcast. Men could not say for a truth, not the wisest of councillors, who received that burden.

Now there is much in this that can be paralleled both from the literature and from the archaeological remains of the North. Abundant traces have been found, either of the burial or of the burning of a chief within a ship. And we are told by different authorities of two ancient Swedish kings who, sorely wounded, and unwilling to die in their beds, had themselves placed upon ships, surrounded by weapons and the bodies of the slain. The funeral pyre was then lighted on the vessel, and the ship sent blazing out to sea. Similarly the dead body of Baldr was put upon his ship, and burnt.

> *Haki konungr fekk svá stór sár, at hann sá, at hans lífdagar mundu eigi langir verða; þá lét hann taka skeið, er hann átti, ok lét hlaða dauðum mönnum, ok vápnum, lét þá flytja út til hafs ok leggja stýri í lag ok draga upp segl, en leggja eld í tyrvið ok gera bál á skipinu; veðr stóð af landi; Haki var þá at kominn dauða eða dauðr, er hann var lagiðr á bálit; siglði skipit síðan loganda út í haf, ok var þetta allfrægt lengi síðan.*

> *(King Haki was so sore wounded that he saw that his days could not be long. Then he had a warship of his taken, and loaded with dead men and weapons, had it carried out to sea, the rudder shipped, the sail drawn up, the fir-tree wood set alight, and a bale-fire made on the ship. The wind blew from the land. Haki was dead or nearly dead, when he was placed on the pyre. Then the ship sailed blazing out to sea; and that was widely famous for a long time after.)*

Ynglinga Saga, Kap. 23, in *Heimskringla*, udg. af Finnur Jónsson, København, 1893, vol. I, p. 43.

The *Skjoldunga Saga* gives a story which is obviously connected with this. King Sigurd Ring in his old age asked in marriage the lady Alfsola; but her brothers scorned to give her to an aged man. War followed; and the brothers, knowing that they could not withstand the hosts of Sigurd, poisoned their sister before marching against him. In the battle the brothers were slain, and Sigurd badly wounded.

Qui, Alfsola funere allato, magnam navim mortuorum cadaveribus oneratam solus vivorum conscendit, seque et mortuam Alfsolam in puppi collocans navim pice, bitumine et sulphure incendi jubet: atque sublatis velis in altum, validis a continente impellentibus ventis, proram dirigit, simulque manus sibi violentas intulit; sese ... more majorum suorum regali pompa Odinum regem (id est inferos) invisere malle, quam inertis senectutis infirmitatem perpeti...

Skjoldungasaga i Arngrim Jónssons udtog, udgiven af Axel Olrik, Kjøbenhavn, 1894, Cap. XXVII, p. 50 [132].
So with the death of Baldr.

En æsirnir tóku lík Baldrs ok fluttu til sævar. Hringhorni hét skip Baldrs; hann var allra skipa mestr, hann vildu goðin framm setja ok gera þar á bálfor Baldrs ... þá var borit út á skipit lík Baldrs,... Oðinn lagði á bálit gullhring þann, er Draupnir heitir ... hestr Baldrs var leiddr á bálit með Ollu reiði.

(But the gods took the body of Baldr and carried it to the sea-shore. Baldr's ship was named Hringhorni: it was the greatest of all ships and the gods sought to launch it, and to build the pyre of Baldr on it... Then was the body of Baldr borne out on to the ship... Odin laid on the pyre the gold ring named Draupnir ... and Baldr's horse with all his trappings was placed on the pyre.)

Snorra Edda: Gylfaginning, 48; udg. af Finnur Jónsson, København, 1900.

We are justified in rendering *setja skip fram* by "launch": Olrik (*Heltedigtning*, I, 250) regards Baldr's funeral as a case of the burning of a body in a ship on land. But it seems to me, as to Mr Chadwick (*Origin*, 287), that the natural meaning is that the ship was launched in the sea.

But the case of Scyld is not exactly parallel to these. The ship which conveyed Scyld out to sea was *not* set alight. And the words of the poet, though dark, seem to imply that it was intended to come to land somewhere: "None could say who received that freight."

Further, Scyld not merely departed over the waves – he had in the first instance come over them: "Not with less treasure did they adorn him," says the poet, speaking of the funeral rites, "than did those who at the beginning sent him forth alone over the waves, being yet a child."

Scyld Scefing then, like Tennyson's Arthur, comes from the unknown and departs back to it.

The story of the mysterious coming over the water was not confined to Scyld. It meets us in connection with King Scef, who was regarded, at any rate from the time of Alfred, and possibly much earlier, as the remotest ancestor of the Wessex kings. Ethelwerd, a member of the West Saxon royal house, who compiled a bombastic Latin chronicle towards the end of the tenth century, traces back the pedigree of the kings of Wessex to Scyld *and his father Scef.* "This Scef," he says, "came to land on a swift boat, surrounded by arms, in an island of the ocean called Scani, when a very young child. He was unknown to the people of that land, but was adopted by them as if of their kin, well cared for, and afterwards elected king." Note here, firstly, that the story is told, not of Scyld Scefing, but of Scef, father of Scyld. Secondly, that although Ethelwerd is speaking of the ancestor of the West Saxon royal house, he makes him come to land and rule, not in the ancient homeland of continental Angeln, but in the "island of Scani," which signifies what is now the south of Sweden, and perhaps also the Danish islands – that same land of *Scedenig* which is mentioned in *Beowulf* as the realm of Scyld. The tone of the narrative is, so far as we can judge from Ethelwerd's dry summary, entirely warlike: Scef is surrounded by weapons.

In the twelfth century the story is again told by William of

Malmesbury. "Sceldius was the son of Sceaf. He, they say, was carried as a small boy in a boat without any oarsman to a certain isle of Germany called Scandza, concerning which Jordanes, the historian of the Goths, speaks. He was sleeping, and a handful of corn was placed at his head, from which he was called 'Sheaf.' He was regarded as a wonder by the folk of that country and carefully nurtured; when grown up he ruled in a town then called Slaswic, and now Haithebi – that region is called ancient Anglia."

William of Malmesbury was, of course, aware of Ethelwerd's account, and may have been influenced by it. Some of his variations may be his own invention. The substitution of the classical form *Scandza* for Ethelwerd's *Scani* is simply a change from popular to learned nomenclature, and enables the historian to show that he has read something of Jordanes. The alteration by which Malmesbury makes Sceaf, when grown up, rule at Schleswig in ancient Angel, may again be his own work – a variant added in order to make Sceaf look more at home in an Anglo-Saxon pedigree.

But William of Malmesbury was, as we shall see later, prone to incorporate current ballads into his history, and after allowing for what he may have derived from Ethelwerd, and what he may have invented, there can be no doubt that many of the additional details which he gives are genuine popular poetry. Indeed, whilst the story of Scyld's *funeral* is very impressive in *Beowulf*, it is in William's narrative that the story of the child coming over the sea first becomes poetic.

Now since even the English historians connected this tale with the Danish territory of *Scani, Scandza*, we should expect to find it again on turning to the records of the Danish royal house. And we do find there, generally at the head of the pedigree, a hero – Skjold – whose name corresponds, and whose relationship to the later Danish kings shows him to be the same as the *Scyld Scefing* of *Beowulf*. But neither Saxo Grammaticus, nor any other Danish historian, knows anything of Skjold having come in his youth or returned in his death over the ocean.

How are we to harmonize these accounts?

Beowulf and Ethelwerd agree in representing the hero as

"surrounded by arms"; William of Malmesbury mentions only the sheaf; the difference is weighty, for presumably the spoils which the hero brings with him from the unknown, or takes back thither, are in harmony with his career. *Beowulf* and Ethelwerd seem to show the warrior king, William of Malmesbury seems rather to be telling the story of a semi-divine foundling, who introduces the tillage of the earth.

In *Beowulf* the child is Scyld Scefing, in Ethelwerd and William of Malmesbury he is Sceaf, father of Scyld.

Beowulf, Ethelwerd and William of Malmesbury agree in connecting the story with *Scedenig, Scani* or *Scandza*, yet the two historians and the *Anglo-Saxon Chronicle* all make Sceaf the ancestor of the West Saxon house. Yet we have no evidence that the English were regarded as having come from Scandinavia.

The last problem admits of easy solution. In heathen times the English traced the pedigree of most of their kings to Woden, and stopped there. For higher than that they could not go. But a Christian poet or genealogist, who had no belief in Woden as a god, would regard the All Father as a man – a mere man who, by magic powers, had made the heathen believe he was a god. To such a Christian pedigree-maker Woden would convey no idea of finality; he would feel no difficulty in giving this human Woden any number of ancestors. Wishing to glorify the pedigree of his king, he would add any other distinguished and authentic genealogies, and the obvious place for these would be at the end of the line, i.e., above Woden. Hence we have in some quite early (not West Saxon) pedigrees, five names given as ancestors of Woden. These five names end in Geat or Geata, who was apparently regarded as a god, and was possibly Woden under another name. Somewhat later, in the *Anglo-Saxon Chronicle*, under the year 855, we have a long version of the West Saxon pedigree with yet nine further names above Geat, ending in Sceaf. Sceaf is described as a son of Noah, and so the pedigree is carried back to Adam, 25 generations in all beyond Woden. But it is rash to assume with Müllenhoff that, because Sceaf comes at the head of this English pedigree, Sceaf was therefore essentially an English hero. *All* these later stages above Woden look like the ornate additions of a later compiler. Some of the figures, Finn, Sceldwa, Heremod, Sceaf himself, we have reason to identify with the primitive heroes of other nations.

The genealogist who finally made Sceaf into a son born to Noah in the ark, and then carried the pedigree nine stages further back through Noah to Adam, merely made the last of a series of accretions. It does not follow that, because he made them ancestors of the English king, this compiler regarded Noah, Enoch and Adam as Englishmen. Neither need he have so regarded Sceaf or Scyld or Beaw. In fact – and this has constantly been overlooked – the authority for Sceaf, Scyld and Beaw as Anglo-Saxon heroes is but little stronger than the authority for Noah and Adam in that capacity. No manuscript exists which stops at Scyld or Sceaf. There is no version which goes beyond Geat except that which goes up to Adam. Scyld, Beaw, Sceaf, Noah and Adam as heroes of English mythology are all alike doubtful.

We must be careful, however, to define what we mean when we regard these stages of the pedigree as doubtful. They are doubtful in so far as they are represented as standing above Woden in the Anglo-Saxon pedigree, because it is incredible that, in primitive and heathen times, Woden was credited with a dozen or more forefathers. The *position* of these names in the pedigree is therefore doubtful. But it is only their connection with the West Saxon house that is unauthentic. It does not follow that the names are, *per se*, unauthentic. On the contrary, it is because the genealogist had such implicit belief in the authenticity of the generations from Noah to Adam that he could not rest satisfied with his West Saxon pedigree till he had incorporated these names. They are not West Saxon, but they are part of a tradition much more ancient than any pedigree of the West Saxon kings. And the argument which applies to the layer of Hebrew names between Noah and Adam applies equally to the layer of Germanic names between Woden and Sceaf. From whatever branch of the Germanic race the genealogist may have taken them, the fact that he placed them where he did in the pedigree is a proof of his veneration for them. But we must not without evidence claim them as West Saxon or Anglo-Saxon: we must not be surprised if evidence points to some of them being connected with other nations – as Heremod, for example, with the Danes.

More difficult are the other problems. William of Malmesbury tells the story of Sceaf, with the attributes of a culture-hero: *Beowulf*, four centuries earlier, tells it of Scyld, a warrior hero: Ethelwerd tells it of Sceaf, but gives him the warrior attributes of Scyld instead of the sheaf of corn.

The earlier scholars mostly agreed in regarding Malmesbury's attribution of the story to Sceaf as the original and correct version of the story, in spite of its late date. As a representative of these early scholars we may take Müllenhoff. Müllenhoff's love of mythological interpretation found ample scope in the story of the child with the sheaf, which he, with considerable reason, regarded as a "culture-myth." Müllenhoff believed the carrying over of the attributes of a god to a line of his supposed descendants to be a common feature of myth – the descendants representing the god under another name. In accordance with this view, Scyld could be explained as an "hypostasis" of his father or forefather Sceaf, as a figure further explaining him and representing him, so that in the end the tale of the boat arrival came to be told, in *Beowulf*, of Scyld instead of Sceaf.

Recent years have seen a revolt against most of Müllenhoff's theories. The view that the story originally belonged to Sceaf has come to be regarded with a certain amount of impatience as "out of date." Even so fine a scholar as Dr Lawrence has expressed this impatience:

"That the graceful story of the boy sailing in an open boat to the land of his future people was told originally of Sceaf … needs no detailed refutation at the present day.

"The attachment of the motive to Sceaf must be, as an examination of the sources shows, a later development."

Accordingly the view of recent scholars has been this: That the story belongs essentially to Scyld. That, as the hero of the boat story is obviously of unknown parentage, we must interpret *Scefing* not as "son of Sceaf" but as "with the sheaf" (in itself a quite possible explanation). That this stage of the story is preserved in *Beowulf*. That subsequently *Scyld Scefing*, standing at the head of the pedigree, came to be misunderstood as "Scyld, son of Sceaf". That consequently the story, which must be told of the earlier ancestor, was thus transferred from Scyld to his supposed father Sceaf – the version which is found in Ethelwerd and William of Malmesbury.

One apparent advantage of this theory is that the oldest version, that of *Beowulf*, is accepted as the correct and original one, and the much later versions of the historians Ethelwerd and William of Malmesbury are regarded as subsequent corruptions. This on the surface seems eminently reasonable. But let us look closer. *Scyld Scefing* in *Beowulf* is to be interpreted "Scyld with the Sheaf." But *Beowulf* nowhere mentions the sheaf as part of Scyld's equipment. On the contrary, we gather that the hero is connected rather with prowess in war. It is the same in Ethelwerd. It is not till William of Malmesbury that the sheaf comes into the story. So that the interpretation of *Scefing* as "with the sheaf" assumes the accuracy of William of Malmesbury's story even in a point where it receives no support from the *Beowulf* version. In other words this theory does the very thing to avoid doing which it was called into being.

Besides this, there are two fundamental objections to the theory that Sceaf is a late creation, a figure formed from the misunderstanding of the epithet *Scefing* applied to *Scyld*. One portion of the poem of *Widsith* consists of a catalogue of ancient kings, and among these occurs *Sceafa*, ruling the Langobards. Now portions of *Widsith* are very ancient, and this catalogue in which Sceafa occurs is almost certainly appreciably older than *Beowulf* itself.

Secondly, the story of the wonderful foundling who comes over the sea from the unknown and founds a royal line, must *ex hypothesi* be told of the first in the line, and we have seen that it is Sceaf, not Scyld, who comes at the head of the Teutonic names in the genealogy in the *Anglo-Saxon Chronicle*.

Now we can date this genealogy fairly exactly. It occurs under the year 855, and seems to have been drawn up at the court of King Æthelwulf. In any case it cannot be later than the latter part of

Alfred's reign. This takes us back to a period when the old English epic was still widely popular. A genealogist at Alfred's court must have known much about Old English story.

These facts are simply not consistent with the belief that Sceaf is a late creation, a figure formed from a misunderstanding of the epithet *Scefing*, applied to Scyld.

To arrive at any definite conclusion is difficult. But the following may be hazarded.

It may be taken as proved that the Scyld or Sceldwa of the genealogists is identical with the Scyld Scefing of *Beowulf*. For Sceldwa according to the genealogy is also ultimately a *Sceafing*, and is the father of Beow; Scyld is *Scefing* and is father of Beowulf.

It is equally clear that the Scyld Scefing of *Beowulf* is identical with the Skjold of the Danish genealogists and historians. For Scyld and Skjold are both represented as the founder and head of the Danish royal house of Scyldingas or Skjoldungar, and as reigning in the same district. Here, however, the resemblance ceases. *Beowulf* tells us of Scyld's marvellous coming and departure. The only Danish authority who tells us much of Skjold is Saxo Grammaticus, who records how as a boy Skjold wrestled successfully with a bear and overcame champions, and how later he annulled unrighteous laws, and distinguished himself by generosity to his court. But the Danish and English accounts have nothing specifically in common, though the type they portray is the same – that of a king from his youth beloved by his retainers and feared by neighbouring peoples, whom he subdues and makes tributary. It looks rather as if the oldest traditions had had little to say about this hero beyond the typical things which might be said of any great king; so that Danes and English had each supplied the deficiency in their own way.

Now this is exactly what we should expect. For Scyld-Skjold is hardly a personality: he is a figure evolved out of the name *Scyldingas*, *Skjoldungar*, which is an old epic title for the Danes. Of this we may be fairly certain: the Scyldingas did not get their name because they were really descended from Scyld, but Scyld was created in order to provide an eponymous father to the Scyldingas. In just the same way tradition also evolved a hero Dan, from whom the Danes were supposed to have their name. Saxo Grammaticus has combined both pedigrees, making Skjold a descendant of Dan; but usually it was agreed that nothing came before Skjold, that he was the beginning of the Skjoldung line. At first a mere name, we should expect that he would have no characteristic save that, like every respectable Germanic king, he took tribute from his foes and gave it to his friends. He differs therefore from those heroic figures like Hygelac or Guthhere (Gunnar) which, being derived from actual historic characters, have, from the beginning of their story, certain definite features attached to them. Scyld is, in the beginning, merely a name, the ancestor of the Scyldings. Tradition collects round him gradually.

Hence it will be rash to attach much weight to any feature which is found in one account of him only. Anything we are told of Scyld in English sources alone is not to be construed as evidence as to his original story, but only as to the form that story assumed in England. When, for example, *Beowulf* tells us that Scyld is *Scefing*, or that he is father of Beowulf, it will be very rash of us to assume that these relationships existed in the Danish, but have been forgotten. This is, I think, universally admitted. Yet the very scholars who emphasize this, have assumed that the marvellous arrival as a child, in a boat, surrounded by weapons, is an essential feature of Scyld's story. Yet the evidence for this is no better and no worse than the evidence for his relationship to Sceaf or Beow – it rests solely on the English documents. Accordingly it only shows what was told about Scyld in England.

Of course the boat arrival *might* be an original part of the story of *Scyld-Skjold*, which has been forgotten in his native country, but remembered in England. But I cannot see that we have any right to assert this, without proof.

What we can assert to have been the original feature of Scyld is this – that he was the eponymous hero king of the Danes. Both *Beowulf* and the Scandinavian authorities agree upon that. The fact that his name (in the form *Sceldwa*) appears in the genealogy of the kings of Wessex is not evidence against a Danish origin. The name appears in close connection with that of Heremod, another Danish king, and is merely evidence of a desire on the part of the genealogist of the Wessex kings to connect his royal house with the most distinguished family he knew: that of the Scyldingas, about whom so much is said in the prologue to *Beowulf*.

Neither do the instances of place-names in England, such as *Scyldes treow*, *Scildes well*, prove Scyld to have been an English hero. They merely prove him to have been a hero who was celebrated in England – which the Prologue to *Beowulf* alone is sufficient to show to have been the case. For place-names commemorating heroes of alien tribes are common enough on English ground.

So much at least is gained. Whatever Müllenhoff and his followers constructed upon the assumption that Scyld was an essentially Anglo-Saxon hero goes overboard. Scyld is the ancestor king of the Danish house – more than this we can hardly with safety assert.

Now let us turn to the figure of Sceaf. This was not necessarily connected with Scyld from the first.

The story of Sceaf first meets us in its completeness in the pages of William of Malmesbury. And William of Malmesbury is a twelfth century authority; by his time the Old English courtly epics had died out – for they could not have long survived the Norman Conquest and the overthrow of Old English court life. But the popular tradition remained, and a good many of the old stories, banished from the hall, must have lingered on at the cross-roads – tales of Wade and Weyland, of Offa and Sceaf. For songs, sung by minstrels at the cross roads, William of Malmesbury is good evidence, and he owns to having drawn information from similar popular sources. William's story, then, is evidence that in his own day there was a tradition of a mythical king Sheaf who came as a child sleeping in a ship with a sheaf of corn at his head How old this tradition may be, we cannot say. Ethelwerd knew the story, though he has nothing to say of the sheaf. But we have seen that when we get back to the ninth century, and the formation of the *Anglo-Saxon Chronicle*, at a court where we may be sure the old English heroic stories were still popular, it is Sceaf and not Sceldwa who is regarded as the beginning of things – the king whose origin is so remote that he is the oldest Germanic ancestor one can get back to: "he was born in Noah's ark."

Whether or no Noah's ark was chosen as Sceaf's birthplace because legend represented him as coming in a boat over the water, we cannot tell. But the place he occupies, with only the Biblical names before him, as compared with Sceldwa the son of Heremod, clearly marks Sceaf rather than Sceldwa as the hero who comes from the unknown. Turning now to the catalogue of kings in *Widsith*, probably the oldest extant piece of Anglo-Saxon verse, some generations more ancient than *Beowulf*, we find a King Sceafa, who ruled over the Langobards. Finally, in *Beowulf* itself, although the story is told of Scyld, nevertheless this Scyld is characterized as *Scefing*. If this means "with the sheaf," then the *Beowulf*-story stands convicted of imperfection, of needing explanation outside itself from the account which William of Malmesbury wrote four centuries later. If it means "son of Sceaf," why should a father be given to Scyld, when the story demands that he should come from the unknown? Was it because, if the boat story was to be attributed to Scyld, it was felt that this could only be made plausible by giving him some relation to Sceaf?

When we find an ancient king bearing the extraordinary name of "Sheaf," it is difficult not to connect this with the honour done to the sheaf of corn, survivals of which have been found in different parts of England. In Herrick's time, the sheaves of corn were still kissed as they were carried home on the Hock-cart, whilst

> *Some, with great*
> *Devotion, stroke the home-borne wheat.*

Professor Chadwick argues, on the analogy of Prussian and Bulgarian harvest customs, that the figure of the "Harvest Queen" in the English ceremony is derived from a corn figure made from the last sheaf, and that the sheaf was once regarded as a religious symbol. But the evidence for this is surely even stronger than would be gathered from Professor Chadwick's very cautious statement. I suppose there is hardly a county in England from Kent to Cornwall and from Kent to Northumberland, where there is not evidence for honour paid to the last sheaf – an honour which cannot be accounted for as merely expressing the joy of the reapers at having got to the end of their task. In Kent "a figure composed of some of the best corn" was made into a human shape: "this is afterwards curiously dressed by the women, and adorned with paper trimmings cut to resemble a cap, ruffles, handkerchief, etc., of the finest lace. It is brought home with the last load of corn." In Northumberland and Durham a sheaf known as the "Kern baby" was made into the likeness of a human figure, decked out and brought home in triumph with dancing and singing. But the most striking form of the sheaf ceremony is found in the honour done to the "Neck" in the West of England.

... After the wheat is all cut, on most farms in the north of Devon the harvest people have a custom of "crying the neck." I believe that this practice is seldom omitted on any large farm in that part of the country. It is done in this way. An old man, or someone else well acquainted with the ceremonies used on the occasion (when the labourers are reaping the last field of wheat), goes round to the shocks and sheaves, and picks out a little bundle of all the best ears he can find; this bundle he ties up very neat and trim, and plats and arranges the straws very tastefully. This is called "the neck" of wheat, or wheaten-ears. After the field is cut out, and the pitcher once more circulated, the reapers, binders, and the women, stand round in a circle. The person with "the neck" stands in the centre, grasping it with both his hands. He first stoops and holds it near the ground, and all the men forming the ring take off their hats, stooping and holding them with both hands towards the ground. They then all begin at once in a very prolonged and harmonious tone to cry "the neck!" at the same time slowly raising themselves upright, and elevating their arms and hats above their heads; the person with "the neck" also raising it on high. This is done three times. They then change their cry to "wee yen!" – "way yen!" – which they sound in the same prolonged and slow manner as before, with singular harmony and effect, three times. This last cry is accompanied by the same movements of the body and arms as in crying "the neck."...

... After having thus repeated "the neck" three times, and "wee yen" or "way yen" as often, they all burst out into a kind of loud and joyous laugh, flinging up their hats and caps into the air, capering about and perhaps kissing the girls. One of them then gets "the neck," and runs as hard as he can down to the farm-house, where the dairy-maid, or one of the young female domestics, stands at the door prepared with a pail of water. If he who holds "the neck" can manage to get into the house, in any way, unseen or openly, by any other way than the door at which the girl stands with the pail of water, then he may lawfully kiss her; but, if otherwise, he is regularly soused with the contents of the bucket. On a fine still autumn evening, the "crying of the neck" has a wonderful effect at a distance, far finer than that of the Turkish muezzin, which Lord Byron eulogizes so much, and which he says is preferable to all the bells in Christendom. I have once or twice heard upwards of twenty men cry it, and sometimes joined by an equal number of female voices. About three years back, on some high grounds, where our people were harvesting, I heard six or seven "necks" cried in one night, although I know that some of them were four miles off.

The account given by Mrs Bray of the Devonshire custom, in her letters to Southey, is practically identical with this. We have plenty of evidence for this ceremony of "Crying the Neck" in the South-Western counties in Somersetshire, in Cornwall, and in a mutilated form in Dorsetshire.

On the Welsh border the essence of the ceremony consisted in tying the last ears of corn – perhaps twenty – with ribbon, and severing this "neck" by throwing the sickle at it from some distance. The custom is recorded in Cheshire, Shropshire, and under a different name in Herefordshire. The term "neck" seems to have been known as far afield as Yorkshire and the "little England beyond Wales" – the English-speaking colony of Pembrokeshire.

Whether we are to interpret the expression "the Neck," applied to the last sheaf, as descended from a time when "the corn spirit is conceived in human form, and the last standing corn is a part of its body – its neck..." or whether it is merely a survival of the Scandinavian word for sheaf – *nek* or *neg*, we have here surely evidence of the worship of the sheaf. "In this way 'Sheaf' was greeted, before he passed over into a purely mythical being."

I do not think these "neck" customs can be traced back beyond the seventeenth century. Though analogous usages are recorded in England (near Eton) as early as the sixteenth century, it was not usual at that time to trouble to record such things.

The earliest document bearing upon the veneration of the sheaf comes from a neighbouring district, and is contained in the Chronicle of the Monastery of Abingdon, which tells how in the time of King Edmund (941–946) a controversy arose as to the right of the monks of Abingdon to a certain portion of land adjoining the river. The monks appealed to a judgment of God to vindicate their claim, and this took the shape of placing a sheaf, with a taper on the top, upon a round shield and letting it float down the river, the shield by its movements hither and thither indicating accurately the boundaries of the monastic domain. At last the shield came to the field in debate, which, thanks to the floods, it was able to circumnavigate.

Professor Chadwick, who first emphasized the importance of this strange ordeal, points out that although the extant MSS of the *Chronicle* date from the thirteenth century, the mention of a *round* shield carries the superstition back to a period before the Norman Conquest. Therefore this story seems to give us evidence for the use of the sheaf and shield together as a magic symbol in Anglo-Saxon times. "An ordeal by letting the sheaf sail down the river on a shield was only possible at a time when the sheaf was regarded as a kind of supernatural being which could find the way itself."

But a still closer parallel to the story of the corn-figure coming over the water is found in Finnish mythology in the person of Sämpsä Pellervoinen. Finnish mythology seems remote from our subject, but if the figure of Sämpsä was borrowed from Germanic mythology, as seems to be thought, we are justified in laying great weight upon the parallel.

Readers of the *Kalewala* will remember, near the beginning, the figure of Sämpsä Pellervoinen, the god of Vegetation. He does not seem to do much. But there are other Finnish poems in his honour, extant in varying versions. It is difficult to get a collected idea from these fragmentary records, but it seems to be this: Ahti, the god of the sea, sends messengers to summon Sämpsä, so that he may bring fertility to the fields. In one version, first the Winter and then the Summer are sent to arouse Sämpsä, that he may make the crops and trees grow. Winter –

> *Took a foal swift as the spring wind,*
> *Let the storm wind bear him forward,*
> *Blew the trees till they were leafless,*
> *Blew the grass till it was seedless,*
> *Bloodless likewise the young maidens.*

Sämpsä refuses to come. Then the Summer is sent with better results. In another version Sämpsä is fetched from an island beyond the sea:

> *It is I who summoned Sämpsä*
> *From an isle amid the ocean,*
> *From a skerry bare and treeless.*
> *In yet another variant we are told how the boy Sämpsä*
> *Took six grains from off the corn heap,*
> *Slept all summer mid the corn heap,*
> *In the bosom of the corn boat.*

Now "It's a long, long way to" Ilomantsi in the east of Finland, where this last variant was discovered. But at least we have evidence that, within the region influenced by Germanic mythology, the spirit of vegetation was thought of as a boy coming over the sea, or sleeping in a boat with corn.

To sum up:

Sceafa, when the Catalogue of Kings in *Widsith* was drawn up – before *Beowulf* was composed, at any rate in its present form – was regarded as an ancient king. When the West Saxon pedigree was drawn up, certainly not much more than a century and a half after the composition of *Beowulf*, and perhaps much less, Sceaf was regarded as the primitive figure in the pedigree, before whom no one lived save the Hebrew patriarchs. That he was originally thought of as a child, coming across the water, with the sheaf of corn, is, in view of the Finnish parallel, exceedingly probable, and acquires some confirmation from the Chronicler's placing him in Noah's ark. But the definite evidence for this is late.

Scyld, on the other hand, is in the first place probably a mere eponym of the power of the Scylding kings of Denmark. He may, at a very early date, have been provided with a ship funeral, since later two Swedish kings, both apparently of Danish origin, have this ship funeral accorded to them, and in one case it is expressly said to be "according to the custom of his ancestors." But it seems exceedingly improbable that his original story represented him as coming over the sea in a boat. For, if so, it remains to be explained why this motive has entirely disappeared among his own people in Scandinavia, and has been preserved only in England. Would the Danes have been likely to forget utterly so striking a story, concerning the king from whom their line derived its name? Further, in England, *Beowulf* alone attributes this story to Scyld, whilst later historians attribute it to Sceaf. In view of the way in which the story of William of Malmesbury is supported by folklore, to regard that story as merely the result of error or invention seems perilous indeed.

On the other hand, all becomes straightforward if we allow that Scyld and Sceaf were both ancient figures standing at the head of famous dynasties. Their names alliterate. What more likely than that their stories should have influenced each other, and that one king should have come to be regarded as the parent or ancestor of the other? Contamination with Scyld would account for Sceaf's boat being stated to have come to land in Scani, Scanza – that Scedeland which is mentioned as the seat of Scyld's rule. Yet this explanation is not necessary, for if Sceaf were an early Longobard king, he would be rightly represented as ruling in Scandinavia.

Beow

T HE ANGLO-SAXON genealogies agree that the son of Sceldwa (Scyld) is Beow (Beaw, Beo). In *Beowulf*, he is named not Beow, but Beowulf.

Many etymologies have been suggested for *Bēow*. But considering that Beow is in some versions a grandson, in all a descendant of Sceaf, it can hardly be an accident that his name is identical with the O.E. word for grain, *bēow*. The Norse word corresponding to this is *bygg*.

Recent investigation of the name is best summed up in the words of Axel Olrik:

"New light has been cast upon the question of the derivation of the name Beow by Kaarle Krohn's investigation of the debt of Finnish to Norse mythology, together with Magnus Olsen's linguistic interpretation. The Finnish has a deity Pekko, concerning whom it is said that he promoted the growth of barley: the Esths, closely akin to the Finns, have a corresponding Peko, whose image – the size of a three-year-old child – was carried out into the fields and invoked at the time of sowing, or else was kept in the corn-bin by a custodian chosen for a year. This Pekko is plainly a personification of the barley; the form corresponding phonetically in Runic Norse would be **beggw-* (from which comes Old Norse *bygg*).

"So in Norse there was a grain **beggw-* (becoming *bygg*) and a corn-god **Beggw-* (becoming *Pekko*). In Anglo-Saxon there was a grain *béow* and an ancestral *Béow*. And all four are phonetically identical (proceeding from a primitive form **beuwa*, 'barley'). The conclusion which it is difficult to avoid is, that the corn-spirit 'Barley' and the ancestor 'Barley' are one and the same. The relation is the same as that between King Sheaf and the worship of the sheaf: the worshipped corn-being gradually sinks into the background, and comes to be regarded as an epic figure, an early ancestor.

"We have no more exact knowledge of the mythical ideas connected either with the ancestor Beow or the corn-god Pekko. But we know enough of the worship of Pekko to show that he dwelt in the corn-heap, and that, in the spring, he was fetched out in the shape of a little child. That reminds us not a little of Sämpsä, who lay in the corn-heap on the ship, and came to land and awoke in the spring."

But it may be objected that this is "harking back" to the old mythological interpretations. After refusing to accept Müllenhoff's assumptions, are we not reverting, through the names of Sceaf and Beow, and the worship of the sheaf, to very much the same thing?

No. It is one thing to believe that the ancestor-king Beow may be a weakened form of an ancient divinity, a mere name surviving from the figure of an old corn-god Beow; it is quite another to assume, as Müllenhoff did, that what we are told about Beowulf was originally told about Beow *and that therefore we are justified in giving a mythological meaning to it.*

All we know, conjecture apart, about Beow is his traditional relationship to Scyld, Sceaf and the other figures of the pedigree. That Beowulf's dragon fight belonged originally to him is only a conjecture. In confirmation of this conjecture only one argument has been put forward: an argument turning upon Beowulf, son of Scyld – that obscure figure, apparently equivalent to Beow, who meets us at the beginning of our poem.

Beowulf's place as a son of Scyld and father of Healfdene is occupied in the Danish genealogies by Frothi, son of Skjold, and father of Halfdan. It has been urged that the two figures are really identical, in spite of the difference of name. Now Frothi slays a dragon, and it has been argued that this dragon fight shows similarities which enable us to identify it with the dragon fight attributed in our poem to Beowulf the Geat.

The argument is a strong one – if it really is the case that the dragon slain by Frothi was the same monster as that slain by Beowulf the Geat.

Unfortunately this parallel, which will be examined in the next section, is far from certain. We must be careful not to argue in a circle, identifying Beowulf and Frothi because they slew the same dragon, and then identifying the dragons because they were slain by the same hero.

Whilst, therefore, we admit that it is highly probable that Beow (grain) the descendant of Sceaf (sheaf) was originally a corn divinity or corn fetish, we cannot follow Müllenhoff in his bold attribution to this "culture hero" of Beowulf's adventures with the dragon or with Grendel.

The House of Scyld and Danish parallels: Heremod-Lotherus and Beowulf-Frotho

SCYLD, ALTHOUGH the source of that Scylding dynasty which our poem celebrates, is *not* apparently regarded in *Beowulf* as the earliest Danish king. He came to the throne after an interregnum; the people whom he grew up to rule had long endured cruel need, "being without a prince." We hear in *Beowulf* of one Danish king only whom we can place chronologically before Scyld – viz. Heremod. The way in which Heremod is referred to would fit in very well with the supposition that he was the last of a dynasty; the immediate predecessor of Scyld; and that it was the death or exile of Heremod which ushered in the time when the Danes were without a prince.

Now there is a natural tendency in genealogies for each king to be represented as the descendant of his predecessor, whether he really was so or no; so that in the course of time, and sometimes of a very short time, the first king of a new dynasty may come to be reckoned as son of a king of the preceding line. Consequently, there would be nothing surprising if, in another account, we find Scyld represented as a son of Heremod. And we *do* find the matter represented thus in the West Saxon genealogy, where Sceldwa or Scyld is son of Heremod. Turning to the Danish accounts, however, we do not find any *Hermóðr* (which is the form we should expect corresponding to *Heremōd*) as father to Skjold (Scyld). Either no father of Skjold is known, or else (in Saxo Grammaticus) he has a father Lotherus. But, although the names are different, there is some correspondence between what we are told of Lother and what we are told of Heremod. A close parallel has indeed been drawn by Sievers between the whole dynasty: on the one hand Lotherus, his son Skioldus, and his descendant Frotho, as given in Saxo: and on the other hand the corresponding figures in *Beowulf*, Heremod, Scyld, and Scyld's son, Beowulf the Dane.

The fixed and certain point here is the identity of the central figure, Skioldus-Scyld. All the rest is very doubtful; not that there are not many parallel features, but because the parallels are of a commonplace type which might so easily recur accidentally.

The story of Lother, as given by Saxo, will be found below: the story of Heremod as given in *Beowulf* is hopelessly obscure – a mere succession of allusions intended for an audience who knew the tale quite well. Assuming the stories of Lother and Heremod to be different versions of one original, the following would seem to be the most likely reconstruction, the more doubtful portions being placed within round brackets thus ( ):

The old Danish prince [Dan in Saxo] has two sons, one a weakling [*Humblus*, Saxo] the other a hero [*Lotherus*, Saxo: *Heremod*, *Beowulf*] (who was already in his youth the hope of the nation). But after his father's death the elder was (through violence) raised to the throne: and Lother-Heremod went into banishment. (But under the rule of the weakling the kingdom went to pieces, and thus) many a man longed for the return of the exile, as a help against these evils. So the hero conquers and deposes the weaker brother. But then his faults break forth, his greed and his cruelty: he ceases to be the darling and becomes the scourge of his people, till they rise and either slay him or drive him again into exile.

If the stories of Lother and Heremod *are* connected, we may be fairly confident that Heremod, not Lother, was the name of the king in the original story.

For Scandinavian literature does know a Hermoth (*Hermóðr*), though no such adventures are attributed to him as those recorded of Heremod in *Beowulf*. Nevertheless it is probable that this Hermoth and Heremod in *Beowulf* are one and the same, because both heroes are linked in some way or other with Sigemund. How these two kings, Heremod and Sigemund, came to be connected, we do not know, but we find this connection recurring again and again. This *may* be mere coincidence: but I doubt if we are justified in assuming it to be so.

It has been suggested that both Heremod and Sigemund were originally heroes specially connected with the worship of Odin, and hence grouped together. The history of the Scandinavian Sigmund is bound up with that of the magic sword which Odin gave him, and with which he was always victorious till the last fight when Odin himself shattered it.

And we are told in the Icelandic that Odin, whilst he gave a sword to Sigmund, gave a helm and byrnie to Hermoth.

Again, whilst in one Scandinavian poem Sigmund is represented as welcoming the newcomer at the gates of Valhalla, in another the same duty is entrusted to Hermoth.

It is clear also that the *Beowulf*-poet had in mind some kind of connection, though we cannot tell what, between Sigemund and Heremod.

We may take it, then, that the Heremod who is linked with Sigemund in *Beowulf* was also known in Scandinavian literature as a hero in some way connected with Sigmund: whether or no the adventures which Saxo records of Lotherus were really told in Scandinavian lands in connection with Hermoth, we cannot say. The wicked king whose subjects rebel against him is too common a feature of Germanic story for us to feel sure, without a good deal of corroborative evidence, that the figures of Lotherus and Heremod are identical.

The next king in the line, Skioldus in Saxo, is, as we have seen, clearly identical with Scyld in *Beowulf*. But beyond the name, the two traditions have, as we have also seen, but little in common. Both are youthful heroes, both force neighbouring kings to pay tribute; but such things are commonplaces.

We must therefore turn to the next figure in the pedigree: the son of Skjold in Scandinavian tradition is Frothi (Frotho in Saxo), the son of Scyld in *Beowulf* is Beowulf the Dane. And Frothi is the father of Halfdan (Haldanus in Saxo) as Beowulf the Dane is of Healfdene. The Frothi of Scandinavian tradition corresponds then in position to Beowulf the Dane in Old English story.

Now of Beowulf the Dane we are told so little that we have really no means of drawing a comparison between him and Frothi. But a *theory* that has found wide acceptance among scholars assumes that the dragon fight of Beowulf the Geat was originally narrated of Beowulf the Dane, and only subsequently transferred to the Geatic hero. Theoretically, then, Beowulf the Dane kills a dragon. Now certainly Frotho kills a dragon: and it has been generally accepted that the parallels between the dragon slain by Frotho and that slain by Beowulf the Geat are so remarkable as to exclude the possibility of mere accidental coincidence, and to lead us to conclude that the dragon story was originally told of that Beowulf who corresponds to Frothi, i.e. Beowulf the Dane, son of Scyld and father of Healfdene; not Beowulf, son of Ecgtheow, the Geat.

But are the parallels really so close? We must not forget that here we are building theory upon theory. That the Frotho of Saxo is the same figure as Beowulf the Dane in Old English, is a theory, based upon his common relationship to Skiold-Scyld before him and to Haldanus-Healfdene coming after him: that Beowulf the Dane was the original hero of the dragon fight, and that that dragon fight was only subsequently transferred to the credit of Beowulf the Geat, is again a theory. Only if we can find real parallels between the dragon-slaying of Frotho and the dragon-slaying of Beowulf will these theories have confirmation.

Parallels have been pointed out by Sievers which he regards as so close as to justify a belief that both are derived ultimately from an old lay, with so much closeness that verbal resemblances can still be traced.

Unfortunately the parallels are all commonplaces. That Sievers and others have been satisfied with them was perhaps due to the fact that they started by assuming as proved that the dragon fight of Beowulf the Geat belonged originally to Beowulf the Dane, and argued that since Frotho in Saxo occupies a place corresponding exactly to that of Beowulf the Dane in *Beowulf*, a comparatively limited resemblance between two dragons coming, as it were, at the same point in the pedigree, might be held sufficient to identify them.

But, as we have seen, the assumption that the dragon fight of Beowulf the Geat belonged originally to Beowulf the Dane is only a theory that will have to stand or fall as we can prove that the dragon fight of Frotho is really parallel to that of Beowulf the Geat, and therefore must have belonged to the connecting link supplied by the Scylding prince Beowulf the Dane. In other words, the theory that the dragon in *Beowulf* is to be identified with the dragon which in Saxo is slain by Frotho the Danish prince, father of Haldanus-Healfdene, is one of the main arguments upon which we must base the theory that the dragon in *Beowulf* was originally slain by the Danish Beowulf, father of Healfdene, not by Beowulf the Geat. We cannot then turn round, and assert that the fact that they were both slain by a Danish prince, the father of Healfdene, is an argument for identifying the dragons.

Turning to the dragon fight itself, the following parallels have been noted by Sievers:

(1) A native (*indigena*) comes to Frotho, and tells him of the treasure-guarding dragon. An informer (*melda*) plays the same part in *Beowulf*.

But a dragon is not game which can be met with every day. He is a shy beast, lurking in desert places. Some informant has very frequently to guide the hero to his foe. And the situation is widely different. Frotho knows nothing of the dragon till directed to the spot: Beowulf's land has been assailed, he knows of the dragon, though he needs to be guided to its *exact* lair.

(2) Frotho's dragon lives on an island. Beowulf's lives near the sea, and there is an island (*ēalond*, 2334) in the neighbourhood.

But *ēalond* in *Beowulf* probably does not mean "island" at all: and in any case the dragon did not live upon the *ēalond*. Many dragons have lived near the sea. Sigemund's dragon did so.

(3) The hero in each case attacks the dragon single-handed.

But what hero ever did otherwise? On the contrary, Beowulf's exploit differs from that of Frotho and of most other dragon slayers in that he is unable to *overcome* his foe single-handed, and needs the support of Wiglaf.

(4) Special armour is carried by the dragon slayer in each case.

But this again is no uncommon feature. The Red Cross Knight also needs special armour. Dragon slayers constantly invent some ingenious or even unique method. And again the parallel is far from close. Frotho is advised to cover his shield and his limbs with the hides of bulls and kine: a sensible precaution against fiery venom. Beowulf constructs a shield of iron: which naturally gives very inferior protection.

(5) Frotho's informant tells him that he must be of good courage. Wiglaf encourages Beowulf.

But the circumstances under which the words are uttered are entirely different, nor have the words more than a general resemblance. That a man needs courage, if he is going to tackle a dragon, is surely a conclusion at which two minds could have arrived independently.

(6) Both heroes waste their blows at first on the scaly back of the dragon.

But if the hero went at once for the soft parts, there would be no fight at all, and all the fun would be lost. Sigurd's dragon-fight is, for this reason, a one-sided business from the first. To avoid this, Frotho is depicted as beginning by an attack on the dragon's rough hide (although he has been specially warned by the *indigena* not to do so):

> *ventre sub imo*
> *esse locum scito quo ferrum mergere fas est,*
> *hunc mucrone petens medium rimaberis anguem.*

(7) The hoard is plundered by both heroes.

But it is the nature of a dragon to guard a hoard. And, having slain the dragon, what hero would neglect the gold?

(8) There are many verbal resemblances: the dragon spits venom, and twists himself into coils.

Some of these verbal resemblances may be granted as proved: but they surely do not prove the common origin of the two dragon fights. They only tend to prove the common origin of the school of poetry in which these two dragon fights were told. That dragons dwelt in mounds was a common Germanic belief, to which the Cottonian Gnomic verses testify. Naturally, therefore, Frotho's dragon is *montis possessor*: Beowulf's is *beorges hyrde*. The two phrases undoubtedly point back to a similar gradus, to a similar traditional stock phraseology, and to similar beliefs: that is all. As well argue that two kings must be identical, because each is called *folces hyrde*.

These commonplace phrases and commonplace features are surely quite insufficient to prove that the stories are identical – at most they only prove that they bear the impress of one and the same poetical school. If a parallel is to carry weight there must be something individual about it, as there is, for example, about the arguments by which the identity of Beowulf and Bjarki have been supported. That a hero comes from Geatland (Gautland) to the court where Hrothulf (Rolf) is abiding; that the same hero subsequently is instrumental in helping Eadgils (Athils) against Onela (Ali) – here we have something tangible. But when two heroes, engaged upon slaying a dragon, are each told to be brave, the parallel is too general to be a parallel at all. "There is a river in Macedon: and there is also moreover a river at Monmouth, and there is salmons in both."

And there is a fundamental difference, which would serve to neutralize the parallels, even did they appear much less accidental than they do.

Dragon fights may be classified into several types: two stand out prominently. There is the story in which the young hero begins his career by slaying a dragon or monster and winning, it may be a hoard of gold, it may be a bride. This is the type of story found, for instance, in the tales of Sigurd, or Perseus, or St George. On the other hand there is the hero who, at the end of his career, seeks to ward off evil from himself and his people.

He slays the monster, but is himself slain by it. The great example of this type is the god Thor, who in the last fight of the gods slays the Dragon, but dies when he has reeled back nine paces from the "baleful serpent."

Now the story of the victorious young Frotho is of the one type: that of the aged Beowulf is of the other. And this difference is essential, fundamental, dominating the whole situation in each case: giving its cheerful and aggressive tone to the story of Frotho, giving the elegiac and pathetic note which runs through the whole of the last portion of *Beowulf*. It is no mere detail which could be added or subtracted by a narrator without altering the essence of the story.

In face of this we must pronounce the two stories essentially and originally distinct. If, nevertheless, there were a large number of striking and specific similarities, we should have to allow that, though originally distinct, the one dragon story had influenced the other in detail. For, whilst each poet who retold the tale would make alterations in detail, and might import such detail from one dragon story into another, what we know of the method of the ancient story tellers does not allow us to assume that a poet would have altered the whole drift of a story, either by changing the last death-struggle of an aged, childless prince into the victorious feat of a young hero, or by the reverse process.

Those, therefore, who hold the parallels quoted above to be convincing, may believe that one dragon story has influenced another, originally distinct. To me, it does not appear that even this necessarily follows from the evidence.

It seems very doubtful whether any of the parallels drawn by Sievers between the stories of Lotherus and Heremod, Skioldus and Scyld, Frotho and Beowulf, are more than the resemblances inevitable in poetry which, like the Old Danish and the Old English, still retains so many traces of the common Germanic frame in which it was moulded.

Indeed, of the innumerable dragon-stories extant, there is probably not one which we can declare to be really identical with that of Beowulf. There is a Danish tradition which shows many similarities, and I have given this below, in Part II; but rather as an example of a dragon-slaying of the *Beowulf* type, than because I believe in any direct connection between the two stories.

Part II

I N THIS section, many of the Old English and Old Norse sources discussed above are presented in lengthy translations. The first extract gives us the comedic tale of a staged dragon slaying, involving the hero Bothvar Bjarki and his protégé, from *Hrólfs saga kraka*. We then have a number of extracts from *Grettis saga*, a second version of Bothvar Bjarki's exploits from the *Bjarkarímur*, and a portion of *Orms þáttr Stórólfssonar*. A dragon-slaying episode from Danish folklore rounds off the Scandinavian material.

The remainder of the section discusses Old English genealogical material, drawn primarily from the *Anglo-Saxon Chronicle*, which includes the names of various heroes and mythological figures also found in *Beowulf*.

Hrólfs Saga Kraka

THEN BOTHVAR went on his way to Leire, and came to the king's dwelling.Bothvar stabled his horse by the king's best horses, without asking leave; and then he went into the hall, and there were few men there. He took a seat near the door, and when he had been there a little time he heard a rummaging in a corner. Bothvar looked that way and saw that a man's hand came up out of a great heap of bones which lay there, and the hand was very black. Bothvar went thither and asked who was there in the heap of bones.

Then an answer came, in a very weak voice, "Hott is my name, good fellow."

"Why art thou here?" said Bothvar, "and what art thou doing?"

Hott said, "I am making a shield-wall for myself, good fellow."

Bothvar said, "Out on thee and thy shield-wall!" and gripped him and jerked him up out of the heap of bones.

Then Hott cried out and said, "Now thou wilt be the death of me: do not do so. I had made it all so snug, and now thou hast scattered in pieces my shield-wall; and I had built it so high all round myself that it has protected me against all your blows, so that for long no blows have come upon me, and yet it was not so arranged as I meant it should be."

Then Bothvar said, "Thou wilt not build thy shield-wall any longer."

Hott said, weeping, "Wilt thou be the death of me, good fellow?" Bothvar told him not to make a noise, and then took him up and bore him out of the hall to some water which was close by, and washed him from head to foot. Few paid any heed to this.

Then Bothvar went to the place which he had taken before, and led Hott with him, and set Hott by his side. But Hott was so afraid that he was trembling in every limb, and yet he seemed to know that this man would help him.

After that it grew to evening, and men crowded into the hall: and Rolf's warriors saw that Hott was seated upon the bench. And it seemed to them that the man must be bold enough, who had taken upon himself to put him there. Hott had an ill countenance when he saw his acquaintances, for he had received naught but evil from them. He wished to save his life and go back to his bone-heap, but Bothvar held him tightly so that he could not go away. For Hott thought that, if he could get back into his bone-heap, he would not be as much exposed to their blows as he was.

Now the retainers did as before; and first of all they tossed small bones across the floor towards Bothvar and Hott. Bothvar pretended not to see this. Hott was so afraid that he neither ate nor drank; and every moment he thought he would be smitten.

And now Hott said to Bothvar, "Good fellow, now a great knuckle bone is coming towards thee, aimed so as to do us sore injury." Bothvar told him to hold his tongue, and put up the hollow of his palm against the knuckle bone and caught it, and the leg bone was joined on to the knuckle bone. Then Bothvar sent the knuckle bone back, and hurled it straight at the man who had thrown it, with such a swift blow that it was the death of him. Then great fear came over the retainers.

Now news came to King Rolf and his men up in the castle that a stately man had come to the hall and killed a retainer, and that the retainers wished to kill the man. King Rolf asked whether the retainer who had been killed had given any offence. "Next to none," they said: then all the truth of the matter came up before King Rolf.

King Rolf said that it should be far from them to kill the man: "You have taken up an evil custom here in pelting men with bones without quarrel. It is a dishonour to me and a great shame to you to do so. I have spoken about it before, and you have paid no attention. I think that this man whom you have assailed must be a man of no small valour. Call him to me, so that I may know who he is."

Bothvar went before the king and greeted him courteously. The king asked him his name. "Your retainers call me Hott's protector, but my name is Bothvar."

The king said, "What compensation wilt thou offer me for my retainer?"

Bothvar said, "He only got what he asked for."

The king said, "Wilt thou become my man and fill his place?"

Bothvar said, "I do not refuse to be your man, but Hott and I must not part so. And we must sit nearer to thee than this man whom I have slain has sat; otherwise we will both depart together." The king said, "I do not see much credit in Hott, but I will not grudge him meat." Then Bothvar went to the seat that seemed good to him, and would not fill that which the other had before. He pulled up three men in one place, and then he and Hott sat down there higher in the hall than the place which had been given to them. The men thought Bothvar overbearing, and there was the greatest ill will among them concerning him.

And when it drew near to Christmas, men became gloomy. Bothvar asked Hott the reason of this. Hott said to him that for two winters together a wild beast had come, great and awful, "And it has wings on its back, and flies. For two autumns it has attacked us here and done much damage. No weapon will wound it: and the champions of the king, those who are the greatest, come not back."

Bothvar said, "This hall is not so well arrayed as I thought, if one beast can lay waste the kingdom and the cattle of the king." Hott said, "It is no beast: it is the greatest troll."

Now Christmas-eve came; then said the king, "Now my will is that men to-night be still and quiet, and I forbid all my men to run into any peril with this beast. It must be with the cattle as fate will have it: but I do not wish to lose my men." All men promised to do as the king commanded. But Bothvar went out in secret that night; he caused Hott to go with him, but Hott did that only under compulsion, and said that it would be the death of him. Bothvar said that he hoped that it would be better than that. They went away from the hall, and Bothvar had to carry Hott, so frightened was he. Now they saw the beast; and thereupon Hott cried out as loud as he could, and said that the beast would swallow him. Bothvar said, "Be silent, thou dog," and threw him down in the mire. And there he lay in no small fear; but he did not dare to go home, any the more.

Now Bothvar went against the beast, and it happened that his sword was fast in his sheath when he wished to draw it. Bothvar now tugged at his sword, it moved, he wrenched the scabbard so that the sword came out. And at once he plunged it into the beast's shoulder so mightily that it pierced him to the heart, and the beast fell down dead to the earth. After that Bothvar went where Hott lay. Bothvar took him up and bore him to where the beast lay dead. Hott was trembling all over. Bothvar said, "Now must thou drink the blood of the beast." For long Hott was unwilling, and yet he did not dare to do anything else. Bothvar made him drink two great sups; also he made him eat somewhat of the heart of the beast.

After that Bothvar turned to Hott, and they fought a long time.

Bothvar said, "Thou hast now become very strong, and I do not believe that thou wilt now fear the retainers of King Rolf."

Hott said, "I shall not fear them, nor thee either, from now on."

"That is good, fellow Hott. Let us now go and raise up the beast, and so array him that others may think that he is still alive." And they did so. After that they went home, and were quiet, and no man knew what they had achieved.

In the morning the king asked what news there was of the beast, and whether it had made any attack upon them in the night. And answer was made to the king, that all the cattle were safe and uninjured in their folds. The king bade his men examine whether any trace could be seen of the beast having visited them. The watchers did so, and came quickly back to the king with the news that the beast was making for the castle, and in great fury. The king bade his retainers be brave, and each play the man according as he had spirit, and do away with this monster. And they did as the king bade, and made them ready.

Then the king faced towards the beast and said, "I see no sign of movement in the beast. Who now will undertake to go against it?"

Bothvar said, "That would be an enterprise for a man of true valour. Fellow Hott, now clear thyself of that ill-repute, in that men hold that there is no spirit or valour in thee. Go now and do thou kill the beast; thou canst see that there is no one else who is forward to do it."

"Yea," said Hott, "I will undertake this."

The king said, "I do not know whence this valour has come upon thee, Hott; and much has changed in thee in a short time."

Hott said, "Give me the sword Goldenboss, Gullinhjalti, which thou dost wield, and I will fell the beast or take my death." Rolf the king said, "That sword cannot be borne except by a man who is both a good warrior and valiant." Hott said, "So shalt thou ween that I am a man of that kind." The king said, "How can one know that more has not changed in thy temper than can be seen? Few men would know thee for the same man. Now take the sword and have joy of it, if this deed is accomplished." Then Hott went boldly to the beast and smote at it when he came within reach, and the beast fell down dead. Bothvar said, "See now, my lord, what he has achieved." The king said, "Verily, he has altered much, but Hott has not killed the beast alone, rather hast thou done it." Bothvar said, "It may be that it is so." The king said, "I knew when thou didst come here that few would be thine equals. But this seems to me nevertheless thy most honourable work, that thou hast made here another warrior of Hott, who did not seem shaped for much luck. And now I will that he shall be called no longer Hott, but Hjalti from this time; thou shalt be called after the sword Gullinhjalti (Goldenboss)."

Translation of Extracts from Grettis Saga

Glam Episode

THERE WAS a man called Thorhall, who lived at Thorhall's Farm in Shadow-dale. Shadow-dale runs up from Water-dale. Thorhall was son of Grim, son of Thorhall, son of Frithmund, who settled Shadow-dale. Thorhall's wife was called Guthrun: their son was Grim, and Thurith their daughter – they were grown up.

Thorhall was a wealthy man, and especially in cattle, so that no man had as much live stock as he. He was not a chief, yet a substantial yeoman. The place was much haunted, and he found it hard to get a shepherd to suit him. He sought counsel of many wise men, what device he should follow, but he got no counsel which was of use to him. Thorhall rode each summer to the All-Thing; he had good horses. That was one summer at the All-Thing, that Thorhall went to the booth of Skapti Thoroddsson, the Law-man.

Skapti was the wisest of men, and gave good advice if he was asked. There was this difference between Skapti and his father Thorodd: Thorodd had second sight, and some men called him underhanded; but Skapti gave to every man that advice which he believed would avail, if it were kept to: so he was called 'Better than his father.' Thorhall went to the booth of Skapti. Skapti greeted Thorhall well, for he knew that he was a prosperous man, and asked what news he had.

Thorhall said, "I should like good counsel from thee." "I am little use at that," said Skapti. "But what is thy need?"

Thorhall said, "It happens so, that it is difficult for me to keep my shepherds: they easily get hurt, and some will not serve their time. And now no one will take on the task, who knows what is before him."

Skapti answered, "There must be some evil being about, if men are more unwilling to look after thy sheep than those of other folk. Now because thou hast sought counsel of me, I will find thee a shepherd, who is named Glam, a Swede, from Sylgsdale, who came out to Iceland last summer. He is great and strong, but not much to everybody's taste."

Thorhall said that he would not mind that, if he guarded the sheep well. Skapti said that if Glam had not the strength and courage to do that, there was no hope of anyone else. Then Thorhall went out; this was when the All-Thing was nearly ending.

Thorhall missed two light bay horses, and he went himself to look for them – so it seems that he was not a great man. He went up under Sledge-hill and south along the mountain called Armannsfell.

Then he saw where a man came down from Gothashaw, bearing faggots on a horse. They soon met, and Thorhall asked him his name, and he said he was called Glam. Glam was tall and strange in bearing, with blue and glaring eyes, and wolf-grey hair. Thorhall opened his eyes when he saw him, but yet he discerned that this was he to whom he had been sent.

"What work art thou best fitted for?" said Thorhall.

Glam said he was well fitted to watch sheep in the winter.

"Wilt thou watch my sheep?" said Thorhall. "Skapti gave thee into my hand."

"You will have least trouble with me in your house if I go my own way, for I am hard of temper if I am not pleased," said Glam.

"That will not matter to me," said Thorhall, "and I wish that thou shouldst go to my house."

"That may I well do," said Glam, "but are there any difficulties?"

"It is thought to be haunted," said Thorhall.

"I am not afraid of such phantoms," said Glam, "and it seems to me all the less dull."

"Thou wilt need such a spirit," said Thorhall, "and it is better that the man there should not be a coward."

After that they struck their bargain, and Glam was to come at the winter-nights [14th–16th of October]. Then they parted, and Thorhall found his horses where he had just been searching. Thorhall rode home and thanked Skapti for his good deed.

Summer passed, and Thorhall heard nothing of his shepherd, and no one knew anything of him; but at the time appointed he came to Thorhall's Farm. The yeoman greeted him well, but all the others could not abide him, and Thorhall's wife least of all. Glam undertook the watching of the sheep, and it gave him little trouble. He had a great deep voice, and the sheep came together as soon as he called them. There was a church at Thorhall's Farm, but Glam would not go to it. He would have nothing to do with the service, and was godless; he was obstinate and surly and abhorred by all.

Now time went on till it came to Yule eve. Then Glam rose early and called for meat. The yeoman's wife answered, "That is not the custom of Christian men to eat meat today, because tomorrow is the first day of Yule," said she, "and therefore it is right that we should first fast today."

He answered, "Ye have many superstitions which I see are good for nothing. I do not know that men fare better now than before, when they had nought to do with such things. It seemed to me a better way when men were called heathen; and I want my meat and no tricks."

The yeoman's wife said, "I know for a certainty that it will fare ill with thee today, if thou dost this evil thing."

Glam bade her bring the meat at once, else he said it should be worse for her. She dared not do otherwise than he willed, and when he had eaten he went out, foul-mouthed.

Now it had gone so with the weather that it was heavy all round, and snow-flakes were falling, and it was blowing loud, and grew much worse as the day went on. The shepherd was heard early in the day, but less later. Then wind began to drive the snow, and towards evening it became a tempest. Then men came to the service, and so it went on to nightfall. Glam did not come home. Then there was talk whether search ought not to be made for him, but because there was a tempest and it was pitch dark, no search was attempted. That Yule night he did not come home, and so men waited till after the service [next, i.e. Christmas, morning]. But when it was full day, men went to search, and found the sheep scattered in the snow-drifts, battered by the tempest, or strayed up into the mountains. Then they came on a great space beaten down, high up in the valley. It looked to them as if there had been somewhat violent wrestling there, because the stones had been torn up for a distance around, and the earth likewise. They looked closely and saw where Glam lay a little distance away. He was dead, and blue like Hel and swollen like an ox. They had great loathing of him, and their souls shuddered at him. Nevertheless they strove to bring him to the church, but they could get him no further than the edge of a ravine a little below, and they went home leaving matters so, and told the yeoman what had happened. He asked what appeared to have been the death of Glam. They said that, from the trodden spot, up to a place beneath the rocks high in the valley, they had tracked marks as big as if a cask-bottom had been stamped down, and great drops of blood with them. So men concluded from this, that the evil thing which had been there before must have killed Glam, but Glam must have done it damage which had been enough, in that nought has ever happened since from that evil thing.

The second day of Yule it was again essayed to bring Glam to the church.

Beasts of draught were harnessed, but they could not move him where it was level ground and not down hill, so they departed, leaving matters so.

The third day the priest went with them, and they searched all day, but Glam could not be found. The priest would go no more, but Glam was found when the priest was not in the company. Then they gave up trying to carry him to the church, and buried him where he was, under a cairn.

A little later men became aware that Glam was not lying quiet. Great harm came to men from this, so that many fell into a swoon when they saw him, and some could not keep their wits. Just after Yule, men thought they saw him at home at the farm. They were exceedingly afraid, and many fled away. Thereupon Glam took to riding the house-roofs at nights, so that he nearly broke them in. He walked almost night and day. Men hardly dared to go up into the dale, even though they had business enough. Men in that country-side thought great harm of this.

In the spring Thorhall got farm-hands together and set up house on his land. Then the apparition began to grow less frequent whilst the sun's course was at its height; and so it went on till midsummer. That summer a ship came out to Hunawater. On it was a man called Thorgaut. He was an outlander by race, big and powerful; he had the strength of two men. He was in no man's service, and alone, and he wished to take up some work, since he had no money. Thorhall rode to the ship, and met Thorgaut. He asked him if he would work for him. Thorgaut said that might well be, and that he would make no difficulties.

"But thou must be prepared," said Thorhall, "that it is no place for weaklings, by reason of the hauntings which have been going on for a while, for I will not let thee into a trap."

Thorgaut answered, "It does not seem to me that I am undone, even though I were to see some little ghosts. It must be no easy matter for others if I am frightened, and I will not give up my place for that."

So now they agreed well, and Thorgaut was to watch the sheep when winter came.

Now the summer passed on. Thorgaut took charge of the sheep at the winter-nights. He was well-pleasing to all. Glam ever came home and rode on the roofs. Thorgaut thought it sporting, and said that the thrall would have to come nearer in order to scare him. But Thorhall bade him keep quiet: "It is best that ye should not try your strength together." Thorgaut said, "Verily, your courage is shaken out of you: I shall not drop down with fear between day and night over such talk."

Now things went on through the winter up to Yule-tide. On Yule evening the shepherd went out to his sheep. Then the yeoman's wife said, "It is to be hoped that now things will not go in the old way."

He answered, "Be not afraid of that, mistress; something worth telling will have happened if I do not come back."

Then he went to his sheep. The weather was cold, and it snowed much. Thorgaut was wont to come home when it was twilight, but now he did not come at that time. Men came to the service, as was the custom. It seemed to people that things were going as they had before. The yeoman wished to have search made for the shepherd, but the church-goers excused themselves, and said they would not risk themselves out in the hands of the trolls by night. And the yeoman did not dare to go, so the search came to nothing.

On Yule-day, when men had eaten, they went and searched for the shepherd. They went first to Glam's cairn, because men thought that the shepherd's disappearance must have been through his bringing-about. But when they came near the cairn they saw great things, for there they found the shepherd with his neck broken and not a bone in him whole. Then they carried him to the church, and no harm happened to any man from Thorgaut afterwards; but Glam began to increase in strength anew. He did so much that all men fled away from Thorhall's Farm, except only the yeoman and his wife.

Now the same cattle-herd had been there a long time. Thorhall would not let him go, because of his good-will and good service. He was far gone in age and was very unwilling to leave: he saw that everything went to waste which the yeoman had, if no one looked after it. And once after mid-winter it happened one morning that the yeoman's wife went to the byre to milk the cows as usual. It was quite light, because no one dared to go out before, except the cattle-herd: he went out as soon as it dawned. She heard great cracking in the byre and a hideous bellowing. She ran back, crying out, and said she did not know what devilry was going on in the byre.

The yeoman went out, and came to the cattle, and they were goring each other. It seemed to him no good to stay there, and he went further into the hay-barn. He saw where the cattle-herd lay, and he had his head in one stall and his feet in the next. He lay on his back. The yeoman went to him and felt him. He soon found that he was dead, and his back-bone broken in two; it had been broken over the partition slab.

Now it seemed no longer bearable to Thorhall, and he left his farm with all that he could carry away; but all the live-stock left behind Glam killed. After that he went through all the dale and laid waste all the farms up from Tongue. Thorhall spent what was left of the winter with his friends. No man could go up into the dale with horse or hound, because it was slain forthwith. But when spring came, and the course of the sun was highest, the apparitions abated somewhat. Now Thorhall wished to go back to his land. It was not easy for him to get servants, but still he set up house at Thorhall's Farm.

All went the same way as before. When autumn came on the hauntings began to increase. The yeoman's daughter was most attacked, and it fared so that she died. Many counsels were taken, but nothing was done. Things seemed to men to be looking as if all Water-dale must be laid waste, unless some remedies could be found.

Now the story must be taken up about Grettir, how he sat at home at Bjarg that autumn, after he had parted from Barthi-of-the-Slayings at Thorey's Peak. And when it had almost come to the winter-nights, Grettir rode from home, north over the neck to Willow-dale, and was a guest at Authun's Farm. He was fully reconciled to Authun, and gave him a good axe, and they spake of their wish for friendship one with the other. (Authun dwelt long at Authun's Farm, and much goodly offspring had he. Egil was his son, who wedded Ulfheith, daughter of Eyjolf Guthmundson; and their son was Eyjolf, who was slain at the All-Thing. He was father of Orm, chaplain to Bishop Thorlak.) Grettir rode north to Water-dale and came on a visit to Tongue. At that time Jokul Barthson lived there, Grettir's uncle. Jokul was a man great and strong and very proud. He was a seafaring man, and very over-bearing, yet of great account. He received Grettir well, and Grettir was there three nights.

There was so much said about the apparitions of Glam that nothing was spoken of by men equally with that. Grettir inquired exactly about the events which had happened. Jokul said that nothing more had been spoken than had verily occurred. "But art thou anxious, kinsman, to go there?"

Grettir said that that was the truth. Jokul begged him not to do so, "For that is a great risk of thy luck, and thy kinsmen have much at stake where thou art," said he, "for none of the young men seems to us to be equal to thee; but ill will come of ill where Glam is, and it is much better to have to do with mortal men than with evil creatures like that."

Grettir said he was minded to go to Thorhall's Farm and see how things had fared there. Jokul said, "I see now that it is of no avail to stop thee, but true it is what men say, that good-luck is one thing, and goodliness another."

"Woe is before one man's door when it is come into another's house. Think how it may fare with thee thyself before the end," said Grettir.

Jokul answered, "It may be that both of us can see somewhat into the future, but neither can do aught in the matter."

After that they parted, and neither was pleased with the other's foreboding.

Grettir rode to Thorhall's Farm, and the yeoman greeted him well. He asked whither Grettir meant to go, but Grettir said he would stay there over the night if the yeoman would have it so. Thorhall said he owed him thanks for being there, "But few men find it a profit to stay here for any time. Thou must have heard what the dealings are here, and I would fain that thou shouldst have no troubles on my account; but though thou shouldst come whole away, I know for certain that thou wilt lose thy steed, for no one who comes here keeps his horse whole."

Grettir said there were plenty of horses, whatever should become of this one.

Thorhall was glad that Grettir would stay there, and welcomed him exceedingly.

Grettir's horse was strongly locked in an out-house. They went to sleep, and so the night passed without Glam coming home. Then Thorhall said, "Things have taken a good turn against thy coming, for every night Glam has been wont to ride the roofs or break up the doors, even as thou canst see."

Grettir said, "Then must one of two things happen. Either he will not long hold himself in, or the wonted haunting will cease for more than one night. I will stay here another night and see how it goes."

Then they went to Grettir's horse, and he had not been attacked. Then everything seemed to the yeoman to be going one way. Now Grettir stayed for another night, and the thrall did not come home. Then things seemed to the yeoman to be taking a very hopeful turn. He went to look after Grettir's horse. When he came there, the stable was broken into, and the horse dragged out to the door, and every bone in him broken asunder.

Thorhall told Grettir what had happened, and bade him save his own life – "For thy death is sure if thou waitest for Glam."

Grettir answered, "The least I must have in exchange for my horse is to see the thrall."

The yeoman said that there was no good in seeing him: "For he is unlike any shape of man; but every hour that thou wilt stay here seems good to me."

Now the day went on, and when bed-time came Grettir would not put off his clothes, but lay down in the seat over against the yeoman's sleeping-chamber. He had a shaggy cloak over him, and wrapped one corner of it down under his feet, and twisted the other under his head and looked out through the head-opening. There was a great and strong partition beam in front of the seat, and he put his feet against it. The doorframe was all broken away from the outer door, but now boards, fastened together carelessly anyhow, had been tied in front. The panelling which had been in front was all broken away from the hall, both above and below the cross-beam; the beds were all torn out of their places, and everything was very wretched.

A light burned in the hall during the night: and when a third part of the night was past, Grettir heard a great noise outside. Some creature had mounted upon the buildings and was riding upon the hall and beating it with its heels, so that it cracked in every rafter. This went on a long time. Then the creature came down from the buildings and went to the door. When the door was opened Grettir saw that the thrall had stretched in his head, and it seemed to him monstrously great and wonderfully huge. Glam went slowly and stretched himself up when he came inside the door. He towered up to the roof. He turned and laid his arm upon the cross-beam and glared in upon the hall. The yeoman did not let himself be heard, because the noise he heard outside seemed to him enough. Grettir lay quiet and did not move.

Glam saw that a heap lay upon the seat, and he stalked in up the hall and gripped the cloak wondrous fast. Grettir pressed his feet against the post and gave not at all. Glam pulled a second time much more violently, and the cloak did not move. A third time he gripped with both hands so mightily that he pulled Grettir up from the seat, and now the cloak was torn asunder between them.

Glam gazed at the portion which he held, and wondered much who could have pulled so hard against him; and at that moment

Grettir leapt under his arms and grasped him round the middle, and bent his back as mightily as he could, reckoning that Glam would sink to his knees at his attack. But the thrall laid such a grip on Grettir's arm that he recoiled at the might of it. Then Grettir gave way from one seat to another. The beams started, and all that came in their way was broken. Glam wished to get out, but Grettir set his feet against any support he could find; nevertheless Glam dragged him forward out of the hall. And there they had a sore wrestling, in that the thrall meant to drag him right out of the building; but ill as it was to have to do with Glam inside, Grettir saw that it would be yet worse without, and so he struggled with all his might against going out. Glam put forth all his strength, and dragged Grettir towards himself when they came to the porch. And when Grettir saw that he could not resist, then all at once he flung himself against the breast of the thrall, as powerfully as he could, and pressed forward with both his feet against a stone which stood fast in the earth at the entrance. The thrall was not ready for this, he had been pulling to drag Grettir towards himself; and thereupon he stumbled on his back out of doors, so that his shoulders smote against the cross-piece of the door, and the roof clave asunder, both wood and frozen thatch. So Glam fell backwards out of the house and Grettir on top of him. There was bright moonshine and broken clouds without. At times they drifted in front of the moon and at times away. Now at the moment when Glam fell, the clouds cleared from before the moon, and Glam rolled up his eyes; and Grettir himself has said that that was the one sight he had seen which struck fear into him. Then such a sinking came over Grettir, from his weariness and from that sight of Glam rolling his eyes, that he had no strength to draw his knife and lay almost between life and death.

But in this was there more power for evil in Glam than in most other apparitions, in that he spake thus: "Much eagerness hast thou shown, Grettir," said he, "to meet with me. But no wonder will it seem if thou hast no good luck from me. And this can I tell thee, that thou hast now achieved one half of the power and might which was fated for thee if thou hadst not met with me. Now no power have I to take that might from thee to which thou hast attained. But in this may I have my way, that thou shalt never become stronger than now thou art, and yet art thou strong enough, as many a one shall find to his cost. Famous hast thou been till now for thy deeds, but from now on shall exiles and manslaughters fall to thy lot, and almost all of thy labours shall turn to ill-luck and unhappiness. Thou shalt be outlawed and doomed ever to dwell alone, away from men; and then lay I this fate on thee, that these eyes of mine be ever before thy sight, and it shall seem grievous unto thee to be alone, and that shall drag thee to thy death."

And when the thrall had said this, the swoon which had fallen upon Grettir passed from him. Then he drew his sword and smote off Glam's head, and placed it by his thigh.

Then the yeoman came out: he had clad himself whilst Glam was uttering his curse, but he dare in no wise come near before Glam had fallen. Thorhall praised God for it, and thanked Grettir well for having vanquished the unclean spirit.

Then they set to work and burned Glam to cold cinders. After, they put the ashes in a skin-bag and buried them as far as possible from the ways of man or beast. After that they went home, and by that time it was well on to day. Grettir lay down, for he was very stiff. Thorhall sent people to the next farm for men, and showed to them what had happened. To all those who heard of it, it seemed a work of great account; and that was then spoken by all, that no man in all the land was equal to Grettir Asmundarson for might and valour and all prowess. Thorhall sent Grettir from his house with honour, and gave him a good horse and fit clothing; for all the clothes which he had worn before were torn asunder. They parted great friends. Grettir rode thence to Ridge in Water-dale, and Thorvald greeted him well, and asked closely as to his meeting with Glam. Grettir told him of their dealings, and said that never had he had such a trial of strength, so long a struggle had theirs been together.

Thorvald bade him keep quiet, "and then all will be well, otherwise there are bound to be troubles for thee."

Grettir said that his temper had not bettered, and that he was now more unruly than before, and all offences seemed worse to him. And in that he found a great difference, that he had become so afraid of the dark that he did not dare to go anywhere alone after night had fallen. All kinds of horrors appeared to him then. And that has since passed into a proverb, that Glam gives eyes, or gives "glam-sight" to those to whom things seem quite other than they are. Grettir rode home to Bjarg when he had done his errand, and remained at home during the winter.

Sandhaugar Episode

There was a priest called Stein who lived at Eyjardalsá (Isledale River) in Barthardal. He was a good husbandman and rich in cattle. His son was Kjartan, a doughty man and well grown. There was a man called Thorstein the White who lived at Sandhaugar (Sandheaps), south of Isledale river; his wife was called Steinvor, and she was young and merry. They had children, who were young then.

People thought the place was much haunted by reason of the visitation of trolls. It happened, two winters before Grettir came North into those districts, that the good-wife Steinvor at Sandhaugar went to a Christmas service, according to her custom, at Isledale river, but her husband remained at home. In the evening men went to bed, and during the night they heard a great rummage in the hall, and by the good-man's bed. No one dared to get up to look to it, because there were very few men about. The good-wife came home in the morning, but her husband had vanished, and no one knew what had become of him.

The next year passed away. But the winter after, the good-wife wished again to go to the church-service, and she bade her manservant remain at home. He was unwilling, but said she must have her own way. All went in the same manner as before, and the servant vanished. People thought that strange. They saw some splashes of blood on the outer door, and men thought that evil beings must have taken away both the good-man and the servant.

The news of this spread wide throughout the country. Grettir heard of it; and because it was his fortune to get rid of hauntings and spirit-walkings, he took his way to Barthardal, and came to Sandhaugar on Yule eve. He disguised himself, and said his name was Guest. The good-wife saw that he was great of stature; and the farm-folk were much afraid of him. He asked for quarters for the night. The good-wife said that he could have meat forthwith, but "You must look after your own safety."

He said it should be so. "I will be at home," said he, "and you can go to the service if you will."

She answered, "You are a brave man, it seems to me, if you dare to remain at home."

"I do not care to have things all one way," said he.

"It seems ill to me to be at home," said she, "but I cannot get over the river."

"I will see you over," said Guest.

Then she got ready to go to the service, and her small daughter with her. It was thawing, the river was in flood, and there were ice-floes in it. Then the good-wife said, "It is impossible for man or horse to get across the river."

"There must be fords in it," said Guest, "do not be afraid."

"Do you carry the child first," said the good-wife, "she is the lighter."

"I do not care to make two journeys of it," said Guest, "and I will carry thee on my arm."

She crossed herself and said, "That is an impossible way; what will you do with the child?"

"I will see a way for that," said he; and then he took them both up, and set the child on her mother's knee and so bore them both on his left arm. But he had his right hand free, and thus he waded out into the ford.

They did not dare to cry out, so much afraid were they. The river washed at once up against his breast; then it tossed a great icefloe against him, but he put out the hand that was free and pushed it from him. Then it grew so deep that the river dashed over his shoulder; but he waded stoutly on, until he came to the bank on the other side, and threw Steinvor and her daughter on the land.

Then he turned back, and it was half dark when he came to Sandhaugar and called for meat; and when he had eaten, he bade the farm folk go to the far side of the room. Then he took boards and loose timber which he dragged across the room, and made a great barrier so that none of the farm folk could come over it. No one dared to say anything against him or to murmur in any wise. The entrance was in the side wall of the chamber by the gable-end, and there was a dais there. Guest lay down there, but did not take off his clothes: a light was burning in the room over against the door: Guest lay there far into the night.

The good-wife came to Isledale river to the service, and men wondered how she had crossed the river. She said she did not know whether it was a man or a troll who had carried her over. The priest said, "It must surely be a man, although there are few like him. And let us say nothing about it," said he, "it may be that he is destined to work a remedy for your evils." The good-wife remained there through the night.

Now it is to be told concerning Grettir that when it drew towards midnight he heard great noises outside. Thereupon there came into the room a great giantess. She had in one hand a trough and in the other a short-sword, rather a big one. She looked round when she came in, and saw where Guest lay, and sprang at him; but he sprang up against her, and they struggled fiercely and wrestled for a long time in the room. She was the stronger, but he gave way warily; and they broke all that was before them, as well as the panelling of the room. She dragged him forward through the door and so into the porch, and he struggled hard against her. She wished to drag him out of the house, but that did not happen until they had broken all the fittings of the outer doorway and forced them out on their shoulders. Then she dragged him slowly down towards the river and right along to the gorge.

By that time Guest was exceedingly weary, but yet, one or other it had to be, either he had to gather his strength together, or else she would have hurled him down into the gorge. All night they struggled. He thought that he had never grappled with such a devil in the matter of strength. She had got such a grip upon him that he could do nothing with either hand, except to hold the witch by the middle; but when they came to the gorge of the river he swung the giantess round, and thereupon got his right hand free. Then quickly he gripped his knife that he wore in his girdle and drew it, and smote the shoulder of the giantess so that he cut off her right arm. So he got free: but she fell into the gorge, and so into the rapids below.

Guest was then both stiff and tired, and lay long on the rocks; then he went home when it began to grow light, and lay down in bed. He was all swollen black and blue.

And when the good-wife came from the service, it seemed to her that things had been somewhat disarranged in her house. Then she went to Guest and asked him what had happened, that all was broken and destroyed. He told her all that had taken place. She thought it very wonderful, and asked who he was. He told her the truth, and asked her to send for the priest, and said he wished to meet him; and so it was done.

Then when Stein the priest came to Sandhaugar, he knew soon that it was Grettir Asmundarson who had come there, and who had called himself Guest.

The priest asked Grettir what he thought must have become of those men who had vanished. Grettir said he thought they must have vanished into the gorge. The priest said that he could not believe Grettir's saying, if no signs of it were to be seen. Grettir said that they would know more accurately about it later. Then the priest went home. Grettir lay many days in bed. The good-wife looked after him well, and so the Christmas-time passed.

Grettir's account was that the giantess fell into the gulf when she got her wound; but the men of Barthardal say that day came upon her whilst they wrestled, and that she burst when he smote her hand off, and that she stands there on the cliff yet, a rock in the likeness of a woman.

The dwellers in the dale kept Grettir in hiding there. But after Christmas time, one day that winter, Grettir went to Isledale river. And when Grettir and the priest met, Grettir said "I see, priest, that you place little belief in my words. Now will I that you go with me to the river and see what the likelihood seems to you to be."

The priest did so. But when they came to the waterfall they saw that the sides of the gorge hung over: it was a sheer cliff so great that one could in nowise come up, and it was nearly ten fathoms from the top to the water below. They had a rope with them. Then the priest said, "It seems to me quite impossible for thee to get down."

Grettir said, "Assuredly it is possible, but best for those who are men of valour. I will examine what is in the waterfall, and thou shalt watch the rope."

The priest said it should be as he wished, drove a peg into the cliff, piled stones against it, and sat by it.

Now it must be told concerning Grettir that he knotted a stone into the rope, and so let it down to the water.

"What way," said the priest, "do you mean to go?"

"I will not be bound," said Grettir, "when I go into the water, so much my mind forebodes me."

After that he got ready for his exploit, and had little on; he girded himself with his short sword, and had no other weapon.

Then he plunged from the cliff down into the waterfall. The priest saw the soles of his feet, and knew no more what had become of him. Grettir dived under the waterfall, and that was difficult because there was a great eddy, and he had to dive right to the bottom before he could come up behind the waterfall. There was a jutting rock and he climbed upon it. There was a great cave behind the waterfall, and the river fell in front of it from the precipice. He went into the cave, and there was a big fire burning. Grettir saw that there sat a giant of frightful size. He was terrible to look upon: but when Grettir came to him, the giant leapt up and seized a pike, and hewed at the new-comer: for with the pike he could both cut and stab. It had a handle of wood: men at that time called a weapon made in such a way a *heptisax*. Grettir smote against it with his short sword, and struck the handle so that he cut it asunder. Then the giant tried to reach back for a sword which hung behind him in the cave. Thereupon Grettir smote him in the breast, and struck off almost all the lower part of his chest and his belly, so that the entrails gushed out of him down into the river, and were swept along the current.

And as the priest sat by the rope he saw some lumps, clotted with blood, carried down stream. Then he became unsteady, and thought that now he knew that Grettir must be dead: and he ran from keeping the rope and went home. It was then evening, and the priest said for certain that Grettir was dead, and added that it was a great loss of such a man.

Now the tale must be told concerning Grettir. He let little space go between his blows till the giant was dead. Then he went further into the cave; he kindled a light and examined it. It is not said how much wealth he took in the cave, but men think that there was something. He stayed there far into the night. He found there the bones of two men, and put them into a bag. Then he left the cave and swam to the rope and shook it, for he thought that the priest must be there. But when he knew that the priest had gone home, then he had to draw himself up, hand over hand, and so he came up on to the cliff.

Then he went home to Isledale river, and came to the church porch, with the bag that the bones were in, and with a rune-staff, on which these verses were exceedingly well cut:

> *There into gloomy gulf I passed,*
> *O'er which from the rock's throat is cast*
> *The swirling rush of waters wan,*
> *To meet the sword-player feared of man.*
> *By giant's hall the strong stream pressed*
> *Cold hands against the singer's breast;*
> *Huge weight upon him there did hurl*
> *The swallower of the changing whirl.*
> *And this rhyme too:*
> *The dreadful dweller of the cave*
> *Great strokes and many 'gainst me drave;*
> *Full hard he had to strive for it,*
> *But toiling long he wan no whit;*
> *For from its mighty shaft of tree*
> *The heft-sax smote I speedily;*
> *And dulled the flashing war-flame fair*
> *In the black breast that met me there.*

These verses told also that Grettir had taken these bones out of the cave. But when the priest came to the church in the morning he found the staff, and what was with it, and read the runes; but Grettir had gone home to Sandhaugar.

But when the priest met Grettir he asked him closely as to what had happened: and Grettir told him all the story of his journey. And he added that the priest had not watched the rope faithfully. The priest said that that was true enough.

Men thought for certain that these monsters must have caused the loss of men there in the dale; and there was never any loss from hauntings or spirit-walkings there afterwards.

Grettir was thought to have caused a great purging of the land. The priest buried these bones in the churchyard.

Translation of Extracts from Bjarka Rímur

Most [of Rolf's retainers] **much tormented Hott [Hjalti];** **he was not cunning in speech. One day Hjalti and Bothvar went out of the hall, in such wise that none of the retainers knew thereof.**

Hjalti spake in great terror, "Let us not go near the wood; here is the she-wolf who eats up men; she will kill us both together."
The she-wolf leapt from a thicket, dread, with gaping jaws. A great terror was it to Hjalti, and he trembled in every limb.

Without delay or hesitation went Bjarki towards her, and hewed at her so that the axe went deep; a monstrous stream of blood gushed from her.

"Choose now, Hjalti, of two things" – so spake Bothvar the champion – "Drink now the blood, or I slay thee here; it seems unto me that there is no valour in thee."

Hjalti replied stoutly enough, "I cannot bring myself to drink blood; but if I needs must, it avails most [to submit], and now is there no better choice."

Hjalti did as Bothvar bade: he stooped down to the blood; then drank he three sups: that will suffice him to wrestle with one man.

Part IV, stanzas 58-64.

He [Hjalti] has gained good courage and keen spirit; he got strength and all valour from the she-wolf's blood.

A grey bear visited the folds at Hleithargarth; many such a ravager was there far and wide throughout the country.

The blame was laid upon Bjarki, because he had slain the herdsmen's dogs; it was not so suited for him to have to strive with men.

Rolf and all his household prepared to hunt the bear; "He who faces the beast shall be greatest in my hall."

Roaring did the bear leap forth from out its den, swinging its evil claws, so that men shrank back.

Hjalti saw, he turned and gazed where the battle began; nought had he then in his hands – his empty fists alone.

Rolf tossed then to Hjalti his wand of war [his sword]; the warrior put forth his hand towards it, and grasped theaaaa pommel.

Quickly then he smote the bear in the right shoulder; Bruin fell to the earth, and bore himself in more lowly wise.

That was the beginning of his exploits: many followed later; his spirit was ever excellent amid the play of battle.

Herefrom he got the name of Hjalti the stout-hearted: Bjarki was no more than his equal.

Part V, stanzas 4-13.

Joyful was the valiant Athils when they [Bjarki and Rolf's champions] came east to that place [Lake Wener]; troops with flashing spears rode quickly forthwith to the battle.

No truce gave they to their foes: well they earned their pay; there fell Ali and all his host, young in the game of swords.

The best of horses, Hrafn by name, they took from Ali; Bjarki chose for his reward the helm Hildisvin.

The prince [Athils] bade them have no talk about the business; he deprived the champions of their treasures – that will be a test of his power.

Ill-pleased was Bothvar: he and Hjalti departed; they declared that before the winter was gone they would seek for the treasure [the malt of Frothi].

Then they rode home and told it to the king [Rolf]; he said it was their business to claim their due outright.

Part VIII, stanzas 23-28.

Translation of Extract from Þáttr Orms Stórólfssonar

Section VII

A little after Orm and Asbiorn had parted, Asbiorn wished to go north to Sandeyar; he went aboard with twenty-four men, went north past Mæri, and landed late in the day at the outermost of the Sandeyar. They landed and pitched a tent, and spent the night there, and met with nothing.

Early in the morning Asbiorn arose, clothed himself, took his arms, went inland, and bade his men wait for him.

But when some time had passed from Asbiorn's having gone away, they were aware that a monstrous cat had come to the door of the tent: she was coal-black in colour and very fierce, for it seemed as if fire was burning from her nostrils and mouth, and her eyes were nothing fair: they were much startled at this sight, and full of fear. Then the cat leapt within the tent upon them, and gripped one after the other, and so it is said that some she swallowed and some she tore to death with claws and teeth. Twenty men she killed in a short time, and three escaped aboard ship, and stood away from the shore.

But Asbiorn went till he came to the cave of Brusi, and hastened in forthwith. It was dim before his eyes, and very shadowy in the cave, and before he was aware of it, he was caught off his feet, and thrown down so violently that it seemed strange to him. Then was he aware that there was come the giant Brusi, and he seemed to him a great one.

Then said Brusi, "Thou didst seek with great eagerness to come hither – now shalt thou have business, in that thou shalt here leave thy life with so great torments that that shall stay others from attacking me in my lair."

Then he stripped Asbiorn of his clothes, forasmuch as so great was their difference in strength that the giant could do as he wished. Asbiorn saw a great barrier standing across the cave, and a mighty opening in the midst of it; a great iron column stood somewhat in front of the barrier. "Now it must be tried," said Brusi, "whether thou art somewhat hardier than other men." "Little will that be to test," said Asbiorn…

[Asbiorn then recites ten stanzas, Brusi tormenting him the while. The first stanza is almost identical with No. 50 in the *Grettis saga*.]

Then Asbiorn left his life with great valour and hardihood.

Section VIII

Now it must be told concerning the three men who escaped; they rowed strongly, and stopped not until they came to land. They told the tidings of what had happened in their journey, and said that they thought that Asbiorn was dead, but that they could not tell how matters had happened concerning his death. They took ship with merchants, and so went south to Denmark: now these tidings were spread far and wide, and seemed weighty.

There had been a change of rulers in Norway: jarl Hakon was dead, and Olaf Tryggvason come to land: and he proclaimed the true faith to all. Orm Storolfson heard, out in Iceland, about the expedition of Asbiorn, and the death which it seemed to men must have come upon him. It seemed to him a great loss, and he cared no longer to be in Iceland, and took passage at Reytharfirth and went abroad. They reached Norway far to the north, and he stayed the winter at Thrandheim: Olaf at that time had reigned three years in Norway.

In the spring Orm made ready for his journey to Sandeyar, and there were nearly as many in the ship as the company of Asbiorn had been.

They landed at Little Sandey late in the evening, and pitched a tent on the land, and lay there the night...

Section IX

Now Orm went till he came to the cave. He saw the great rock, and thought it was impossible for any man to move it. Then he drew on the gloves that Menglath had given him, and grasped the rock and moved it away from the door; this is reckoned Orm's great feat of strength. Then he went into the cave, and thrust his weapon against the door. When he came in, he saw a giantess (she-cat) springing towards him with gaping jaws. Orm had a bow and quiver; he put the arrow on the string, and shot thrice at the giantess. But she seized all the arrows in her mouth, and bit them asunder. Then she flung herself upon Orm, and thrust her claws into his breast, so that Orm stumbled, and her claws went through his clothes and pierced him to the bone. She tried then to bite his face, and Orm found himself in straits: he promised then to God, and the holy apostle Peter, to go to Rome, if he conquered the giantess and Brusi her son. Then Orm felt the power of the giantess diminishing: he placed one hand round her throat, and the other round her back, and bent it till he broke it in two, and so left her dead.

Then Orm saw where a great barrier ran across the cave: he went further in, and when he came to it he saw a great shaft coming out through the barrier, both long and thick. Orm gripped the shaft and drew it away; Brusi pulled it towards himself, but it did not yield. Then Brusi wondered, and peeped up over the barrier. But when Orm saw that, he gripped Brusi by the beard with both hands, but Brusi pulled away, and so they tugged across the barrier. Orm twisted the beard round his hand, and tugged so violently that he pulled the flesh of Brusi away from the bone – from chin, jaws, cheeks, right up to the ears. Brusi knitted his brows and made a hideous face. Then Orm leapt in over the barrier, and they grappled and wrestled for a long time. But loss of blood wearied Brusi, and he began to fail in strength. Orm pressed on, pushed Brusi to the barrier, and broke his back across it. "Right early did my mind misgive me," said Brusi, "even so soon as I heard of thee, that I should have trouble from thee: and now has that come to pass. But now make quick work, and hew off my head. And true it is that much did I torture the gallant Asbiorn, in that I tore out all his entrails – yet did he not give in, before he died." "Ill didst thou do," said Orm, "to torture him, so fine a man as he was, and thou shalt have something in memory thereof." Then he drew his knife, and cut the "blood eagle" in the back of Brusi, shore off his ribs and drew out his lungs. So Brusi died in cowardly wise. Then Orm took fire, and burned to ashes both Brusi and the giantess. And when he had done that, he left the cave, with two chests full of gold and silver.

And all that was most of value he gave to Menglath, and the island likewise. So they parted with great friendship, and Orm came to his men at the time appointed, and then they sailed to the mainland. Orm remained a second winter at Thrandheim.

A Danish Dragon-Slaying of the Beowulf-Type

I N THE DAYS when King Gram Guldkølve ruled in Leire, there were two ministers at court, Bessus and Henry. And at that time constant complaints came to the court from the inhabitants of Vendsyssel, that a dread monster, which the peasants called a Drake, was destroying both man and beast. So Bessus gave counsel, that the king should send Henry against the dragon, seeing that no one in the whole kingdom was his equal in valour and courage. Henry answered that

assuredly he would undertake it; but he added that he thought it impossible to escape from such a struggle with his life. And he made himself ready forthwith for the expedition, took a touching farewell of his lord and king, and said among other things: "My lord, if I come not back, care thou for my wife and my children."

Afterwards, when he crossed over to Vendsyssel, he caused the peasants to show him the place where the monster had its lair, and learnt how that very day the drake had been out of its den, and had carried off a herdsman and an ox; how, according to its wont, it would now not come out for three hours, when it would want to go down to the water to drink after its meal. Henry clothed himself in full armour, and inasmuch as no one dared to stand by him in that task, he lay down all alone by the water, but in such wise that the wind did not blow from him toward the monster. First of all he sent a mighty arrow from his bow: but, although it exactly hit the spot at which he had aimed, it darted back from the dragon's hard scales. At this the monster was so maddened, that it attacked him forthwith, reckoning him but a little meal. But Henry had had a mighty barbed crook prepared by a smith beforehand, which he thrust into the beast's open mouth, so that it could not get rid of it, however much it strove, although the iron rod broke in Henry's hands. Then it smote him to the ground with its mighty tail, and although he was in complete armour, clutched at him with its dread claws, so that he fell in a swoon, wounded almost to death. But when he came somewhat to his senses again, after the drake for some time had had him lying under its belly, he rallied his last strength and grasped a dagger, of which he carried several with him in his belt, and smote it therewith in the belly, where the scales were weakest. So the monster at last breathed out its poisoned breath, whilst he himself lay half crushed under its weight. When the Vendsyssel peasants, who stood some distance away, in great fear and little hope, at last noticed that the battle had slackened, and that both combatants were still, they drew near and found Henry almost lifeless under the slain monster. And after they for some time had tended him well, he returned to die by his king, to whom he again commended his offspring. From him descends the family Lindenroth, which in memory of this mighty contest carries a drake on its coat of arms.

This story resembles the dragon fight in *Beowulf*, in that the hero faces the dragon as protector of the land, with forebodings, and after taking farewell; he attacks the dragon in its lair, single-handed; his first attack is frustrated by the dragon's scales; in spite of apparatus specially prepared, he is wounded and stunned by the dragon, but nevertheless smites the dragon in the soft parts and slays him; the watchers draw near when the fight is over. Yet these things merely prove that the two stories are of the same type; there is no evidence that this story is descended from *Beowulf*.

Part III

HERE CHAMBERS takes a close look at The Finnsburh Fragment, a partially surviving Old English poem translated in the appendix to this volume, and its relationship to a seemingly parallel passage in *Beowulf* (Sections XVI–XVII in the translation above).

This is a thorny problem; characters and actions do not neatly align across the two texts, and it is clear that the audience is expected to provide a good deal of background knowledge no longer available to us. These difficulties are fleshed out in detail, followed by a more general discussion of the conduct of early medieval feuds, and then an attempt to reconcile the two texts. Once again, Chambers calls upon a treasure trove of Scandinavian sources to supplement the sparse Old English material.

The Finnsburg Fragment

THE FINNSBURG FRAGMENT was discovered two centuries ago in the library of Lambeth Palace by George Hickes. It was written on a single leaf, which was transcribed and published by Hickes: but the leaf is not now to be found. This is to be regretted for reasons other than sentimental, since Hickes' transcript is far from accurate.

The *Fragment* begins and breaks off in the middle of a line: but possibly not much has been lost at the beginning. For the first lines of the fragment, as preserved, reveal a well-loved opening motive – the call to arms within the hall, as the watcher sees the foes approach. It was with such a call that the *Bjarkamál*, the poem on the death of Rolf Kraki, began: "a good call to work" as a fighting king-saint thought it. It is with a similar summons to business that the *Finnsburg Fragment* begins. The watchman has warned the king within the hall that he sees lights approaching – so much we can gather from the two and a half words which are preserved from the watchman's speech, and from the reply made by the "war-young" king: "This is not the dawn which is rising, but dire deeds of woe; to arms, my men." And the defending warriors take their posts: at the one door Sigeferth and Eaha: at the other Ordlaf and Guthlaf, and Hengest himself.

Then the poet turns to the foes, as they approach for the attack. The text as reported by Hickes is difficult: but it seems that Garulf[1] is the name of the warrior about to lead the assault on the hall. Another warrior, Guthere, whether a friend, kinsman, or retainer we do not know, is dissuading him, urging him not to risk so precious a life in the first brunt. But Garulf pays no heed; he challenges the champion on guard: "Who is it who holds the door?"

"Sigeferth is my name," comes the reply, "Prince I am of the Secgan: a wandering champion known far and wide: many a woe, many a hard fight have I endured: from me canst thou have what thou seekest."

So the clash of arms begins: and the first to fall is Garulf, son of

Guthlaf: and many a good man round him. "The swords flashed as if all Finnsburg were afire."

Never, we are told, was there a better defence than that of the sixty champions within the hall. "Never did retainers repay the sweet mead better than his bachelors did unto Hnæf. For five days they fought, so that none of the men at arms fell: but they held the doors." After a few more lines the piece breaks off.

There are many textual difficulties here. But these, for the most part, do not affect the actual narrative, which is a story of clear and straightforward fighting. It is when we try to fit this narrative into relationship with the *Episode* in *Beowulf* that our troubles begin. Within the *Fragment* itself one difficulty only need at present be mentioned. Guthlaf is one of the champions defending the hall. Yet the leader of the assault, Garulf, is spoken of as Guthlaf's son. Of course it is possible that we have here a tragic incident parallel to the story of Hildebrand and Hadubrand: father and son may have been separated through earlier misadventures, and now find themselves engaged on opposite sides. This would harmonize with the atmosphere of the *Finnsburg* story, which is one of slaughter breaking out among men near of kin, so that afterwards an uncle and a nephew are burnt on the same pyre. And it has been noted that Garulf rushes to the attack only after he has asked "Who holds the door?" and has learnt that it is Sigeferth: Guthlaf had gone to the opposite door. Can Garulf's question mean that he knows his father Guthlaf to be inside the hall, and wishes to avoid conflict with him? Possibly; but I do not think we can argue much from this double appearance of the name Guthlaf. It is possible that the occurrence of Guthlaf as Garulf's father is simply a scribal error. For, puzzling as the tradition of *Finnsburg* everywhere is, it is peculiarly puzzling in its proper names, which are mostly given in forms that seem to have undergone some alteration. And even if *Gūðlāfes sunu* be correctly written, it is possible that the Guthlaf who is father of Garulf is not to be identified with the Guthlaf whom Garulf is besieging within the hall.

One or other of these rather unsatisfactory solutions must unfortunately be accepted. For no theory is possible which will save us from admitting that, according to the received text, Guthlaf is fighting on the one side, and a "son of Guthlaf" on the other.

Episode in Beowulf

FURTHER DETAILS of the story we get in the *Episode* of *Finnsburg*, as recorded in *Beowulf* (ll. 1068-1159).

Beowulf is being entertained in the court of the king of the Danes, and the king's harper tells the tale of Hengest and Finn. Only the main events are enumerated. There are none of the dramatic speeches which we find in the *Fragment*. It is evident that the tale has been reduced in scope, in order that it may be fitted into its place as an episode in the longer epic.

The tone, too, is quite different. Whereas the *Fragment* is inspired by the lust and joy of battle, the theme of the *Episode*, as told in *Beowulf*, is rather the pity of it all; the legacy of mourning and vengeance which is left to the survivors:

For never can true reconcilement grow

Where wounds of deadly hate have struck so deep.

It is on this note that the *Episode* in *Beowulf* begins: with the tragic figure of Hildeburh. Hildeburh is closely related to both contending parties. She is sister to Hnæf, prince of the "Half-Danes," and she is wedded to Finn, king of the Frisians. Whatever may be obscure in the story, it is clear that a fight has taken place between the men of Hnæf and those of Finn, and that Hnæf has been slain: probably by Finn directly, though perhaps by his followers. A son of Finn has also fallen.

With regard to the peoples concerned there are difficulties. Finn's Frisians are presumably the main Frisian race, dwelling in and around the district still known as Friesland; for in the Catalogue of Kings in *Widsith* it is said that "Finn Folcwalding ruled the kin of the Frisians¹." Hnæf and his people are called Half-Danes, Danes and Scyldings; Hnæf is therefore presumably related to the Danish royal house. But, in no account which has come down to us of that house, are Hnæf or his father Hoc ever mentioned as kings or princes of Denmark, and their connection with the family of Hrothgar, the great house of Scyldings who ruled Denmark from the capital of Leire, remains obscure. In

Widsith, the people ruled over by Hnæf are called "children of Hoc" (*Hōcingum*), and are mentioned immediately after the "Sea-Danes."

Then there is a mysterious people called the *Eotens*, upon whom is placed the blame of the struggle: "Verily Hildeburh had little reason to praise the good faith of the Eotens." This is the typical understatement of Old English rhetoric: it can only point to deliberate treachery on the part of the Eotens. Our interpretation of the poem will therefore hinge largely upon our interpretation of this name. There have been two views as to the Eotens. The one view holds them to be Hnæf's Danes, and consequently places on Hnæf the responsibility for the aggression. This theory is, I think, quite wrong, and has been the cause of much confusion: but it has been held by scholars of great weight[1]. The other view regards the Eotens as subjects of Finn and foes of Hnæf. This view has been more generally held, and it is, as I shall try to show, only along these lines that a satisfactory solution can be found.

The poet continues of the woes of Hildeburh. "Guiltless, she lost at the war those whom she loved, child and brother. They fell as was fated, wounded by the spear, and a sad lady was she. Not for naught did the daughter of Hoc [i.e. Hildeburh] bewail her fate when morning came, when under the sky she could behold the murderous bale of her kinsfolk…"

Then the poet turns to the figure of Finn, king of the Frisians. His cause for grief is as deep as that of Hildeburh. For he has lost that body of retainers which to a Germanic chief, even as to King Arthur, was dearer than a wife. "War swept away all the retainers of Finn, except some few."

What follows is obscure, but as to the general drift there is no doubt. After the death of their king Hnæf, the besieged Danes are led by Hengest. Hengest must be Hnæf's retainer, for he is expressly so called (*þēodnes þegn*) "the king's thegn." So able is the defence of Hengest, and so heavy the loss among Finn's men, that Finn has to come to terms. Peace is made between Finn and Hengest, and the terms are given fully in the *Episode*. Unfortunately, owing to the confusion of pronouns, we soon lose our way amidst the clauses of this treaty, and it becomes exceedingly difficult to say who are the people who are alluded to as "they." This is peculiarly unlucky because here again the critical word *Eotena* occurs, but amid such a tangle of "thems" and "theys" that it is not easy to tell from this passage to which side the Eotens belong.

But one thing in the treaty is indisputable. In the midst of these complicated clauses, it is said of the Danes, the retainers of Hnæf, that they are not to be taunted with a certain fact: or perhaps it may be that they are not, when speaking amongst themselves, to remind each other of a certain fact. However that may be, what *is* clear is the *fact*, the mention of which is barred. Nothing is to be said of it, even though "*they were following the slayer (bana) of their lord, being without a prince, since they were compelled so to do*." Here, at least, are two lines about the interpretation of which we can be certain: and I shall therefore return to them. We must be careful, however, to remember that the word *bana*, "slayer," conveys no idea of fault or criminality. It is a quite neutral word, although it has frequently been mistranslated "murderer," and has thus helped to encourage the belief that Finn slew Hnæf by treachery. Of course it conveys no such implication: *bana* can be applied to one who slays another in self-defence: it implies neither the one thing nor the other.

Then the poet turns to the funeral of the dead champions, who are burned on one pyre by the now reconciled foes. The bodies of Hnæf and of the son (or sons) of Hildeburh are placed together, uncle and nephew side by side, whilst Hildeburh stands by lamenting.

Then, we are told, the warriors, deprived of their friends, departed to Friesland, to their homes and to their high-city.

Hengest still continued to dwell for the whole of that winter with Finn, and could not return home because of the winter storms. But when spring came and the bosom of the earth became fair, there came also the question of Hengest's departure: but he thought more of vengeance than of his sea-journey: "If he might bring about that hostile meeting which he kept in his mind concerning the child (or children) of the Eotens." Here again the word *Eotena* is used ambiguously, but, I think, this time not without some indication of its meaning. It has indeed been urged that the child or children of the Eotens are Hnæf, and any other Danes who may have fallen with him, and that when it is said that Hengest keeps them in mind, it is meant that he is remembering his fallen comrades with a view to taking vengeance for them. But this would be a queer way of speaking, as Hengest and his living comrades would on this theory be also themselves children of the Eotens. We should therefore need the term to be further defined: "children of the Eotens *who fell at Finnsburg*." It seems far more likely, from the way in which the expression is used here, that the children of the Eotens are the people *upon* whom Hengest intends to take vengeance.

Then, we are further told, Hunlafing places in the bosom of Hengest a sword of which the edges were well known amongst the Eotens. Here again there has been ambiguity, dispute and doubt. Hunlafing has been even bisected into a chief "Hun," and a sword "Lafing" which "Hun" is supposed to have placed in the bosom of Hengest (or of someone else). Upon this act of "Hun" many an interpretation has been placed, and many a theory built. Fortunately it has become possible, by a series of rather extraordinary discoveries, such as we had little reason to hope for at this time of day, to put Hunlafing together again. We now know (and this I think should be regarded as outside the region of controversy) that the warrior who put the sword into Hengest's bosom *was* Hunlafing. And about Hunlafing we gather, though very little, yet enough to help us. He is apparently a Dane, the son of Hunlaf, and Hunlaf is the brother of the two champions Guthlaf and Ordlaf[1]. Now Guthlaf and Ordlaf, as we know from the *Fragment*, were in the hall together with Hengest: it was "Guthlaf, Ordlaf and Hengest himself" who undertook the defence of one of the doors against the assailants. Guthlaf and Ordlaf were apparently sons of the king of Denmark. As Scyldings they would be Hnæf's kinsmen, and accompanied him to his meeting with Finn. Hunlafing, then, is a nephew of two champions who were attacked in the hall, and it is possible, though we cannot prove this, that his father Hunlaf was himself also in the hall, and was slain in the struggle. At any rate, when Hunlaf's son places a sword in the bosom of Hengest, this can only mean one thing. It means mischief. The placing of the sword, by a prince, in the bosom of another, is a symbol of war-service. It means that Hengest has accepted obligations to a Danish lord, a Scylding, a kinsman of the dead Hnæf, and consequently that he means to break the troth which he has sworn to Finn.

Further, we are told concerning the sword, that its edges were well known amongst the Eotens. At first sight this might seem, and to many has seemed, an ambiguous phrase, for a sword may be well known amongst either friends or foes. The old poets loved nothing better than to dwell upon the adornments of a sword, to say how a man, by reason of a fine sword which had been given to him, was honoured amongst his associates at table. But if this had been the poet's meaning here, he would surely have dwelt, not upon the edges of the sword, but upon its gold-adorned hilt, or its jewelled pommel. When he says the *edges* of the sword were well known amongst the Eotens, this seems to convey a hostile meaning. We know that the ill-faith of the Eotens was the cause of the trouble. The phrase about the sword seems therefore to mean that Hengest used this sword in order to take vengeance on the Eotens, presumably for their treachery.

The *Eotenas*, therefore, far from being the men of Hnæf and Hengest, must have been their foes.

Then the poet goes on to tell how "Dire sword-bale came upon the valiant Finn likewise." The Danes fell upon Finn at his own home, reddened the floor of his hall with the life-blood of his men, slew him, plundered his town, and led his wife back to her own people.

Here the *Episode* ends.

The Eotens

FINN IS surely entitled to be held innocent till he can be proved guilty. And the argument for his guilt comes to this: the trouble was due to the bad faith of the Eotens: "Eotens" means "Jutes": "Jutes" means "Frisians": "Frisians" means "Finn": therefore the trouble was due to the treachery of Finn.

Now I agree that it is probable that *Eotenas* means Jutes; and, as I have said, there is nothing improbable in a Frisian king having had a clan of Jutes, or a body of Jutish mercenaries, subject to him. But that the Frisians as a whole should be called Jutes is, *per se*, exceedingly improbable, and we have no shadow of evidence for it. Lawrence tries to justify it by the authority of Siebs:

"Siebs, perhaps the foremost authority on Frisian conditions, conjectures that … the occupation by the Frisians of Jutish territory after the conquest of Britain assisted the confusion between the two names."

But *did* the Frisians occupy Jutish territory? When we ask what is Siebs' authority for the hypothesis that Frisians occupied Jutish territory, we find it to be this: that because in *Beowulf* "Jute" means "Frisian," some such event must have taken place to account for this nomenclature[1]. So it comes to this: the Frisians must have been called Jutes, because they occupied Jutish territory: the Frisians must have occupied Jutish territory because they are called Jutes. I do not think we could have a better example of what Prof. Tupper calls "philological legend."

Siebs rejects Bede's statement, which places the Jutes in what is now Jutland: he believes them to have been immediately adjacent to the Frisians. For this belief that the Jutes were immediate neighbours of the Frisians there is, of course, some support, though not of a very convincing kind: but the belief that the Frisians occupied the territory of these adjacent Jutes rests, so far as I know, solely upon this identification of the *Eotenas*-Jutes with the Frisians, which it is then in turn used to prove.

But if by Jutes we understand (following Bede) a people dwelling north of the Angles, in or near the peninsula of Jutland, then it is of course true that (at a much later date) a colony of Frisians *did* occupy territory which is near Jutland, and which is sometimes included in the name "Jutland." But, as I have tried to show above, this "North Frisian" colony belongs to a period much later than that of the Finn-story: we have no reason whatever to suppose that the Frisians of the Finn story are the North Frisians of Sylt and the adjoining islands and mainland – the *Frisiones qui habitabant Juthlandie*.

And when we have assumed, without evidence, that, at the period with which we are dealing, Frisians had occupied Jutish territory, we are then further asked to assume that, from this settlement in Jutish territory, such Frisians came to be called Jutes. Now this is an hypothesis *per se* conceivable, but very improbable. Throughout the whole Heroic Age, for a thousand years after the time of Tacitus, Germanic tribes were moving, and occupying the territory of other people. During this period, how many instances can we find in which a tribe took the name of the people whose territory it occupied? Even where the name of the new home is adopted, the old tribal name is *not* adopted. For instance, the Bavarians occupied the territory of the Celtic Boii, but they did not call themselves Boii, but Bai(haim)varii, "the dwellers in the land of the Boii" – a very different thing. In the same way the Jutes who settled in the land of the Cantii did not call themselves *Kente*, but *Cantware*, "dwellers in Cantium." Of course, where the old name of a country survives, it does often *in the long run* come to be applied to its new inhabitants; but this takes many ages. It was not till a good thousand years after the English had conquered the land of the Britons, that Englishmen began to speak and think of themselves as "Britons." In feudal or 18th century days all the subjects of the ruler of Britain, Prussia, Austria, may come to be called British, Prussians, Austrians. But this is no argument for the period with which we are dealing. The assumption, then, that a body of Frisians, simply because they inhabited land which had once been inhabited by Jutes, should have called themselves Jutes, is so contrary to all we know of tribal nomenclature at this date, that one could only accept it if compelled by very definite evidence to do so. And of such evidence there is no scrap. Neither is there a scrap of evidence for the underlying hypothesis that any Frisians *were* settled at this date in Jutish territory.

And as if this were not hypothetical enough, a further hypothesis has then to be built upon it: viz., that this name "Jutes," belonging to such of the Frisians as had settled in Jutish territory, somehow became applicable to Frisians as a whole. Now this might conceivably have happened, but only as a result of certain political events. If the Jutish Frisians had become the governing element in Frisia, it would be conceivable. But after all, we know something about Frisian history, and I do not think we are at liberty to assume any such changes as would have enabled the Frisian people, as a whole, to be called Jutes. How is it that we never get any hint anywhere of this Jutish preponderance and Jutish ascendancy?

The argument that the "treachery of the Jutes" means the treachery of Finn, King of the Frisians, has, then, no support at all.

One further argument there is, for attributing treason to Finn.

It has been urged that in other stories a husband entraps and betrays the brother of his wife. But we are not justified in reading pieces of one story into another, unless we believe the two stories to be really connected. The Signy of the *Vǫlsunga Saga* has been quoted as a parallel to Hildeburh. Signy leaves the home of her father Volsung and her brother Sigmund to wed King Siggeir. Siggeir invites the kin of his wife to visit him, and then slays Volsung and all his sons, save Sigmund. But it is the difference of the story, rather than its likeness, which is striking. No hint is ever made of any possibility of reconciliation between Siggeir and the kin of the men he has slain. The feud admits of no atonement, and is continued to the utterance. Siggeir's very wife helps her brother Sigmund to his revenge.

How different from the attitude of Sigmund and Signy is the willingness of Hengest to come to terms, and the merely passive and elegiac bearing of Hildeburh! These things do not suggest that we ought to read a King Siggeir treachery into the story of Finn.

Again, the fact that Atli entices the brother of his wife into his power, has been urged as a parallel. But surely it is rather unfair to erect this into a kind of standard of conduct for the early Germanic brother-in-law, and to assume as a matter of course that, because Finn is Hnæf's brother-in-law, therefore he must have sought to betray him. The whole atmosphere of the Finn-Hnæf story, with its attempted reconciliation, is as opposed to that of the story of Atli as it is to the story of Siggeir.

The only epithet applied to Finn is *ferhð-freca*, "valiant in soul." Though *freca* is not necessarily a good word, and is applied to the dragon as well as to Beowulf, yet it denotes grim, fierce, almost reckless courage. It does not suggest a traitor who invites his foes to his house, and murders them by night.

I interpret the lines, then, as meaning that the trouble arose from the Jutes, and, since the context shows that these Jutes were on Finn's side, and against the Danes, we must hold them to be a body of Jutes in the service of Finn.

Ethics of the Blood Feud

BUT, AS we have seen, it is objected that this interpretation of the situation, absolving Finn from any charge of treachery or aggression, does not "help matters." Or, as Prof. Lawrence puts it, "the hurt to Danish pride [in entering the service of Finn] would be very little lessened by the assumption that someone else [than Finn] started the quarrel."

These objections seem to me to be contrary to the whole spirit of the old heroic literature.

I quite admit that there is a stage in primitive society when the act of slaying is everything, and the circumstances, or motives, do not count. In the Levitical Law, it is taken for granted that, if a man innocently causes the death of another, as for instance if his axe break, and the axe-head accidentally kill his comrade, then the avenger of blood will seek to slay the homicide, just as much as if he had been guilty of treacherous murder. To meet such cases the Cities of Refuge are established, where the homicide may flee till his case can be investigated; but even though found innocent, the homicide may be at once slain by the avenger, should he step outside the City of Refuge. And this "eye for eye" vengeance yields slowly: it took long to establish legally in our own country the distinction between murder and homicide.

For "The thought of man" it was held "shall not be tried: as the devil himself knoweth not the thought of man." Nevertheless, even the Germanic *wer-gild* system permits consideration of circumstances: it often happens that no *wer-gild* is to be paid because the slain man has been unjust, or the aggressor, or no *wer-gild* will be accepted because the slaying was under circumstances making settlement impossible.

Doubtless in Germanic barbarism there was once a stage similar to that which must have preceded the establishment of the Cities of Refuge in Israel; but that stage had passed before the period with which we are dealing; in the Heroic Age the motive *did* count for a very great deal. Not but what there were still the literal people who insisted upon "an eye for an eye," without looking at circumstances; and these people often had their way; but their view is seldom the one taken by the characters with whom the poet or the saga-man sympathises. These generally hold a more moderate creed. One may almost say that the leading motive in heroic literature is precisely this difference of opinion between the people who hold that under any circumstances it is shameful to come to an agreement with the *bana* of one's lord or friend or kinsman, and the people who are willing *under certain circumstances* to come to such an agreement.

It happens not infrequently that after some battle in which a great chief has been killed, his retainers are offered quarter, and accept it; but I do not remember any instance of their doing this if, instead of an open battle, it is a case of a treacherous attack. The two most famous downfalls of Northern princes afford typical examples: after the battle of Svold, Kolbjorn Stallari accepts quarter from Eric, the chivalrous *bani* of his lord Olaf; but Rolf's men refuse quarter after the treacherous murder of their lord by Hiarwarus.

That men, after a fair fight, could take quarter from, or give it to, those who had slain their lord or closest kinsman, is shown by abundant references in the sagas and histories. For instance, when Eric, after the fight with the Jomsvikings, offers quarter to his prisoners, that quarter is accepted, even though their leaders, their nearest kin, and their friends have been slain. The first to receive quarter is young Sigurd, whose father Bui has just been killed: yet the writer obviously does not the less sympathize with Sigurd, or with the other Jomsviking survivors, and feels the action to be generous on the part of Eric, and in no wise base on the part of the Jomsvikings. But this is natural, because the Jomsvikings have just been defeated by Eric in fair fight. It would be impossible, if Eric were represented as a traitor, slaying the Jomsvikings by a treacherous attack, whilst they were his guests. Is it to be supposed that Sigurd, under such circumstances, would have taken quarter from the slayer of Bui his father?

In the *Laxdæla Saga*, Olaf the Peacock, in exacting vengeance for the slaying of his son Kjartan, shows no leniency towards the sons of Osvif, on whom the moral responsibility rests. But he accepts compensation in money from Bolli, who had been drawn into the feud against his will. Yet Bolli was the actual slayer of Kjartan, and he had taken the responsibility as such. And Olaf is not held to have lowered himself by accepting a money payment as atonement from the slayer of his son – on the contrary "he was considered to have grown in reputation" from having thus spared Bolli. But after Olaf's death, the feud bursts out again, and revenge in the end falls heavily upon Bolli, as it does upon Finn.

On this question a fairly uniform standard of feeling will be found from the sixth century to the thirteenth. That it *does* make all the difference in composing a feud, whether the slaying from which the feud arises was treacherous or not, can be abundantly proved from many documents, from Paul the Deacon, and possibly earlier, to the Icelandic Sagas. Such composition of feuds may or may not be lasting; it may or may not expose to taunt those who make it; but the questions which arise are precisely these: Who started the quarrel? Was the slaying fair or treacherous? Upon the answer depends the possibility of atonement. There may be some insult and hurt to a man's pride in accepting atonement, even in cases where the other side has much to say for itself. But if the slaying has been fair, composition is felt to be possible, though not without danger of the feud breaking out afresh.

Prof. Lawrence has suggested that perhaps, in the original version of the *Finnsburg* story, the Danes were reduced to greater straits than is represented to be the case in the extant *Beowulf Episode*. He thinks that it is "almost incomprehensible" that Hengest should make terms with Finn, if he had really reduced Finn and his thegns to such a degree of helplessness as the words of the *Episode* state. It seems to me that the matter depends much more upon the treachery or the honesty of Finn. If Finn was guilty of treachery and slaughter of his guests, then it *is* "unintelligible" that Hengest should spare him: but if Finn was really a respectable character, then the fact that Hengest was making headway against him is rather a reason why Hengest should be moderate, than otherwise. To quote the *Laxdæla Saga* again: though Olaf the Peacock lets off Bolli, the *bani* of his son Kjartan, with a money payment, he makes it clear that he is master of the situation, before he shows this mercy. Paradoxical as it sounds, it was often easier for a man to show moderation in pursuing a blood feud, just *because* he was in a strong position. It is so again in the *Saga of Thorstein the White*. But the adversary must be one who deserves to be treated with moderation.

Of course it is quite possible that Prof. Lawrence is right, and that in some earlier and more correct version the Danes may have been represented as so outnumbered by the Frisians that they had no choice except to surrender to Finn, and enter his service, or else to be destroyed. But, whether this be so or no, all parallel incidents in the old literature show that their choice between these evil alternatives will depend upon whether Finn, the *bana* of their lord, slew that lord by deliberate and premeditated treachery whilst he was his guest, or whether he was embroiled with him through the fault of others, under circumstances which were perfectly honourable. If the latter is the case, then Hnæf's men *might* accept quarter. Their position is comparable with that of Illugi at the end of the *Grettis Saga*[1]. Illugi is a prisoner in the hands of the slayers of Grettir and he charges them with having overcome Grettir, when already on the point of death from a mortifying wound, which they had inflicted on him by sorcery and enchantment. The slayers propose to Illugi terms parallel to those made to the retainers of Hnæf. "I will give thee thy life," says their leader, "if thou wilt swear to us an oath not to take vengeance on any of those who have been in this business."

Now, note the answer of Illugi: "That might have seemed to me a matter to be discussed, if Grettir had been able to defend himself, and if ye had overcome him with valour and courage; but now it is not to be looked for that I will save my life by being such a coward as art thou. In a word, no man shall be more harmful to thee than I, if I live, *for never can I forget how it was that ye have vanquished Grettir*. Much rather, then, do I choose to die."

Now of course it would have been an "insult and hurt" to the pride of Illugi, or of any other decent eleventh century Icelander, to have been compelled to swear an oath not to avenge his brother, even though that brother had been slain in the most chivalrous way possible; and it would doubtless have been a hard matter, even in such a case, for Illugi to have kept his oath, had he sworn it. But the treachery of the opponents puts an oath out of the question, just as it must have done in the case of the followers of King Cynewulf or of Rolf Kraki, and as it must have done in the case of the followers of Hnæf, had the slaying of Hnæf been a premeditated act of treachery on the part of Finn.

In the *Njáls Saga*, Flosi has to take up the feud for the slain Hauskuld. Flosi is a moderate and reasonable man, so the first thing he does is to enquire into the *circumstances* under which Hauskuld was slain. Flosi finds that the circumstances, and the outrageous conduct of the slayers, give him no choice but to prosecute the feud. So in the end he burns Njal's hall, and in it the child of Kari.

Now to have burned a man's child to death might well seem a deed impossible of atonement. Yet in the end Flosi and Kari are reconciled by a full atonement, *the father of the slain child actually taking the first step*[1]. And all this is possible because Flosi and Kari recognise that each has been trying to play his part with justice and fairness, and that each is dragged into the feud through the fault of others. When Flosi has said of his enemy, "I would that I were altogether such a man as Kari is," we feel that reconciliation is in sight.

Very similar is the reconciliation between Alboin and Thurisind in Longobard story, but with this difference, that here it is Alboin who seeks reconciliation by going to the hall of the man whose son he has slain, thus reversing the parts of Flosi and Kari; and reconciliation is possible – just barely possible.

Again, when Bothvar comes to the hall of Rolf, and slays one of Rolf's retainers, the other retainers naturally claim full vengeance. Rolf insists upon investigating the *circumstances*. When he learns that it was his own man who gave the provocation, he comes to terms with the slayer.

Of course it was a difficult matter, and one involving a sacrifice of their pride, for the retainers of Hnæf to come to any composition with the *bana* of their lord; but it is not unthinkable, if the quarrel was started by Finn's subordinates without his consent, and if Finn himself fought fair. But had the slaying been an act of premeditated treachery on the part of Finn, the atonement would, I submit, have been not only difficult but impossible. If the retainers of Hnæf had had such success as our poem implies, then their action under such circumstances is, as Lawrence says, "almost incomprehensible." If they did it under compulsion, and fear of death, then their action would be contrary to all the ties of Germanic honour, and would entirely deprive them of any sympathy the audience might otherwise have felt for them. Yet it is quite obvious that the retainers of Hnæf are precisely the people with whom the audience is expected to sympathise[.]

In any case, the feud was likely enough to break out again as it did in the case of Alboin and Thurisind, and equally in that of Hrothgar and Ingeld.

Indeed, the different versions of the story of the feud between the house of Hrothgar and the house of Froda are very much to the point.

Much the oldest version – probably in its main lines quite historical – is the story as given in *Beowulf*. Froda has been slain by the Danes in pitched battle. Subsequently Hrothgar, upon whom, as King of the Danes, the responsibility for meeting the feud has devolved, tries to stave it off by wedding his daughter Freawaru to Ingeld, son of Froda. The sympathy of the poet is obviously with the luckless pair, Ingeld and Freawaru, involved as they are in ancient hatreds which are not of their making. For it is foreseen how some old warrior, who cannot forget his loyalty to his former king, will stir up the feud afresh.

But Saxo Grammaticus tells the story differently. Froda (Frotho) is treacherously invited to a banquet, and then slain. By this treachery the whole atmosphere of the story is changed. Ingeld (Ingellus) marries the daughter of his father's slayer, and, for this, the old version reproduced by Saxo showers upon him literally scores of phrases of scorn and contempt. The whole interest of the story now centres not in the recreant Ingeld or his wife of treacherous race, but in the old warrior Starkad, whose spirit and eloquence is such that he can bring Ingeld to a sense of his "vast sin," can burst the bonds of his iniquity, and at last compel him to take vengeance for his father.

In the *Saga of Rolf Kraki* the story of Froda is still further changed. It is a tale not only of treachery but also of slaying of kin. Consequently the idea of any kind of atonement, however temporary, has become impossible; there is no hint of it.

Now the whole atmosphere of the Hengest-story in *Beowulf* is parallel to that of the *Beowulf* version of the Ingeld-story: agreement is possible, though it does not prove to be permanent. There is room for much hesitation in the minds of Hengest and of Ingeld: they remain the heroes of the story. But if Finn had, as is usually supposed, invited Hnæf to his fort and then deliberately slain him by treachery, the whole atmosphere would have been different. Hengest could not then be the hero, but the foil: the example of a man whose spirit fails at the crisis, who does the utterly disgraceful thing, and enters the service of his lord's treacherous foe. The hero of the story would be some other character – possibly the young Hunlafing, who, loyal in spite of the treachery and cowardice of his leader Hengest, yet, remaining steadfast of soul, is able in the end to infuse his own courage into the heart of the recreant Hengest, and to inspire all the perjured Danish thegns to their final and triumphant revenge on Finn.

But that is not how the story is presented.

An Attempt at Reconstruction

THE THEORY, then, which seems to fit in best with what we know of the historic conditions at the time when the story arose, and which fits in best with such details of the story as we have, is this:

Finn, King of Frisia, has a stronghold, Finnsburg, outside the limits of Frisia proper. There several clans and chieftains are assembled: Hnæf, Finn's brother-in-law, prince of the Hocings, the Eotens, and Sigeferth, prince of the Secgan; whether Sigeferth has his retinue with him or no is not clear.

But the treachery of the Eotens causes trouble: they have some old feud with Hnæf and his Danes, and attack them by surprise in their hall. There is no proof that Finn has any share in this treason. It is therefore quite natural that in the *Episode* – although the treachery of the Eotens is censured – Finn is never blamed; and that in the *Fragment*, Finn has apparently no share in the attack on the hall, at any rate during those first five days to which the account in the *Fragment* is limited.

The attack is led by Garulf (*Fragment*, l. 20), presumably the prince of the Eotens: and some friend or kinsman is urging Garulf not to hazard so precious a life in the first attack. And here, too, the situation now becomes clearer: if Garulf is the chief of the attacking people, we can understand one of his kinsmen or friends expostulating thus: but if he is merely one of a number of subordinates despatched by Finn to attack the hall, the position would not be so easily understood.

Garulf, however, does not heed the warning, and falls, "first of all the dwellers in that land." The *Fragment* breaks off, but the fight goes on: we can imagine that matters must have proceeded much as in the great attack upon the hall in the *Nibelungen lied*. One man after another would be drawn in, by the duty of revenge, and Finn's own men would wake to find a battle in progress. "The sudden bale (*fær*) came upon them." Finn's son joins in the attack, perhaps in order to avenge some young comrade in arms; and is slain, possibly by Hnæf. Then Finn *has* to intervene, and Hnæf in turn is slain, possibly, though not certainly, by Finn himself. But Hengest, the thegn of Hnæf, puts up so stout a defence, that Finn is unable to take a full vengeance upon all the Danes. He offers them terms. What are Hengest and the thegns to do?

Finn has slain their lord. But they are Finn's guests, and they have slain Finn's son in his own house. Finn himself is, I take it, blameless. *It is here that the tragic tension comes in.* We can understand how, even if Hengest had Finn in his power, he might well have stayed his hand. So peace is made, and all is to be forgotten: solemn oaths are sworn. And Finn keeps his promise honestly. He resumes his position of host, making no distinction between Eotens, Frisians and Danes, who are all, for the time at least, his followers.

I think we have here a rational explanation of the action of Hengest and the other thegns of Hnæf, in following the slayer of their lord.

The situation resembles that which takes place when Alboin seeks hospitality in the hall of the man whose son he has slain, or when Ingeld is reconciled to Hrothgar. Very similar, too, is the temporary reconciliation often brought about in an Icelandic feud by the feeling that the other side has something to say for itself, and that both have suffered grievously. The death of Finn's son is a set off against the death of Hnæf. But, as in the case of Alboin and of Ingeld, or of many an

Icelandic Saga, the passion for revenge is too deep to be laid to rest permanently. This is what makes the figure of Hengest tragic, like the figure of Ingeld: both have plighted their word, but neither can keep it.

The assembly breaks up. Finn and his men go back to Friesland, and Hengest accompanies them: of the other Danish survivors nothing is said for the moment: whatever longings they may have had for revenge, the poet concentrates all for the moment in the figure of Hengest.

Hengest spends the winter with Finn, but he cannot quiet his conscience: and in the end, he accepts the gift of a sword from a young Danish prince Hunlafing, who is planning revenge. The uncles of Hunlafing, Guthlaf and Oslaf [Ordlaf], had been in the hall when it was attacked, and had survived. It is possible that the young prince's father, Hunlaf, was slain then, and that his son is therefore recognised as having the nominal leadership in the operations of vengeance. Hengest, by accepting the sword, promises his services in the work of revenge, and makes a great slaughter of the treacherous Eotens. Perhaps he so far respects his oath that he leaves the simultaneous attack upon Finn to Guthlaf and Oslaf [Ordlaf]. Here we should have an explanation of *swylce*: "in like wise"; and also an explanation of the omission of Hengest's name from the final act, the slaying of Finn himself. Hengest made the Eotens feel the sharpness of his sword: and in like wise Guthlaf and Oslaf conducted their part of the campaign. Of course this is only a guess: but it is very much in the manner of the Heroic Age to get out of a difficulty by respecting the letter of an oath whilst breaking its spirit – just as Hogni and Gunnar arrange that the actual slaying of Sigurd shall be done by Guttorm, who had not personally sworn the oath, as they had.

Gefwulf, Prince of the Jutes

CONCLUSIVE EXTERNAL evidence in favour of the view just put forward we can hardly hope for: for this reason, amongst others, that the names of the actors in the Finn

tragedy are corrupted and obscured in the different versions. Hnæf and Hengest are too well known to be altered: but most of the other names mentioned in the *Fragment* do not agree with the forms given in other documents. Sigeferth is the Sæferth of *Widsith*: the Ordlaf (correct) of the *Fragment* is the Oslaf of the *Episode*. The first Guthlaf is confirmed by the Guthlaf of the *Episode*: the other names, the second Guthlaf, Eaha and Guthere, we cannot control from other sources: but they have all, on various grounds, been suspected.

Tribal names are equally varied. Sigeferth's people, the Secgan, are called Sycgan in *Widsith*. And he would be a bold man who would deny (what almost all students of the subject hold) that *Eotena, Eotenum* in the *Episode* is yet another scribal error: the copyist had before him the Anglian form, *eotna, eotnum*, and miswrote *eotena, eotenum*, when he should have written the West-Saxon equivalent of the tribal name, *Ӯtena, Ӯtum* – the name we get in *Widsith*:

Ӯtum [weold] Gefwulf
Fin Folcwalding Frēsna cynne.

But in *Widsith* names of heroes and tribes are grouped together (often, but not invariably) according as they are related in story. Consequently Gefwulf is probably (not certainly) a hero of the Finn story. What part does he play? If, as I have been trying to show, the Jutes are the aggressors, then, as their chief, Gefwulf would probably be the leader of the attack upon the hall. This part, in the *Fragment*, is played by Garulf.

Now *Gārulf* is not *Gefwulf*, and I am not going to pretend that it is. But *Gārulf* is very near *Gefwulf*: and (what is important) more so in Old English script than in modern script. It stands to *Gefwulf* in exactly the same relation as *Heregār* to *Heorogār* or *Sigeferð* to *Sǣ⁻ferð* or *Ordlāf* to *Ōslāf*: that is to say the initial letter and the second element are identical. And no serious student, I think, doubts that *Heregā⁻r* and *Heorogā⁻r*, or *Sigeferð* and *Sǣ⁻ferð*, or *Ordlāf* and *Ōslāf* are merely corruptions of one name. And if it be admitted to be probable that *Gefwulf* is miswritten for *Gārulf*, then the theory that Garulf was prince of the Jutes, and the original assailant of Hnæf, in addition to being the only theory which satisfactorily explains the internal evidence of the *Fragment* and the *Episode*, has also powerful external support.

Conclusion

BUT, APART from any such confirmation, I think that the theory offers an explanation of the known facts of the case, and that it is the only theory yet put forward which does. It enables us to solve many minor difficulties that hardly otherwise admit of solution. But, above all, it gives a tragic interest to the story by making the actions of the two main characters, Finn and Hengest, intelligible and human: they are both great chiefs, placed by circumstances in a cruel position.

Finn is no longer a treacherous host, plotting the murder of his guests, without even having the courage personally to superintend the dirty work: and Hengest is not guilty of the shameful act of entering the service of a king who had slain his lord by treachery when a guest. The tale of *Finnsburg* becomes one of tragic misfortune besetting great heroes – a tale of the same type as the stories of Thurisind or Ingeld, of Sigurd or Theodric.

Part IV

THIS FINAL section is the most wide-ranging in the work, picking up as it does various loose and lingering threads. It begins with a catalogue of early medieval place names associated with the name Grendel. Given that no other Old English literary sources mention *Beowulf*, the poem or the character, it is documents such as these charters that provide our strongest evidence for contemporary knowledge of the story.

The section on Beowulf and archaeology is somewhat outdated now; Sutton Hoo had not yet been excavated and many of the artefacts that are today intrinsically bound up with our conception of early medieval England were still undiscovered. Nevertheless, the section includes a wealth of Scandinavian finds, including the famous Gokstad and Oseberg ships. The final two sections firstly return to the theme of Beowulf's name, tracing further literary and folkloric analogues, then discuss the date of Hygelac's death as attested in historical documents.

Grendel

It may be helpful to examine the places where the name of Grendel occurs in English charters.

A.D. 708. Grant of land at Abbots Morton, near Alcester, co. Worcester, by Kenred, King of the Mercians, to Evesham (extant in a late copy).

> *Ærest of grindeles pytt on wīðimære; of wīðimære on þæt rēade slōh ... of ðēre dīce on þene blace pōl; of þām pōle æfter long pidele in tō þām mersce; of þām mersce þā æft on grindeles pytt.*

The valley of the Piddle Brook is about a mile wide, with hills rising on each side till they reach a height of a couple of hundred feet above the brook. The directions begin in the valley and run "From Grindel's 'pytt' to the willow-mere; from the willow-mere to the red morass"; then from the morass the directions take us up the hill and along the lea, where they continue among the downs till we again make our descent into the valley, "from the ditch to the black pool, from the pool along the Piddle brook to the marsh, and from the marsh back to Grindel's 'pytt.'" In modern English a "pit" is an artificial hole which is generally dry: §but the word is simply Latin *puteus,* "a well," and is used in this sense in the Gospel translations. Here it is a hole, and we may be sure that, with the willow-mere and the red slough on the one side, and the black pool and the marsh on the other, the hole was full of water.

A.D. 739. Grant of land at Creedy, co. Devon, by Æthelheard, King of Wessex, to Bishop Forthhere.

> *of doddan hrycge on grendeles pyt; of grendeles pytte on ifigbearo (ivy-grove)...*

The spot is near the junction of the rivers Exe and Creedy, with Dartmoor in the distance. The neighbourhood bears uncanny names,

Cāines æcer, egesan trēow. If, as has been suggested by Napier and Stevenson, a trace of this pit still survives in the name Pitt farm, the mere must have been in the uplands, about 600 feet above sea level.

A.D. 931. Grant of land at Ham in Wiltshire by Athelstan to his thane Wulfgar. It is in this charter that *on Bēowan hammes hecgan, on Grendles mere* occur. "Grendel pits or meres" are in most other cases in low-lying marshy country: but this, like (perhaps) the preceding one, is in the uplands – it must have been a lonely mere among the hills, under Inkpen Beacon.

Circa A.D. 957. A list of boundaries near Battersea.

Đis synd ðā landgemǣre tō Batriceseie. Ǣrst at hēgefre; fram hēgefre to gætenesheale; fram gæteneshæle to gryndeles syllen; fram gryndeles sylle to russemere; fram ryssemere to bælgenham...

All this is low-lying land, just south of the Thames. *Hēgefre* is on the river; *Bælgenham* is Balham, co. Surrey. "From Grendel's mire to the rushy mere" harmonizes excellently with what we know of the swampy nature of this district in early times.

A.D. 958. Grant of land at Swinford, on the Stour, co. Stafford, by King Eadred to his thane Burhelm.

Ondlong bæces wið neoþan eostacote; ondlong dīces in grendels-mere; of grendels-mere in stāncōfan; of stāncōfan ondlong dūne on stiran mere...

A.D. 972. Confirmation of lands to Pershore Abbey (Worcester) by King Edgar.

of Grindles bece swā þæt gemǣre ligð...

A.D. 972. Extract from an account of the descent of lands belonging to Westminster, quoting a grant of King Edgar.

andlang hagan to grendeles gatan æfter kincges mearce innan brægentan...

The property described is near Watling Street, between Edgware, Hendon, and the River Brent. It is a low-lying district almost surrounded by the hills of Hampstead, Highgate, Barnet, Mill Hill, Elstree, Bushey Heath and Harrow. The bottom of the basin thus formed must have been a swamp. What the "gate" may have been it is difficult to say. A foreign scholar has suggested that it may have been a narrow mountain defile or possibly a cave: but this suggestion could never have been made by anyone who knew the country. The "gate" is likely to have been a channel connecting two meres – or it might have been a narrow piece of land between them – one of those *enge ānpaðas* which Grendel and his mother had to tread. Anyway, there is nothing exceptional in this use of "gate" in connection with a water-spirit. Necker, on the Continent, also had his "gates." Thus there is a "Neckersgate Mill" near Brussels, and the name "Neckersgate" used also to be applied to a group of houses near by, surrounded by water

All the other places clearly point to a water-spirit: two meres, two pits, a mire and a beck: for the most part situated in low-lying country which must in Anglo-Saxon times have been swampy. All this harmonizes excellently with the *fenfreoðo* of *Beowulf* (l. 851). Of course it does not in the least follow that these places were named after the Grendel of our poem. It may well be that there was in England a current belief in a creature Grendel, dwelling among the swamps. Von Sydow has compared the Yorkshire belief in Peg Powler, or the Lancashire Jenny Greenteeth. But these aquatic monsters are not exactly parallel; for they abide in the water, and are dangerous only to those who attempt to cross it, or at any rate venture too near the bank whilst Grendel and even his mother are capable of excursions of some distance from their fastness amid the fens.

Of course the mere-haunting Grendel *may* have been identified only at a comparatively late date with the spirit who struggles with the hero in the house, and flees below the earth in the folk-tale.

At any rate belief in a Grendel, haunting mere and fen, is clearly demonstrable for England – at any rate for the south and west of England: for of these place-names two belong to the London district, one to Wiltshire, one to Devonshire, two to Worcester and one to Stafford. The place-name *Grendele* in Yorkshire is too doubtful to be of much help. (*Domesday Book*, I, 302.) It is the modern village Grindale, four miles N.W. of Bridlington. From it, probably, is derived the surname *Grindle, Grindall* (Bardsley).

Abroad, the nearest parallel is to be found in Transsylvania, where there is a *Grändels môr* among the Saxons of the Senndorf district, near Bistritz. The Saxons of Transsylvania are supposed to have emigrated from the neighbourhood of the lower Rhine and the Moselle, and there is a *Grindelbach* in Luxemburg which may possibly be connected with the marsh demon.

Most of the German names in *Grindel-* or *Grendel-* are connected with *grendel*, "a bar," and therefore do not come into consideration here: but the Transsylvanian "Grendel's marsh," anyway, reminds us of the English "Grendel's marsh" or "mere" or "pit." Nevertheless, the local story with which the Transsylvanian swamp is connected – that of a peasant who was ploughing with six oxen and was swallowed up in the earth – is such that it requires considerable ingenuity to see any connection between it and the *Beowulf-Grendel*-tale.

The Anglo-Saxon place-names may throw some light upon the meaning and etymology of "Grendel." The name has generally been derived from *grindan*, "to grind"; either directly[1], because Grendel grinds the bones of those he devours, or indirectly, in the sense of "tormentor." Others would connect with O.N. *grindill*, "storm," and perhaps with M.E. *gryndel*, "angry."

It has recently been proposed to connect the word with *grund*, "bottom": for Grendel lives in the *mere-grund* or *grund-wong* and his mother is the *grund-wyrgin*. Erik Rooth, who proposes this etymology, compares the Icelandic *grandi*, "a sandbank," and the common Low German dialect word *grand*, "coarse sand." This brings us back to the root "to grind," for *grand*, "sand" is simply the product of the grinding of the waves. Indeed the same explanation has been given of the word "ground."

However this may be, the new etymology differs from the old in giving Grendel a name derived, not from his grinding or tormenting others, but from his dwelling at the bottom of the lake or marsh. The name would have a parallel in the Modern English *grindle*, *grundel*, German *grundel*, a fish haunting the bottom of the water.

The Old English place-names, associating Grendel as they do with meres and swamps, seem rather to support this.

As to the Devonshire stream *Grendel* (now the Grindle or Greendale Brook), it has been suggested that this name is also connected with the root *grand*, "gravel," "sand." But, so far as I have been able to observe, there is no particular suggestion of sand or gravel about this modest little brook. If we follow the River Clyst from the point where the Grindle flows into it, through two miles of marshy land, to the estuary of the Exe, we shall there find plenty. But it is clear from the charter of 963 that the name was then, as now, restricted to the small brook. I cannot tell why the stream should bear the name, or what, if any, is the connection with the monster Grendel. We can only note that the name is again found attached to water, and, near the junction with the Clyst, to marshy ground.

Anyone who will hunt Grendel through the shires, first on the 6-in. ordnance map, and later on foot, will probably have to agree with the Three Jovial Huntsmen

This huntin' doesn't pay,

But we'n powler't up an' down a bit, an' had a rattlin' day.

But, if some conclusions, although scanty, can be drawn from place-names in which the word *grendel* occurs, nothing can be got from the numerous place-names which have been thought to contain the name *Bēow*. The clearest of these is the *on Bēowan hammes hecgan*, which occurs in the Wiltshire charter of 931. But we can learn nothing definite from it: and although there are other instances of strong and weak forms alternating, we cannot even be quite certain that the Beowa here is identical with the Beow of the genealogies.

The other cases, many of which occur in *Domesday Book* are worthless. Those which point to a weak form may often be derived from the weak noun *bēo*, "bee": "The Anglo-Saxons set great store by their bees, honey and wax being indispensables to them."

Bēas brōc, Bēas feld(*Bewes feld*) occur in charters: but here a connection with *bēaw*, "horsefly," is possible: for parallels, one has only to consider the long list of places enumerated by Björkman, the names of which are derived from those of beasts, birds, or insects. And in such a word as *Bēolēah*, even if the first element be *bēow*, why may it not be the common noun "barley," and not the name of the hero at all?

No argument can therefore be drawn from such a conjecture as that of Olrik, that *Bēas brōc* refers to the water into which the last sheaf (representing Beow) was thrown, in accordance with the harvest custom, and in the expectation of the return of the spirit in the coming spring.

Beowulf and the Archeologists

THE PEAT-BOGS of Schleswig and Denmark have yielded finds of the first importance for English archæology. These "moss-finds" are great collections, chiefly of arms and accoutrements, obviously deposited with intention. The first of these great discoveries, that of Thorsbjerg, was made in the heart of ancient Angel: the site of the next, Nydam, also comes within the area probably occupied by either Angles or Jutes; and most of the rest of the "moss-finds" were in the closest neighbourhood of the old Anglian home. The period of the oldest deposits, as is shown by the Roman coins found among them, is hardly before the third century A.D., and some authorities would make it considerably later.

An account of these discoveries will be found in Engelhardt's *Denmark in the Early Iron Age*, 1866: a volume which summarizes the results of Engelhardt's investigations during the preceding seven years. He had published in Copenhagen *Thorsbjerg Mosefund*, 1863; *Nydam*

Mosefund, 1865. Engelhardt's work at Nydam was interrupted by the war of 1864: the finds had to be ceded to Germany, and the exploration was continued by German scholars. Engelhardt consoled himself that these "subsequent investigations ... do not seem to have been carried on with the necessary care and intelligence," and continued his own researches within the narrowed frontiers of Denmark, publishing two monographs on the mosses of Fünen: *Kragehul Mosefund*, 1867; *Vimose Fundet*, 1869.

These deposits, however, obviously belong to a period much earlier than that in which *Beowulf* was written: indeed most of them certainly belong to a period earlier than that in which the historic events described in *Beowulf* occurred; so that, close as is their relation with Anglian civilization, it is with the civilization of the Angles while still on the continent.

The Archæology of *Beowulf* has been made the subject of special study by Knut Stjerna, in a series of articles which appeared between 1903 and his premature death in 1909. A good service has been done to students of *Beowulf* by Dr Clark Hall in collecting and translating Stjerna's essays. They are a mine of useful information, and the reproductions of articles from Scandinavian grave-finds, with which they are so copiously illustrated, are invaluable. The magnificent antiquities from Vendel, now in the Stockholm museum, are more particularly laid under contribution[1]. Dr Clark Hall added a most useful "Index of things mentioned in *Beowulf*," well illustrated. Here again the illustrations, with few exceptions, are from Scandinavian finds.

Two weighty arguments as to the origin of *Beowulf* have been based upon archæology. In the first place it has been urged by Dr Clark Hall that:

"If the poem is read in the light of the evidence which Stjerna has marshalled in the essays as to the profusion of gold, the prevalence of ring-swords, of boar-helmets, of ring-corslets, and ring-money, it becomes clear how strong the distinctively Scandinavian colouring is, and how comparatively little of the *mise-en-scène* must be due to the English author."

Equally, Prof. Klaeber finds in Stjerna's investigations a strong argument for the Scandinavian character of *Beowulf*.

Now Stjerna, very rightly and naturally, drew his illustrations of *Beowulf* from those Scandinavian, and especially Swedish, grave-finds which he knew so well: and very valuable those illustrations are. But it does not follow, because the one archæologist who has chosen to devote his knowledge so wholeheartedly to the elucidation of *Beowulf* was a Scandinavian, using Scandinavian material, that therefore *Beowulf* is Scandinavian. This, however, is the inference which Stjerna himself was apt to draw, and which is still being drawn from his work. Stjerna speaks of our poem as a monument raised by the Geatas to the memory of their saga-renowned king, though he allows that certain features of the poem, such as the dragon-fight, are of Anglo-Saxon origin.

Of course, it must be allowed that accounts such as those of the fighting between Swedes and Geatas, if they are historical (and they obviously are), must have originated from eyewitnesses of the Scandinavian battles: but I doubt if there is anything in *Beowulf* so purely Scandinavian as to compel us to assume that any line of the story, in the poetical form in which we now have it, was *necessarily* composed in Scandinavia. Even if it could be shown that the conditions depicted in *Beowulf* can be better illustrated from the grave-finds of Vendel in Sweden than from English diggings, this would not prove *Beowulf* Scandinavian. Modern scientific archæology is surely based on chronology as well as geography. The English finds date from the period before 650 A.D., and the Vendel finds from the period after. *Beowulf* might well show similarity rather with contemporary art abroad than with the art of earlier generations at home. For intercourse was more general than is always realized. It was not merely trade and plunder which spread fashions from nation to nation. There were the presents of arms which Tacitus mentions as sent, not only privately, but with public ceremony, from one tribe to another. Similar presentations are indicated in *Beowulf* we find them equally at the court of the Ostrogothic Theodoric; Charles the Great sent to Offa of Mercia *unum balteum et unum gladium huniscum*; according to the famous story in the *Heimskringla*, Athelstan sent to Harold Fairhair of Norway a sword and belt arrayed with gold and silver; Athelstan gave Harold's son Hakon a sword which was the best that ever came to Norway. It is not surprising, then, if we find parallels between English poetry and Scandinavian grave-finds, both apparently dating from about the year 700 A.D. But I do not think that there is any *special* resemblance, though, both in *Beowulf* and in the Vendel graves, there is a profusion lacking in the case of the simpler Anglo-Saxon tomb-furniture.

Let us examine the five points of special resemblance, alleged by Dr Clark Hall, on the basis of Stjerna's studies.

"The profusion of gold." Gold is indeed lavishly used in *Beowulf*: the golden treasure found in the dragon's lair was so bulky that it had to be transported by waggon. And, certainly, gold is found in greater profusion in Swedish than in English graves: the most casual visitor to the Stockholm museum must be impressed by the magnificence of the exhibits there. But, granting gold to have been rarer in England than in Sweden, I cannot grant Stjerna's contention that therefore an English poet could not have conceived the idea of a vast gold hoard; or that, even if the poet does deck his warriors with gold somewhat more sumptuously than was actually the case in England, we can draw any argument from it. For, if the dragon in *Beowulf* guards a treasure, so equally does the typical dragon of Old English proverbial lore. Beowulf is spoken of as *gold-wlanc*, but the typical thegn in *Finnsburg* is called *gold-hladen*. The sword found by Beowulf in the hall of Grendel's mother has a golden hilt, but the English proverb had it that "gold is in its place on a man's sword." Heorot is hung with golden tapestry, but gold-inwoven fabric has been unearthed from Saxon graves at Taplow, and elsewhere in England. Gold glitters in other poems quite as lavishly as in *Beowulf*, sometimes more so. Widsith made a hobby of collecting golden *bēagas*. The subject of *Waldere* is a fight for treasure. The byrnie of Waldere is adorned with gold: so is that of Holofernes in *Judith*, so is that of the typical warrior in the *Elene*. Are all these poems Scandinavian?

"The prevalence of ring-swords." We know that swords were sometimes fitted with a ring in the hilt. It is not clear whether the object of this ring was to fasten the hilt by a strap to the wrist, for convenience in fighting (as has been the custom with the cavalry sword in modern times) or whether it was used to attach the "peace bands," by which the hilt of the sword was sometimes fixed to the scabbard, when only being worn ceremonially. The word *hring-mæl*, applied three times to the sword in *Beowulf*, has been interpreted as a reference to these "ring-swords," though it is quite conceivable that it may refer only to the damascening of the sword with a ringed pattern[1]. Assuming that the reference in *Beowulf is* to a "ring-sword," Stjerna illustrates the allusion from seven ring-swords, or fragments of ring-swords, found in Sweden. But, as Dr Clark Hall himself points out (whilst oddly enough accepting this argument as proof of the Scandinavian colouring of *Beowulf*) four ring-swords at least have been found in England. And these English swords are *real* ring-swords; that is to say, the pommel is furnished with a ring, within which another ring moves (in the oldest type of sword) quite freely. This freedom of movement seems, however, to be gradually restricted, and in one of these English swords the two rings are made in one and the same piece. In the Swedish swords, however, this restriction is carried further, and the two rings are represented by a knob growing out of a circular base. Another sword of this "knob"-type has recently been found in a Frankish tomb, and yet another in the Rhineland. It seems to be agreed among archæologists that the English type, as found in Kent, is the original, and that the Swedish and continental "ring-swords" are merely imitations, in which the ring has become conventionalized into a knob. But, if so, how can the mention of a ring-sword in *Beowulf* (if indeed that be the meaning of *hring-mæl*) prove Scandinavian colouring? If it proved anything (which it does not) it would tend to prove the reverse, and to locate *Beowulf* in Kent, where the true ring-swords have been found.

"The prevalence of boar-helmets." It is true that several representations of warriors wearing boar-helmets have been found in Scandinavia. But the only certainly Anglo-Saxon helmet yet found in England has a boar-crest; and this is, I believe, the only actual boar-helmet yet found. How then can the boar-helmets of *Beowulf* show Scandinavian rather than Anglo-Saxon origin?

"The prevalence of ring-corslets." It is true that only one trace of a byrnie, and that apparently not of ring-mail, has so far been found in an Anglo-Saxon grave. (We have somewhat more abundant remains from the period prior to the migration to England: a peculiarly fine corslet of ring-mail, with remains of some nine others, was found in the moss at Thorsbjerg in the midst of the ancient Anglian continental home; and other ring-corslets have been found in the neighbourhood of Angel, at Vimose in Fünen.) But, for the period when *Beowulf* must have been composed, the ring-corslet is almost as rare in Scandinavia as in England; the artist, however, seems to be indicating a byrnie upon many of the warriors depicted on the Vendel helm (Grave 14: seventh century). Equally, in England, warriors are represented on the Franks Casket as wearing the byrnie: also the laws of Ine (688-95) make it clear that the byrnie was by no means unknown. Other Old English poems, certainly not Scandinavian, mention the ring-byrnie. How then can the mention of it in *Beowulf* be a proof of Scandinavian origin?

"The prevalence of ring-money." Before minted money became current, rings were used everywhere among the Teutonic peoples. Gold rings, *intertwined* so as to form a chain, have been found throughout Scandinavia, presumably for use as a medium of exchange. The term *locenra bēaga* (gen. plu.) occurs in *Beowulf*, and this is interpreted by Stjerna as "rings *intertwined or locked* together." But *locen* in *Beowulf* need not have the meaning of "intertwined"; it occurs elsewhere in Old English of a single jewel, *sincgim locen*. Further, even if *locen* does mean "intertwined," such intertwined rings are not limited to Scandinavia proper. They have been found in Schleswig. And almost the very phrase in *Beowulf*, *londes ne locenra bēaga* recurs in the *Andreas*. The phrase there may be imitated from *Beowulf*, but, equally, the phrase in *Beowulf* may be imitated from some earlier poem. In fact, it is part of the traditional poetic diction: but its occurrence in the *Andreas* shows that it cannot be used as an argument of Scandinavian origin.

Whilst, therefore, accepting with gratitude the numerous illustrations which Stjerna has drawn from Scandinavian grave-finds, we must be careful not to read a Scandinavian colouring into features of *Beowulf* which are at least as much English as Scandinavian, such as the ring-sword or the boar-helmet or the ring-corslet.

There is, as is noted above, a certain atmosphere of profusion and wealth about some Scandinavian grave-finds, which corresponds much more nearly with the wealthy life depicted in *Beowulf* than does the comparatively meagre tomb-furniture of England. But we must remember that, after the spread of Christianity in the first half of the seventh century, the custom of burying articles with the bodies of the dead naturally ceased, or almost ceased, in England. Scandinavia continued heathen for another four hundred years, and it was during these years that the most magnificent deposits were made. As Stjerna himself points out, "a steadily increasing luxury in the appointment of graves" is to be found in Scandinavia in these centuries before the introduction of Christianity there. When we find in Scandinavia things (complete ships, for example) which we do not find in England, we owe this, partly to the nature of the soil in which they were embedded, but also to the continuance of such burial customs after they had died out in England.

Helm and byrnie were not necessarily unknown, or even very rare in England, simply because it was not the custom to bury them with the dead. On the other hand, the frequent mention of them in *Beowulf* does not imply that they were common: for *Beowulf* deals only with the aristocratic adherents of a court, and even in *Beowulf* fine specimens of the helm and byrnie are spoken of as things which a king seeks far and wide to procure for his retainers. We cannot, therefore, argue that there is any discrepancy. However, if we do so argue, it would merely prove, not that *Beowulf* is Scandinavian as opposed to English, but that it is comparatively late in date. Tacitus emphasizes the fact that spear and shield were the Teutonic weapons, that helmet and corslet were hardly known. Pagan graves show that at any rate they were hardly known *as tomb-furniture* in England in the fifth, sixth, and early seventh centuries. The introduction of Christianity, and the intercourse with the South which it involved, certainly led to the growth of pomp and wealth in England, till the early eighth century became "the golden age of Anglo-Saxon England."

It might therefore conceivably be argued that *Beowulf* reflects the comparative abundance of early Christian England, as opposed to the more primitive heathen simplicity; but to argue a Scandinavian origin from the profusion of *Beowulf* admits of an easy *reductio ad absurdum*. For the same arguments would prove a heathen, Scandinavian origin for the *Andreas*, the *Elene*, the *Exodus*, or even for the Franks Casket, despite its Anglo-Saxon inscription and Christian carvings.

However, though the absence of helm and byrnie from Anglo-Saxon graves does not prove that these arms were not used by the living in heathen times, one thing it assuredly *does* prove: that the Anglo-Saxons in heathen times did not sacrifice helm and byrnie recklessly in funeral pomp. And this brings us to the second argument as to the origin of *Beowulf* which has been based on archæology.

Something has been said above of this second contention – that the accuracy of the account of Beowulf's funeral is confirmed in every point by archæological evidence: that it must therefore have been composed within living memory of a time when ceremonies of this kind were still actually in use in England: and that therefore we cannot date *Beowulf* later than the third or fourth decade of the seventh century.

To begin with; the pyre in *Beowulf* is represented as hung with helmets, bright byrnies, and shields. Now it is impossible to say exactly how the funeral pyres were equipped in England. But we *do* know how the buried bodies were equipped. And (although inhumation cemeteries are much more common than cremation cemeteries) all the graves that have been opened have so far yielded only one case of a helmet and byrnie being buried with the warrior, and one other very doubtful case of a helmet without the byrnie. Abroad, instances are somewhat more common, but still of great rarity. For such things could ill be spared. Charles the Great forbade the export of byrnies from his dominions. Worn by picked champions fighting in the forefront, they might well decide the issue of a battle. In the mounds where we have reason to think that the great chiefs mentioned in *Beowulf*, Eadgils or Ohthere, lie buried, any trace of weapons was conspicuously absent among the burnt remains. Nevertheless, the belief that his armour would be useful to the champion in the next life, joined perhaps with a feeling that it was unlucky, or unfair on the part of the survivor to deprive the dead of his personal weapons, led in heathen times to the occasional burial of these treasures with the warrior who owned them. The fifth century tomb of Childeric I, when discovered twelve centuries later, was found magnificently furnished – the prince had been buried with treasure and much equipment, sword, scramasax, axe, spear. But these were his own. Similarly, piety might have demanded that Beowulf should be burnt with his full equipment. But would the pyre have been hung with helmets and byrnies? Whose? Were the thegns asked to sacrifice theirs, and go naked into the next fight in honour of their lord? If so, what archæological authority have we for such a custom in England?

Then the barrow is built, and the vast treasure of the dragon (which included "many a helmet") placed in it. Now there are instances of articles which have not passed through the fire being placed in or upon or around an urn with the cremated bones. But is there any instance of the thing being done on this scale – of a wholesale burning of helmets and byrnies followed by a burial of huge treasure? If so, one would like to know when, and where. If not, how can it be argued that the account in *Beowulf* is one of which "the accuracy is confirmed in every point by archæological or contemporary literary evidence?" Rather we must say, with Knut Stjerna, that it is "too much of a good thing."

Scandinavian Burial Mounds

The three great "Kings' Mounds" at Old Uppsala were explored between 1847 and 1874: cremated remains from them can be seen in the Stockholm Museum. An account of the tunnelling, and of the complicated structure of the mounds, was given in 1876 by the Swedish State-Antiquary. From these finds Knut Stjerna dated the oldest of the "Kings' Mounds" about 500 A.D., and the others somewhat later. Now, as we are definitely told that Athils (Eadgils) and the two kings who figure in the list of Swedish monarchs as his grandfather and great-grandfather (Aun and Egil) were "laid in mound" at Uppsala, and as the chronology agrees, it seems only reasonable to conclude that the three Kings' Mounds were raised over these three kings.

That Athils' father Ottar (Ohthere) was not regarded as having been buried at Uppsala is abundantly clear from the account given of his death, and of his nickname Vendel-crow. A mound near Vendel north of Uppsala is known by his name. Such names are often the result of quite modern antiquarian conjecture: but that such is not the case here was proved by the recent discovery that an antiquarian survey (preserved in MS in the Royal Library at Stockholm) dating from 1677, mentions in Vendel "widh Hussby, [en] stor jorde högh, som heeter Otters högen." An exploration of Ottar's mound showed a striking similarity with the Uppsala mounds. The structure was the same, a cairn of stones covered over with earth; the cremated remains were similar, there were abundant traces of burnt animals, a comb, half-spherical draughts with two round holes bored in the flat side, above all, there was in neither case any trace of weapons. In Ottar's mound a gold Byzantine coin was found, pierced, having evidently been used as an ornament. It can be dated 477-8; it is much worn, but such coins seldom remained in the North in use for a century after their minting. Ottar's mound obviously, then, belongs to the same period as the Uppsala mounds, and confirms the date attributed by Stjerna to the oldest of those mounds, about 500 A.D.

Weapons

The Sword. The sword of the Anglo-Saxon pagan period (from the fifth to the seventh century) "is deficient in quality as a blade, and also ... in the character of its hilt." In this it contrasts with the sword found in the peat-bogs of Schleswig from an earlier period: "these swords of the Schleswig moss-finds are much better weapons as well as with the later Viking sword of the ninth or tenth century, which "is a remarkably effective and well-considered implement¹." It has been suggested that both the earlier Schleswig swords and the later Viking swords (which bear a considerable likeness to each other, as against the inferior Anglo-Saxon sword) are the product of intercourse with Romanized peoples¹, whilst the typical Anglo-Saxon sword "may represent an independent Germanic effort at sword making." However this may be, it is noteworthy that nowhere in *Beowulf* do we have any hint of the skill of any sword-smith who is regarded as contemporary. A good sword is always "an old heirloom," "an ancient treasure." The sword of Wiglaf, which had belonged to Eanmund, or the sword with which Eofor slays Ongentheow, are described by the phrase *ealdsweord eotenisc*, as if they were weapons of which the secret and origin had been lost – indeed the same phrase is applied to the magic sword which Beowulf finds in the hall of Grendel's mother.

The blade of these ancestral swords was sometimes damascened or adorned with wave-like patterns. The swords of the Schleswig moss-finds are almost all thus adorned with a variegated surface, as often are the later Viking swords; but those of the Anglo-Saxon graves are *not*. Is it fanciful to suggest that the reference to damascening is a tradition coming down from the time of the earlier sword as found in the Nydam moss? A few early swords might have been preserved among the invaders as family heirlooms, too precious to be buried with the owner, as the product of the local weapon-smith was.

The Helmet. The helmet found at Benty Grange in Derbyshire in 1848 is now in the Sheffield Museum: little remains except the boar-crest, the nose-piece, and the framework of iron ribs radiating from the crown, and fixed to a circle of iron surrounding the brow (perhaps the *frēawrāsn* of *Beowulf*, 1451). Mr Bateman, the discoverer, described the helmet as "coated with narrow plates of horn, running in a diagonal direction from the ribs, so as to form a herring-bone pattern; the ends were secured by strips of horn, radiating in like manner as the iron ribs, to which they were riveted at intervals of about an inch and a half: all the rivets had ornamented heads of silver on the outside, and on the front rib is a small cross of the same metal. Upon the top or crown of the helmet, is an elongated oval brass plate, upon which stands the figure of an animal, carved in iron, now much rusted, but still a very good representation of a pig: it has bronze eyes[.]." Helmets of very similar construction, but without the boar, have been found on the Continent and in Scandinavia (Vendel, Grave 14, late seventh century). The continental helmets often stand higher than the Benty Grange or Vendel specimens, being sometimes quite conical (cf. the epithet "war-steep," *heaðo-stēap*, *Beowulf*). Many of the continental helmets are provided with cheek-protections, and these also appear in the Scandinavian representations of warriors on the Torslunda plates and elsewhere. These side pieces have become detached from the magnificent Vendel helmet, which is often shown in engravings without them[.], but they can be seen in the Stockholm Museum[.]. If it ever possessed them, the Benty Grange helmet has lost these side pieces. Such cheek-protections are, however, represented, together with the nose-protection, on the head of one of the warriors depicted on the Franks Casket. In the Vendel helms, the nose-pieces were connected under the eyes with the rim of the helmet, so as to form a mask; the helmet in *Beowulf* is frequently spoken of as the battle-mask.

Both helmet and boar-crest were sometimes gold-adorned: the golden boar was a symbol of the god Freyr: some magic protective power is still, in *Beowulf*, felt to adhere to these swine-likenesses, as it was in the days of Tacitus.

In Scandinavia, the Torslunda plates show the helmet with a boar-crest: the Vendel helmet has representations of warriors whose crests have an animal's head tailing off to a mere rim or roll: this may be the *walu* or *wala* which keeps watch over the head in *Beowulf*. The helmet was bound fast to the head; exactly how, we do not know.

The Corslet. This in *Beowulf* is made of rings, twisted and interlaced by hand. As stated above, the fragments of the only known Anglo-Saxon byrnie were not of this type, but rather intended to have been sewn "upon a doublet of strong cloth. Byrnies were of various lengths, the longer ones reaching to the middle of the thigh (*byrnan sīde*, *Beow.* 1291, cf. *loricæ longæ, síðar brynjur*).

The Spear. Spear and shield were the essential Germanic weapons in the days of Tacitus, and they are the weapons most commonly found in Old English tombs. The spear-shaft has generally decayed, analysis of fragments surviving show that it was frequently of ash. The butt-end of the spear was frequently furnished with an iron tip, and the distance of this from the spear-head, and the size of the socket, show the spear-shaft to have been six or seven feet long, and three-quarters of an inch to one inch in diameter.

The Shield. Several round shields were preserved on the Gokstad ship, and in the deposits of an earlier period at Thorsbjerg and Nydam. These are formed of boards fastened together, often only a quarter of an inch thick, and not strengthened or braced in any way, bearing out the contemptuous description of the painted German shield which Tacitus puts into the mouth of Germanicus. It was, however, intended that the shield should be light. It was easily pierced, but, by a rapid twist, the foe's sword could be broken or wrenched from his hand. Thus we are told how Gunnar gave his shield a twist, as his adversary thrust his sword through it, and so snapped off his sword at the hilt. The shield was held by a bar, crossing a hole some four inches wide cut in the middle. The hand was protected by a hollow conical boss or umbo, fixed to the wood by its brim, but projecting considerably. In England the wood of the shield has always perished, but a large number of bosses have been preserved. The boss seems to have been called *rond*, a word which is also used for the shield as a whole. In *Beowulf*, 2673, *Gifts of Men*, 65, the meaning "boss" suits *rond* best, also in *rand sceal on scylde, fæst fingra gebeorh* (*Cotton. Gnomic Verses*, 37-8). But the original meaning of *rand* must have been the circular rim round the edge, and this meaning it retains in Icelandic (Falk, 131). The linden wood was sometimes bound with bast, whence *scyld (sceal) gebunden, lēoht linden bord* (*Exeter Gnomic Verses*, 94-5).

The Bow is a weapon of much less importance in *Beowulf* than the spear. Few traces of the bow have survived from Anglo-Saxon England, though many wooden long-bows have been preserved in the moss-finds in a remarkably fine state. They are of yew, some over six feet long, and in at least one instance tipped with horn. The bow entirely of horn was, of course, well known in the East, and in classical antiquity, but I do not think traces of any horn-bow have been discovered in the North. It was a difficult weapon to manage, as the suitors of Penelope found to their cost. Possibly that is why Hæthcyn is represented as killing his brother Herebeald accidentally with a horn-bow: he could not manage the exotic weapon.

The Hall

It may perhaps be the fact that in the church of Sta. Maria de Naranco, in the north of Spain, we have the hall of a Visigothic king driven north by the Mohammedan invasion. But, even if this surmise be correct, the structure of a stone hall of about 750 A.D. gives us little information as to the wooden halls of early Anglo-Saxon times. Heorot is clearly built of timber, held together by iron clamps. These halls were oblong, and a famous passage in Bede makes it clear that, at any rate at the time of the Conversion, the hall had a door at both ends, and the fire burnt in the middle. (The smoke escaped through a hole in the roof, through which probably most of the light came, for windows were few or none.) The *Finnsburg Fragment* also implies two doors. Further indications can be drawn from references to the halls of Norse chiefs. The Scandinavian hall was divided by rows of wooden pillars into a central nave and side aisles. The pillars in the centre were known as the "high-seat pillars." Rows of seats ran down the length of the hall on each side. The central position, facing the high-seat pillars and the fire, was the most honourable. The place of honour for the chief guest was opposite: and it is quite clear that in *Beowulf* also the guest did not sit next his host.

Other points we may note about Heorot, are the tapestry with which its walls are draped, and the paved and variegated floor. Unlike so many later halls, Heorot has a floor little, if anything, raised above the ground: horses can be brought in.

In later times, in Iceland, the arrangement of the hall was changed, and the house consisted of many rooms; but these were formed, not by partitioning the hall, but by building several such halls side by side: the *stufa* or hall proper, the *skáli* or sleeping hall, *etc.*

Ships

IN A TUMULUS near Snape in Suffolk, opened in 1862, there were discovered, with burnt bones and remains thought to be of Anglo-Saxon date, a large number of rivets which, from the positions in which they were found, seemed to give evidence of a boat 48 feet long by over nine feet wide. A boat, similar in dimensions, but better preserved, was unearthed near Bruges in 1899, and the ribs, mast and rudder removed to the Gruuthuuse Museum.

Three boats were discovered in the peat-moss at Nydam in Schleswig in 1863, by Engelhardt. The most important is the "Nydam boat," clinker-built (i.e. with overlapping planks), of oak, 77 feet [23.5 m.] long, by some 11 [3.4 m.] broad, with rowlocks for fourteen oars down each side. There was no trace of any mast. Planks and framework had been held together, partly by iron bolts, and partly by ropes of bast. The boat had fallen to pieces, and had to be laboriously put together in the museum at Flensborg. Another boat was quite fragmentary, but a third boat, of fir, was found tolerably complete. Then the war of 1864 ended Engelhardt's labours at Nydam.

The oak-boat was removed to Kiel, where it now is.

The fir-boat was allowed to decay: many of the pieces of the oak-boat had been rotten and had of necessity been restored in facsimile, and it is much less complete than might be supposed from the numerous reproductions, based upon the fine engraving by Magnus Petersen. The rustic with a spade, there depicted as gazing at the boat, is apt to give a wrong impression that it was dug out intact.

Such was, however, actually the case with regard to the ship excavated from the big mound at Gokstad, near Christiania, by Nicolaysen, in 1880. This was fitted both as a rowing and sailing ship; it was 66 feet [20.1 m.] long on the keel, 78 feet [23.8 m.] from fore to aft and nearly 17 feet [5.1 m.] broad, and was clinker-built, out of a much larger number of oaken planks than the Nydam ship. It had rowlocks for sixteen oars down each side, the gunwale was lined with shields, some of them well preserved, which had been originally painted alternately black and yellow. The find owed its extraordinary preservation to the blue clay in which it was embedded. Its discoverer wrote, with pardonable pride: "Certain it is that we shall not disinter any craft which, in respect of model and workmanship, will outrival that of Gokstad."

Yet the prophecy was destined to prove false: for on Aug. 8, 1903, a farmer came into the National Museum at Christiania to tell the curator, Prof. Gustafson, that he had discovered traces of a boat on his farm at Oseberg. Gustafson found that the task was too great to be begun so late in the year: the digging out of the ship, and its removal to Christiania, occupied from just before Midsummer to just before Christmas of 1904. The potter's clay in which the ship was buried had preserved it, if possible, better than the Gokstad ship: but the movement of the soft subsoil had squeezed and broken both ship and contents. The ship was taken out of the earth in nearly two thousand fragments. These were carefully numbered and marked: each piece was treated, bent back into its right shape, and the ship was put together again plank by plank, as when it was first built. With the exception of a piece about half a yard long, five or six little bits let in, and one of the beams, the ship as it stands now consists of the original woodwork. Two-thirds of the rivets are the old ones. Till his death in 1915 Gustafson was occupied in treating and preparing for exhibition first the ship, and then its extraordinarily rich contents: a waggon and sledges beautifully carved, beds, chests, kitchen utensils which had been buried with the princess who had owned them. A full account of the find is only now being published.

The Oseberg ship is the pleasure boat of a royal lady: clinker-built, of oak, exquisitely carved, intended not for long voyages but for the land-locked waters of the fiord, 70½ feet [21.5 m.] long by some 16½ feet [5 m.] broad. There are holes for fifteen oars down each side, and the ship carried mast and sail.

The upper part of the prow had been destroyed, but sufficient fragments have been found to show that it ended in the head of a snake-like creature, bent round in a coil. This explains the words *bringed-stefna*, *bring-naca*, *wunden-stefna*, used of the ship in *Beowulf*. A similar ringed prow is depicted on an engraved stone from Tjängvide, now in the National Historical Museum at Stockholm. This is supposed to date from about the year 1000.

The Gokstad and Oseberg ships, together with the ship of Tune, a much less complete specimen (unearthed in 1867, and found like the others on the shore of the Christiania fiord) owe their preservation to the clay, and the skill of Scandinavian antiquaries. Yet they are but three out of thousands of ship- or boat-burials. Schetelig enumerates 552 known instances from Norway alone. Often traces of the iron rivets are all that remain.

Ships preserved from the Baltic coast of Germany can be seen at Königsberg, Danzig and Stettin; they are smaller and apparently later; the best, that of Brösen, was destroyed.

The seamanship of *Beowulf* is removed by centuries from that of the (? fourth or fifth century) Nydam boat, which not only has no mast or proper keel, but is so built as to be little suited for sailing. In *Beowulf* the sea is a "sail-road," the word "to row" occurs only in the sense of "swim," sailing is assumed as the means by which Beowulf travels between the land of the Geatas and that of the Danes. Though he voyages with but fourteen companions, the ship is big enough to carry back four horses. How the sail may have been arranged is shown in many inscribed stones of the eighth to the tenth centuries: notably those of Stenkyrka, Högbro, and Tjängvide.

The Oseberg and Gokstad ships are no doubt later than the composition of *Beowulf*. But it is when looking at the Oseberg ship, especially if we picture the great prow like the neck of a swan ending in a serpent's coil, that we can best understand the words of *Beowulf*

> *flota fāmī-heals fugle gelīcost,*
> *wunden-stefna,*

well rendered by Earle "The foamy-necked floater, most like to a bird – the coily-stemmed."

Bee-wolf and Bear's Son

THE OBVIOUS interpretation of the name *Bēowulf* is that suggested by Grimm, that it means "wolf, or foe, of the bee." Grimm's suggestion was repeated independently by Skeat, and further reasons for the interpretation "bee-foe" have been found by Sweet (who had been anticipated by Simrock in some of his points), by Cosijn, Sievers, von Grienberger, Panzer and Björkman.

From the phonological point of view the etymology is a perfect one, but many of those who were convinced that "Beowulf" meant "bee-foe" had no satisfactory explanation of "bee-foe" to offer. Others, like Bugge, whilst admitting that, so far as the form of the words goes, the etymology is satisfactory, rejected "bee-foe" because it seemed to them meaningless.

Yet it is very far from meaningless. "Bee-foe" means "bear." The bear has got a name, or nickname, in many northern languages from his habit of raiding the hives for honey. The Finnish name for bear is said to be "honey-hand": he is certainly called "sweet-foot," *sötfot*, in Sweden, and the Old Slavonic name, "honey-eater," has come to be accepted in Russian, not merely as a nickname, but as the regular term for "bear."

And "bear" is an excellent name for a hero of story. The O.E. *beorn*, "warrior, hero, prince" seems originally to have meant simply "bear." The bear, says Grimm, "is regarded, in the belief of the Old Norse, Slavonic, Finnish and Lapp peoples, as an exalted and holy being, endowed with human understanding and the strength of twelve men. He is called 'forest-king,' 'gold-foot,' 'sweet-foot,' 'honey-hand,' 'honey-paw,' 'honey-eater,' but also 'the great,' 'the old,' 'the old grandsire.'" "Bee-hunter" is then a satisfactory explanation of *Bēowulf*: while the alternative explanations are none of them satisfactory.

Many scholars have been led off the track by the assumption that Beow and Beowulf are to be identified, and that we must therefore assume that the first element in Beowulf's name is *Bēow* – that we must divide not *Bēo-wulf* but *Bēow-ulf*, "a warrior after the manner of Beow." But there is no ground for any such assumption. It is true that in ll. 18, 53, "Beowulf" is written where we should have expected "Beowa." But, even if two words of similar sound have been confused, this fact affords no reason for supposing that they must necessarily have been in the first instance connected etymologically. And against the "warrior of Beow" interpretation is the fact that the name is recorded in the early Northumbrian *Liber Vitae* under the form "Biuuulf." This name, which is that of an early monk of Durham, is presumably the same as that of the hero of our poem, though it does not, of course, follow that the bearer of it was named with any special reference to the slayer of Grendel. Now *Biuuulf* is correct Northumbrian for "bee-wolf," but the first element in the word cannot stand for *Bēow*, unless the affinities and forms of that word are quite different from all that the evidence has hitherto led us to believe. So much at least seems certain. Besides, we have seen that Byggvir is taunted by Loki precisely with the fact that he *is* no warrior. If we can estimate the characteristics of the O.E. Beow from those of the Scandinavian Byggvir, the name "Warrior after the manner of Beow" would be meaningless, if not absurd. Bugge, relying upon the parallel O.N. form *Bjólfr*, which is recorded as the name of one of the early settlers in Iceland, tried to interpret the word as *Bœjólfr* "the wolf of the farmstead," quoting as parallels *Heimulf, Gardulf*. But *Bjólfr* itself is best interpreted as "Bee-wolf." And admittedly Bugge's explanation does not suit the O.E. *Bēowulf*, and necessitates the assumption that the word in English is a mere meaningless borrowing from the Scandinavian: for *Bēowulf* assuredly does not mean "wolf of the farmstead."

Neither can we take very seriously the explanation of Sarrazin and Ferguson that *Bēowulf* is an abbreviation of *Beadu-wulf*, "wolf of war." Our business is to interpret the name *Bēowulf*, or, if we cannot, to admit that we cannot; not to substitute some quite distinct name for it, and interpret that. Such theories merely show to what straits we may be reduced, if we reject the obvious etymology of the word.

And there are two further considerations, which confirm, almost to a certainty, this obvious interpretation of "Beowulf" as "Bee-wolf" or "Bear." The first is that it agrees excellently with Beowulf's bear-like habit of hugging his adversaries to death – a feature which surely belongs to the original kernel of our story, since it is incompatible with the chivalrous, weapon-loving trappings in which that story has been dressed. The second is that, as I have tried to show, the evidence is strongly in favour of Bjarki and Beowulf being originally the same figure: and Bjarki is certainly a bear-hero. His name signifies as much, and in the *Saga of Rolf Kraki* we are told at length how the father of Bjarki was a prince who had been turned by enchantment into a bear.

If, then, Beowulf is a bear-hero, the next step is to enquire whether there is any real likeness between his adventures at Heorot and under the mere, and the adventures of the hero of the widely-spread "Bear's Son" folk-tale. This investigation has, as we have seen above, been carried out by Panzer in his monumental work, which marks an epoch in the study of *Beowulf*.

Panzer's arguments in favour of such connection would, I think, have been strengthened if he had either quoted textually a number of the more important and less generally accessible folk-tales, or, since this would have proved cumbersome, if he had at least given abstracts of them. The method which Panzer follows, is to enumerate over two hundred tales, and from them to construct a story which is a compound of them all. This is obviously a method which is liable to abuse, though I do not say that Panzer has abused it. But we must not let a story so constructed usurp in our minds the place of the actual recorded folk-tales. Folk-tales, as Andrew Lang wrote long ago, "consist of but few incidents, grouped together in a kaleidoscopic variety of arrangements." A collection of over two hundred cognate tales offers a wide field for the selection therefrom of a composite story. Further, some geographical discrimination is necessary: these tales are scattered over Europe and Asia, and it is important to keep constantly in mind whether a given type of tale belongs, for example, to Greece or to Scandinavia.

A typical example of the Bear's son tale is *Der Starke Hans* in Grimm. Hans is brought up in a robber's den: but quite apart from any of the theories we are now considering, it has long been recognized that this is a mere toning down of the original incredible story, which makes a bear's den the nursery of the strong youth. Hans overcomes in an empty castle the foe (a mannikin of magic powers) who has already worsted his comrades Fir-twister and Stone-splitter. He pursues this foe to his hole, is let down by his companions in a basket by a rope, slays the foe with his club and rescues a princess. He sends up the princess in the basket; but when his own turn comes to be pulled up his associates intentionally drop the basket when halfway up. But Hans, suspecting treason, has only sent up his club. He escapes by magic help, takes vengeance on the traitors, and weds the princess.

In another story in Grimm, the antagonist whom the hero overcomes, but does not in this case slay, is called the Earthman, *Dat Erdmänneken*. This type begins with the disappearance of the princesses, who are to the orthodox number of three; otherwise it does not differ materially from the abstract given above. Grimm records four distinct versions, all from Western Germany.

The versions of this widespread story which are most easily accessible to English readers are likely to prejudice such readers against Panzer's view. The two versions in Campbell's *Popular Tales of the West Highlands*, or the version in Kennedy's *Legendary Fictions of the Irish Celts* are not of a kind to remind any unprejudiced reader strongly of *Beowulf*, or of the *Grettir*-story either. Indeed, I believe that from countries so remote as North Italy or Russia parallels can be found which are closer than any so far quoted from the Celtic portions of the British Isles. Possibly more Celtic parallels may be forthcoming in the future: some striking ones at any rate are promised.

So, too, the story of the "Great Bird Dan" (*Fugl Dam*), which is accessible to English readers in Dasent's translation, is one in which the typical features have been overlaid by a mass of detail.

A much more normal specimen of the "Bear's son" story is found, for example, in a folk-tale from Lombardy – the story of *Giovanni dell' Orso*. Giovanni is brought up in a bear's den, whither his mother has been carried off. At five, he has the growth of a man and the strength of a giant. At sixteen, he is able to remove the stone from the door of the den and escape, with his mother. Going on his adventures with two comrades, he comes to an empty palace. The comrades are defeated: it becomes the turn of Giovanni to be alone. An old man comes in and "grows, grows till his head touched the roof." Giovanni mortally wounds the giant, who however escapes. They all go in search of him, and find a hole in the ground. His comrades let Giovanni down by a rope. He finds a great hall, full of rich clothes and provision of every kind: in a second hall he finds three girls, each one more beautiful than the other: in a third hall he finds the giant himself, drawing up his will. Giovanni kills the giant, rescues the damsels, and, in spite of his comrades deserting the rope, he escapes, pardons them, himself weds the youngest princess and marries his comrades to the elder ones.

I cannot find in this version any mention of the hero smiting the giant below with a magic sword which he finds there, as suggested by Panzer. But even without this, the first part of the story has resemblances to *Beowulf*, and still more to the *Grettir*-story.

There are many Slavonic variants. The South Russian story of the Norka begins with the attack of the Norka upon the King's park. The King offers half his kingdom to whomsoever will destroy the beast. The youngest prince of three watches, after the failure of his two elder brothers, chases and wounds the monster, who in the end pulls up a stone and disappears into the earth. The prince is let down by his brothers, and, with the help of a sword specially given him in the underworld, and a draught of the water of strength, he slays the foe, and wins the princesses. In order to have these for themselves, the elder brothers drop what they suppose to be their youngest brother, as they are drawing him up: but it is only a stone he has cautiously tied to the rope in place of himself. The prince's miraculous return in disguise, his feats, recognition by the youngest princess, the exposure of the traitors, and marriage of the hero, all follow in due course.

A closer Russian parallel is that of *Ivashko Medvedko*. "John Honey-eater" or "Bear." John grows up, not by years, but by hours: nearly every hour he gains an inch in height. At fifteen, there are complaints of his rough play with other village boys, and John Bear has to go out into the world, after his grandfather has provided him with a weapon, an iron staff of immense weight. He meets a champion who is drinking up a river: "Good morning, John Bear, whither art going?" "I know not whither; I just go, not knowing where to go." "If so, take me with you." The same happens with a second champion whose hobby is to carry mountains on his shoulder, and with a third, who plucks up oaks or pushes them into the ground. They come to a revolving house in a dark forest, which at John's word stands with its back door to the forest and its front door to them: all its doors and windows open of their own accord. Though the yard is full of poultry, the house is empty. Whilst the three companions go hunting, the river-swallower stays in the house to cook dinner: this done, he washes his head, and sits at the window to comb his locks. Suddenly the earth shakes, then stands still: a stone is lifted, and from under it appears Baba Yaga driving in her mortar with a pestle: behind her comes barking a little dog. A short dialogue ensues, and the champion, at her request, gives her food; but the second helping she throws to her dog, and thereupon beats the champion with her pestle till he becomes unconscious; then she cuts a strip of skin from his back, and after eating all the food, vanishes. The victim recovers his senses, ties up his head with a handkerchief, and, when his companions return, apologizes for the ill-success of his cooking: "He had been nearly suffocated by the fumes of the charcoal, and had had his work cut out to get the room clear." Exactly the same happens to the other champions. On the fourth day it is the turn of John Bear, and here again the same formulas are repeated. John does the cooking, washes his head, sits down at the window and begins to comb his curly locks. Baba Yaga appears with the usual phenomena, and the usual dialogue follows, till she begins to belabour the hero with her pestle. But he wrests it from her, beats her almost to death, cuts three strips from her skin, and imprisons her in a closet. When his companions return, they are astonished to find dinner ready. After dinner they have a bath, and the companions try not to show their mutilated backs, but at last have to confess. "Now I see why you all suffered from suffocation," says John Bear. He goes to the closet, takes the three strips cut from his friends, and reinserts them: they heal at once. Then he ties up Baba Yaga by a cord fastened to one foot, and they all shoot at the cord in turn. John Bear hits it, and cuts the string in two; Baba Yaga falls to the earth, but rises, runs to the stone from under which she had appeared, lifts it, and vanishes. Each of the companions tries in turn to lift the stone, but only John can accomplish it, and only he is willing to go down. His comrades let him down by a rope, which however is too short, and John has to eke it out by the three strips previously cut from the back of Baba Yaga. At the bottom he sees a path, follows it, and reaches a palace where are three beautiful maidens, who welcome him, but warn him against their mother, who is Baba Yaga herself: "She is asleep now, but she keeps at her head a sword. Do not touch it, but take two golden apples lying on a silver tray, wake her gently, and offer them to her. As soon as she begins to eat, seize the sword, and cut her head off at one blow." John Bear carries out these instructions, and sends up the maidens, two to be wives to his companions, and the youngest to be his own wife. This leaves the third companion wifeless and, in indignation, he cuts the rope when the turn comes to pull John up. The hero falls and is badly hurt. [John has forgotten, in this version, to put his iron club into the basket instead of himself – indeed he has up to now made no use of his staff.] In time the hero sees an underground passage, and makes his way out into the white world. Here he finds the youngest maiden, who is tending cattle, after refusing to marry the false companion. John Bear follows her home, slays his former comrades with his staff, and throws their bodies on the field for the wild beasts to devour. He then takes his sweetheart home to his people, and weds her.

The abstract given above is from a translation made by one of my students, Miss M. Steine, who tells me that she had heard the tale in this form many times from her old nurse "when we were being sent to sleep, or sitting round her in the evening." I have given it at this length because I do not know of any accessible translation into any Western language.

Panzer enumerates two hundred and two variants of the story: and there are others. But there is reason in the criticism that what is important for us is the form the folk-tale may have taken in those countries where we must look for the original home of the *Beowulf*-story. The Mantuan folk-tale may have been carried down to North Italy from Scandinavia by the Longobards: who can say? But Panzer's theory must stand or fall by the parallels which can be drawn between the *Beowulf-Grettir*-story on the one hand, and the folk-tales as they have been collected in the countries where this story is native: the lands, that is to say, adjoining the North Sea.

Now it is precisely here that we do find the most remarkable resemblances: in Iceland, the Faroes, Norway, Denmark, Jutland, Schleswig, and the Low German lands as far as the Scheldt.

An Icelandic version exists in an unprinted MS at Reykjavik which can be consulted in a German translation. In this version a bear, who is really an enchanted prince, carries off a princess. He resumes his human form and weds the princess, but must still at times take the bear's form. His child, the Bear-boy (Bjarndreingur), is to be kept in the house during the long periods when the enchanted husband is away. But at twelve years old the Bear-boy is too strong and unmanageable, bursts out, and slays a bear who turns out to be his father. His mother's heart is broken, but Bear-boy goes on his adventures, and associates with himself three companions, one of whom is Stein. They build a house in the wood, which is attacked by a giant, and, as usual, the companions are unable to withstand the attacks. Bear-boy does so, ties the giant's hands behind his back, and fastens him by his beard. But the giant tears himself free. As in *Beowulf*, Bear-boy and his companions follow the track by the drops of blood, and come to a hole. Stein is let some way down, the other companions further, but only Bear-boy dares to go to the bottom. There he finds a weeping princess, and learns that she, and her two sisters, have been carried off by three giants, one of whom is his former assailant. He slays all three, and sends their heads up, together with the maidens and other treasures. But his companions desert the rope, and he has to climb up unaided. In the end he weds the youngest princess.

The story from the Faroe Islands runs thus:

Three brothers lived together and took turns, two to go out fishing, and one to be at home. For two days, when the two elder brothers were at home, came a giant with a long beard (Skeggjatussi) and ate and drank all the food. Then comes the turn of the despised youngest brother, who is called in one version Øskudólgur – "the one who sits and rakes in the ashes" – a kind of male Cinderella. This brother routs the giant, either by catching his long beard in a cleft tree-trunk, or by branding him in the nose with a hot iron. In either case the mutilated giant escapes down a hole: in one version, after the other brothers come home, they follow him to this hole by the track of his blood. The two elder brothers leave the task of plunging down to the youngest one, who finds below a girl (in the second version, two kidnapped princesses). He finds also a magic sword hanging on the wall, which he is only able to lift when he has drunk a magic potion. He then slays the giant, rescues the maiden or maidens, is betrayed in the usual way by his brothers: in the one version they deliberately refuse to draw him up: in the other they cut the rope as they are doing so: but he is discreetly sending up only a big stone. The hero is helped out, however, by a giant, "Skræddi Kjálki" or "Snerkti risi," and in the end marries the princess.

In the Norwegian folk-tale the three adventurers are called respectively the Captain, the Lieutenant and the Soldier. They search for the three princesses, and watch in a castle, where the Captain and Lieutenant are in turn worsted by a strange visitor – who in this version is not identical with the troll below ground who guards the princesses. When the turn of the Soldier comes, he seizes the intruder (the man, as he is called).

"Ah no, Ah no, spare my life," said the man, "and you shall know all. East of the castle is a great sandheap, and down in it a winch, with which you can lower yourself. But if you are afraid, and do not dare to go right down, you only need to pull the bell rope which you will find there, and up you will come again. But if you dare venture so far as to come to the bottom, there stands a flask on a shelf over the door: you must drink what is in it: so will you become so strong that you can strike the head off the troll of the mountain. And by the door there hangs a Troll-sword, which also you must take, for no other steel will bite on his body."

When he had learnt this, he let the man go. When the Captain and the Lieutenant came home, they were not a little surprised to find the Soldier alive. "How have you escaped a drubbing," said they, "has not the man been here?" "Oh yes, he is quite a good fellow, he is," said the Soldier, "I have learnt from him where the princesses are," and he told them all. They were glad when they heard that, and when they had eaten, they went all three to the sandheap.

As usual, the Captain and the Lieutenant do not dare to go to the bottom: the hero accomplishes the adventure, is (as usual) betrayed by his comrades, but is saved because he has put a stone in the basket instead of himself, and in the end is rescued by the interposition of "Kløverhans."

What is the explanation of the "sandheap" (*sandhaug*) I do not know. But one cannot forget that Grettir's adventure in the house, followed by his adventure with the troll under the earth, is localized at Sandhaugar. This may be a mere accident; but it is worth noting that in following up the track indicated by Panzer we come across startling coincidences of this kind. As stated above, it can hardly be due to any influence of the *Grettis Saga* upon the folk-tale. The likeness between the two is too remote to have suggested a transference of such details from the one story to the other.

We find the story in its normal form in Jutland. The hero, a foundling, is named Bjørnøre (Bear-ears). There is no explanation offered of this name, but we know that in other versions of the story, where the hero is half bear and half man, his bear nature is shown by his bear's ears. "Bear-ears" comes with his companions to an empty house, worsts the foe (the old man, *den gamle*) who has put his companions to shame, and fixes him by his beard in a cloven tree. The foe escapes nevertheless; they follow him to his hole: the companions are afraid, but "Bear-ears" is let down, finds the enemy on his bed, and slays him. The rest of the story follows the usual pattern. "Bear-ears" rescues and sends up the princesses, his comrades detach the rope, which however is hauling up only the hero's iron club. He escapes miraculously from his confinement below, and returns to marry the youngest princess. In another Danish version, from the South of Zealand[1], the hero, "Strong Hans" (nothing is said about his bear-origin), comes with his companions to a magnificent but empty castle. The old witch worsts his comrades and imprisons them under the trap-door: but Hans beats her and rescues them, though the witch herself escapes. Hans is let down, rescues the princesses, is betrayed by his comrades (who, thinking to drop him in drawing him up, only drop his iron club), and finally weds the third princess.

A little further South we have three versions of the same tale recorded for Schleswig-Holstein. The hero wins his victory below by means of "a great iron sword" (*en grotes ysernes Schwäert*) which he can only wield after drinking of the magic potion.

From Hanover comes the story of Peter Bär, which shows all the familiar features: from the same district came some of Grimm's variants. Others were from the Rhine provinces: but the fullest version of all comes from the Scheldt, just over the Flemish border. The hero, Jean l'Ourson, is recovered as a child from a bear's den, is despised in his youth, but gives early proof of his strength. He defends an empty castle *un superbe château*, when his companion has failed, strikes off an arm of his assailant *Petit-Père-Bidoux*, chases him to his hole, *un puits vaste et profond*. He is let down by his companion, but finding the rope too short, plunges, and arrives battered at the bottom. There he perceives *une lumière qui brillait au bout d'une longue galerie*. At the end of the gallery he sees his former assailant, attended by *une vieille femme à cheveux blancs, qui semblait âgée de plus de cent ans,* who is salving his wounded arm. The hero quenches the light (which is a magic one) smites his foe on the head and kills him, and then rekindles the lamp. His companion above seeks to rob him of the two princesses he has won, by detaching the rope. Nevertheless, he escapes, weds the good princess, and punishes his faithless companion by making him wed the bad one.

The white-haired old woman is not spoken of as the mother of the foe she is nursing, and it may be doubted whether she is in any way parallel to Grendel's mother. The hero does not fight her: indeed it is she who, in the end, enables him to escape. Still the parallels between Jean l'Ourson and Beowulf are striking enough. Nine distinct features recur, in the same order, in the *Beowulf*-story and in this folk-tale. It needs a more robust faith than I possess to attribute this solely to chance.

Unfortunately, this French-Flemish tale is found in a somewhat sophisticated collection. Its recorder, as Sainte-Beuve points out in his letter introductory to the series, uses literary touches which diminish the value of his folk-tales to the student of origins. Any contamination from the *Beowulf*-story or the *Grettir*-story is surely improbable enough in this case: nevertheless, one would have liked the tale taken down verbatim from the lips of some simple-minded narrator as it used to be told at Condé on the Scheldt.

But if we take together the different versions enumerated above, the result is, I think, convincing. Here are eight versions of one folk-tale taken as representatives from a much larger number current in the countries in touch with the North Sea: from Iceland, the Faroes, Norway, Jutland, Zealand, Schleswig, Hanover, and the Scheldt. The champion is a bear-hero (as Beowulf almost certainly is, and as Bjarki quite certainly is); he is called, in Iceland, *Bjarndreingur*, in Jutland, *Bjørnøre*, in Hanover, *Peter Bär*, on the Scheldt *Jean l'Ourson*. Like Beowulf, he is despised in his youth (Faroe, Scheldt). In all versions he resists his adversary in an empty house or castle, after his comrades have failed. In most versions of the folk-tale this is the third attack, as it is in the case of Grettir at Sandhaugar and of Bjarki: in *Beowulf*, on the contrary, we gather that Heorot has been raided many times. The adversary, though vanquished, escapes; in one version after the loss of an arm (Scheldt): they follow his track to the hole into which he has vanished, sometimes, as in *Beowulf*, marking traces of his blood (Iceland, Faroe, Schleswig). The hero always ventures down alone, and gets into an underworld of magic, which has left traces of its mysteriousness in *Beowulf*. In one tale (Scheldt) the hero sees a magic lamp burning below, just as he sees the fire in *Beowulf* or the *Grettis Saga*. He overcomes either his original foe, or new ones, often by the use of a magic sword (Faroe, Norway, Schleswig); this sword hangs by the door (Norway) or on the wall (Faroe) as in *Beowulf*. After slaying his foe, the hero rekindles the magic lamp, in the Scheldt fairy tale, just as he kindles a light in the *Grettis Saga*, and as the light flashes up in *Beowulf* after the hero has smitten Grendel's mother. The hero is in each case deserted by his companions: a feature which, while it is marked in the *Grettis Saga*, can obviously be allowed to survive in *Beowulf* only in a much softened form. The chosen retainers whom Beowulf has taken with him on his journey could not be represented as unfaithful, because the poet is reserving the episode of the faithless retainers for the death of Beowulf. To have twice represented the escort as cowardly would have made the poem a satire upon the *comitatus*, and would have assured it a hostile reception in every hall from Canterbury to Edinburgh. But there is no doubt as to the faithlessness of the comrade Stein in the *Grettis Saga*. And in Zealand, one of the faithless companions is called *Stenhuggeren* (the Stone-hewer), in Schleswig *Steenklöwer*, in Hanover *Steinspieler*, whilst in Iceland he has the same name, *Stein*, which he has in the *Grettis Saga*.

The fact that the departure home of the Danes in *Beowulf* is due to the same cause as that which accounts for the betrayal of his trust by Stein, shows that in the original *Beowulf*-story also this feature must have occurred, however much it may have become worn down in the existing epic.

I think enough has been said to show that there is a real likeness between a large number of recorded folk-tales and the *Beowulf-Grettir* story. The parallel is not merely with an artificial, theoretical composite put together by Panzer. But it becomes equally clear that *Beowulf* cannot be spoken of as a version of these folk-tales. At most it is a version of a portion of them. The omission of the princesses in *Beowulf* and the *Grettis Saga* is fundamental. With the princesses much else falls away. There is no longer any motive for the betrayal of trust by the watchers. The disguise of the hero and his vengeance are now no longer necessary to the tale.

It might be argued that there was something about the three princesses which made them unsatisfactory as subjects of story. It has been thought that in the oldest version the hero married all three: an awkward episode where a *scop* had to compose a poem for an audience certainly monogamous and most probably Christian. The rather tragic and sombre atmosphere of the stories of Beowulf and Grettir fits in better with a version from which the princesses, and the living happily ever afterwards, have been dropped. On the other hand, it might be argued that the folk-tale is composite, and that the source from which the *Beowulf-Grettir*-story drew was a simpler tale to which the princesses had not yet been added.

And there are additions as well as subtractions. Alike in *Beowulf* and in the *Grettis Saga*, the fight in the house and the fight below are associated with struggles with monsters of different sex. The association of "The Devil and his Dam" has only few and remote parallels in the "Bear's-son" folk-tale.

The Date of the Death of Hygelac

GREGORY OF TOURS mentions the defeat of Chochilaicus (Hygelac) as an event of the reign of Theudoric. Now Theudoric succeeded his father Chlodoweg, who died 27 Nov. 511. Theudoric died in 534. This, then, gives the extreme limits of time; but as Gregory mentions the event among the first occurrences of the reign, the period 512–520 has generally been suggested, or in round numbers about 515 or 516.

Nevertheless, we cannot attach much importance to the mere order followed by Gregory. He may well have had no means of dating the event exactly. Of much more importance than the order, is the fact he records, that Theodoric did not defeat Chochilaicus in person, but sent his son Theudobert to repel the invaders.

Now Theudobert was born before the death of his grandfather Chlodoweg. For Gregory tells us that Chlodoweg left not only four sons, but a grandson Theudobert, *elegantem atque utilem*: *utilem* cannot mean that, at the time of the death of Chlodoweg, Theudobert was of age to conduct affairs of state, for Chlodoweg was only 45 at death. The Merovingians were a precocious race; but if we are to allow Theudobert to have been at least fifteen before being placed in charge of a very important expedition, and Chlodoweg to have been at least forty before becoming a grandfather, the defeat of Hygelac cannot be put before 521; and probability would favour a date five or ten years later.

There is confirmation for this. When Theudobert died, in 548, he left one son only, quite a child and still under tutelage; probably therefore not more than twelve or thirteen at most. We know the circumstances of the child's birth. Theudobert had been betrothed by his father Theodoric to a Longobardic princess, Wisigardis. In the meantime he fell in love with the lady Deoteria, and married her[1]. The Franks were shocked at this fickleness (*valde scandalizabantur*), and Theudobert had ultimately to put away Deoteria, although they had this young son (*parvulum filium*), who, as we have seen, could hardly have been born before 535, and possibly was born years later. Theudobert then married the Longobardic princess, in the seventh year after their betrothal. So it cannot have been much before 530 that Theudobert's father was first arranging the Longobardic match. A king is not likely to have waited to find a wife for a son, upon whom his dynasty was to depend, till fifteen years after that son was of age to win a memorable victory.

Appendix: The Finnsburh Fragment, Deor, Widsith, Tribes and Genealogies

The three Old English poems here present intriguing – though ambiguous – analogues to the much longer narratives presented in *Beowulf*. The Finnsburh Fragment is a portion of what was clearly once a longer work. Opening with a stirring call to arms, it tells of a battle – seemingly also narrated in *Beowulf* – fought at a place called Finnsburh.

The exact relationship between the two works is complicated; the details are teased out by R.W. Chambers above. The other two poems, 'Deor' and 'Widsith', are both catalogue poems from the Exeter Book manuscript. The first has an elegiac tone, the latter is more boasting. Both are spoken by poet-narrators showcasing the richness of their wordhord, their store of tales, through a collage of enigmatic allusions. All three poems make references to characters or places given much fuller treatment in *Beowulf*, although none mentions Beowulf himself. Also included here are a list of tribes and further genealogies, for those who would like to delve further into the background of Beowulf as discussed by Chambers.

The Finnsburh Fragment

...Then the young king spoke:
"This is no dawn from the east, no dragon flies here,
nor do the gables of this hall burn,
but here they bear forth, birds call,
wolves howl, the spear crashes,
the shield answers the shaft. Now the moon shines,
shifting under the clouds; now evil doings arise,
will bring to fruition this people's enmity.
But awaken now, my warriors,
grab your shields, think of courage,
strive to the front, be single-minded!"

Then arose many a gold-laden warrior,
readied himself with his sword.
Then the noble warriors, Sigeferth and Eaha,
strode to the door, they drew their swords,
and at the other door Ordlaf and Guthlaf,
and Hengest himself went behind them.

Then Guthere still exhorted Garulf
that he should not take such a noble spirit
in the first wave to the door of the hall,
now that one hard in enmity wished to seize it.
But he asked clearly over all of them,
the brave-hearted hero, who held that door.

"Sigeferth is my name", he said, "I am a man of the Secgan,
an wanderer widely known; I have endured many trials,
hard battles. You'll get what's coming to you,
whatever you wish to seek from me."

Then the sound of slaughter rose in the hall;
the firm shield, the bone-protector

held in brave hands, must shatter – the floor resounded –
until Garulf fell in the fight,
the first of all the men on earth,
Guthlaf's son, and around him many good men,
mortal bodies. The raven wandered,
black and glossy. Swords flashed
as though all of Finnsburh were aflame.

I have never heard that sixty warriors
bore themselves better in a clash of men,
nor ever more fully repaid the sweet mead
than his retainers repaid Hnæf.
They fought for five days, so fiercely that
not a single warrior fell, but they held that door.
Then the wounded hero departed on the way from them,
he said that his mail was broken,
the weakened war-gear, and his helmet was pierced.
Then immediately the leader of the army asked him
how the warriors dealt with their wounds,
or whether those young men's…

Deor

Weland knew for himself the torment of serpents:
that stubborn man suffered tortures,
he had sorrow and longing as his companions,
and winter-cold exile. He often found woes,
when Nithhad compelled him,
laid supple sinew-bonds on the better man.
That came to an end, so may this.

Beadohild wasn't as sorry for her brothers' deaths
as for her own trouble,
in that she could clearly tell

that she was pregnant; she could not ever
fearlessly conceive what that would mean.
That came to an end, so may this.

We have all heard that the laments of Maethhild,
Geat's lady, knew no end,
that the bitter desire entirely deprived her of sleep.
That came to an end, so may this.

Theodric held the Merovingian's fortress
for thirty winters. That was known to many.
That came to an end, so may this.

We learnt about Eormanric's
wolfish thought; he ruled widely over the people
of the kingdom of the Goths. That was one grim king.
Many a man sat bound with sorrows,
in expectation of misery, constantly wished
that the kingdom's time was up.
That came to an end, so may this.

The one who sits with sorrow-cares, deprived of joys,
with a darkening heart, who thinks to himself
that his share of troubles is endless,
he might then consider that the wise Lord
always moves throughout this world,
shows prosperity to many men,
a choice gift, to others a share of woes.

Of myself, I will say this:
that I was for a while the poet of the Heodingas,
dear to that king. Deor was my name.
For many winters I had a good position,
a gracious lord, until now Heorrenda,
that song-skilled man, has taken those rights

which the king of men previously bestowed on me.
That came to an end, so may this.

Widsith

Widsith spoke, unlocked his word-hoard,
he who had travelled most widely of men,
through the nations across earth. Often he had received
many treasures in the hall. He was born to the
Myrgingas. With Ealhhild,
the noble peaceweaver, he first
sought Eormanric's home,
king of the Ostrogoths, to the east of Anglen,
the enemy of traitors. Then he began to speak many things:

"I have heard of many men who ruled over nations!
Every prince should live rightly,
the noble one rule the land through custom,
he who wishes to keep his throne.
For a while Hwala was the greatest of them,
and Alexander the mightiest of all
of mankind, and he prospered most
of all of those who I have heard of across the earth.

Attila ruled the Huns, Eormanric the Goths,
Becca the Baningas, the Burgundinians – Gifica.
Caesar ruled the Greeks and Cælic the Finns,
Hagena the Holmrygas and Heoden the Glommas.
Witta ruled the Swæfas, Wada the Hælsingas,
Meaca the Myrgingas, Mearchealf the Hundingas.
Theodric ruled the Franks, Thyle the Rondingas,
Breoca the Brodingas, Billing the Wernas.
Oswine rules the Eowan, and the Jutes – Gefwulf.
Finn, son of Folcwalda, the Frisian people.

Sigehere ruled the Sea-Danes the longest,
Hnæf the Hocingas, Helm the Wulfingas,
Wald the Woingas, Wod the Thuringians,
Sæferth the Secgan, the Swedes – Ongentheow,
Sceafthere the Ymbras, Sceafa the Langobards,
Hun the Hætwere and Holen the Wrosnas.
Hringweald was called the king of the Herefaran.

Offa ruled the Angles, Alewih the Danes;
he was the boldest of all these men,
however he did not gain glory over Offa,
rather Offa, the first of men,
while still a boy, subdued most of his kingdom.
No one of his age ever achieved
greater glory. With a single sword
he marked the border with the Myrgingas
at Fifeldor; afterwards they held it,
Angles and Swedes, as Offa had forged it.

Hrothwulf and Hrothgar, uncle and nephew,
held the longest peace together,
after they drove out the Viking people,
and humbled Ingeld's sword,
killed at Heorot the Heathobard force.

So I travelled widely in the lands of strangers,
through distant grounds. I experienced there
both good and evil, separated from my kin,
far from friends, and served widely.
Therefore I can sing, and tell the tale,
declare before men in the meadhall
how noble people rewarded me with riches.

I was with the Huns and with the glorious Goths,
with the Swedes and with the Geats and with the South-Danes.

I was with the Wendlas and with the Wærnas and with the Vikings.
I was with the Gefthas and with the
Winedas and with the Gefflegas.
I was with the Angles and with the Swæfas and with the Ænenas.
I was with the Saxons and the Secgan and with the Sweordweras.
I was with the Hronas and with the Danes
and with the Heathoremas.
I was with the Thuringians and with the Throwendas,
and with the Burgundians, where I received a ring;
Guthhere there gave me welcome treasure
in payment for a song. That was no idle king!

I was with the Franks and the Frisians and with the Frumtingas.
I was with the Rugas and with the
Glommas, and with the Romans.
Likewise I was in Italy, with Ælfwine,
he had, I have heard, of all men
the quickest hand to do good,
the most generous heart in the dealing of rings,
and bright jewellery, Eadwine's son.

I was with the Saracens and with the Seringas;
I was with the Greeks and with the Finns and with Caesar,
he who ruled over wine-halls,
riches and slaves, and the kingdom of Rome.
I was with the Scots and the with the Picts
and with the Scridefinnas;
I was with the Lidwicingas and with the
Leonas and with the Langobards,
with heathens and with heroes and with the Hundingas.
I was with the Israelites and with the Assyrians,
with the Hebrews and with the Indians and with the Egyptians.
I was with the Medes and with the Persians
and with the Myrgingas,
and the Mofdingas and against the Myrgingas,

and with the Amothingas. I was with the East Thuringians
and with the Eolas and with the Iste and the Idumingas.

And I was with Eormanric all of a while,
where the Goth king did right by me;
he gave me a ring, the lord of cities,
of pure gold reckoned at
six hundred shillings' worth,
when I came home I gave it
into the keeping of Eadgils, ruler of the Myrgingas,
a mark of gratitude to my lord,
because he had given me land, my father's homestead.

And then Ealhhild, Eadwine's daughter,
the noble queen of troops, gave me another one.
Her glory spread throughout many lands,
when I could tell through song
where under the heavens I knew the greatest
gold-decked queen dispensing gifts.

Then Scilling and I together, with bright voices,
raised up a song for our shared lord,
loud with the harp, sang with voices,
then many men, those in the know,
proud in their hearts, said with their words
that they had never heard a better song.

From there I travelled throughout all the homeland of the Goths,
I always sought the best of companies;
that was Eormanric's household.
I sought Hethca and Beadeca and the Herelingas,
I sought Emerca and Fridla and Eastgota,
the wise and the good, father of Unwen.
I sought Secca and Becca, Seafola and Theodric,
Heathoric and Sifeca, Hlith and Incgentheow.

I sought Eadwine and Elsa, Ægelmund and Hungar,
and the proud retinue of the Withmyrgingas.
I sought Wulfhere and Wyrmhere; there war did not often sleep,
when the force of Goths with hard swords,
around the Vistula Woods had to defend
the old homestead against Attila's people.

I sought Rædhere and Rondhere, Rumstan and Gislhere,
Withergield and Freotheric, Wudga and Hama;
they were not at all the least of companions,
though I may have named them last.
Very often from the army a screaming spear
flew whistling to the opposing troop:
the exiles, Wudga and Hama, gained
twisted gold there, and men and women.

So I always found, wherever I fared,
that whoever is dearest to his people
is the one who God gives a kingdom of men
to rule, as long as he lives."

So wandering, poets of men
are moved by fate through many lands,
they state their need, speak their gratitude,
and always, north or south, they meet someone
well-versed in song, liberal with gifts,
someone who wishes to beef up his fame amongst his forces,
to demonstrate his prowess, until it all crumbles,
light and life together; he who holds fame
has a sure glory under the heavens.

Tribes Mentioned in the Story of Beowulf

1. *Brondings*. Breca was a Bronding. After his famous swimming-match with Beowulf (Chapter VIII.), he is said to have sought out his 'pleasant fatherland the land of the Brondings.' Arnold suggests that they were located in Mecklenburg or Pomerania.

2. *Danes*, also called Bright-Danes, Ring-Danes, Spear-Danes, because of their warlike character; and North Danes, South Danes, &c., because of their wide distribution. They are said to have inhabited the Scede lands and Scedenig and 'between the seas'; that is, they were spread over the Danish Islands, the southern province of Sweden, and the seas between them.

3. *Jutes* (Eotenas), probably people ruled over by Finn, King of Friesland, and identical with the Frisians.

4. *Franks* and Frisians. The Franks were ancestors of the modern French. After the conversion of Clovis (A.D. 496), they gradually encroached on the Frisians.

5. *Frisians* include the Frisians, the Franks, the Hetware, and the Hugs. Friesland was the country between the River Ems and the Zuyder Zee.

6. *Geats*. They dwelt in the south of Sweden between the Danes and the Swedes. Bugge sought to identify them with the Jutes, and held that Gautland was Juteland. He based this theory on certain phrases: e.g. Chapter XXXIII., where the Swedes (the sons of Ohthere) are said to have visited the Geats 'across the sea,' and again in Chapter XXXV. The Swedes and the Geats are said to have fought 'over wide water'; but, as Arnold points out, these phrases can be interpreted in such a way as not to be incompatible with the theory that they dwelt on the same side of the Cattegat, i.e. on the northern side, and in the extreme south of Sweden.

The question as to whether they are identical with the Goths of Roman history is still an open one. Arnold says, 'There is a great weight of evidence tending to identify the Geats with the Goths,' and he quotes evidence from Gibbon (Chapter X.). Pytheas of Marseilles, in the fourth century, says that, passing through the Baltic Sea, he met with tribes of Goths, Teutons, and Ests.

Tacitus, in Chapter XLIII. of Germania, speaks of the Goths as dwelling near the Swedes. Jornandes traces the Goths to Scanzia, an island in the

Northern Sea. It is probable, then, that the Goths had a northern and indeed a Scandinavian origin. If so, Beowulf the Geat was probably a Goth.

7. *Healfdenes*. The tribe to which Hnaef belonged.

8. *Heathoremes*. The people on whose shores Beowulf was cast up after his swimming-match with Breca.

9. *Ingwine*. Friends of Ing – another name for the Danes.

10. *Scyldingas*. Another name for the Danes, as descended from Scyld.

11. *Scylfingas*. Name for the Swedes.

12. *Waegmundings*. The tribe to which both Beowulf and Wiglaf belonged.

13. *Wylfings*. Probably a Gothic tribe.

The Old English Genealogies

enealogical tables allowed Anglo-Saxon royalty to claim authority by tracing their descent back to mythical gods and heroes. They provide a different sort of analogue to *Beowulf* than the more obvious literary and archaeological parallels. First and foremost, they were produced in England, and largely in Old English. *Beowulf* is so lauded as a cornerstone of English literature, it is easy to forget that the poem's setting, its characters, and many of its closest analogues are Scandinavian. And so when we find familiar characters such as Scyld and Beow listed in the pedigree of Anglo-Saxon kings, we catch a glimpse of how *Beowulf*'s original audience may have related to the poem. Similarly reminiscent of *Beowulf* is the ease with which these tables weave together Christian and Germanic mythology. It may be surprising to find Woden, pagan god that he is, listed proudly amongst the ancestors of these Christian kings. No less surprising, though, is the detail that Scyf was *geboren on þære earce Nóes* 'born in Noah's ark'. Delighting as he does in the nuance of detail, Chambers showcases the individual quirks of these genealogies by presenting various versions side-by-side. The short Latin notes are untranslated, but primarily list proper names.

The Mercian Genealogy

Of the Old English Genealogies, the only one which, in its stages *below* Woden, immediately concerns the student of *Beowulf* is the Mercian. This contains three names which also occur in *Beowulf*, though two of them in a corrupt form – Offa, Wermund (Garmund, *Beowulf*), and Eomær (Geomor, *Beowulf*).

This Mercian pedigree is found in its best form in *MS Cotton Vesp. B. VI*, fol. 109 *b*, and in the sister MS at Corpus Christi College, Cambridge (*C.C.C.C.* 183). Both these MSS are of the 9th century. They contain lists of popes and bishops, and pedigrees of kings. By noting where these lists stop, we get a limit for the final compilation of the document. It must have been drawn up in its present form between 811 and 814. But it was obviously compiled from lists already existing, and some of them were even at that date old. For the genealogy of the Mercian kings, from Woden, is not traced directly down to this period 811-814, but in the first place only as far as Æthelred (reigning 675-704), son of Penda: that is to say, it stops considerably more than a century before the date of the document in which it appears. Additional pedigrees are then appended which show the subsequent stages down to and including Cenwulf, king of Mercia (reigning 796-821). It is difficult to account for such an arrangement except on the hypothesis that the genealogy was committed to writing in the reign of Æthelred, the monarch with whose name it terminates in its first form, and was then brought up to date by the addition of the supplementary names ending with Cenwulf. This is confirmed when we find that precisely the same arrangement holds good for the accompanying Northumbrian pedigree, which terminates with Ecgfrith (670-685), the contemporary of Æthelred of Mercia, and is then brought up to date by additional names.

Genealogies which draw from the same source as the *Vespasian* genealogies, and show the same peculiarities, are found in the *Historia Brittonum* (§§ 57–61). They show, even more emphatically than do the *Vespasian* lists, traces of having been originally drawn up in the time of Æthelred of Mercia (675–704) or possibly of his father Penda, and of having then been brought up to date in subsequent revisions.

One such revision must have been made about 796: it is a modification of this revision which is found in the *Historia Brittonum*. Another was that which, as we have seen, must have been made between 811–814, and in this form is found in *MS Cotton Vespasian B. VI*, *MS C.C.C.C.* 183, both of the 9th century, and in the (much later) *MS Cotton Tiberius B. V.*

The genealogy up to Penda is also found in the *A.-S. Chronicle* under the year 626 (accession of Penda).

This Mercian list, together with the Northumbrian and other pedigrees which accompany it, can claim to be the earliest extant English historical document, having been written down in the 7th century, and recording historic names which (allowing thirty years for a generation) cannot be later than the 4th century A.D. In most similar pedigrees the earliest names are meaningless to us. But the Mercian pedigree differs from the rest, in that we are able from *Beowulf*, *Widsith*, Saxo Grammaticus, Sweyn Aageson and the *Vitae Offarum*, to attach stories to the names of Wermund and Offa. How much of these stories is history, and how much fiction, it is difficult to say – but, with them, extant English history and English poetry and English fiction alike have their beginning.

MS Cotton Vesp. B. VI.		**MS C.C.C.C. 183.**	
Aeðilred	Peding	Æðelred	Pending
Penda	Pypbing	Penda	Pybbing
Pypba	Crioding	Pybba	Creoding
Crioda	Cynewalding	Creoda	Cynewalding
Cynewald	Cnebbing	Cynewald	Cnebbing
Cnebba	Icling	Cnebba	Icling
Icil	Eamering	Icel	Eomæring
Eamer	Angengeoting	Eomær	Angengeoting
Angengeot	Offing	Angengiot	Offing
Offa	Uærmunding	Offa	Wærmunding
Uermund	Uihtlaeging	Wærmund	Wihtlæging
Uihtlaeg	Wioðulgeoting	Wihtlæg	Wioþolgeoting
Weoðulgeot	Wodning	Weoþolgiot	Wodning
Woden	Frealafing	Woden	Frealafing

Historia Brittonum MS Harl 3859.	*Anglo-Saxon Chronicle* MSS Cotton Tib. A. VI. and B.I.	
Penda	Penda	Pybbing
Pubba	Pybba	Creoding
	Creoda	Cynewalding
	Cynewald	Cnebbing
	Cnebba	Iceling
	Icel	Eomæring
Eamer	Eomær	Angelþeowing
Ongen	Angelþeow	Offing
Offa	Offa	Wærmunding
Guerdmund	Wærmund	Wihtlæging
Guithleg	Wihtlæg	Wodening
Gueagon		
Guedolgeat		
[U]Uoden		

The Stages Above Woden
Woden to Geat

The stages above Woden are found in two forms: a short list which traces the line from Woden up to Geat: and a longer list which carries the line from Geat to Sceaf and through Noah to Adam.

The line from Woden to Geat is found in the *Historia Brittonum*, not with the other genealogies, but in § 31, where the pedigree of the Kentish royal family is given, when the arrival of Hengest in Britain is recounted. Notwithstanding the dispute regarding the origin and date of the *Historia Brittonum*, there is a pretty general agreement that this *Woden to Geat* pedigree is one of the more primitive elements, and is not likely to be much later than the end of the 7th century[1]. The original nucleus of the *Historia Brittonum* was revised by Nennius in the 9th century, or possibly at the end of the 8th. The earliest MS of the *Historia*, that of Chartres, belongs to the

9th or 10th century – this is fragmentary and already interpolated; the received text is based upon *MS Harleian* 3859, dating from the end of the 11th century, or possibly somewhat later.

I give the pedigree in four forms:

A. The critical text of the *Historia Brittonum* as edited by Th. Mommsen (*Monumenta Germaniae Historica, Auct. Antiq., Chronica Minora*, III, Berolini, 1898, p. 171).

B. *MS Harl.* 3859, upon which Mommsen's text is based, fol. 180.

C. The *Chartres MS.*

D. Mommsen's critical text of the later revision, *Nennius interpretatus*, which he gives parallel to the *Historia Brittonum*.

A	B	C	D
Hors et Hengist	Hors & Hengist	Cors et Haecgens	Hors et Hengist
filii Guictgils	filii Guictgils	filii Guictils	filii Guictgils
Guigta	Guitta	Guicta	Guigta
Guectha	Guectha	Gueta	Guectha
VVoden	VVoden	VVoden	Voden
Frealaf	Frealaf	Frelab	Frealaf
Fredulf	Fredulf	Freudulf	Fredolf
Finn	Finn	Fran	Finn
			Frenn
Fodepald	Fodepald	Folcpald	Folcvald
Geta	Geta	G[e]uta	Gaeta
qui fuit, ut aiunt,	qui fuit, ut aiunt,	qui sunt [sic], ut	Vanli
filius dei	filius dei	aiunt, filius dei	Saxi
			Negua

MS Cotton Vespasian B. VI (9th century) contains a number of Anglo-Saxon genealogies and other lists revised up to the period 811-14. The genealogy of the kings of Lindsey in this list has the stages from Woden to Geat. This genealogy is also found in the sister list in the 9th century MS at Corpus Christi College, Cambridge (*MS C.C.C.C.* 183).

A similar list is to be found in the *Anglo-Saxon Chronicle* (entered under the year 547). But there it is appended to the genealogy of the Northumbrian kings. This genealogy has been erased in the oldest MS (Parker, end of the 9th century) to make room for later additions, but is found in *MSS Cotton Tiberius A. VI* and *B. I.*

Cotton (Vespasian) MS.	Corpus MS.	A.-S. Chronicle
UUoden Frealafing	Woden Frealafing	Woden Freoþolafing
Frealaf Frioðulfing	Frealaf Frioþowulsing (sic)	Freoþelaf Freoþulfing
Frioðulf Finning	Freoþowulf Godwulfing	Friþulf Finning
Finn Goduulfing		Finn Godulfing
Godulf Geoting	Godwulf Geating	Godulf Geating

The *Fodepald* or *Folcpald* who, in the *Historia Brittonum*, appears as the father of Finn, is clearly the *Folcwalda* who appears as Finn's father in *Beowulf* and *Widsith*. The Old English *w* (*ᵽ*) has been mistaken for *p*, just as in *Pinefred* for *Winefred* in the *Life of Offa II*. In the *Vespasian MS* and in other genealogies Godwulf is Finn's father. It has been very generally held that Finn and his father Godwulf are mythical heroes, quite distinct from the presumably historic Finn, son of Folcwalda, mentioned in *Beowulf* and *Widsith*: and that by confusion *Folcwald* came to be written instead of *Godwulf* in the genealogy, as given in the *Historia Brittonum*. I doubt whether there is sufficient justification for this distinction between a presumed historic Finn Folcwalding and a mythical Finn Godwulfing. Is it not possible that Godwulf was a traditional, probably historic, king of the Frisians, father of Finn, and that *Folcwalda* was a *title* which, since it alliterated conveniently, in the end supplanted the proper name in epic poetry?

The Stages Above Woden
Woden to Sceaf

The stages above Geat are found in the genealogy of the West-Saxon kings only. This is recorded in the Chronicle under the year 855 (notice concerning Æthelwulf) and it was probably drawn up at the court of that king. Though it doubtless contains ancient names, it is apparently not so ancient as the Woden-Geat list. It became very well known, and is also found in Asser and the Textus Roffensis. It was copied by later historians such as William of Malmesbury, and by the Icelandic genealogists.

The principal versions of this pedigree are given in tabular form below; omitting the merely second-hand reproductions, such as those of Florence of Worcester.

Extract from the Chronicle Roll

This roll was drawn up in the reign of Henry VI, and its compiler must have had access to a document now lost.

There are many copies of the roll extant – the "Moseley" Roll at University College, London (formerly in the Phillipps collection); at Corpus Christi College, Cambridge (No. 98 A); at Trinity College, Cambridge; and in the Bibliothèque Nationale, Paris; and one which recently came into the market in London.

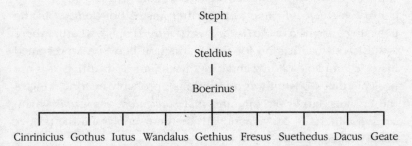

Steph
|
Steldius
|
Boerinus

Cinrinicius Gothus Iutus Wandalus Gethius Fresus Suethedus Dacus Geate

Chambers leaves the following Latin notes, consisting mostly of names, from the 'Moseley' Roll untranslated:

William of Malmesbury. Wodenius fuit filius Fridewaldi, Fridewaldus Frelafii, Frelafius Finni, Finnus Godulfi, Godulfus Getii, Getius Tetii, Tetius Beowii, Beowius Sceldii, Sceldius Sceaf. Iste, ut ferunt, in quandam insulam Germaniae Scandzam... appulsus, navi sine remige, puerulus, posito ad caput frumenti manipulo, dormiens, ideoque Sceaf nuncupatus, ab hominibus regionis illius pro miraculo exceptus et sedulo nutritus, adulta aetate regnavit in oppido quod tunc Slaswic, nunc vero Haithebi appellatur ... Sceaf fuit filius Heremodii, Heremodius Stermonii, Stermonius Hadrae, Hadra Gwalae, Gwala Bedwigii, Bedwegius Strephii; hic, ut dicitur, fuit filius Noae in arca natus.

The following marginal note occurs:

Iste Steldius primus inhabitator Germanie fuit. Que Germania sic dicta erat, quia instar ramorum germinancium ab arbore, sic nomen regnaque germania nuncupantur. In nouem filiis diuisa a radice Boerini geminauerunt. Ab istis nouem filiis Boerini descenderunt nouem gentes septentrionalem partem inhabitantes, qui quondam regnum Britannie inuaserunt et optinuerunt, videlicet Saxones, Angli, Iuthi, Daci, Norwagences, Gothi, Wandali, Geathi et Fresi.

West-Saxon Genealogy — Stages Above Woden

CHRONICLE PARKER MS	ASSER	TEXTUS ROFFENSIS I
Woden Fribowalding	Uuoden	Woden
Friþuwald Freawining	Frithowald	Friþewold
Frealaf Friþuwulfing	Frealaf	Frealaf
Friþuwulf Finning	Frithuwulf	Friþewulf
Fin Godwulfing	Fingodwulf	Finn
Godwulf Geating		Godwulf
Geat Tætwaing	Geata* ...	Geata* ...
Tætwa Beawing	Caetuua	Teþwa
Beaw Sceldwaing	Beauu	Beaw
Sceldwea Heremoding	Sceldwea	Scaldwa
Heremod Itermoning	Heremod	Heremod
Itermon Hraþraing	Itermod	Iterman
	Hathra	Haþra
	Huala	Hwala
	Beduuig	Bedwig
se wæs geboren in	Seth	Scyf, se wæs
þære earce Noe etc.	Noe, etc.	in ðam arken
		geboran [but son
		of Sem, not Noe]
	* quem Getam	* ðene ða
	iamdudum	hæþena
	pagani pro	wuþedon for god
	deo venerabantur	

ETHELWERD	CHRONICLE MSS COTT. TIB. A. VI [& B. I]
Uuothen	Woden Frealafing
Frithouuald	
Frealaf	
Frithouulf	Frealaf Fin[n]ing
Fin	Finn Godwulfing
	[Godulfing]
Goduulfe	Godulf Geat[t]ing
Geat	Geata [Geatt] Tætwaing
Tetuua	Tætwa Beawing
Beo	Beaw Sceldweaing
Scyld	

Scef

CHRONICLE MS COTT. TIB. B. IV	TEXTUS ROFFENSIS II	MS COTT. TIB. B. V
Woden Frealafing	Woden Frealafing	Woden Frealafing
Frealaf Finning	Frealaf Finning	Frealaf Finning
Fin Godulfing	Finn Godulfing	Finn Godulfing
Godulf Gating	Godulf Eating	Godulf Eating
Geat Tætwaing	Eata Teþwafing	Eat Beawing
Tætwa Beawing	Teþwa Beawing	
Beaw Scealdwaing	Beaw Scealdwaging	Beaw Scealdwaging
Scealdhwa Heremoding	Scealwa Heremoding	Scealwa Heremoding
Heremod Itermoning	Heremod Hermanning	Heremod Itermoning
Itermon Haðrahing	Herman Haþraing	Iterman Haðraing
Haþra	Haðra Hwalaing	Haðra Bedwiging
Hwala Beowung	Hwala Bedwining	
Beowi Sceafing, id	Beadwig Sceafing	Bedwig Sceafing
est filius Noe, se wæs	Se Scef wæs Noes sunu	se Scef wæs Nóes sunu
geboren on þære	and he wæs innan	and he wæs innan
arce Nones ...	ðære earce geboren	þære earce geboren